D1535348

*Devastating news triggers Dr. Curt Nover's PTSD and depression as he is unknowingly lured into danger, orchestrated by a vengeful Don Denney. Curt's friends race to save him from Don and a sinister Serbian oligarch. Meanwhile, war drums pound in the Balkans as Washington D.C. sits idle. Kosovo, facing imminent invasion and potentially its very existence, stands ready to face the massive Serbian Army, but who will stand with them in the face of yet another all-out war in the hotbed of the Balkans?*

# Balkan Reprisal

By:

Jeffrey H. Fischer
Colonel (Retired), U.S. Air Force

Website: www.jeffreyhfischer.com
Facebook: www.facebook.com/ColonelFisch
LinkedIn: www.LinkedIn.com/in/jeffreyfisch/
Twitter: @jefffisch

*"The views expressed in this publication are those of the author and do not necessarily reflect the official policy or position of the Department of Defense or the U.S. government."*

**DEPARTMENT OF DEFENSE**
DEFENSE OFFICE OF PREPUBLICATION AND SECURITY REVIEW
1155 DEFENSE PENTAGON
WASHINGTON, DC 20301-1155

Ref: 22-SB-0055
July 08, 2022

Colonel (Retired) Jeffrey Fischer

Dear Colonel (Ret.) Fischer:

This responds to your January 23, 2022, correspondence requesting public release clearance of the manuscript titled, "Balkan Reprisals." The manuscript submitted for prepublication security review is **CLEARED** for public release. This clearance does not include any photograph, picture, exhibit, caption, or other supplemental material not specifically approved by this office, nor does this clearance imply Department of Defense (DoD) endorsement or factual accuracy of the material.

This office notes that your manuscript may include personally identifiable information (PII) of former or active duty Service members, DoD employees, and third party individuals, the release of which could be a violation of the privacy rights of these individuals. As the author, you are solely responsible for the release of any PII and its legal implications. If necessary, you may wish to consult these individuals and obtain permission to include their PII in the manuscript.

This office requires that you add the following disclaimers prior to publishing the manuscript: "The views expressed in this publication are those of the author and do not necessarily reflect the official policy or position of the Department of Defense or the U.S. government." and; "The public release clearance of this publication by the Department of Defense does not imply Department of Defense endorsement or factual accuracy of the material." A copy of the first page of the manuscript with our clearance stamp is enclosed. Please direct any questions regarding this case to paul.j.jacobsmeyer.civ@mail.mil .

Sincerely,

Chief

# DEDICATION

To fellow veterans and service members who struggle with the wounds of war.  Perhaps more importantly, to those who stand by their side, love them, remain loyal, and accept their faults.

To my friends and family who stand by me, know fully well that today I am a far different person than I was before partaking in the horrors of combat.

To Philip 'Monk' Baylis.  One of the smartest intelligence officers I ever met.  God must have needed better intel.  You were taken way too soon.  It never gets easier to lose brothers and sisters in arms.
Until Valhalla,
Rest in Peace

# ACKNOWLEDGMENTS

I am blessed to have a team of warrior editors.  Thanks to all of you for your time, energy, candidness and support!!!

Thanks to the Twin Otter (DHC-6 100/200/300/400) Facebook group for helping craft a realistic scenario.  I hope I got that part of this story right!  Awesome group!

To Joel Taylor, a childhood friend who kicks butt at graphics.  Thanks for the cover.  More importantly, thanks for remaining my friend after all my queepish requests... over and over and over.

## NOTICES TO READER

This book contains a glossary of acronyms on page 365.

The map on the cover of the book may help the reader to geographically frame the story.

This book is the second in a series. Some characters and their backgrounds were first detailed in *LIVE RANGE*. Scan the QR code below to purchase and begin reading the first Dr. Curt Nover novel.

# Foreword

by

## *Greg Delawie*

### *Former U.S Ambassador to the Republic of Kosovo*

Sometimes fiction cuts disturbingly close to fact.   A key theme of *Balkan Reprisal* deals with the always-torturous relationship between Kosovo – the newest state in Europe – and its neighbor and former ruler Serbia, which formed the core of Yugoslavia.  The evening I stayed up to finish a galley copy of this book, gunfire was reported in the northern section of Kosovo as its government prepared to enforce its own laws on its own territory, laws that Serbia opposed.  Fortunately, that August evening ended peacefully; nevertheless, as those of us who have worked to keep the peace on the Kosovo – Serbia border know, another problem is inevitably just around the corner.

USAF Colonel Jeff Fischer, AKA "Fisch," arrived in the summer of 2016 to assume the position of Defense Attaché at the United States embassy in Pristina, Kosovo, where I had been the U.S. Ambassador for a year.  Being Defense Attaché is a big job at any embassy, since it is usually the most-senior military officer there, someone who represents not only the Secretary of Defense and the Chairman of the Joint Chiefs, but also important components like the defense intelligence agency and the European Command.  In fact, Fisch told me he had more bosses than anyone else at the embassy due to his responsibility to report to all these different superiors – although he assured me, I would be his number one boss.  Did he use the same line with all his superiors?  Who knows; in any case, we got along well.*

In our first meeting, I asked Fisch to focus his policy attention on increasing the professionalism of the still young Kosovo Security Force (KSF), the country's army in waiting; without tromping on our own government's "slow and steady" approach to KSF development, he should look at available tools, ranging from the help of the Iowa

National Guard, to DOD training classes, to non-lethal-equipment sales, that we could employ to prepare the force, increase its abilities, and reduce the time it would require to become a true partner for the militaries of NATO nations. I was pleased to get a quick "Roger that, sir," because I had not developed a plan any more detailed than just described. In the coming years, Fisch and his team delivered in spades; with their assistance, the KSF's growth into the Kosovo Armed Forces and its ongoing transformation into a fully NATO-capable military should be completed by 2028.

The KSF plays a key role in *Balkan Reprisal*, but in real life its role is just as important. With neighboring Serbia periodically staging provocations and deploying its army along Kosovo's borders, it is important for the young country to develop a credible deterrent to supplement the Kosovo Force, the 3,000-soldier NATO peacekeeping force that has been in place since NATO drove Serbian troops out during the 1999 Kosovo War. Fisch's novel may blend fact and fiction in the Balkans, but it realistically portrays the level of tension that Kosovo's government and citizens must live with every day in the shadow of Serbia's hostile government and much larger and better-equipped military.

*Balkan Reprisal* takes place in well-described exotic locations from Key West to Washington to Belgrade. It was a fun read, although a nail-biter at times. Those like me whose hearts belong to the wonderful people of the Balkans will enjoy catching up with characters representing many friends – and a few adversaries as well. Enjoy!

Greg Delawie

Former Ambassador to the Republic of Kosovo

*\* I should note that disputes one sees so often in movies and books between State Department folk like me and military officers like Fisch are mostly fiction – they occur, but they are the exception rather than the rule.*

Balkan Reprisal

# Chapters

*Chapter One*

# The Confrontation

Craig and Kelly Hewlett were flush with anticipation.  The sun had set on their quaint Elizabeth Street AirBnB, and they'd soon be stumbling down Duval Street in Key West, Florida.  It would be their first time taking on the famed 'Duval Crawl,' the local's term for pub crawling along the street.  Jimmy Buffett tunes filled the rental house, margaritas topped their glasses, and they felt like teenagers again as they prepared for their night of debauchery.

"Hey darlin.'  You almost ready?" Craig asked.

"Almost," Kelly replied.  "Two more minutes.  I just need to get my shoes on and finish my drink."  It was the same line Craig had heard for the past twenty years.  He just grinned, poured another margarita, and watched the sunset fill the evening sky while sitting on the back deck.  No worries.  It was only 1900Hrs.  The two of them, well into their forties, wouldn't be starting their evening after ten like the teens and twenty somethings who ravage Key West every spring break.

Fifteen minutes later, Kelly was ready.  It took thirteen minutes longer than she'd promised.  Craig didn't say a word.  He kissed her; she polished off her margarita, and the two stepped out, ready to take on the bars of Duval Street.

"Where do you want to go first?" Kelly asked.  She knew Craig had done a minor bit of research on the city.

"I don't care what's first, but we need to make it to Sloppy Joe's and to Captain Tony's.  Sloppy Joe's is the historic Hemingway bar, but the truth is, it originally was located where Captain Tony's is today.  So, we gotta drink at both."

Kelly smiled and sarcastically replied, "Darn."  Craig hugged her as they walked down Eaton Street towards Duval.

As they neared the corner of Easton and Duval, the Wendy's hamburger shop parking lot came into view.  There, they saw a

1

man hunched over a homeless individual. The two were in the back of the parking lot, near the dumpsters. To Craig, it appeared suspect and, as a 20-year police officer from the East Coast, he felt the urge to investigate.

Kelly was in no mood. "Craig, can you please let it go? We are on vacation."

"Just a minute, Kelly. I promise."

Craig walked a few steps towards them and hollered from about twenty yards away. "Hey, you guys OK?"

Standing up quickly, the man on top yelled, "Thank God someone is here! Please get help! I think this guy is overdosing! He's convulsing and unresponsive. I don't know, man. This is bad!"

Craig ran over and looked down. The man was right. Craig had seen a handful of overdose victims in his career. This was textbook. "Kelly!" he yelled. "Call 911 and get an ambulance! Probable overdose. Also get the police!" Craig turned his attention towards the other man. "Hey, I'm an off-duty cop. I need your help to lay him down." Craig and the tourist laid the victim flat. He clearly was homeless. His clothes tattered, unshaven for weeks and, by the smell of it, his last shower was likely aligned with his last shave. As he convulsed, Craig rolled him to his side to keep the man from choking on his own vomit. His muscles seized and relaxed, uncontrolled.

Kelly ran inside the Wendy's presuming they would have a better chance explaining the situation to the police. As an out of towner, she was not exactly sure where she was.

The man helping Craig kept looking around as if for more help. "Hey! A police car just drove into the parking lot! I'm going to go get them." Before Craig could respond, he jumped to his feet and ran to the police car. "Officers! Officers! There's a homeless man over there who appears to be overdosing!"

One of the police officers jumped out of the car, opened the trunk, and pulled out a small medic bag. The other transmitted on the radio. "Dispatch, Unit 27. Be advised, we have a med call, possible 10-85 at the corner of Duval and Eaton in the Wendy's parking lot. Request 10-41."

As the radio call was made, the other officer expeditiously took the medic bag to the homeless man. By now, the man had stopped breathing. Craig was administering CPR as best he could, given the vomit and other secretions retching out of the victim. The homeless man's pulse was shallow and beginning to wane. Between breaths, Craig looked up, "Officer, my name is Craig Hewlett. I'm an off-duty police officer from North Carolina."

"Got it. I'm Shawn. Keep him breathing. I'm breaking out the NARCAN." Craig had heard of NARCAN, but never seen it. In his small town, the need for an overdose remedy was nothing compared to Key West.

Shawn opened the NARCAN and as Craig pulled away, he shoved it into the victim's nose and administered one dose. "OK. Keep him breathing," Shawn told Craig.

The other officer made his way over to the commotion. He quickly scanned the area. It was a well-known homeless hangout, as it offered plenty of leftover food from restaurant goers. The victim's ragged backpack leaned against the back of the dumpster. The officer began to investigate the contents. "Craig, just keep him breathing. If the first dose doesn't work, we can give him a second one after three minutes," Shawn told him.

No sooner had Shawn stopped talking than the victim coughed. His eyes widened, then closed, and he began to breathe. He was despondent and uncommunicative, but he was alive and breathing. The officers transmitted an update, stating the NARCAN dose appeared to be successful. That information would be relayed to the ambulance en route. It would be there in minutes.

As the second officer continued rummaging through the victim's belongings, he found an identification card. He looked at the photo and then at the victim. While they were the same face, the images were far from similar. The man in the photo was clean cut and in great health, a far cry from the homeless man they were assisting. That said, it was all they had to go on. Shawn looked at his partner, who was holding the ID card. "You got a name?"

"Possibly," he responded. "If this is our guy, the ID says he's a doctor in Chicago. His name is Curt Nover."

## *Chapter Two*
# The Divisional Playoffs
### (Three Months Earlier)

It was late January, and the NFL playoffs were the talk of the nation. At their condominium, Curt and Allison would soon host a party for some close friends. Their newly acquired condo was the perfect location. It sat aloft in a high rise building that towered over Chicago's beautiful Lake Shore Drive. The glass windows from floor to ceiling provided a stunning view of not only the Chicago skyline but also the waterfront and Navy Pier. Such a place was not in an average person's budget, but Curt was recently hired back to the John H. Stroger, Jr. Cook County Medical Center. It was the same place the chiseled chest former Navy SEAL had completed his residency. Despite the cliché descriptions of U.S. Special Operations Forces during the Global War on Terror, Curt was one of those that joined to punish those who assaulted American on September 11th. His medical career after service was a step that moved him from hurting people to helping them.

Allison was in the kitchen, preparing food for the party. She was a professional freelance journalist who'd made many connections, and after the fall of Nissassa, she'd received several offers from major outlets. Those offers were on standby. Today, she'd be party planning. Much of the food would be southwestern style due to her Arizona childhood. Aside from the party, Allison was busy planning their wedding later that summer. The doorbell rang.

Allison jumped, and said, "Curt! Are the guests already coming? Please God, no! Can you get that? I'm swamped in here!"

Curt laughed. "Baby, you still have about a half hour. I had Smitty come by a bit early to help set up the surround sound on the TV." Curt walked to the door and opened it. Smitty stood there, decked out in an overstuffed winter jacket, an

Indianapolis Colts football jersey, sunglasses, jeans, a small backpack and holding a twelve pack of Bud Light.

"I brought ya a gift." Smitty said with a smile.

"Yes, I see that. Classy. Very, uh… you. Hey, did you get the memo? The Colts finished last in their division. The only Colts players at the playoffs this year will be ticket holders in the stands."

"Fuck off. They're my team, man!" Smitty tossed the twelve pack at Curt, walked into the condo and straight to the kitchen. "Hey beautiful," he said to Allison. "I have no idea how you put up with that man." He dropped his backpack, which contained overnight amenities. Smitty planned on couch-crashing as the drive back to Northwest Indiana would be too far on a full belly of beer. Allison and Curt didn't mind one bit.

Allison threw her arms around him. "Smitty!!! Hello you stud! It's great to see you! As for Curt, I found our marriage is likely to work out perfectly if I just ignore 50% of everything he says." They smiled and hugged again.

Curt had heard and seen enough. "OK, you two, knock it off. Smitty, get two beers out of the fridge and bring them into the living room. I need help with the TV audio."

"Got it," Smitty replied. He did as instructed, and the two moved into the living room. Allison smiled as she heard them squabble over activating the surround sound. Neither would read the instructions, but each was absolutely certain they knew how to make it work. Her heart filled with warmth as she reflected. It was only a few short months ago when they were all in Casablanca and Curt proposed.

The TV audio setup banter reached a fevered pitch until Allison finally yelled, "Gentlemen! You can't fight in there! It's the war room!"

The two were instantly muted. Smitty looked at Curt and said, "Really? Dr. Strangelove?" Allison's comment clearly was a line from the famous classic comedy 'Dr. Strangelove,' revered by many past and present military members.

"What can I say?" Responded Curt. "She's a quick learner and a great catch!"

"I gotta get me one of those." Smitty and Curt grinned, then restarted their arguing, just at a lower decibel setting.

An hour or so later, the party was in full swing. Food was out on the kitchen island for folks to self-serve. Drinks were at the bar, in the fridge, and in a cooler next to the large sofa. Everyone was having a wonderful time. The game was about to start and almost all the guests had arrived. Then another knock. Curt walked into the hallway and opened the door.

"Hey Doc, I got a horrible case of '*Mahballzitch*' and was wondering if you could help?" It was Buck... being Buck. He stood there in well-traveled clothing, a five o'clock shadow and a small suitcase.

"Buck! You're late! What did you say your condition was?" Curt knew it wasn't a medical condition but felt obliged to let Buck finish out his most likely inappropriate and lewd joke.

"You know doc! 'My Balls Itch!' Ha! Ha! Great to see ya, Doc! Sorry, my flight was delayed out of Frankfurt. I got here as quick as I could."

Curt was right. The joke was not appropriate, but it was Buck, and one must take the good with the bad. "No worries! Come in! I'm glad you made it!" They hugged like old friends, and both were extremely pleased to be in each other's company once again.

Curt walked Buck into the party and said, "Look, honey! Look who it is. It's old Peter Bailey, back from the War!" The line was quoted from the classic film, 'A Wonderful Life,' a film both Curt and Allison, as well as millions of Americans, had just watched over the Christmas Holidays.

Buck continued into the condo, heading straight for Allison. He picked her up in a bear hug, spinning her around in a circle as if they were swing dancing. "There you are, young lady! So wonderful to see you again!" Allison was startled at first and blushed a bit at the attention. Then again, she too loved Buck. She smiled, laughed, hugged him back, and then kissed his cheek. "Oh, Peter Bailey!"

Buck began tickling her ribs, as if they were siblings. For most, this would be inappropriate, but then again... it was Buck.

Allison laughed wildly. "Buck! You're flipping crazy!"

"Damn! Have you been talking to my therapist?" Buck didn't miss a beat. They both laughed. He put Allison back down as Curt handed him a beer. Buck was a former U.S. Air Force Special Operations pilot. After an incident caused him to separate, he flew as an independent operator in Northern Africa, where he met Curt and saved his life. Buck was crazy, inappropriate, and obnoxious at times, but lovable. With Buck nearby, one was assured boredom would not set in.

"Buck, make yourself at home, grab some food, and enjoy the game. I'll take your luggage to the guest room. I can't wait for us to catch up."

"Will do, Doc!" Buck headed straight for the kitchen island. He was starving after the flight and needed some good American junk food.

The games continued into the night. Like most NFL playoff matches, these weren't close enough to be exciting, but the commercials and the time spent with friends made up for the lacking playoff hype. Along with many of the other friends, Smitty, Buck, Allison, and Curt were all able to catch up with each other. It was a great night and Curt looked forward to the morning. He couldn't wait to have time with Buck and Smitty.

# *Chapter Three*
# Sprung

Monday morning, roughly five hundred miles east of Chicago at a sterile and secure facility in rural Maryland, a loud klaxon horn blared. It was followed by the sound of large metal electric locks unlatching. A nasally voice cracked over a loudspeaker. "Donald Denney. Step forward." At floor level, a set of freshly polished black shoes emerged from an industrial-looking doorway. Hems from a sharp Italian suit gently lay across the top of two shoes, forming a soft crease in the pants pleat. These clothes were far from the standard issue Federal Correctional Institution Cumberland uniform that other inmates were wearing. Wearing these clothes was a fit man in his early forties. He walked towards a desk. His visitor raised from the desk to meet him. "Good afternoon, Mr. Denney. I am Matt Henderson, an attorney from Baker, Allen, and Hobbs. I have some good news for you. Please sit down." The two were alone in a private prison room, reserved for attorney-client discussions.

Donald Denney sat down. "Mr. Henderson, good morning. Please call me Don."

"Sure, Don. And please call me Matt. As I said, Don, there appears to be some good news for you. I see your clothing has been returned. That's a great start."

"Matt, you seem to have me at a disadvantage. I don't understand what is going on."

"Yes, I realize that. Don, there is a current motion in the Alexandria Federal District Court of Virginia to have all charges against you dropped in relation to the Federal case regarding Nissassa, Inc. The DA is not going to challenge the motion."

Don made a fist pump, realizing his family's political connections had come through. He also knew of Baker, Allen, and Hobbs. Everyone did. It was one of, if not, the top law firms in the U.S. litigating white collar crime. They were exceptional, but they were not cheap. "Sir, this is great news. May I ask, what is the legal precedence for the dismissal?"

Matt looked squarely into Don's eyes and spoke slowly. "Well, as you may remember, when you were initially arrested, the arresting officer failed to read you your Miranda Rights." Don knew this was not true. So did Matt, as he continued. "During depositions, the arresting officer has now recanted his story under oath and confesses he did not read you your rights. Therefore, your statements and the vast majority of evidence against you were obtained illegally. The prosecuting attorney has agreed to dismiss the charges. At this point, your release is a matter of time based on legal formalities."

Don knew there was some serious legal mumbo jumbo going on. The case against him was airtight. And now the DA was dropping charges on a Miranda Rights technicality? It was unbelievable. If it was a dream, he prayed it would come true and responded, "Sir, I can't thank you enough. What about Jerry and the others?"

Matt again looked at Don seriously. "Mr. Denney, it would be best if you considered your dismissal as a gift from God. Our firm was not hired to represent anyone but you." He paused. "Do you understand?"

Don completely understood. Nothing more needed to be said. Within hours, he would be a free man. "Yes, I get it. Thanks."

"Don, I was asked to give you this phone number. Please call it once you are out of prison. Do you have any questions for me?" Don took the paper; it contained the number +381 62 8130760. There was no name or other information.

"Sir, no. I'm good. Again, thank you."

"Don, may I suggest you not thank me. You may want to save that for your phone call." Mr. Henderson rose out of his seat and extended his hand. Don also stood, reaching out to shake hands. Matt picked up his briefcase and walked out. It would be the last time Don ever saw Matt.

Don remained in a holding cell for a few hours until his papers were in order. Once complete, he was escorted out of the prison.  As he walked through the hallways, he couldn't wait to be free.  He longed to see his family; the ones he believed were responsible for facilitating his release.  A final door opened, and the sunlight shone down onto a sidewalk.  The two guards that had been escorting him down the hallway stopped at the door's threshold.  One said, "You're free to go."  Both guards looked at him with disgust.  They, just like Don, knew the dismissal was a sham.

Don didn't care.  He walked away from the building towards the parking lot, scanning for his parents or any other individual to meet him.  Nobody was there.  He looked down at his recently reacquired phone and tried to call his parents.  Unfortunately, his phone contract was canceled, and the call would not go through.  Don stood in the parking lot alone.  He began walking down the street until he found a sign of life.  After walking for 15 minutes, he was at Western Maryland Distributing, Inc.  He entered and asked the secretary if he could use the phone.  She hesitated at first, but after a few pleas and explaining the situation (omitting he'd just been released from prison), she relented.

He called his parents.  The phone rang and an elderly male voice answered.  "Hello, Andrew Denney."

"Hello!  Dad!  It's Don."

"Don, hey, it's good to hear from you.  Are you OK?  Normally you don't call until Thursday, in another few days."

Don was puzzled.  "Dad, I'm free!  I'm out of jail!  My case was dismissed."

Don's father was shocked.  "Really?  What happened?  Where are you?"

"Dad, I'll explain later.  Can you either pick me up or send a vehicle to get me?  I'll give you the address where I am."

With that, his father dispatched an Uber to recover his son.  He then shared the good news with his wife.  They both were elated, but completely blindsided by this amazing turn of fate.  Clearly, it had not been the Denney family ties that had secured his release, regardless of how influential (and shady) they may be.

## *Chapter Four*

# The Morning After

Back in Chicago, it was morning and Buck had been up for hours alone in Curt's condo. Living in Europe and just arriving in the U.S., his jet lag and circadian rhythm were a mess. Back in his Brussels apartment, it was daytime. In his mind, it was also daytime, and there was no possibility of sleeping. Buck sat in the kitchen, scrolling through trivial information and social media on his phone. It was the only thing to do, other than clean the kitchen after the playoff bash; something far beyond Buck's ability and desire. He eventually heard rumblings from the master bedroom. Soon, he saw Curt coming towards him.

"Good morning, sunshine," Buck said.

"That was a rockin party, but I am going to reserve judgement as to the status of this morning. Did you make coffee?" Curt was still groggy.

"Make coffee? Buddy, I wouldn't even know where to start in this kitchen. Just look at it. Your place is a train wreck. If I wanted this level of customer service, I would have stayed at the Motel 6." Buck may have been sleep deprived, but he was clearly his ornery self.

"Yeah, well, show me a Motel 6 with a view like that one," as Curt pointed out the windows over Lake Michigan. The view looked eastward, and the sun was already casting beautiful colors across the clouds. It truly was a spectacular view.

"Fair point. You win," Buck replied.

"Hey, did you sleep OK?"

"Eh, I was up early. I think at three. Time zone challenges and all."

"Yeah, about that. Buck, why don't you just move back to the U.S. like Smitty and I. There's plenty of work here for you and the truth is, I'd like you closer."

"Doc, I appreciate that, but I just got a fantastic job. NATO hired me to fly VIP travel for their senior personnel out of

Brussels. It's a sweet gig, pays great, and I get to travel all over Europe. Through some of our mutual friends, I was able to craft a competitive bid relative to other contracts with an exception to policy letter, allowing me to fly single pilot in and around Europe as long as the flight duration was under four hours. Buddy... I'm my own boss. I fly by myself. It's a dream for me."

"Buck, that may be true, but your friends are here in the States. And how on earth am I supposed to get married this summer if my best man is stuck in Europe?"

Buck was stunned. He didn't know what to say. Curt stared at him and smiled. "What's the matter, Buck? Did I finally catch you speechless?"

"OK, you win. You got me. I knew it was just a joke, anyway."

"Buck, it's not a joke. I want you to be my best man."

"Doc, come on. What about Smitty? He's the odds-on favorite?

"Well, you may think that, but you'd be wrong. Look, Smitty will be a groomsman, that's for certain. But the truth is, he betrayed me at one point and that still needs time to heal. Both Allison and I have discussed it. If it weren't for you, I would not be here today. That matters to me. You matter to me. So, will you do it?"

Buck was speechless, and even if he could talk, he didn't know what to say. He had very few friends, and even fewer that were close. Military life afforded many an opportunity to make friends, but somehow, he never really did. Sadly, a military lifestyle of moving every few years also created a condition for losing many. One way to deal with such a dilemma was to build walls and isolate oneself from the pain. That had been Buck's strategy throughout his military career; however, Curt was throwing a massive wrench into the plan. How could he say no? "Doc, I'd be honored. Thanks."

"Good, it's settled. You're moving back and we can begin planning."

"Look, Doc. If the plan was to ask me to be your best man just to convince me about moving back, the deal is off. I'm happy in Europe. And let's be honest, the bachelor party I throw you in Europe will be far superior to any you'd have in the States."

Unbeknownst to the two of them, Allison had awakened and was standing roughly 10 feet away. "I don't believe we agreed on a European bachelor party," she said.

Both of their eyes widened as if they were kids caught with a pre-dinner cookie. A brief hush fell across the kitchen, then Curt spoke, "Good morning, sweetheart. I was just telling Buck he needs to move back to the U.S."

"Well, that's a conversation I condone far more than one regarding bachelor parties. Yes, Buck, come back to the States. Lord knows you don't need the money!" They all laughed, as they all knew Buck was loaded. Back in North Africa, his plane had been filled with Nissassa funds that were never recovered.

"Aww. Rolling in the female persuasion, eh? Look, you guys. I appreciate it. I really do. But I love owning my own plane. I love living in Europe. I now have a one-year contract flying NATO senior leaders. Let's see how things pan out. I can't commit to coming back to live here, but if you still want a best man, again, I'd be honored."

Curt looked at Allison. There was no point pushing Buck further. He wanted to be in Europe. There was no changing that.

## *Chapter Five*
# The Anonymous Benefactor

Don finished dinner with his family. His mother was overjoyed that her son would neither be a convicted felon nor serve significant amounts of jail time. His father, Andrew, was far more skeptical as to the day's developments. While Don had shared most of his conversation with Attorney Matt Henderson, he didn't share the information regarding the international phone number.

His mother, Becky Denney, finished cleaning the table and kitchen along with their in-home staff help. The Denney home was enormous, ornate, and exactly what one would expect from the man who was one of the largest political donors in America.

Andrew looked at Don. "Well, son, I am thrilled for you. Tomorrow, I will reach out to my contacts and find out how all of this evolved."

"Actually, dad. I was hoping you could just let me figure it out. I am not sure if it was Jerry or even perhaps Steve's influence in the West Wing." Andrew, like Don, also knew both these individuals and their connections. He also knew that Jerry was still in jail with little chance of freedom and Steve remained the White House Chief of Staff, not implicated in the Nissassa activities. If it was Steve who helped secure his release, Andrew should have known. He was one of the top contributors to the President's campaign coffers. If the White House had secured Don's release, the President himself would have called to take a victory lap.

While Andrew remained extremely skeptical, he would not push it. "Maybe you're correct. Maybe Steve or Jerry. Yes, I'll let you figure it out. I just ask that you keep me informed. I love you, son. But you got lucky."

"Yes dad, but didn't you say it was better to be lucky than good?"

"Perhaps, but you take too much risk. It frustrates me to see you fail and tarnish our family name." It was always the same with Andrew. The Denney name always seemed to be more important than the Denney family. Don ignored it.

They hugged, like they always did, awkwardly, with limited emotion. Andrew had just promised Don he wouldn't meddle. Of course, the Denney family didn't get where they were by remaining idle in the face of such things. In the morning, Andrew would break his promise to Don.

Retiring to the study, Andrew left Don alone in the living room. After a few phone calls to his mobile carrier, Don's cellular phone was reactivated. He was alone. Pulling out the paper that Matt gave him back in prison, Don sat on the couch and dialed the number.

The phone line began to ring. A burly voice in a thick foreign and indistinguishable language answered on a prerecorded voice mail. Don couldn't understand any of it and hung up. *'Strange,'* he thought. *'Why an unmonitored number and a voicemail?'* He then searched for the country code. It was Serbia and the local time there was 0300Hrs. Understandably, no one would answer.

Don got up from the sofa and went to his bedroom. For the first time in months, he would sleep in privacy, in a familiar and comfortable setting. No other prisoners singing, snoring, talking. No klaxons, buzzers, or alarm bells throughout the night. The day's events were staggering. He still could not believe he was free. As he lay in bed, the silence was so odd, he could not stand it. Don moved back down to the living room, turned on the TV and fell asleep on the sofa. Oddly, he needed noise to sleep. Prison had conditioned him.

Don awoke at 0630Hrs Virginia time. It was slightly past noon in Belgrade, Serbia. He made some coffee in the kitchen, then returned to the living room sofa. Don pulled out his phone and once again attempted a call to the mysterious number. This time, a human answered. Again, the language was undiscernible. The voice was thick and burly.

"Hello? Yes, this is Don. Don Denney. I was instructed to call this number?"

The party on the other end of the line responded with two words in extremely poor English, "Vait Pleez." Don did as instructed. Roughly thirty seconds later, another individual spoke on the phone. It was far better English, albeit with a thick Serbian accent. "Mr. Denney. Good morning. My name is Nikola. Nikola Stojanović. But we will just stick with first names, OK? How does your freedom feel?"

"Mr. Nikola, hello. Yes, yes. It feels great. I understand I perhaps owe you my thanks."

"Say nothing of it. I believe we both have a common interest, and I could not very well share it with you in prison." With that, Nikola began laughing in a deep, husky voice at his own attempted humor.

Don felt awkward. "Ha…. Ha, yes. I guess not."

"Don, I wish to invite you to Belgrade. I'd like to discuss a business proposal."

As Nikola had abated Don's incarceration, it was perhaps the least Don could do. "Sure, yes. Let's look at calendars and see what may work."

"Don, I think we may be on different timelines. I have booked you on a flight tomorrow from Washington Dulles to Vienna, Austria, on Austrian Airlines flight 94 departing at 6:05 PM. From there, your flight itinerary will continue to Belgrade. At the Belgrade airport, I will have someone meet you. I don't have time to discuss much more. I will see you when you are in Belgrade. Until then, goodbye." Before Don could respond, the line was dead.

## *Chapter Six*
# Into the Abyss

Don was conflicted. The chances that Nikola would accept Don's refusal to travel were remote. He wasn't sure exactly what his freedom had cost, but he was not naïve enough to think it did not come with strings attached. Given the context of the discussion he had with Nikola and that he had already booked flights, it was clear Nikola expected him on that aircraft and to arrive in Belgrade. It was also clear sharing any of this with his father at this point would be unwise. Perhaps later, but not now.

A few minutes after the call, Don's mother entered the kitchen. "Good morning, son. How did you sleep?"

"Great, mom." He leaned into her as she hugged him. It felt great to be in his mother's arms.

"So, what is your plan?" Becky asked. "Will you stay with us for a while until you get back on your feet?"

"I think I'll stay again tonight, but tomorrow I'll go find an apartment. I don't want to be a burden to you and dad." In reality, he had no intent in finding an apartment but was instead laying the foundation of a lie, covering his international travel to see his newfound friend.

"Well, you're welcome here as long as you wish. I'm just so happy to have you home."

"That makes two of us, mom. I love you." His mom turned to make coffee and Don began to check the news on his phone. Odd, he thought. There is not one mention of his case dismissal. Months ago, his face was splashed across every mainstream media outlet for nearly a week straight. How could it be possible no media covered his release?

A day passed and the next afternoon, Don began planning his travel. He packed for a few days, grabbed his passport, then called for a cab to take him to Dulles International Airport. After paying the cabbie, Don entered the airport and approached the check-in counter, saying, "Good afternoon. Don

Denney traveling to Belgrade."

"Yes, Mr. Denney," the attendant said. "I see your reservation right here. Will you be checking any bags?"

"Yes, please. Just this one. Also, I seem to have misplaced my itinerary. Could you please print off the entire trip?"

"Certainly, Mr. Denney." She typed rapidly into her computer and within seconds, a sheet of paper emerged. The attendant took his bag, tagged it, and then handed Don his tickets, his bag tag, and his full itinerary. "Here you are, Mr. Denney. You are booked to Vienna leaving in a few hours, then following on to Belgrade. According to my system, your flight to Austria is on time and the aircraft is at the gate. Will there be anything else?"

"No. Thank you for your help."

"Great, the business class lounge will be near your gate. May I suggest you wait there?"

Don looked down at his ticket. It was business class. Whoever Nikola was and whomever he worked with; they were not short on resources. Don turned away from the counter and glanced down at the paper he'd received with his entire flight reservation. It did not take long to realize there was no return trip. His concern about traveling increased, but again, what were his options? A man as powerful and wealthy as this Nikola character, who could spring someone from an American jail that easily, would likely be able to take an alternate course of action, or worse. Don kept calm by reminding himself he was strong, smart, and well trained in several skill sets. As a West Point graduate and a former U.S. Army Special Forces officer, this was something he could manage.

Don continued through customs and security to the lounge. He had a few drinks until the boarding announcement softly filled the business class lounge. Don was one of the first to board and settled into his reclining seat. It was wonderful. After takeoff, a chef for Austrian Airlines took his personalized order and served dinner. Just days before, Don was eating prison food. Now he was being pampered by a private chef in business class on an international flight. *'Not a bad transition over the past week,'* he thought.

The landing in Vienna was uneventful. Don cleared customs arriving into the European Union Schengen Zone and awaited his follow-on flight to Belgrade. It was 0900Hrs local in Vienna, and Don had been up all night. He needed something to drink. He pulled up a chair at 'Bierbar-Oida!' and ordered an Austrian coffee. He looked around the bar and noticed he was the only customer drinking coffee. Next to him, an attractive woman was drinking a beer and others around the bar were doing the same. Don finished his coffee and ordered a local beer named 'Ottakringer,' a Vienna lager. It tasted great and reminded him of days long past, when he was stationed in Stuttgart, Germany and attended Munich's world-famous Oktoberfest. He savored the beer, slowly wasting time as he scrolled through the web browser on his cell phone while monitoring his surroundings. It was the Special Forces in him. He could never really just let go.

After finishing his beer, Don got up and headed to the gate. Once boarded, he placed his coat in the overhead bin, sat down and watched as other passengers boarded. The vast majority were clearly Serbian. If one did not already know where the aircraft was headed, Belgrade would have been a top guess. Don watched the other passengers board. One caught his eye. It was the same woman from the bar. He'd noticed her attractive face at the bar, but now, as she walked, he was even more impressed. She was a tall, thin, blonde with clearly dark roots and dark eyebrows. She was attractive, but had a demeanor of being distant, even cold, looking down and making eye contact with no one. Don presumed she was in her early thirties and was by far the most attractive woman on the plane. *'God Bless Serbia,'* he thought to himself.

The flight to Belgrade was a bit bumpy. The mid-day sun warmed up the earth at various locations, causing thermals. While slightly uncomfortable, the aircraft landed safely, which was all that mattered. As the aircraft flaps and slats retracted, the Airbus A320 turned towards the Nikola Tesla International Airport Terminal.

Don was a fan of Nikola Tesla, studying him back at West

Point during electrical engineering classes. He knew the scientist was born in present-day Croatia, but most of his discoveries took place in Belgrade. What Balkan nation possesses the 'rights' to claim Tesla's heritage depended on who you spoke to; much like everything in Balkan history. Back in Tesla's day, most of the region had been at one time part of the Austrian-Hungarian Empire and then Yugoslavia, which served as a thorny history in diplomatic relations between Serbia and the United States, even in present day.

Don exited the aircraft and recovered his luggage from baggage claim. A grumpy customs officer stamped his passport with a scowl. It was quite the common occurrence for Americans entering Serbia. Don finally passed through the controlled area of the airport and walked out into the public area, psyching himself up for his first meeting with Nikola or to see some cabbie standing there with the name "Denney" on a makeshift sign. As he made his way through the arrival terminal, Don would find neither. He stood there for a moment, then pulled out his cell phone to call Nikola.

As he raised his phone, a raspy yet seductive feminine voice said, "Mr. Denney. Are you ready to go?" He turned to see where it came from. As he did, he realized it was the attractive woman from the flight. '*Strange coincidence*,' he thought.

"Uh? Yes. Um, excuse me. Who are you?" Don asked.

"Katarina." The answer was short. There'd be no small talk. "Come with me." She didn't wait and walked in front of him. Her long legs were wrapped in skintight black leggings and had a half shirt that barely covered her midriff. On the aircraft, she had also dressed attractively, but far more conservatively. As she walked away, Don attempted to divert his eyes away from staring at Katrina's backside and remain professional. It was not easy, and that was exactly how Katarina wanted it.

Don followed her to a cab. They both got in. She rattled something off in Serbian and the driver sped away. In roughly 20 minutes, the cab stopped. She paid, and they both exited in front of the 'Russian Tsar' restaurant. Don's travel mate did not wait for him. She walked in, and he closely followed.

The restaurant was beautifully upscale. Off in a corner sat a man in his early forties, well dressed and casually observing the surroundings as they approached. Katarina said something in Serbian, bent over him and kissed the man on the cheek. He halfheartedly leaned up to meet her kiss. The majority of the effort fell on her, and she was more than happy to oblige. Whoever the gentleman was, he exuded power.

Katarina took a seat next to the man and Don walked up. Katarina remained silent, clearly with no intent to introduce the two. The man spoke. "Don. We finally meet. I am Nikola. Please sit."

Nikola did not stand but rather slowly waved his hand towards the chair across from him.

Don grabbed the empty chair at the small table and as he sat, Katarina jumped up, shifted her chair, and sat back down. Don was puzzled.

Nikola laughed. "Don't mind her. Serbians like us are quite superstitious. Katarina believes in one of our old stories that if she sits at the corner of a table, she won't get married. Somewhat comical given another Serbian superstition suggests that if a woman shows her stomach in public, her ovaries will freeze, and she won't have children." Nikola said this as he stared at Katarina. She pulled her half shirt down as far as it would go, demonstrating she too might believe in that old wives' tale as well.

Katarina rattled off something in Serbian. She clearly was displeased with Nikola's comments. Nikola ignored her with clear overtones of chauvinism.

"Don, you must be hungry." Nikola raised his hand, and a waiter approached. After exchanging a few words, the waiter vanished and reappeared with a menu, handing it to Don. Katarina sat at the table silently. She would not be getting a menu.

"Thank you. Yes. I am a bit hungry." As he opened the menu, Don continued, "Nikola, it is a pleasure to finally meet you, but I must confess, all of this has me confused, if not a bit on edge. I am curious as to why..."

Nikola cut him off. "Don, we shall chat later. Let's eat and get to know each other. I can assure you of two things. One, you are in no danger when you are with me. Two, I have an opportunity of a lifetime for you. Please order your meal. How do you say in English? Let's get…. akuant… Oh, I forgot the word."

Don helped him out. "Sir, do you mean, 'acquainted?'"

"Yes! Yes. But you will not call me sir. We use first names and, perhaps in the near future, 'comrade.' May I propose a toast to our new friendship?"

"Živeli!!" Nikola said, with a slight raise to his voice.

Don looked down and grabbed one of the shot glasses of clear liquid on the table.

Don raised it, staring at the glass and responded, "Živeli!"

Nikola quickly lowered his glass and stopped Don in his tracks. "Forgive me, my friend. Here in Serbia, if you toast and do not look someone in the eyes, you will have seven years of bad sex. I can't let that happen to my friend." Nikola began again, staring intently into Don's eyes.

"Thanks for saving my sex life," Don joked. Again, he said, "Živeli," returning the stare. They both drank.

For the next hour, they would talk about nothing of substance. Family, schooling, history, politics and other subjects. None of it would come close to touching on their future business venture. Again, through the entire event, Katarina remained silent, intently listening to the conversation.

## *Chapter Seven*
# Back to the Grind

Buck's visit to Chicago was nothing short of perfect. They ate deep-dish pizza from Gino's East and had drinks at the Signature Lounge on the top floor of the John Hancock building – formerly referred to by locals as the no longer politically correct, "Top of the Cock Bar." They listened to excellent music at a few of the amazing Chicago Blues bars, then took a walk down the Magnificent Mile. They'd relish in yet another local custom, ducking under Michigan Ave onto Wacker Drive, for some burgers, beers and banter at the Billy Goat Tavern, an old school Chicago staple frequented by famous SCTV cast members, past and present, such as John Belushi, Dan Aykroyd and others. To be honest, though, their location did not truly matter. Time together was special, particularly given their shared traumatic experiences in North Africa. Because of it, they would always remain the closest of friends.

Unfortunately, Buck needed to return to Europe. Allison and Curt took him to O'Hare Airport. The goodbyes were difficult, and Allison wept a bit. Buck and Curt hugged and made cursory plans for the wedding.

Buck settled into his seat on flight United 972 for the long flight back to Brussels, back to the 'real world' and his new job. The trip was uneventful and after landing, Buck departed the commercial terminal and walked over to the private one where his aircraft was parked. With his recent windfall from the Nissassa money, Buck had traded in his old aircraft for a used but good condition DHC-6 400 Twin Otter. Years in the African sun had taken a toll on his old Cessna, and he needed a more reliable aircraft for the contract. The Twin Otter was a workhorse and provided greater passengers and cargo space, a key requirement that helped him secure the NATO bid for VIP airlift support.

After a quick scan, the aircraft was clearly just as Buck had left it. Buck would polish it one last time. For the NATO mission, it was configured with four extremely comfortable seats, six average seats and then room in the back for cargo, as well as an aft door to facilitate on and off loading. Many would argue the aircraft wasn't much to look at, but to Buck, she was a beaut. After cleaning the aircraft, Buck headed to his apartment. Time to get some rest. Tomorrow morning, he would fly NATO Assistant Secretary General for Emerging Security Challenges Janis Van de Veer and two staffers from Brussels to Ramstein Air Base (AB), Germany. There, the assistant secretary would give a keynote speech at NATO Allied Air Command. The planned departure was from the Fixed Base Operations (FBO) executive terminal at Brussels International Airport around 0800Hrs, arriving in Ramstein approximately an hour later.

For the first 120 days, Buck's contract with NATO was under a probationary status. He needed to prove reliability, security, and flexibility beyond what commercial airlines could offer. Clearly, the cost for Buck's operation was far more expensive than commercial airlines, but it also afforded NATO senior civilian leaders the flexibility they often envied of their military counterparts. Buck was up to the challenge.

\*\*\*\*\*\*\*\*\*\*\*\*\*\*\*\*\*\*\*\*\*\*\*\*\*\*\*\*\*\*\*\*\*\*\*\*\*\*\*\*

The next morning, Buck waited, leaning up against the aircraft at the FBO executive terminal. Two black SUVs approached like clockwork, and three individuals emerged from the vehicles. Buck greeted them, took their bags, and set them into the cargo area. He quickly showed them to their seats, then tied down the cargo. It was a bit much for a one-man show, but that's the way Buck wanted it. *'Partners were for dancing'* as far as he was concerned.

Once ready, Buck fired up the engines, taxied out, and took off. The flight was extremely smooth, and he landed at Ramstein Air Base, Germany, roughly 10 minutes ahead of schedule. As he pulled up to the terminal at Base Operations, another set of SUVs was waiting. His passengers stepped off the aircraft and headed to the vehicles. One staffer turned around and said, "Sir, we are planning to depart around 2:00 p.m. Please be ready."

"No problem, ma'am. I'll be here. Also, here is my card, should anything change."

"Perfect, thanks." The three were soon in the vehicles and they departed.

Buck's first mission was a success. He spent the next few hours refueling the aircraft, filing a return flight plan with air traffic control, grabbing some lunch at the world famous Ramstein food court and hanging out. Around 1300Hrs, his phone rang; it was a Belgian number.

"Hello, Buck here."

"Hello, yeah. Uh, is this our pilot?"

"Yes, ma'am. What can I do for you?"

"The assistant secretary general has been asked to attend dinner tonight with U.S. Air Forces in Europe, Commander General Harrigian. She'd like to know if you'd be able to remain overnight and then fly us back tomorrow morning."

The sound of that question was music to Buck's ears. "Yes, ma'am. As long as the contracting officer approves the layover, I am happy to help." The NATO contracting officer was about ten rungs down on the seniority ladder from the Assistant Secretary. There was little chance the request would be denied. Buck's flexibility was already proving to be worth the contract. Had the three flown commercial, there would be ticket change fees as well as travel to and from Frankfurt airport, roughly 1.5 hours each way. Without question, Buck was saving NATO time and money. Now, to find a place to stay.

Buck grabbed his emergency overnight bag and walked over to the military base billeting office. He secured a charming hotel room for the night and took a stroll through the Kaiserslautern Military Community Center, a huge U.S. style mall on Ramstein Air Base, nestled in the middle of Germany. He enjoyed a nice dinner at Macaroni Grill, a glass of wine, and a chance to buy a few American knickknacks not available in Brussels. Life was good.

The next morning, Buck met his passengers and flew back to Brussels. A first of what would hopefully become many successful missions. After landing, Buck took a gander at his schedule. The next few weeks would include flights to Rome, Vienna, Helsinki, Belgrade, Pristina, Sigonella and other beautiful European cities. Buck pinched himself. This truly was his dream job.

## *Chapter Eight*
# The Offer

Don and Nikola's lunch ended, and a cab took Don to the Belgrade Hyatt, where his upgraded room was waiting. Don had traveled halfway around the world and had not spent a dime. All of this made him uneasy, but the need for sleep overwhelmed him. In five minutes, Don had passed out from jet lag. He'd sleep for a few hours and awake to meet Nikola again for dinner. Just the two of them, and an expectation for a more serious discussion.

Back at the restaurant, Nikola and Katarina got up and departed the restaurant. They walked down the street.

The two communicated in Serbian. "Anything out of the ordinary?" Nikola inquired.

Katarina responded, "No. He engaged with no one throughout the entire travel."

"And his communications?" Nikola's questions were all business.

"While in Vienna, he accessed the free airport Wi-Fi. When he did, I was able to clone the Wi-Fi, routing his data through my laptop. I have sorted through most of it on the flight from Vienna to Belgrade. Again, there was nothing of significance. Before he left Vienna, I installed an access app in the background of his phone to monitor all future activity. I also dropped an Apple AirTag into his backpack in Vienna. The Air Tag's speaker is disabled, and the software has been altered to prevent it reporting to anyone but us. It's amazing how off-the-shelf technology is making it so easy for our efforts."

"Very good. We need Mr. Denney, if only for a while. Are the plans for tonight in place?"

Her response continued in Serbian, "Da."

"Well done." Nikola stopped walking, kissed the blonde woman on her forehead, clearly with feeling but not passionately. He pulled back and smiled. She fawned back at him. As they separated, a black limousine pulled up as if on cue.

Nikola got in and, within seconds, was whisked away.

\*\*\*\*\*\*\*\*\*\*\*\*\*\*\*\*\*\*\*\*\*\*\*\*\*\*\*\*\*\*\*\*\*\*\*\*\*\*\*\*

In D.C., Andrew Denney waited at a lunch table inside The Capital Grille. The restaurant was one of the better places to discuss business in the city. It was dark, and the booths had extremely high backs, which blocked both nosey ears and wandering eyes. He wouldn't wait long.

A man approached the table. "Hello, Mr. Denney." His guest would be the President's White House Chief of Staff Steve Lewis; a key individual that Don worked with in the Nissassa days. Steve was an overly ambitious man and extremely loyal to his boss. Chief of Staff would be a steppingstone for Steve. Like many others in D.C., he had strong aspirations for higher authorities and greater power.

"Hello, Steve. Very good to see you. How is the President?"

"Sir, he is well, and he asked me to send his best regards." Steve sat down and as he did, a waiter stood by diligently to take his drink order. "Unsweet tea, please."

"Yes, sir, immediately." And with that, the waiter departed.

"Very nice of the President to share good wishes. I am glad to hear he is doing well." In actuality, Mr. Denney was far less impressed to hear of the President's good wishes as he was to learn he was still on the President's radar.

While staring Steve in the eye, Andrew pulled out his phone and turned it off. His actions were intentional. Steve did not miss the message and copied Andrew's actions. Once the screens were blank, Steve continued talking.

"Mr. Denney, I want you to know, the President and I are doing everything we can to get as much leniency as possible for Don."

Andrew just looked at Steve. There was a long pause and Steve mentally rewound what he just said, trying to figure out if he had mis-stepped. "Yes, Steve…. about that. I am not sure how this news has escaped you, but all charges against Don have been dropped. He is a free man and was home earlier this week.

As I understand, he has run off to find an apartment. The question I had planned to ask you was *'how did you get the charges dropped?'* Now, I'd like to understand how you do not know about his freedom?"

Steve was dumbfounded. Part of him contemplated if this was Andrew's attempt at a horrible joke. It only took a few seconds looking at Mr. Denney that he realized Don's freedom was not a joke. Andrew was telling the truth.

"Sir, I, um, I don't know, but this is great news. Perhaps some of the wheels we set in motion came through and we just haven't been informed yet."

"Son, don't bullshit me. I've been in the game for far too long. I'd wager that prior to our meeting, you checked with each of your 'wheels' regarding efforts to help my son. Before you learned of his freedom, you were likely well prepared to tell me everything they were doing. The notion that one of them succeeded two days ago and failed to tell you is preposterous. I'd kindly ask, do not take me for a fool." Andrew could be a very charming man. He could also be a raging asshole. Steve knew this and realized it would be wise to find ways to avoid the latter.

"Mr. Denney, you are correct. My apologies. But given Don is free, why did you ask to meet me?"

"I want to know who did this. If it wasn't you, it's clear it was someone. The notion that the arresting officer forgot Miranda Rights and the prosecuting attorney no longer sees enough evidence to continue is utter horseshit. Someone wanted my son out of jail, and I want to know who."

"Sir, I can do that. Give me a few days and I'll get back to you." Andrew nodded and raised his glass of water for a drink. As he did, the waiter, standing a decent distance away, took that as his opportunity to set down Steve's tea.

"Steve, one final issue. Don is not to learn of our discussion. Do you understand?"

"Yes, sir. This stays between us."

Andrew raised his phone and turned it back on, as did Steve. The subject would change to a topic that allowed the presence of active cell phones.

"I noticed the President believes his national security bill doesn't have enough votes in the House."

"Funny, it's what the President and I just spoke about before arriving here. We are hopeful at this point, but not confident. There are still some strings to pull."

"Good. I hope the bill succeeds. It would be good for the nation, for the President and for me."

"I concur on all counts, sir."

Over the next hour, Steve and Andrew would continue with what they both saw as political small talk. To nearly every other American, the discussion would have been fascinating. It's how D.C. worked. Small talk among the elite was like verbal crack cocaine to the media and average American.

\*\*\*\*\*\*\*\*\*\*\*\*\*\*\*\*\*\*\*\*\*\*\*\*\*\*\*\*\*\*\*\*\*\*\*\*\*\*\*\*

Two black sedans in Belgrade would soon converge at a downtown dock on the Danube River. Nikola and Don were both traveling to dinner in separate vehicles. Dinner would be served on a beautiful yacht that was converted into a restaurant. Nikola arrived first, closely followed by Don. The ship's crew, a captain, a cook and a waiter, were the only others who'd be aboard. Nikola bought out the entire boat for the night. With a short blast of the ship's horn, the engine revolutions increased, and the vessel pulled out onto the black Danube water as a cool winter evening air blanketed the river.

"Good evening, Don. Welcome aboard."

"Thank you, Nikola." They both walked into the main dining area and sat down. The boat would slowly steam down the Danube. In the bitter cold, Nikola's private yacht for the night was the only pleasure craft on the river, occasionally passed by a commercial barge. They were alone inside a warm glass dining cabin, with an exceptional view of the Belgrade Fortress on the river's edge lit up against the night sky. The view was magnificent. Vast, beautifully illuminated stone walls rose at 90-degree angles from the shoreline, accompanied by spires and a statue atop a lone pillar. All blanketed with flood lights, high into the air from the river's edge. It was far more than just a castle and was appropriately named a fortress.

After some more small talk, Nikola broached the subject Don longed to hear, "Don, may we discuss why I have brought you here?"

"Yes, Nikola. I'd welcome that conversation."

"You were one of the senior officers of Nissassa. Is that correct?"

Immediately, Don was uneasy. "Nikola, with all due respect, my attorneys have asked me to avoid discussions...."

Nikola cut him off. "Don, I am not the U.S. Government, nor do I care about legalities." Nikola grinned. "And let's not forget, I am the one who paid your attorneys. Don, I don't have much time for such things. Let's talk. Your concept of operating a live training range in Africa is not the first of its kind. Do you not think that many of the 'freedom fighters' in the breakaway sections of Ukraine, Georgia, North Africa and other places have received similar training?"

Don, like many others, had heard several allegations that Russian mercenaries were heavily involved in Crimea, Donetsk, and Luhansk, the three breakaway regions of Ukraine. There were also reports they were in North Africa. "Interesting. I was unaware. To answer your first question, yes. I contracted Nissassa efforts for the U.S. Government."

"Thank you for your honesty. Now we are getting somewhere. I have friends with similar companies that could use your unique skill set. May I ask you what your exact role was and what you controlled?"

Don explained the operation over the next ten minutes. It was clear Nikola knew the framework of the operation. Don just provided the detail. Nikola focused on how Don secured the contracts and the payments.

"I see," said Nikola. "This is exactly why I wanted to speak with you. Currently, I have a minor problem with one of my colleague's operations. You see, he has well-trained teams, but few opportunities. I am interested in seeing what partnerships we may be able to establish using your unique contacts." Don had not shared any information about his White House contacts, but he had a strong hunch Nikola knew about Steve.

Nikola continued. "It is unfortunate your operation was disrupted. I presume you are not very fond of those who exposed Nissassa. I have friends who are also, let's say, 'disenchanted,' with those responsible for imprisoning you. Curt Nover, Mark Smith, Allison Donley, and some pilot named Doug Thiessen. My friends may welcome the opportunity to help you enact some level of retribution."

Don's pulse quickened. He had cursed those names nightly for months while sitting in a jail cell awaiting trial. "Yes, I'm listening. You have my attention."

"Great. My proposal has two parts. First, I'd like you to sit down with Katarina tomorrow morning and try to provide a dossier of sorts on each of them. After that, I'd like to have you meet the head of our training operation. You two could discuss opportunities that could gainfully employ our teams. Are you interested?"

Don did not need to hesitate long. "Nikola, it sounds like a promising opportunity. I can't commit to anything, but let's start with the discussions you mentioned."

"Excellent. Katarina will be at your hotel in the morning. As for tonight, let's continue our wonderful meal." Nikola was engaging. He was an excellent storyteller and an intent listener. The discussion would wind around various. By the minute, Don's comfort level with Nikola was bolstered.

\*\*\*\*\*\*\*\*\*\*\*\*\*\*\*\*\*\*\*\*\*\*\*\*\*\*\*\*\*\*\*\*\*\*\*\*\*\*\*\*

The next day in D.C., three men dressed in conservative business suits sat inside a West Wing waiting room. They were not FBI agents, but based on their dress and demeanor, that would have been a great guess. Steve opened his office door, looked at the three and said, "Gentlemen, come in, please."

The three stood and followed Steve into his office.

"I had lunch recently with a powerful individual. I was blindsided by his news that the charges against Don Denney were dismissed, and he was released from prison. Does anyone care to tell me how that happened?"

Before the meeting, the three had also learned the news of Don's release. Ironically, it was Steve who had covertly tasked them months ago to try and mitigate or eliminate the charges against Don. Each of them, however, was just as surprised as Steve and were smart enough not to take the credit. Finally, one spoke. "Sir, it's clear someone got to the arresting officer and the DA. I have spoken with both, and neither will say a word. They are both sticking to their stories."

"Thanks, Dick Tracy, but that's not helpful." Steve already knew this. "OK. Then why no press or media? Jerry is rotting in another prison awaiting his trial and seems to be in the news every freakin' week."

Another spoke, "Sir, we've asked. But nearly every media executive has refused to even listen to the notion of running a story about Don's freedom. Excuses ranged from '*it isn't newsworthy*' to '*such a story would only weaken our citizens' belief in the judicial system*.' Both excuses are bullshit, but no one is talking."

Steve was not pleased with the answer, but it was far more informative than the one from Dick Tracy. "OK. New mission for you. Find out who sprung Don. And more importantly, what they are after. Do you understand?"

All three nodded.

"Great. Now get out." The three arose and departed the office. Steve was no closer to providing Andrew an answer than he had been at lunch. The key question was whether or not to tell the President. After a short personal mental debate, Steve knew if he brought it up, he could only explain the surface and the President would want far more answers; answers Steve did not have.  There was no point in informing the President at this time.  More answers were needed.

*****************************************

Don awoke early in Belgrade and hit the hotel gym.  After a shower, he strolled down to the restaurant for a casual breakfast.  Sitting at a window table, Don watched the streets of Belgrade come alive.  A bit dirtier and grittier than the U.S., but there was a warmth to the city.  His phone rang at 0700Hrs.  It was Katarina.  The two spent the morning together.  He shared everything he knew about Curt and the others.  Katarina made a point to ask Don if she could record the meeting, as English was her second language.  Don obliged.  Even though it was recorded, Katarina also took notes.

By noon, they would finish in the hotel and head south to the Serbian city of Novi Sad.  There, he'd have dinner with a man who called himself 'Bull' in English, or 'Bik' in Serbian.  He was a beast of a fellow, drank heavily, and boasted of the capabilities of his trained teams of mercenaries.  If they could do half the things Bull suggested, Don was certain he could find them work.

Throughout the meal, Bull drank beer nonstop and must have challenged Don to fifteen arm wrestling matches.  Each time, Katarina smiled.  They both knew Bull would have easily won.  After dinner, Katarina drove Don back to his hotel in Belgrade.  When he entered his room, a small envelope was on the dresser in front of the TV.  He opened the envelope, discovering it contained a business-class ticket back to Dulles, through Vienna, departing in the morning.  Next to the envelope was a bottle of champagne, chilling in a sterling silver ice bucket and a small tin of caviar.  In front of the food and drink was a handwritten note from Nikola which merely said, '*Thank you for your time.*'  After the previous days' dinner, Don's apprehensions about Nikola had eased.  This, however, was too much, and some of his concerns returned.  He was far from comfortable with the items left in his room while he was absent. '*What else was left?*' He thought.  No matter, in a day he would be back in the U.S., still a free man, and with an opportunity.

## *Chapter Nine*
# Long Tall Natalie

The next weeks flew past. March would soon arrive and the relenting wintry weather in Chicago and Brussels would also soon ease. Allison continued with the wedding plans. Curt was proving his worth at the Hospital, and Smitty landed a management position at U.S. Steel in Gary, Indiana, overseeing security operations. As for Buck, he had flown into darn near every European capital.

At the Brussels FBO, Buck awaited his next mission out of the Executive Terminal. He'd be flying the NATO Assistant Secretary General for Policy to Vienna where she would speak at the Organization for Security and Cooperation in Europe (OSCE), a far more diplomatic and political entity than NATO although it shared some similar structures and missions. The trip would be an overnighter and Buck's second time in Vienna.

Buck's passengers arrived and within a half hour they were on their way. It was a quick flight over the Alps, and Buck loved the scenery. Once at Vienna's VIP terminal, Buck shut down the aircraft. As he did, a small fleet of vehicles pulled in front of it. Two were there to take the assistant secretary general and her staff to the OSCE. As Buck refueled the plane, performed his post flight inspection and then sealed up the aircraft, another beautiful black Mercedes Benz waited.

Buck walked past the Mercedes towards the terminal offices. As he did, the driver of the vehicle began walking towards him and said, "Mr. Thiessen? Doug Thiessen?"

Buck was a bit surprised. "Yes. That's me. What can I do for you?"

"Sir, I am your driver."

Buck was a bit shocked. He knew the OSCE had a substantial budget, but when the executive pilot gets a chauffeured ride, life is good. "OK then. I'd like to go to Vienna."

"Yes, sir. I was instructed to take you to your hotel."

"My hotel?"

"Yes. Reservations were made for you at the Marriott on Parkringstrasse across from Stadtpark, or, in English, the City Park. It's a beautiful hotel, sir. I think you'll like it."

Again, Buck did not know what to think, but he really was growing fond of the service in Austria. "Alright. What are we waiting for?" Buck got in the car, and they drove off.

The car pulled in front of the hotel and the driver was not wrong. The hotel, the park, the ring street or 'Parkringstrasse'... none of it was a disappointment. Buck jumped out of the Mercedes, checked into his room, changed clothes, and strolled through Vienna looking ever the tourist. Hofburg Palace, Kohlmarkt, Stephansdom, Votivkirche, Naschmarkt, Karlsplatz, and so much more. It was a city one could fall in love with. Buck could not be happier.

That evening, Buck walked down to the lobby, looking for a place to eat. He heard roars of cheering emanating from the hotel bar named Champions. On the TVs, college basketball's March Madness was playing. Buck could not pass it up. He walked into the restaurant, snuggled up to the bar, and ordered a beer. While waiting for his drink, Buck perused a menu and watched the game along with other traveling Americans and locals who loved college hoops.

During the games and dinner, Buck struck up a conversation with a fellow American a few seats down. He was a computer engineer, on a business trip with Siemens. Buck was not completely sure what the man did, but it had to do with next generation magnetic resonance imaging. Brian was his name, a good guy and easy to talk to.

During a pause in their conversation as they both were looking up at the game, another patron walked up to the bar and took the seat right in between both of them. A well dressed, stunningly beautiful blond. It was no other than Katarina.

"Excuse me," she said to Buck. "Is this seat taken?"

"It's yours if you want it," Buck replied hastily.

"Great. Being stuck in Europe, I just miss good American basketball." She ordered a Budweiser and chicken wings. "Who won the earlier games?" She asked Buck.

"Sorry, I don't know. We've only been here a half hour. I'm sure they'll cover the scores during the halftime break."

"Oh, excuse me. Where are my manners? My name is Natalie. Natalie Brandstetter."

Buck thought he had traveled to another universe. Never in his life had such a situation with a strikingly beautiful woman happened. Vienna was quickly becoming his favorite city. "Hi, Natalie. My name is Doug. Doug Thiessen, but my friends call me Buck."

Natalie downed her new beer in roughly fifteen seconds. Not stopping until it was finished. She looked Buck in the eyes, coyly. "Well, Doug, can I be your friend?" She waved the empty beer glass in front of her as she said it.

"Absolutely! Bartender. Can we get another round?" With that, Buck was hooked. The bartender brought two drinks, and Buck raised his glass. "Cheers!"

Natalie too raised her glass with one hand and grabbed Buck by the chin with her other. She turned his face, so they were staring each other in the eye. "Cheers," she replied. Even during a 'honey trap' sting and international espionage, Katarina would not risk seven years of bad sex. Superstitions were particularly important to her.

After putting their glasses down, Buck inquired, "What was that?"

"I saved you. Where I come from, if you don't look your drinking partner in the eye when toasting, it's seven years of bad sex. Given our new friendship, I couldn't let that happen now, could I?" Her hand rested on Buck's thigh.

Buck laughed. "No. Ha! I guess not. I should thank you later!"

"I plan on it." She answered quickly. Buck's heart melted, as a tingling was felt in his nether regions.

They spent the evening in the bar, laughing, flirting, and talking. Buck's other new friend, Brian, no longer existed. Katarina played him perfectly. She'd accompany Buck to his hotel room and woke up with him the next morning.

"Hey, Natalie. It was a perfect night, but I gotta go. I had a great time, and I am hoping I can see you again next time I am in Vienna."

"I'd really like that, Buck. You're a doll. Maybe I can visit you in Brussels, too."

"Sure. That would be great!" They exchanged numbers and said goodbye. Buck ran to the lobby to turn in his hotel key card and then hailed a cab. Waiting for him in front of the hotel was the same Mercedes and driver that brought him to the hotel. "Mr. Thiessen. Good morning. Are you ready?"

Buck slowed his pace. "Yes... Yes, I am. Thank you." He got into the vehicle and proceeded to the airport. On the way, he programmed Natalie's number into his phone. He was as giddy as a teenager.

At the Vienna airport, Buck performed his preflight and opened the aircraft. Everything was ready, and he awaited his passengers. Once they arrived, he sealed up the aircraft and opened his checklist.

He turned to the 'Starting Engine Checklist.' He cranked engine one. It started just as quickly as it ever had. Oil pressure, revolutions per minute, temperatures gauges all climbed into tolerances. *'Good girl,'* Buck thought, as if talking to the first engine. Once online and in operational limits, he quickly scanned out at engine two on the right and depressed the start button. The blades began to turn, but after three rotations, they came to a standstill. He took his finger off the button, waited, and pushed it another time. This time, the propeller blades stood still. Buck scanned all his instruments, switches, knobs, and all the other zillion things in the cockpit. Everything was set correctly. There was no more troubleshooting to do. It was no use. Buck cut the fuel to engine one and finished the engine shutdown checklist. He unstrapped and trudged to the back of the airplane to tell his passengers the unwelcome news. It was his first delayed flight for maintenance. He escorted his passengers into the VIP terminal lounge, then returned to the aircraft. A few aircraft maintainers at the terminal helped him pull off the engine two cowling. Everything looked fine. Buck checked the starter wiring, and it too was perfect. He then took a few bolts off from the starter block. As he gently pulled back the starter block to peek inside, he heard a loud 'clunk.' The other maintainers with Buck said, "Well, that didn't sound good."

"No. It didn't." Buck replied. Investigating further, he found the problem. The starter gear shaft had sheared off and was laying in the bottom of starter block. He would be flying nowhere today.

Buck worked with the local maintainers and ordered a new starter. It would be there in two days. Buck returned to the VIP terminal lounge and informed his passengers of the bad news. He helped them secure commercial travel. It killed him to think they'd fly commercial. Once complete, he took a cab back to the Vienna Marriott and asked if they had a room for two more days. As luck would have it, they did. And as luck would have it, Natalie would also have a free calendar for the two days. Over the next two days, Buck fell hard and fast for her. It was just as she'd planned and extremely easy since she knew everything about him before they met. It also helped that one of the maintainers was happy to set a piece of metal in the starter block that upon engine start would damage the main shaft.

Buck would never learn the actual financier for his hotel reservations and limo. He also would never learn that the entity which secured those assets was also the one that sabotaged his aircraft.

## Chapter Ten
# Mending Fences

Don had secured a small apartment near Verizon center in downtown D.C., spending time furnishing it and settling in. It was a great location, full of bars, restaurants and an easy commute to catch a Capitals or Wizards game. After catching up on some much-needed sleep, Don pulled out his cell phone and typed in a text message.

'Hey stranger. Remember me?'

Steve looked down at his phone. A text from Don. *'Jesus!'* he thought and quickly responded.

'Where are you!?'

Don replied, and the exchange continued....

'D.C. Near Verizon Center.' (Don)

'Can we meet, now?' (Steve)

'Sure, shall we meet at Clyde's in an hour' (Don)

'Make it 30 minutes' (Steve)

Steve needed answers from Don. There had to be some clues that would help provide answers to Andrew, a key donor to the President. Steve ordered his secretary to clear his schedule and tell the President that an emergency had arisen, should he ask. Steve jumped in a staff car and was at Clyde's in fifteen minutes.

Steve sat at the bar and drank a lemonade. Eventually, Don came strolling in as if he owned the place. At the bar, Steve settled his tab, and the two moved to a table.

Steve started. "Well. Freedom looks good on you."

Don smiled. "Yeah. I think it suits me. I must confess, when I walked out of prison and didn't see my family, you or any of our mutual friends, I was somewhat perplexed."

Steve paused. He realized that was a slight dig from Don, and partially deserved. Steve knew Don would never turn on the President. Don's loyalty, much like Steve's, was unwavering. And while Don sat in prison without parole, it was Nikola who proved more powerful than the Executive Branch in garnering his freedom. "Yes. I can imagine. Don, I want you to know we were doing everything to get you out and were attacking the issue from every angle."

"I don't doubt that, Steve. Look. Enough. I am out. I trust you." Don had taken his shot. He need not overplay his hand. The next few minutes would be crucial. "Steve, I do have perhaps some interesting information for you." Don paused. Then made his pitch, "If you're seeking more of the services I previously provided, I can meet your requirements."

Steve was dumbfounded. "Excuse me? How are..."

Don cut him off. "Steve. Our long-standing agreement has always relied on limited knowledge and plausible deniability. The less you know, the better. Let's just say I have an offer to join a similar outfit as their contracting officer. If you or your boss are interested, I'm ready to fulfill your requirements."

While Don was correct about their long-standing agreement, he also knew if he shared information that the teams would not solely be former American Special Operations Forces, but also from other nations to include former Eastern Bloc nations as well as potentially Russians, Steve would never consider the offer. But in Don's mind, there was a gray area as to 'who' completed the mission... as long as it was a success. Somewhat ironically, Don believed he could make a good argument it was actually better to use non-Americans given it provided even greater distance from the White House should a team get exposed or fail. Still, at this point, it was better to keep such information to himself.

"Don, I don't know. The whole Nissassa thing is still too

fresh." Steve was not receptive.

"Fair. But promise me you'll ask your boss."

"Sure, Don, but if I do that, you need to tell me who facilitated your release? At some point, the President is going to ask, and I don't have anything close to an answer."

Don knew Steve was right. He had to expose some of his relationship with Nikola. "OK. I can't say much, but a very philanthropic individual who runs an operation similar to my last one. He realizes my talents and seeks to employ me. He is the man I owe my freedom to."

"Good start. More, please." Steve was not satisfied.

"In time. That's all I can say at this point. Look, I gotta go. It's good to see you, Steve, and I look forward to the chance to do business again." In actuality, Don did not have to go. But he also did not want to stay and answer any more questions about Nikola.

"Yeah. OK. Sounds good. I'll be in touch." With that, they both got up, shook hands, and went their separate ways. Don was pleased with the meeting's outcome. Steve? Not so much.

\*\*\*\*\*\*\*\*\*\*\*\*\*\*\*\*\*\*\*\*\*\*\*\*\*\*\*\*\*\*\*\*\*\*\*\*\*\*\*\*

On the Vienna airport ramp, aircraft maintainers were completing the repair work on Buck's aircraft. After a quick engine run check, he'd be flying back to Brussels. Buck would not have a scheduled VIP mission from NATO, but he also would not be flying alone. Over the course of two days, Natalie had convinced him to fly her back to Brussels so she could stay with him, at least for a while. He did not think twice about the offer. Within an hour, they were airborne.

He'd be in Brussels in a few hours and would work with the NATO contractor for his next flight. Taking Assistant Secretary General of Operations Dan Manzina to Belgrade and then onto Kosovo. That flight would be in two days and from that point on, Buck would be back on schedule with his contractor.

## *Chapter Eleven*
# Befuddled

The United Center in Chicago was rocking. Over twenty thousand screaming fans were going wild watching one of the NCAA Sweet Sixteen Basketball matchups. Thirty rows up near center court, Curt and Smitty sat there watching the game. Duke and Indiana were into their second overtime and, with fifteen seconds left, Duke was up by two. It was a game for the ages.

Indiana in-bounded the ball and transitioned with ease to their half-court game. From there, the Blue Devil's defense became stifling. The clock ticked and the Hoosiers desperately tried to penetrate the ball inside, continuing to pass it around the horn. With only seconds left, Indiana's star forward caught the ball and was smothered with two defenders. He tried to pass to an open guard, but the ball bounced off his leg and out of bounds. The Hoosiers were eliminated. Curt and Smitty would wait yet another year for the Hoosiers to win a National Championship.

After the game, the two headed back to Curt's apartment. Smitty would spend the night, then head to the steel mill in the morning. Once at the house, the two cracked a beer and turned on the TV. The news rumbled in the background as they spoke.

"Buddy, that was a shit game."

Curt responded. "I agree. On one hand, I really appreciate the parity that has developed in college basketball. On the other hand, I also really liked when Indiana was a powerhouse. Sadly, both cannot coexist."

"How are the wedding plans going?"

"Good. I think. I try to give Allison a huge amount of space on that issue. I think my only job is to show up."

"Yeah. Try not to fuck that up." Smitty smiled at his own joke.

"How is your work going at the mill?"

"It's all right. Gary is a shithole though, and I'd really like to get out of there. I'm looking for other options."

"Smitty, why don't you come to the city? I am sure I can put in a good word at the hospital. Lord knows Cook County Medical could use more security because of the amount of gang members we treat in the emergency room."

"Yeah, I appreciate that, Curt. Chicago is a wonderful place for me to visit, but I love Northwest Indiana. The small-town squares like Crown Point, Hobart, or Valparaiso. Corn fields for miles. Sure, I can rage in Chi-Town for a night or two, but I need to hear corn rustling as it grows in the night, and I need to smell pig shit as I drive old county roads."

"Smitty. You are one crazy cat. OK. I guess I should just be happy you're close. It still bums me out Buck is so far away." And with that, as if by magic, Curt's phone rang. It was a video call from Buck.

"Buck! What are you doing?"

"Doc! I stayed up all night just to give you shit about your Hoosiers getting crushed by Duke! Great game, eh?"

"Buck, it was two points. Fuck off…. never mind. Look who's here!" Curt swung the phone around.

"Buck, you crazy fucker! Why are you awake?" Smitty said.

"Smitty! Great to see you. Are you two guys cuddling and hugging one out after Indiana's loss?"

"Funny. Do you write these lame jokes or pay for them? If it's the latter, you're getting robbed."

"Hahahaha! Anyway. It's good to see you two. Guess what? I found a chick!" Curt and Smitty looked at each other in disbelief.

Smitty spoke, "Do you mean a human female or one of the high-tech sex dolls?"

Buck did not even flinch at the question. Knowing who Buck was as a human, the question was fair. "No, an actual human! Here look." With that, Buck held up a 5x7 photo of the two in the camera lens. The photo clearly displayed two things. First, Natalie was beautiful, and second, Buck was extremely smitten. "If you guys want, I can go into the bedroom and show you some video of her sleeping."

"There's the Buck we know and love!" Smitty said.

Curt jumped in. "No, Buck! That's ok. Hey buddy, we are thrilled for ya. Give us the details." And with that, Buck told Smitty and Curt all about Natalie. As he spoke, both could hear how happy Buck was. As Buck finished, he said, "Hey Doc, I hope there's room for one more at the wedding. If things progress, I'd like to bring Natalie. You guys are gonna love her!"

"Sure, Buck. For you, there's always room for one more." The three continued to talk. It was almost 0400Hrs in Belgium, but Buck didn't care. The three amigos were together, albeit via technology.

Eventually, Buck hung up. Smitty grabbed another beer from the kitchen. It was now pushing midnight in Chicago. Just one more as a nightcap. From the family room, Smitty heard Curt say, "No fucking way!"

Smitty saw Curt watching the television and walked in. "What's up, buddy?"

"According to this news, Jerry's trial will start soon."

Smitty smiled, "Good. I hope that fucker rots in jail."

Curt continued. "Yeah, me too, but as a side note in the report, it seems all the charges against Denney were dropped weeks ago. He's a free man."

Smitty was dumbfounded. "That can't be right." They both began scouring the news on their iPhones. Sure enough, there it was… one obscure news reference to Denney's release in the *Cumberland Times*.

Smitty looked at Curt. "Well, what by chance do you think Mr. Denney is up to then?"

"Buddy, I don't know. But I think it may be wise to watch our backs for a while."

"Fair. Well, with that news, I no longer want this beer. I'm off to bed. Good night, Curt." Smitty said.

"Night, Smitty. See ya in the morning."

## *Chapter Twelve*
# The Deadly Double-Cross

Buck and Natalie were out on the town in Brussels. She told Buck it was her first time there; far from the truth. She'd frequented Vienna, Brussels, and New York City multiple times. They were the top three cities in the world for espionage. She faked it well and Buck took on the role of tour guide, leading her to see the ancient 'Mannequin Piss' (the Peeing Boy) followed by the newer Peeing Girl and Peeing Dog. Clearly, Belgians have a strange sense of humor. They walked through the city square, took photos of the Beer Museum, and then settled into a fire-warmed restaurant ordering the standard tourist staples; mussels, frites and beer.

"Bucky (her pet name for Buck), this is just wonderful. I can't thank you enough for today. I wish I could spend every day with you."

"Baby. I wish that too. I really do. You are the best thing that's ever happened to me."

"Do you really have to leave tomorrow??" Natalie shot her puppy dog eyes at Buck. They were lethal in more ways than one.

"Yes. Duty calls. I must fly to Belgrade and then Pristina. I should be back the next day. Do you want to wait here for me? You can stay in the apartment." Buck thought he'd offered a wonderful solution, but she had other plans.

Natalie's eyes lit up. "Belgrade? I have a friend there! Can I come with you?"

Buck had not considered this. "Sweetheart, I fly some fairly powerful people. I can't just have extra people in the aircraft when they are paying for their privacy; no matter how awesome you are."

"I understand, but what if I flew up front with you in the cockpit, like we did when we flew here together? Bucky, I could be your copilot." Her smile turned sheepishly coy.

Buck's mind churned. "That's an option I hadn't even thought about." He sat there. Sure, he won the NATO contract on a low bid with a single pilot operator waiver in Europe. Would the NATO contractor mind? It was his contract. If he chose to have a second pilot for safety, wouldn't that make NATO happier... even if the second pilot had no skills? In Buck's mind, it made perfect sense.

"You know what? Yes. Let's try it. But you have to act the part of a copilot when the customers are onboard. Okay?"

"YES, BUCK! I can be an EXCEPTIONAL actress! That's more than OK! Thank you! You are the BEST!" Little did Buck know how good Katarina's acting abilities truly were.

Buck cracked a small joke back, "Aww... shucks. You probably say that to all the guys." How unwittingly and unfortunately true his statement was.

That night, as Buck slept, Natalie sent a quick text in Serbian to Nikola.

*'I'm on the flight. Belgrade tomorrow.'*

The next afternoon, they both arrived at the plane and Natalie offered to help Buck get everything ready. She was, after all, his copilot. Buck gave her a few menial tasks. There was nothing, really, but he wanted her to feel like part of his crew. The passengers arrived. There were two, as expected. Natalie helped with the luggage in the back, as Buck settled the passengers into the cabin. Afterwards, he checked the cargo area and the bags. Natalie actually had done a great job strapping down and securing the items. He was impressed.

The two of them entered the cockpit and Buck started the aircraft. After a brief taxi, they took off for a two-and-a-half-hour flight to Belgrade.

Unbeknown to Buck, this was an important event for NATO. Assistant Secretary General Manzina would be meeting with the Serbian President in Belgrade and then later, the President of Kosovo in Pristina. There were hopes he could deescalate some of the rising tensions between the nations. Disappointingly, the rhetoric and pressure had escalated to where the two Presidents refused to meet on common ground, hence the separate trips to both countries. Although the Kosovo War officially had ended in 1999 under U.N. Security Council Resolution 1244 (UNSCR 1244), decades later, the area was still a tinderbox, with NATO peacekeeping forces called 'KFOR' still assigned to Kosovo. Most Western nations had long recognized Kosovo's independence; however, some still abstained from recognition, even to this day. Russia, China, and some of their other allies remain staunchly opposed to officially recognizing Kosovo, supporting the Serbian position. As the talk in Serbian coffee shops goes, NATO cannot afford to keep troops in Kosovo forever. It was merely a matter of time before present day Kosovo territory would return to Serbia.

Buck's aircraft landed in Belgrade and the welcoming committee was nonexistent. Assistant Secretary Manzina was met by a taxi. The cab driver was the highest-level dignitary sent to greet the senior diplomat. Given the cold relationship between Serbia and NATO, Mr. Manzina did not expect more. Since the bombing of Belgrade by NATO in 1999, many Serbians thoroughly disliked NATO. Government leaders who wished to remain in office took little opportunity to afford the appropriate level of recognition to NATO, even if it was warranted.

The NATO personnel entered the cab and departed for the President's office. They'd return to the aircraft in three hours. Natalie looked at Buck and said, "Hey baby, I'm going to get a cab and grab a coffee with my friend. Is that OK?"

Buck was slightly taken aback; he had expectations he'd accompany her. She saw this in his eyes. Natalie tried to ease the situation. "Baby, look. I really like you. But our relationship is still new, and I don't want to jeopardize it by introducing friends too early. Plus, I want to tell her all about you! Does that make sense? I hope you understand."

Her point was fair, albeit a lie. Buck had not really considered an intro of his friends back in the U.S. "Sure. I understand. Go have fun. I'll see you in a few hours."

"Thanks, Bucky. You're the best!" Soon, a cab would arrive

and whisk Natalie away.  She'd be meeting Nikola in a half-hour.

Buck remained at the aircraft.  He had it refueled, did a post flight inspection and then walked into the Belgrade executive services terminal.  He jotted off a quick text back to Curt and Smitty:

> *'Dudes.  Great talking to you the other night.  In Belgrade, then onto Kosovo – if I recall, some of your old stomping grounds.  I'm trying out a new copilot this trip.  Natalie is with me.  Buddies, I tell ya, I think she could be the one!  Catch up with you later!'*

Neither Curt nor Smitty were on their phones to respond.  No matter.  They'd eventually get back to him.  Buck surfed through the internet on his phone, checked the weather for the flight into Pristina and then filed his flight plan.  Three minutes after he submitted the plan into the system, it was rejected.  He called base operations and a man with a thick Serbian accent answered.  "Hello, base operations."

"Yes, sir, I am Mr. Thiessen, the pilot for callsign NATO 02.  I see my flight plan was denied.  Can you please explain?"

"Mr. Thiessen, Serbia does not authorize any direct flights between Belgrade and Pristina.  You will need to alter your flight plan."

"Yes.  I am aware of that policy, but I was told by the NATO Kosovo Forces Commander (COMKFOR) that he and the Serbian Defense Chief had worked out an exception to policy."  Buck was right.  Assistant Secretary Manzina had spoken with Italian Major General Mario Torres, COMKFOR.  According to the general, a waiver was approved.

"Mr. Thiessen, please hold."  After a brief five minutes, the base operator returned.  "Sir, yes, I have your approval here, but this is highly irregular.  You must not make this a routine flight.  Do you understand?"

Buck had no intent to make it routine.  "Yes, sir.  This is my only flight here... far from routine.  I really appreciate it.  I will resubmit the flight plan now.  Have a good day."  Buck hung up.

The distance between Belgrade and Pristina was 150 miles as the crow flies.  However, for the average traveler, movement between the two was a nightmare.  For ground movement, it was extremely difficult to cross through the Administrative Boundary Line or 'ABL' (per UNSCR 1244, there was no border between Serbia and Kosovo but rather an ABL).  Most traffic needed to drive south along the ABL until it neared North Macedonia and then into Kosovo.  It turned a typical two-and-a-half-hour journey into a four-hour drive.  Buck would fly between the two capitals in approximately 45 minutes.  For the average traveler, direct flights were prohibited.  Anyone wishing to fly between the two would require a layover somewhere.  Also, in most cases, all flights into Kosovo had to enter through Albanian airspace, a ridiculous waste of time and fuel for flights approaching Kosovo from the north.

After a few hours, Natalie returned by cab with a fairly sizeable box.  She walked up to Buck and kissed him.  "Hey Bucky!  How are you doing, baby?  Look at this!  I told my friend about you, and she gave us a 'new relationship' gift!  Isn't that sweet?"

"Awesome.  That's really nice.  What is it?"

"A surprise!  Don't worry.  It only weighs about fifteen kilos.  It's nothing.  I'll strap it in behind the passenger seats and we can open it back in Brussels."

"Perfect.  I'll finish up the preflight.  Our customers will be here soon."  She kissed him again, a long kiss as if to say everything was going to be fine.  The two separated to complete their respective tasks.  Soon, another cab pulled up.  Mr. Manzina and his staffer exited the cab and headed to the aircraft.

The sunset departure out of Belgrade was beautiful and uneventful, right up to the point when Buck spoke to air traffic control and requested direct to Pristina.  Much like Belgrade base operations, the air traffic controllers had not got the waiver memo and were trying to force him to fly to Albania.  After a few minutes, the controller transmitted, "NATO 02, you are cleared direct Pristina, but you must maintain under 10,000 feet." Buck responded, "Copy, cleared direct Pristina at or below 10K." Buck turned the plane south. It was not the preferred altitude Buck wanted to fly at, but it was better than nothing. *'Just another air traffic controller asshole, trying to get in his last jab,'* Buck thought.

Natalie looked at her watch. Over the headset she said, "Well, that added a few minutes to our flight. Very frustrating, Bucky. Sorry."

Buck replied. "Eh, it is what it is. No worries. COMKFOR told me this was a likely response. The only assets that are ever allowed between the two cities are NATO KFOR helicopters, which operate in lower altitudes. No big deal. The views will be better, and I won't have to bleed oxygen out of the pressurization system." Buck set the autopilot for 10,000 feet after adjusting the altimeter.

They were quickly at altitude and would be crossing the Serbian-Kosovo ABL in approximately twenty minutes.

As they flew, Buck noticed Natalie grabbing at her stomach. Finally, he asked, "Are you OK?"

"Yeah, I think so. I may have eaten some rotten food. I had a cake with my coffee, and it isn't settling very well. Do you mind if I get up and walk around?"

"No, not at all. Go ahead. Get better. We have great dinner plans in Pristina. I hear Sarajeva Steak House is one of the best in the entire Balkans."

"OK, Bucky, thanks." She leaned over and kissed him softly with her hand on his chin. It was a kiss full of feeling for both. Unfortunately, each had wildly opposite feelings. Pulling off her headset and unstrapping, she opened the flight deck curtain, walked through, and closed it once on the other side.

Both passengers were trying to catch a quick catnap. She walked past both quietly. As she passed, the warm face of Natalie rapidly transitioned to Katarina's business face. It was stern, cold, and deadly. Natalie opened the gift from her friend. Neatly packed on top were two syringes. She grabbed them, removed their safety caps, and slowly tiptoed towards the passengers. Standing behind them, she quickly injected both. They woke for mere seconds, disoriented, and soon fell unconscious. Natalie returned to the box. She removed a neatly packed, professional grade parachute and quietly put it on. Next, she grabbed a helmet with a mounted commercial night vision device. Once her gear was on, she removed the last two items in the box, an aerosol can, and screwdriver.

Slowly, she moved forward in the aircraft, stopping near Flight Station 130 or 130 inches back from the front of the aircraft. It was just aft of the flight deck, where the wing line adjoined the fuselage. At face level on the starboard side was a metal plate with four fasteners holding it secure. She began unscrewing the fasteners, quickly but with precision. Unfortunately, one screw was stripped. She did not have time to wrestle with it and bent the metal plate up, exposing the main power distribution box. Natalie raised the aerosol can and sprayed highly caustic acid all over the wires and fuses. With that, her task of sabotaging the aircraft was nearly complete.

In the cockpit, Buck was just staring out the window. The flight was somewhat boring. That would change soon. As the initial acid spray hit the breakers, the cockpit LED displays flickered. Next, the master caution light illuminated. Buck sat up in his seat and he switched off the master caution light, then knocked off the autopilot, scanning the instruments. He ran a check internal in his head. *'What the fuck?!'* He had never seen something like this. His night was about to get far worse.

A loud thump was heard throughout the aircraft, then a rush of freezing air flooded the cabin. Buck turned around and slung open the cockpit curtain just in time to see Natalie's legs disappear from the aircraft through the cargo door.

"Natalie!" He Screamed. *'Holy Shit! Did she just get sucked out? NO!'* He thought.

The violent wind in the cabin was overwhelming, yet as he looked back, both of his passengers remained asleep. *'Unbelievable,'* he thought.

Buck quickly reengaged the autopilot, unstrapped, and ran back and closed the cargo door. A quick scan of the door area showed there was no structural damage. He also noticed the gift box was open and empty. *'What the fuck is going on!?'* No matter. Now was not the time to solve that mystery. Buck returned to the cockpit, unfortunately failing to notice the power distribution box cover was removed. Buck re-assumed controls of the aircraft and made another methodical scan of the instruments. *'What are you telling me, old girl? What's wrong?'* he thought. The glass cockpit displays flickered worse than before. On the cockpit circuit board, breakers began to pop. Buck tried to push them in for a reset…. most just popped again. Then the engines began to chug. The Twin Otter's two main fuel tanks are located on the aircraft underbelly, requiring pumps to get the fuel up into the wing root and out to the engines. In the situation of an electrical failure, the main boost pumps would likely fail. Buck tried to push the breakers back in, but they popped again.

Fuel flow to the engines was nearing zero. Buck rapidly activated both emergency boost pumps, and the engines began to calm down and run smoothly. Then more breakers popped. Navigation systems, hydraulic pumps, communications. Some breakers reset when Buck pushed on them. Others did not. Within another 30 seconds, the power to the right emergency boost pump failed and the right engine could take no more. It shut down. Buck shut off the right engine in accordance with the checklist and focused all his efforts on his one remaining good engine. The aircraft began to descend out of 10,000ft. The left engine was now sputtering as well. As a former Special Operations pilot in the Air Force, Buck was disciplined enough to do exceptional mission planning. Today, that paid off. Pristina airport was off the nose for sixty miles. Now at 9,500 feet, he was praying he could make it. Pristina's Adem Jashari Airport had a field elevation of 1,500ft and the mountains he was currently over, topped out at 3,500ft. Buck had a bit of time. "MAYDAY, MAYDAY, MAYDAY. NATO 02 declaring an emergency." As he spoke, he turned his transponder to emergency.

The controller reposed within seconds. "NATO 02, Pristina

Control. Please state the nature of your emergency."

"NATO 02 is a Twin Otter, now single engine with fuel flow problems. Four, er ah, three, three souls, 1.5 hours of fuel onboard."

"NATO 02, climb and maintain 10,000 feet. Will you need emergency vehicles at Pristina?"

"Control, if I could climb to 10,000 feet, I probably wouldn't be talking to you. As it stands, I don't know if I can make Pristina. Please advise on divert fields."

Within fifteen seconds, control responded, "NATO 02, your closest divert fields are Tirana and Skopje. Please advise."

Buck immediately knew both of those airfields were even farther away. He looked out at the night sky and saw a town just off his nose. It was Mitrovica.

"Pristina control. NATO 02. Is there any kind of dirt strip in Mitrovica or the vicinity?"

"NATO 02, negative." As Buck continued flying and descending, he could see the streetlights of a road beyond Mitrovica, which appeared to continue towards Pristina. A quick look at the map and he could see it was the M2. A highway by Kosovo standards, but far from what a western society would call a highway. If worst came to worst, that would be his divert. Soon thereafter, that decision was made for him as the second engine quit. The Twin Otter was now a glider. Buck saw no further value in talking to Pristina Control. They could do nothing for him. He needed to nurse this plane as best he could. Buck cinched down his seatbelt straps, turned around to his passengers and screamed, "Strap in tight!" They didn't hear a word.

Pristina was now thirty miles in front of him and he could see the city lights. Frustratingly, the airport was three more miles south of the city. He was now only 3,500 feet above the terrain. He looked at his instruments. His descent rate was 600 feet per minute. Quick math. There was no chance to make Pristina airfield.

As he flew over the M2 highway, he saw what appeared to be a fairly straight section with limited traffic. Tonight, that was going to be his runway. "Pristina control, NATO 02. Be advised, I can't make PRN. Send emergency vehicles to the M2 highway north of Pristina."

This transmission was something Pristina approach control had never heard. "NATO 02, Pristina Control. Please confirm. You are landing on the road?"

"Pristina Control. Affirm. NATO 02." It would be his last transmission as now all power in the aircraft was dead. The emergency battery had finally failed too.

Buck slowly circled the plane back towards the section of road he had previously spotted. It was eerie. The only sound was the wind whistling by the aircraft. With all the systems failed, he'd need to dead stick the aircraft, using just his own strength. Buck lined up the aircraft and descended. 1000 feet. 750 feet, 500 feet. Buck manually set the flaps to 100%. He could see some vehicle traffic, but none that would affect him. The lights of the houses and the smoke from their chimneys were visible in the streetlights. 100 feet now.

50 feet. Buck's heart raced. His passengers were asleep. Clueless.

Unfortunately, Buck did not see a power-line stretched across the road. At 30 feet, his left main landing gear snagged the wire. The force of the aircraft snapped the cable quickly, but it sent the airplane into a nose down, left yaw. Buck did his best to recover, pulling back on the yoke and stepping on the right rudder, but the flight speed was too low to fully correct the aircraft attitude. The nose landing gear hit first. Then his left wing. The force of the left wing smashing into the ground rolled the aircraft to the right, slamming the fuselage, main landing gear, and then the right wing onto the road. The empennage could withstand no more. It snapped off, exposing the cargo area. As fuel spilled, a fireball erupted on the broken tail section, which was now behind the main aircraft, tumbling down the road. Buck, still conscious, continued to try to induce controls to the aircraft, but there was little use. The elevators and rudder were gone, now 50 feet behind him; part of the empennage. As the plane skidded down the highway, the strain on the right wing was too much and it snapped at the fuselage, again sparking another fire. Without a right wing, the aircraft began rolling. The two passengers in the back, poorly strapped in, were thrown around the fuselage, smashing into the sides as the aircraft tumbled. Eventually, they were both thrown clear of the wreckage at nearly 80 miles an hour. Their bodies would tumble down the road. The staffer slammed into a tree next to the road. He stopped but would be dead within minutes. Mr. Manzina would not feel any of the pain from tumbling down the road. Inside the fuselage, his head had wedged into a piece of the metal ribbing as his body rolled. His neck snapped, and he was dead the moment he was tossed from the aircraft.

Buck continued to hold on. His body flailing in the seat and his head violently shaking. The roll rate was increasing and the bolts holding his seat in place gave way. Buck and his chair flew towards the ceiling of the cockpit. Buck received a massive blow near the front crown of his skull. He was knocked unconscious. The freed seat hit the ceiling with such force, it had wedged into the cabin and now rolled in concert with the fuselage until it came to rest.

There, in the middle of the M2, a 1,000-foot trail of aircraft wreckage lay scattered down the road. The tail section, wing, and fuselage slowly burned. The few vehicles on the road stopped.

Valton, a resident of Pristina who was driving home that night, stopped his car 100 feet in front of the fuselage. He jumped out and ran to the piece of wreckage. Looking in from the open back, he could see Buck, unconscious through the smoke. Without hesitation, he ran into the fuselage and began trying to free Buck from the chair. Coughing on smoke, wincing from the heat and receiving superficial cuts from the exposed metal, Valton finally freed Buck, dragging him from the wreckage. Once clear of danger, Valton laid Buck on the street and collapsed next to his body. Within ten minutes, emergency vehicles arrived and took Buck to the hospital. He was alive, for now. Barely.

\*\*\*\*\*\*\*\*\*\*\*\*\*\*\*\*\*\*\*\*\*\*\*\*\*\*\*\*\*\*\*\*\*\*\*\*\*\*

Twenty minutes earlier, north of the ABL, a parachute quietly fell from the sky. Katarina flipped down her night vision device and scanned the ground. She found the infrared beacon light she was looking for and steered her parachute towards it. On the ground, a small team of former military men jumped in their vehicles and hastily drove to where they believed Katarina would land. She'd be safe. Katarina and Nikola's plan to sabotage Buck's aircraft had worked.

## *Chapter Thirteen*
# Breaking News

Allison was at the condo, working on a piece for the Chicago Tribune, while mainstream news softly played in the background. She'd been commissioned to write a puff piece on a local sailor from Naval Station Great Lakes. It was a straightforward task, and the money was good. As she typed, a 'Breaking News' banner flashed across the television screen, followed by an impassioned host explaining the events as if it were her family member. The story was about a small twin-engine plane with NATO markings, identifiable from privately taken on-scene video. Allison's heart raced, and she picked up the phone to call Curt. He was in the Emergency Room, finishing up a cast on a young boy who'd become a bit too brave on a skateboard. Curt saw the inbound call, stepped away from the child and mom. "Hello baby, what's up?"

"Curt! Turn on the news. There was a plane wreck in Kosovo, and they say it was a NATO plane."

Curt responded, "OK. Slow down. I'll turn it on. But realize, there is still an ongoing NATO mission in Kosovo and there are many aircraft in the area."

His comments eased Allison. "OK. Just turn it on."

"I will. I love you. We can talk later." Curt sat down in the E.R.'s staff break room. The TV was already on the news channel, and he turned up the volume. As he did, he looked down at his phone, which he had not checked for a long while. There was Buck's message.

> *'Dudes. Great talking to you the other night. In Belgrade, then onto Kosovo – if I recall, some of your old stomping grounds. I'm trying out a new copilot this trip. Natalie is with me. Buddies... I tell ya, I think she could be the one! Catch up with you later!'*

Curt's concern began to increase. He called Buck's phone.

The call went straight to voicemail. He then called Smitty and told him to turn on the news. The two spoke for a few minutes, agreeing everything was fine. From Curt's time in Kosovo, he knew the types of aircraft NATO KFOR operated in Kosovo. They were mainly helicopters, Blackhawk, Puma, etc. Curt kept watching the live scene video, hoping to see some of the wreckage and eliminate the possibility it was Buck. Then he saw it. A flaming tail section of a fixed-wing aircraft. '*Fuck*,' he thought. Curt's heart sank. He called back Smitty. "Hey dude. I just saw some of the wreckage. It's a fixed wing, not rotary. Man, I think it's Buck. I also tried to call him. No answer."

"Yeah, I tried to call too. Same result. Let me see if I still have any KFOR contacts and I'll get you what I can."

"Got it, Smitty. I'll do the same. Thanks." Curt hung up and scrolled through his phone. He found the number he was looking for and hit dial.

"Congressman Donegan's Office, Andrea speaking. Can I help you?"

"Yes, it's Curt Nover. I'm a friend of Jack's. Is he available?"

"Hold one moment, sir." The line cut out. Jack, now a congressman, was a former SEAL teammate of Smitty and Curt.

In under a minute, Jack answered. "Nover! Are you in D.C.!? What's going on?"

"Jack, no. In Chicago. Look. I think I have bad news but need some help running it to ground."

"Sure, what's up?"

"You remember Doug Thiessen, the pilot that helped us expose Nissassa, right?"

"I think so. Callsign was Buck or something. Right?"

"Yeah. Well, there's been a plane crash in Kosovo. Smitty and I think it might be him, but you and I know the media won't release names for the next 24-48 hours. Can you find out? Not sure I can stomach waiting that long."

"Yeah. I got it. But I can tell you this. Rumor right now is a NATO assistant secretary general was on that aircraft, too."

"Fuck."

"Why fuck?"

"Well, Buck's new job was flying VIPs and dignitaries out of NATO Brussels."

"OK. Not good. But we don't know much yet. Let me get back to you."

"Thanks Jack. Take care." Curt hung up. He knew in his heart that the aircraft was Buck's. Now he just had to pray Buck was OK. Back on the E.R. floor, Curt sought out and found Wanda. Wanda, Curt's favorite nurse during his residency, had recently been promoted to E.R. charge nurse. She was the one person he could trust in that medical facility.

"Hey, Wanda. I just got some bad news and need to run home to Allison. I'll coordinate with Doctor Agnew and see if he can cover down. OK?"

Wanda understood. "Sure Doc. I got you. Let me know if I can help." She meant it. Not only was she his confidant, but Wanda was also instrumental in helping him take down Nissassa, something he'd never forget.

Curt left the hospital. His mind wasn't clear, and he forgot to coordinate with Dr. Agnew. Halfway home, he remembered. *'No worries, he thought. Wanda will take care of it.'*

Curt got back to the condo and told Allison everything. She wept out of nervousness. There was no one to call. The waiting game started, and the minutes felt like hours.

# *Chapter Fourteen*
# A New Proposition

Back in the White House, a presidential staff meeting was wrapping up. Steve, the office secretary and others had received their weekly directives from the President and made their way out of the conference room. Steve looked up and said, "Mr. President, may I walk back to the Oval Office with you? I have some news that may be of interest."

"Sure, Steve. Let's walk. Your dime."

"Well, sir. It appears Don Denney's charges were dropped, and he's a free man."

"Yes, I heard that. I was wondering why you hadn't shared the news with me before. Frankly, I don't want to know how you did it, but excellent job."

"Sir, that's the thing. Neither I, nor my contacts, were the ones who freed him."

The President kept walking. "OK. Interesting. Who did it?"

"Well, Mr. President. At this point, I don't know, but I met with Don and have some other news. It appears Don is back in the same line of business and has solicited me regarding any future tasks we may have."

The two were finally in the Oval Office now. "Steve, close the door." Steve did as he was instructed. The two were alone. "So, if I am to understand this, Don is again in the same line of services that landed him in jail?"

"Yes, sir."

"Does Andy know?" Andy was how the President addressed Don's father, Andrew Denney.

"Sir, I do not know. I do know that Andrew is also unaware who secured Don's freedom. He asked me to get to the bottom of it, but also told me to not say anything to Don."

"Interesting." The President paused. Let me "do some thinking about missions we could consider for Don. Also, I welcome your thoughts on this."

"Yes, Mr. President."

"And, Steve, find out who freed Don. I am going to guess that's a key piece of information in this puzzle."

"Will do, sir." And with that, Steve opened the door and exited the Oval Office. As he did, a female U.S. Army Presidential Aide knocked at the door. The President looked up. "Major Buckhout, yes, please enter. What is it?"

"Mr. President, sir. A flash message from the Chairman and the Secretary of Defense." She approached and handed him a note. He took it. She stepped back in professional military fashion, spun around, and walked out.

The President opened the note.

"FLASH – NATO ASSISTANT SECREATRY GENERAL FOR OPERATIONS, DANIEL MANZINA KILLED IN PLANE CRASH. END.

The president laid the paper down on his desk and picked up the phone.

"Yes, Mr. President," his secretary said.

"Please send in my prep material for the next meeting." His secretary did as requested. The President digested the material quickly. 10 minutes later, he called her again. "Please, get Steve and then send in my appointment."

"Yes, Mr. President."

He sat down in his chair. Disappointing news, he thought, but accidents happen.

# *Chapter Fifteen*
# Under Pressure

The phone rang at 0300Hrs. Curt jumped out of bed. He really had not been sleeping. Nor had Allison. "Hello!"

"Curt. Jack here. I have an update for you. I put one of my staff on this and they relayed that your fears were warranted. It was Buck's aircraft. Buck is clinging to life in a Pristina hospital. His brain is swelling uncontrollably, and they are saying he likely won't make it. His two passengers are both dead. From what we know, he declared an inflight emergency with engine trouble. As is typical in the Balkans, the speculation is rampant across the media. Getting ground truth is challenging. Kosovo is claiming Serbia shot the aircraft down and Serbia is blaming Kosovo for the same. From what we believe, neither is true."

"Damn it. OK. I'm gonna pack and get there as soon as possible."

"Curt, I can't stop you, but I've already talked to the Chairman of the Joint Chiefs. Admiral Hershey remembers Buck and the instrumental role he played taking down Nissassa. The Admiral has made a few calls and via Buck's Veterans Administration benefits, they've made some very generous arrangements. U.S. Doctors from Camp Bondsteel south of Pristina are being flown up to Pristina to oversee his medical care. If they can stabilize him, Blackhawks will fly him from the hospital to Pristina airport, where a medevac will take him to Landstuhl. He is getting the best care available. I likely need not tell you that Buck's care is highly irregular, and the Department of Defense (DoD) would not just step in like this for other similar cases. I know you think you are a great doctor, and buddy, I think you are, too. But there are five thousand miles between you and Buck. Let's see what happens."

"OK. Got it. Thanks. One question. Is there going to be any investigation about the accident?"

"That's a great question. Right now, the Kosovo Security

Force (KSF) is responsible for disaster response and has secured the scene. Unfortunately, Kosovo doesn't have the capacity for an investigation like our National Transportation Safety Board. The NATO KFOR Commander, Major General Torres, has offered his assistance to the KSF, and it appears KSF Commander Lieutenant General Krasniqi is receptive. I've heard good things about both generals, so there's optimism. The embassies in Kosovo right now are a bit chaotic. The two passengers were from Spain and England. Spain is a bit of a challenge as it is one of the few Western countries which does not recognize Kosovo, thus it has limited diplomatic relations. The U.S. Embassy is involved, and I have spoken directly with the Ambassador. I believe they are doing everything they can. It's about 1000Hrs in Pristina now. I am hopeful we will know more soon. Does that answer your questions?"

"Jack, thanks. This sucks, but I really appreciate your efforts."

"Buddy, I know it sucks. We've both lost friends. It's always been the ugly part of our old business. Keep your chin up and if you need to talk, I'm here."

Curt appreciated his comments. "Got it, Jack. Thanks. I'll talk to you soon. Goodbye." Curt hung up the phone. Allison was awake and had heard the whole story. Her head lay sideways on her pillow. A small tear trickled out of her lower eye. She could not bear to talk to Curt right now. He was not much for conversation, either. He got out of bed, made coffee, and called Smitty. Much like Jack's conversation, the discussion was almost businesslike, almost sterile, in the way you'd expect two former Special Forces operatives to talk about combat operations. It was not a discussion about a dear friend.

Smitty hung up and sent a text to the only friend he knew in Germany. Another Special Forces colleague named Ian.

> *'Ian, possible inbound medivac coming your way. Former USAF SOF pilot crashed in Kosovo. Outlook grim. Can you please keep me updated?'*

Minutes later, a response came back.

>*'Too easy. On it. We have a detachment at Landstuhl Medical. I'll have them update me regularly and pass words. Prayers, brother.'*

\*\*\*\*\*\*\*\*\*\*\*\*\*\*\*\*\*\*\*\*\*\*\*\*\*\*\*\*\*\*\*\*\*\*\*\*\*\*\*\*\*\*

Lunch was being prepared in a fancy Belgrade restaurant. It would be served at noon. Nikola sat at the table reading the news, old school style, out of a newspaper. Katarina walked up, kissed him on the cheek, and sat down. She addressed him in Serbian, "Greetings, Nikola."

"Hello, Katarina. It seems you had a very interesting evening yesterday."

"Interesting, yes. But just as planned."

"Very good. The Belgrade and Pristina news media outlets are both in hysterics, blaming each other's nation for the accident. Just as we expected." Katarina sat down. As she did, Nikola's phone rang. He looked at the number and answered immediately.

In Russian, he spoke, "Yes. I will wait.' Nikola was receiving a call from someone important, and he waved his hand for Katarina to remain quiet.

"Good morning," Nikola continued in Russian. "Yes, the news today is quite interesting." There was a pause. Nikola continued with a smile on his face, "Yes, you can presume the plan is underway. In fact, I was just preparing to talk with my contact regarding our next step."

Katarina watched as there was another long pause and Nikola listened intently.

"Thank you, Mr. President. I don't plan to fail. Goodbye." They both hung up.

Katarina spoke, "I presume he is pleased?"

"Katarina. This is only step one of our plan. I am proud of you, my little sister. You've done well, but we are far from complete. Let's put step two into motion."

Nikola picked up his phone and dialed a number. Back in D.C., Don's phone rang on his nightstand. It was 0600Hrs. "Hello," he answered groggily.

"Hello, Don. It's Nikola."

Don sat up in bed and rubbed his eyes. "Yes, Nikola. Hello. Good morning. Or, what time is it there? Should I say good afternoon?" Don was trying to clear the sleep cobwebs from his head.

"Don. None of that matters. Did you happen to see the news? Sadly, Mr. Thiessen, the man you knew as Buck, appears to have had a very tragic flying accident last night in Kosovo."

A grin washed over Don's face. Revenge is a powerful emotion, and he relished the information. 'Revenge' was akin to a professional level full contact sport in the Balkans. Nikola, too, was enjoying the moment.

Don finally spoke, "Well, that is very unfortunate to hear. I thank you for the news."

"Don, say nothing of it." Nikola changed the subject. "Did you have a chance to talk to your contacts in the U.S. Government about our offer?"

"Yes, Nikola, I raised the opportunity with the right folks who are considering it. I'll keep you posted."

"Don, we really need you to try and move on this. We are paying our teams a significant amount of money to just sit around and wait for a mission. Can you elevate this to a higher decision maker?"

"Nikola, I assure you, there is no one higher. My contact is in the White House and one of the closest to the President."

"Don, I don't doubt you, but perhaps you can get to the President himself."

"Nikola, you need to believe in me. I am doing my best. And I can assure you, while I don't speak to the President, he's fully aware, as is the decision maker. Look, we've said enough. I will be in touch later."

"OK, Don. I appreciate it. I want to believe you can deliver. I tell you what, now that Mr. Thiessen is gone, perhaps your contacts can find out where Dr. Nover is? Do you think that is possible?"

Don knew Steve had assets that could easily ping Curt's phone. "Sure, I'll get that for you, but last I heard, he was in Chicago."

"Yes, but one never knows. I think it is perhaps time for Dr. Nover to suffer an unfortunate accident. Let's talk next week." They both said goodbye and Nikola hung up the phone. He then quickly switched apps and turned off the program that was recording the conversation. He smiled at Katarina. "Our fish has swallowed the bait whole."

Katarina smiled. Lunch was served. They relished their meal. Appropriately, a lovely white fish.

As they ate, Katarina shared the details of her time with Buck. Nikola enjoyed the story greatly. After she finished, she asked Nikola, "So, is Dr. Nover next?"

"Hmmm… I think so."

Katarina grinned as she swirled the wine in her glass.

\*\*\*\*\*\*\*\*\*\*\*\*\*\*\*\*\*\*\*\*\*\*\*\*\*\*\*\*\*\*\*\*\*\*\*\*\*\*\*\*

Curt could not sleep. He threw on some warm running clothes and headed out to the beach along Lake Shore Drive. The air was icy and burned his lungs. Oddly, the pain helped clear Buck's crash from his head. After three miles, the endorphins still had not kicked in. Something was wrong. Curt turned around. He ran even faster back towards his residence. Sweat was soaking through his clothes. His heart raced. Still, there were no endorphins. '*What the fuck*,' he thought. He slowed to a walk. For the last half mile, he'd calmly stroll back to his building. The sun slowly emerged over Lake Michigan. The air was clear, and a wispy cloud deck floated in the sky, all the required ingredients for a beautiful sunrise. It did nothing to inspire or affect Curt. He entered his high-rise and headed up to the condo.

The morning sun flooded into Curt and Allison's kitchen. Curt was making coffee and Allison entered. As predicted, it was a gorgeous morning, but did little to alleviate the sadness and gloom. "Good morning, baby." She walked up to Curt and held him. She did not care how bad he smelled from the workout.

Curt replied, "Good morning, sweetheart. Did you sleep at all?"

"I think I did, but it doesn't feel like it." Allison was tired. So was Curt.

"Hey, I am going to ask the hospital for some time off and fly out to Europe today. I need to do something. I need to be there."

"Curt, I can't stop you, but I heard Jack last night. They are doing everything they can."

Curt snapped. "Look! I need to do something. I got to go!"

Allison knew Curt was mad at the situation, not her. "Baby, I get it. You're upset. So am I, and there's likely a million things running through our heads right now. Things like *'we should have tried harder to get him to move to the U.S.,' 'we should have written him more, called him more.'* None of those thoughts are helpful at the moment."

Allison was right, but Curt could not turn off the thoughts. They were overwhelming and consuming him. His shoulders slumped. His head dropped. He began to weep. She held him. "Look, go if you need to. I will be here." After a few minutes, he slowly pulled away. Curt slowly walked to the bathroom, took a shower, and prepared to go to work.

At the hospital, Curt walked in and said hello to Wanda. Before she could warn him, a male voice from behind him in an angry tone spoke, "Doctor Nover!"

Curt turned around. It was Shawn Walker, one of the senior hospital administrators. "Yes, Mr. Walker. What can I do for you?"

"Do you mind telling me where you were yesterday during your shift? We had an understaffed emergency room and nearly lost three lives. I had to call two other doctors down from their specialty duties to cover for you."

None of this was what Curt wanted to hear. "Yes, sir. I am sorry about that. I had a personal issue."

"Personal issue? Are you serious? I don't give a fuck about

your personal issues.  You are on thin ice right now.  Consider this your probation notice.  Do you understand?"

Curt's pulse raced.  His pupils restricted to near specs.  He could feel some of his muscle's spasm.  Slowly, he addressed Shawn.  "So, Shawn.  It's disappointing you somehow failed to be informed that the plane which just crashed in Kosovo was piloted by a guy who was to be my best man.  It's infuriating that it also 'doesn't rise to your give a fuck' level of concern.  I can see why you are an administrator and not a caregiver.  Your compassion for humanity is nearly nonexistent.  As for me, I do have compassion.  I have enough to tell you I'm requesting two weeks of personal time off.  I am going to fly to Kosovo and try to do everything I can to save my best man's life."

Shawn was steaming.  Hospital staff in the vicinity overheard the discussion up to this point and had stopped to watch the fireworks.  After a pause, Shawn spoke.  "Doctor Nover.  Listen clearly.  Your request is denied, and should you fly out of the country, you'll never secure employment as a doctor again.  Do I make myself clear?"

Curt stared at Shawn.  About ten different ways of how to kill him flashed through his brain.   Curt remained silent.

Shawn spoke again.  "Do I make myself clear?"

Curt just grinned at Shawn.  Slowly, Curt turned away.  As he did, he shed his medical smock.  It dropped to the floor.  Curt continued out the hospital doors and didn't stop.  He pulled out his phone and called Allison.  "Hey.  I just quit the hospital."

"You What!!!?" Allison was floored.

"Fuck them.  I'm done."

"Curt, you're not thinking clearly.  Go back, now!  Please!"

"Allison, I love you, but I made my mind up.  I'll be home later."

"Curt.  STOP.  Listen to me, God damn it!"  With that, Curt hung up.  Allison tried to call him back, but it was pointless.  He would not answer.

Next, Allison called Smitty and relayed the news.

Smitty hung up with Allison and then rang Curt.  He answered, "Wow.  Only took three minutes.  She told ya, huh?"

"Dude. What the fuck are you doing? Go back in there. I know in your heart you NEED to help people heal. If you don't go back, where are you going to go?"

"Smitty, you don't understand."

"Fuck you! I do understand. I'm one of the few who do. You are NOT thinking straight and if you don't snap out of it, this is only going to get worse."

"Smitty, I'm not in the mood for this. Sorry. I gotta go." Curt hung up and turned off his phone. It was only 0900Hrs, but he needed a drink. Curt stopped in a grocery store and exited with a 12 pack of Pabst Blue Ribbon. He cracked one open and headed down the sidewalk.

"You gonna drink all those?" A voice spoke out as he passed. It was a homeless man who Curt had never spoken to but passed nearly every day on his way to work over the past few months.

"I may," Curt responded. "Do you want one?"

"Sure. If you're offering. I don't have no money."

"No problem. It's on me. What's your name?" Curt handed him a beer.

"Darryl is the name." Curt noticed Darryl's hands were chaffed, blistered, and had signs of frostbite scarring. His clothes were soiled and smelled.

"Hey, I'm Curt."

"Cool, come in and sit down." Darryl led him to where the sidewalk met the wall of the building. There, an old refrigerator packing box served as Darryl's home, and inside were a few ripped sleeping bags and blankets. It was all he had to offer.

"Thanks," Curt responded. They both sat down. Over the course of the next few hours, the two polished off the 12 pack. Darryl shared his entire story. Curt was amazed. His new friend was a military veteran, was 100% disabled and received over $3,000 a month tax free but didn't care. All the money would go to his kids. He took none of it. He also refused to stay in any homeless shelters. They scared him. While serving in the Marines, Darryl had spent several nights outside the wire in Afghanistan. The first few nights, he was scared. Over time, he not only shed those fears, but he also began to enjoy it, gaining a sense of freedom. He slept with his weapon under the stars, with fellow Marines at his side. It was hard to explain, but to Darryl, it was the most secure feeling in the world. As he told Curt, "Walls work two ways. To some, they serve to protect them from the outside. To others, they serve to deny a clear view of an incoming threat. They can be extremely comforting or extremely threatening." To Darryl, it was the latter.

The time was getting late, and Curt felt the need to go home. Before he did, he walked back into the grocery store and bought a decent amount of food. Returning to Darryl, he handed the food over. "Here you go, Darryl. It was great meeting you."

"Curt, thanks. But if you want to give me food, I only ask you stay and eat it with me. I don't want no handouts. I want a meal with a fellow warrior."

Curt was moved. He sat back down and ate with Darryl. Potato chips, beef jerky, Slim Jims and other junk food. It was the unhealthiest dinner Curt had for the past few months. Also, one of the most rewarding. Darryl was exactly what Curt needed that day. The time grew even later. Curt looked at Darryl. He had learned more about himself from Darryl in the past day than he'd learned from others over the past few years. "Hey Darryl, you got an extra blanket?"

"Sure do, Curt. You gonna spend the night at my place?"

"I'd like to if that's OK?"

"Yup. Let me make you some room." Darryl moved over.

The two grown men curled up in the broken apart refrigerator box, covered in blankets and lay on old carpet insulation for protection from the cold cement. One of them was homeless, the other strangely wishing he was.

The next morning, Curt awoke shivering cold. His back was sore, and he had a tremendous urge to urinate. He also had a warped but positive feeling he had not experienced for years. Darryl was still asleep. Curt stood up, pulled $50 out of his wallet, and tucked it into Darryl's pocket. He walked down the street, breathing the air and sensing colors with a vibrant clarity.

He was alive, as if something had switched in his head.

Curt walked back towards his condo and entered the coffee shop across the street. Turning on his phone, text and voice messages flooded in. He sent a text to Allison. "Hey, sorry I didn't come home. I needed space. I'm at the Billy Goat Tavern and I am OK." He again turned off his phone and watched the entrance to his condo. As expected, Allison raced away in her car 15 minutes later. The condo was empty.

Curt quickly entered and grabbed his backpack. He filled it with blankets and a few sets of clothes. He took off his work clothes and put on a set of heavy utility pants and an old crewneck sweatshirt. In the kitchen, he opened a cupboard and pulled out a fifth of Jack Daniels. He also grabbed photos of Allison, Buck, and Smitty. The only people left in his life and hopefully the only ones who would understand.

30 minutes later, Curt was out of the house. He'd stop at the bank and withdraw $5,000, most of it in $100 bills. He tucked the two stacks of cash, which were as thick as decks of cards, in his backpack. After leaving the bank, he took the 'L,' Chicago's elevated train to the bus station.

Curt sat in the station, watching people come and go. There was no rush. It was the atmosphere he was digesting. After an hour, he approached a man in an old camouflage jacket who was sitting against the wall in the corner. "Hey, is the seat next to you taken?"

"Nope. Free country buddy."

Curt sat down on the ground next to the man, placing his backpack against the wall. "My name is Curt. What's yours?"

"Kev is what they call me."

"OK, Kev. Nice to meet you. How long have you been here?"

"Oh, for a few days. Trying to get together enough money to go south."

Curt tried to fit in. "Yeah, I know the feeling." It was a ridiculously ironic statement from a man with $5,000 in his backpack.

"I see your jacket.... You former military?"

"Army.  Was with 3rd ID.  What about you?"

"Navy.  I was a SEAL."

"Ha!  Bullshit, and I was a general."  Kev laughed at Curt's comment, no matter how true it was.  Truth be told, there were very few Navy SEAL veterans that frequented the homeless crowd, but there were many veterans who claimed to be.  Curt decided to let it go.

"Hey Kev, when you say south, where are you trying to go?"

"Don't really know.  Just know this town is too damn cold."

Curt looked up at the departure board.  A bus would soon be leaving for Atlanta.  "Kev, well, I am going to Atlanta.  Do you want to go with me?"

Kev laughed again.  "Curt, you are full of funny jokes today.  I just told you I don't have no money."

"Don't worry.  I want to pay for your ticket.  We can go together."

Kev stared at Curt for a few seconds and could tell he was serious.  "OK.  I'll go.  But let's be clear.  I ain't gay and I ain't gonna do no weird shit."

Curt smiled.  "Kev, I ain't gay either, but if you were, I wouldn't care.  I'm just trying to get us both out of here."  While that comment was true in the current construct, the undertones of it also applying in a military rescue operation could not be avoided in Curt's mind.  He was helping people, and he was doing good.  The news of Buck's crash had resided in his mind for over a day, but still had not registered.  It was something he still could not process.

Curt paid cash for the two tickets: a little over $100.  The two boarded the bus and slept.  The musty bus seats were far more luxurious than the bus terminal tile floor or Darryl's carpet padding.  The bus would travel down I-65 through Indiana and Kentucky.  Once in Tennessee, it would transition onto I-75.  The overall trip would take nearly 24 hours, with stops in Indianapolis, Louisville, and Chattanooga.  Somewhere between Indy and Louisville, Curt awoke.  He opened his backpack and took a long swig of whiskey from his fifth of Jack.  It was his fourth drink since meeting Kev.  Next, he pulled out his phone and powered it up in airplane mode.  There would be no transmissions or receptions.  He ensured the geolocation was turned off.  Curt knew Allison and Smitty would be trying to locate him.  He did not want to be found.

Curt read through the text messages from Allison and Smitty that were downloaded when he had been in the coffee shop across from his condo.   They were worried and, deep inside, Curt felt bad, but where he was, and what he was doing were important.  A few of the messages were updates on Buck's medical status.  Jack Donegan had come through.  Buck was in critical condition, but on a Medical Evacuation mission headed to the U.S. Military's Landstuhl Medical Center in Germany.  That was the good news.  Unfortunately, Buck was in a coma with a swollen brain.  He was on life support and even the best prognosis was grim.  Curt turned off his phone.  In his mind, he prayed, *'God, I know we don't speak much, but please take care of Buck.  Also, please help Allison and Smitty understand.  Someday, I will need their love and friendship again.  -- Amen'*

## *Chapter Sixteen*
# The Pains of Loss

"Smitty! I'm worried to death. I'm physically shaking! I can't find Curt. He said he was at the Billy Goat Tavern. I am standing in here now and the staff say he never walked in." Allison was crying as she spoke.

"Allison. I know. He's not returning my calls or texts, either. I realize you're hurting. Do you need me to come to Chicago?"

"I need you to do something! Please! I can't take this. I feel like I am back in Akjoujt." Smitty was not fond of the reference to Akjoujt. It was the location where Smitty took Curt hostage, separating Allison and Curt, then tried to hunt Curt down and kill him.

"Allison, I am worried too, but I think we both know Curt is in exceptionally good physical health. He's smart, well trained, and probably fine. Unfortunately, we also know if he doesn't want to be found, our likelihood of finding him is a smidge over nil."

Allison realized Smitty was right. But she was not going to give up. "Yes… I know." Allison took a deep breath. Freaking out was not going to help solve the problem. "Smitty, I'm gonna be fine. I'm going to go to the hospital and talk to Curt's colleagues."

"OK. Keep me informed…" The call waiting function on Smitty's phone beeped. "Hey, I have another call coming in. I'll call you back."

"OK. Goodbye, and thanks, Smitty."

He switched over to the other line. "Smitty."

"Hey, Smitty, Jack here in D.C. What are you doing right now?"

"Jack, I'm at work. Why, what's up?"

"I think there's some value in you heading to Kosovo. U.S. Embassy Pristina is reporting the crash investigation is going poorly and being leveraged for the purposes of Serbian and Kosovar propaganda. Both sides are spinning the cause of the incident to fit their narrative, devoid of factual data. It very well may be an accident or a number of other reasons, but I am convinced the truth isn't going to rise to the top under the current circumstances."

"OK. Let me see what I can do. I'll call you back. Cheers." Smitty hung up his phone. He walked up to his boss's office.

"Hey, Tommy. You got a minute?"

Smitty's boss, Tommy Taylor, was a former Navy Petty Officer. He'd exited the Navy early on a medical discharge after driving over an improvised explosive device in Afghanistan. He walked with a slight limp but refused to complain. Daily, he wore a miniature Purple Heart medal ribbon on his shirt. "Yeah, Smitty. What's up?"

Smitty explained what had happened. His supervisor, given his former military service, completely understood. Smitty would have at least two weeks off if he needed it.

After a quick 'thanks,' Smitty booked flights to Pristina that evening out of Chicago O'Hare. Once his reservations were secure, he checked back in with Congressman Donegan.

"Jack, I'll be in Pristina tomorrow around noon their time. Can you pass me a contact or any info?"

"Yes. I'll send you a contact. He's a prominent local Kosovar named Erolld. He's got the right connections. Good luck."

"Thanks. Funny, after I left Kosovo in 2004, I was hopeful I'd never go back. Good times. Cheers." Smitty hung up the phone and went home to pack.

Once done, he looked at his phone again. A message had come in while he prepared for the trip.

> *'Your PAX arrived. Induced coma, brain swelling. Limited brain activity. No plans to do anything until the swelling eases. Sorry – Ian'*

Smitty quickly sent another message to both Curt and Allison, sharing Ian's news that Buck was still alive. The one he sent, however, was far more optimistic than the one he had received. Smitty plugged his phone in, set it down, and sat on his bed, ready to leave for his flight.  He thought to himself, *'Come on, Buck.  Fight you fucker.'*

## *Chapter Seventeen*
# The Dinner Discussion

The dining room table was set beautifully.  While it was large enough to seat ten comfortably, tonight there would only be three.  Off in the entryway, the front door opened and then closed.  Shuffling could be heard in the foyer.

A woman's voice from the kitchen piped up, "Hello!?"

A quick response.  "Hello, mom!" Don walked into the dining room and met his mom who'd entered from the kitchen.

"Hello Donny!  Welcome home!  Your father is running a bit late.  He's upstairs in the study."

"No rush, mom.  What's for dinner?"

"Your favorite!  Lasagna!"

"Mom… you're too good to me."  He hugged her, then grabbed a glass off the table, filling it with red wine.

"How was your day?"

"Good.  I am anxiously waiting for the tulips to pop.  Spring is almost here!"

Another voice joined the conversation.  "Good evening, Don."

"Hey, dad.  Good evening."  Don and Andrew hugged.  It was awkward, as always.  The men sat as Don's mother ran to the kitchen to get the lasagna.  She returned seconds later, set it on the table and took her seat, only to pop up again, run to the kitchen to get a spatula.  She returned a second time and started serving the lasagna.

Andrew would be the first to break the silence.  "So, son, how is the new apartment?"

"Really nice, dad.  I enjoy being downtown."

"I remember being your age.  I truly relished that fast pace of life.  No more though.  The Virginia countryside is for me.  Any ideas on a new job or a source of income?"  The second part of that question was intended to sting.  It didn't, as Don had grown immune to his father's needling.

"Actually, yes.  I've been approached by a foreign investor

who'd like to leverage some of my contacts for future contracts." Both Andrew and Don knew what that meant. Don's mom acted ignorant to the deeper meaning. It wasn't clear if she didn't understand, or just chose not to. While Andrew wasn't pleased with the new arrangement, Don was quite proud of his new relationship, as it was yet again a chance to do something beyond simply relying on his father or the family name.

"Interesting. What do you know about this contact?" His father's skepticism was obvious, but Don couldn't decipher its origin. Was he truly concerned for his son's wellbeing or was he yet again shocked his son could secure such a role, given the perpetual perceptions, if Don would never amount to much? Don estimated that answer at 50/50 odds.

"Well, he's wealthy. He has an existing operation and is seeking opportunities." The fact Don did not share the nationality of this investor was not lost on his father. The lack of this information was curious.

"You said foreign investor. What nation?" Andrew inquired.

"Father," a name Don only used at times when the discussion would turn to debate then potentially become argumentative, "What difference does it make? You initially questioned my efforts with Nissassa, only to later support it. Once it was exposed, you again reversed course, acting as if you were opposed to it all along." Don leaned back and let out a blatant snicker. "Hell. At one point, you even said Nissassa was doing the nation's bidding in a way the nation itself could not."

"Son, Nissassa, while a private firm, was still a U.S. entity. Frankly, I don't think I need to tell you why some foreign nations wouldn't be appropriate. The fact you won't mention the nation is a strong indicator that you, in your heart, know there's potential conflict. Lord knows I can't prevent you from making stupid mistakes if you don't wish to entertain my wisdom."

Don's mom could take no more. "Would anyone like cake? I baked it today. German Chocolate!"

"No thank you, mom. I've lost my appetite. And I don't think dad will want any. German cake is foreign."

Andrew ignored the comment. "Darling, I will have some. The lasagna, by the way, was fantastic, as always."

Don's mom blushed as she floated into the kitchen, weightless from the lovely compliment.

Don was steaming. His father's last comments, especially about stupid mistakes, hurt. "Dad, I've always respected your wisdom, but I'm done hearing about your perception of my 'stupid mistakes.' Congrats to you... and your successful career in which, evidently, you made no errors. It must be tough for you, continually being compared to the Lord." Don's sarcasm turned to one last effort of honest dialogue. "Look, I know in your career there were risks taken. Please let me take mine in a measured fashion."

The effort was pointless. His father's temper had been sparked. "Son, if I'm God, then you sure as hell are no Jesus. Do what you will, but you will NOT speak to me like that in my house. Do not call me when you get yourself in trouble. I'm sure it won't be long."

Don slid back his chair and stood up. "No worries. I won't." He began to leave, then stopped and looked back. "Man, you're a real peach. You refuse to hire any of your kids, demanding they carve their own path, and then criticize the very path they chose." Don walked into the kitchen, kissed his mom, then walked out to his car. '*Screw dad*,' he thought. Things were going as planned. The pilot that ruined him was dead or at least dying, and the others would soon suffer the same fate. Don also knew he could get some missions for Nikola. He just needed time. Before driving away, he texted Steve and asked to meet. After 10 minutes of driving away, Steve replied he could meet tomorrow at their usual spot near the WWII memorial. 1100Hrs.

## *Chapter Eighteen*
# Things Going South

The Atlanta homeless scene was substantial.  Curt found himself among dozens of other veterans camping out under an I-75 overpass.  He drank with them.  Talked with them.  Learned their stories.  To Curt, it was the most fascinating part.  War wounds, both physical and mental, were common.  Broken families, fear of loneliness, anxiety, PTSD, drugs, alcohol.  Some of the homeless argued they were 'forgotten' and given no chance to improve their lives.  That was perhaps true.  Others simply said this was the life they wished to live.  A few days ago, it would have been nearly impossible for Curt to understand this.  Every hour he spent with other veterans helped him understand how homelessness is a home.   As night fell, Curt was inebriated, but one of the few still awake.

About twenty yards away from him on the other side of the viaduct, two homeless men began to squabble.  Over the next minute, their argument grew more heated.  Evidently, the fight was over real estate, close to the oil drum fire.  Curt began walking that direction.  The two were cursing.  Then, the smaller man cracked an empty glass bottle against the wall, pointing the jagged glass at his adversary.

"Whoa, whoa!" Curt said as he was running, if not staggering, towards the two.

"That fucker took my spot.  For the last three nights, that's my spot."

"You on crack, boy.  You was gone all night.  Now you come back and think you own this.  Bullshit.  Ain't nobody own no homeless real estate."

The two circled.  Sizing each other up.  It was getting tense.  Then, they charged each other.

"No!" Curt screamed and jumped on them both.  His arms felt like cement as he tried to apply close combat techniques he'd learned and when sober, could execute flawlessly.  One of them swung wildly, hitting Curt on the cheek.  It was nothing but would generate a decent shiner for the next few days. Finally, Curt was able to pull the one with the glass bottle away. As he did, they both looked down. The other was bleeding from his stomach.

"Look! You asshat! Look what you did! Damn it! He's one of us!" Curt tossed the aggressor to the side. He quickly knelt down and tried to treat the abdomen wound. He applied pressure with scraps of cloth that were far from sterile, but at least somewhat clean, given the environment.

"Who's got Vodka?" No one answered. "For Fuck's sake! Do you want him to die?" About 30 seconds later, a half full bottle of Smirnoff magically appeared. Curt poured the alcohol onto the wound, then reapplied the cloth. The guy would be OK but would need stitches.

"Hey buddy, what's your name?" Curt asked.

"Trevor," the black man replied.

"Great to meet you, buddy. I'm Curt. I'm a doctor."

"You a doctor? Great. I'm an astronaut." Clearly, Trevor had little faith in Curt's claimed profession.

"Seriously. And I'm going to tell you, this wound needs stitches. You need to go to a hospital."

Unbeknownst to Curt, the word 'hospital' was a trigger for Trevor's PTSD.

"I ain't going to no hospital." Trevor's anxiety was growing.

"Trevor, I'm not messing with you. If you don't get this sewn up, you're going to bleed out or get an infection."

Trevor's veins began to pulse in his temples. His heart was racing. As he thought about hospitals, he recalled being twelve years old in the Montgomery, Alabama, Emergency Room with his mom and older brother. As they waited, in walked a crazed white male, clearly on some illicit drug. He swung a knife wildly. Trevor's brother jumped up and stood between the man and his mom. It would be the last act of heroism Trevor's brother would make. In a single, swift motion, the man mowed the boy down, slashing his neck open. Trevor sat there with his mom, holding their sibling as he bled out on the hospital floor.

"I SAID NO HOSPITAL!" Trevor screamed, jumping up and

running off into the night.

Curt tried to chase him but was unable. He was too drunk. After about 50 yards, he fell to the ground. He tried to help, but failed. Slowly, Curt struggled back to his feet and walked back under the overpass. No one really paid attention to Trevor's outburst, and it appeared few cared. They were all asleep again.

Quietly, Curt picked up his backpack. He opened it and reached inside. As he passed by each homeless member, he silently placed a $100 bill near them.

Curt staggered down the road. Alone, he leaned against a telephone pole, pulled out his phone, turned it on and wrote a text to Allison:

> *'Allison. I'm sorry. I know I'm hurting u and I don't mean to. I have to run for a while. Someday, I hope u understand. I love you, Curt.'*

Curt turned off his phone and returned it to his backpack. Leaning forward, he was again erect, but far from stable. Curt needed to keep moving. He needed to be 'out.' It was freeing to run, but he still wasn't certain as to 'what' he was running from. It certainly wasn't Allison. It wasn't Smitty. He'd keep running. He'd eventually figure it out.

Curt staggered up the hill of the I-75 overpass. Once on the shoulder of the highway, he threw out his thumb, attempting to hitchhike. After an hour, around 0200Hrs, a semi-truck pulled over. Curt shuffled towards it and opened the passenger door. The driver was a burly man with a beard. "Where ya headed?" The driver asked.

"South, sir. Orlando, Miami. It doesn't matter." Curt was just running.

"OK. I can get you to Fort Lauderdale. After that, you're on your own."

"I'd be much obliged." Curt slung up his backpack and jumped in. "My name's Curt."

"Hey. I'm Jamie. Jamie Brumfiel." Jamie started the big rig

rumbling on the shoulder, looked out the side-view mirror and then merged into I-75 South traffic. "What takes you to Fort Lauderdale?" Curt asked.

"For me, it's work. What are you going for?" Jamie responded.

"Honestly, I am not sure. I quit my job yesterday and just started going south." Curt pulled out a half-drank bottle of Jim Beam and gulped a few swigs. "I'd offer you some, but I doubt that's a good idea," he said to Jamie.

"Yeah, aside from the obvious driving issues, I gave that stuff up seven years ago. It nearly ruined my life and me. I got no time for it."

To Curt, the notion of giving up drinking alcohol was as distant as Mars at that point. Curt looked down at Jamie's arm and saw a tattoo of a turtle shell crossed by anchors.

"Hey, you former Navy? Curt asked.

"Yup. Good guess." Jamie replied.

"I saw your shellback tattoo. I was also in the Navy. What was your rate?"

"I was a Seabee. One tour on the Reagan and two tours in Afghanistan. I loved it and I hated it. The whole chain of command, stupid orders, time away from family, missed holidays. All that crap. Then, there are the great times with shipmates, the friends I made, the lessons I learned, the challenges I overcame. I'm happy I did it, but I wouldn't do it again."

"I understand. Hey, I actually just left a homeless camp under I-75 and was hanging out with other veterans. The stories are fascinating; they're sad; and they're real." Curt's inebriation had taken over. He was blurting out anything and everything. Jamie had been in such a condition many times. He humored Curt, halfheartedly listening to the gibberish.

"Yeah. We have a bunch out there."

"Mind if I ask you a personal question?" Curt asked.

"Nope. Go ahead. It's a long ride."

"Was it because of the Navy that you gave up alcohol?"

Jamie paused... "Curt, that's a good question. I don't know

if it was only the Navy. Like many of us, I came back to the U.S. as a very different man after my second tour in Afghanistan. At times, I was numb. In my mind, there were times I couldn't tell if my wife was yelling at me or making love to me. If I wasn't drinking, I was scared. If I was drinking, I was a zombie. Before Afghanistan, I could drink socially with friends and family. After Afghanistan, that changed."

Curt listened as intently as possible through his insobriety. Jamie's experience was similar to many other homeless veterans he'd met. They were also drunk and numb or sober and scared. It was far too binary... too black and white. Where had the shades of gray gone that existed before PTSD? "Jamie, what do you think changed you?"

"I don't know. All of it? None of it? Maybe it was trying to explain Afghanistan to those who just couldn't understand. One time, I tried to tell my wife about an incident that, to this day, still plays in my head. I was working on a water well at a Fire Base in Helmand. The fighting was awful, and most of the deaths were Afghan soldiers. For days, bodies after bodies kept stacking up on the base. The first ones I saw made me vomit. After a week, I remember one of my colleagues driving up on a little single seat quad that had a small trailer, like ones used on golf courses. The trailer was full of Afghan soldier body parts. The soldiers were discovered out in the desert a few days after their little Toyota truck drove over an Improvised Explosive Device intended to blow up a tank. Feet in boots, detached torsos, arms, heads, organs-some in clothing, some exposed, and everything was filthy, covered with flies. I didn't flinch. In fact, I asked my friend, *'Hey, do you know what's on the menu for lunch?'* Later that day, I reflected on that moment. How could I have grown so numb to death? How could I even consider lunch at a time like that? My wife tried to understand, but I know she doesn't, and she never will. She feels for me, but honestly, that comes across more like a pity party. It's not sympathy I want. It's understanding. And frankly, I don't think I'll ever get that from anyone other than fellow veterans."

The details of the story were new to Curt, but it had a similar theme to many other stories he'd heard or lived through. "Thanks for telling me. Especially the last part. I almost said, *'I'm sorry,'* which clearly would have been wrong."

Curt continued, "I too have skeletons, and I understand the feeling you shared about receiving sympathy from others. But, if we don't want them to say, 'I'm sorry,' what do we want them to say?"

This was perhaps the first time Jamie had considered such a question. What would be the 'right' answer? *'I understand?'* *'That's horrible?'* "Good question. I don't know what I want others to say. But I do know this. When I tell you, or perhaps other veterans who've been to Afghanistan, such a story, I know you can process it. That it's not some alien concept. Others can't... and yet they keep asking, 'What was it like? What happened?' When I was young, I could never understand why my grandfathers never talked about WWII or Korea. Now, I completely understand why older vets rarely spoke about past wars. There really was no one other than other combatants that could understand. There was no point." Jamie chuckled. "I guess it would be like Steven Hawking attempting to passionately explain quantum physics to me. Frankly, he'd just be wasting oxygen."

Curt took another swig of Jim Beam. "Maybe it's best to just not say anything."

"Maybe."

"Hey, do you mind if I doze off?" Curt was growing tired.

"Nope. Have at it."

Curt leaned into the truck window, holding his backpack tight. He'd sleep for the next few hours.

\*\*\*\*\*\*\*\*\*\*\*\*\*\*\*\*\*\*\*\*\*\*\*\*\*\*\*\*\*\*\*\*\*\*\*\*\*\*\*\*


Allison had received Curt's message instantaneously. As it came in, she immediately tried to call, but it was too late. His phone was off. She responded to his text, hoping he'd get it soon. She fell down on the floor of her condo and cried. The man she loved was lost, literally and figuratively.  He was hurting her, and while she knew it wasn't intentional, that did little to ease the pain.

# Chapter Nineteen
# On the Verge

Smitty's flight landed in Pristina around noon. The recently built Adem Jashari airport was impressive and far better than the one he remembered from years ago. It was built with part of the massive influx of humanitarian and infrastructure assistance. Much of Kosovo would differ from how he remembered. Once on the ground, Smitty immediately turned on his phone. No messages from Curt, but Ian had an update.

> *'Brain swelling finally shrinking. Still limited brain activity. Lungs filling with fluid and now on respiratory life support. – Sorry, buddy.'*

He relayed to Allison that Buck was still among the living. If Curt wanted updates on Buck, he was going to have to grow a pair and call for them.

Smitty departed the plane, cleared customs, and received his luggage. As he walked out, a tall, black-haired man held a sign that said "Mr. Smith." Smitty walked up. "Hello, I think I am the guy you're lookin' for."

"Mr. Smith, hello. Welcome to Pristina. My name is Erolld. Congressman Donegan's office asked if I could help you. I was more than honored. I hope your flight was good."

"Yes, all good. Nice to meet you. Did Jack's office explain why I am here?"

"I understand you want to try and find out about the aircraft accident. Is that correct?"

"Yup, but I am not an airplane investigator, so my success might be limited. The pilot of that flight was a best friend of mine."

"Mr. Smith, I have taken some liberties to help you. I hope that's OK. Tomorrow, we will work to get your answers, as for now, how about we get you into a hotel and some rest?"

"Sounds good."

Erolld drove out of the airport parking lot.  As he drove, Smitty was amazed.  While there were still a few Yugoslavian era vehicles on the road, the vast majority were newer cars. Toyotas, Nissans, Audis, BMWs, and Mercedes.  Also, there were highways.  Real highways around Pristina.  It wasn't Chicago, but it was much improved.  Kosovo was going in the right direction.

As they pulled into a subdivision named Marigona Residence, a guard raised a gate arm.  Erolld drove in on the main road named 'California Street.'  Smitty's jaw dropped.  The neighborhood street was wide enough for parking on both sides. It also had sidewalks - on both sides.  Houses were separated by a generous distance, much greater than other parts of Europe. It was as if someone had teleported a middle-class American neighborhood into Kosovo.  Even other parts of Europe didn't have this type of housing development.  In the center of the neighborhood, a small strip mall stood; within walking distance of each house.  A supermarket, restaurants, a gym, and a Sheraton hotel that was exquisite.

"Erolld.  We are in Kosovo?  Right?"

Erolld just laughed.  "Yes, Mr. Smith.  This is Kosovo.  Has it changed since your last time here?"

"Just a bit.  Where are all the bullet-riddled houses?"

"Some of them still stand, but only a few.  My nation owes a significant amount of thanks to America and Americans like you. We would have none of this if it weren't for you."

Smitty wasn't sure what to say.  Kosovo had advanced further and faster in the past few decades than the U.S. had.

Once at the Four Points Sheraton, Smitty checked in.  The hotel was less than two years old and still had that 'new smell.' Smitty recalled his first night in Kosovo back in 2004.  He had arrived in country wearing a bullet-proof vest and a Kevlar helmet and slept in a 20-man tent on Camp Bondsteel.  Change was a good thing.

The hotel room bed was firm and comfortable.  Smitty slept like a rock.  He didn't know what he would find tomorrow, but he knew he needed to find something, anything to understand what happened to Buck.

\*\*\*\*\*\*\*\*\*\*\*\*\*\*\*\*\*\*\*\*\*\*\*\*\*\*\*\*\*\*\*\*\*\*\*\*\*\*\*\*

Jamie pulled his big rig into Fort Lauderdale and tapped Curt on the shoulder. "Hey buddy. Gonna have to drop ya here."

Curt awoke with a hangover. His head throbbed. "Yeah. OK. Hey, can I give you some money?"

"No need, man. You probably need it more than me. Take care out there, Curt. And thanks for helping me reflect on some things I hadn't considered."

"No, thank you Jamie. It may sound weird, but I'm on a mission here, and your information helped."

They shook hands and Curt jumped out of the truck. He walked for a while, finding a small diner. It was morning, and Curt needed coffee, aspirin, and food. The diner seemed like a mirage.

Curt entered and saw an empty seat at the bar. Next to it was an elderly biker. Jeans and leather, head to boot, long hair on his head and longer on his beard. His jacket had a massive 'Vietnam Veteran' patch on the back.

"Sir, is this seat taken?"

"Nope. Yours if you want it," the biker replied.

"Thanks. Hey, I'm new here. What's good?"

"Dunno. My first time here too. Just passin' through. Headed to Key West."

"Cool. I'm passin' through too. Guess I'll test the coffee and take my chances on some eggs." Curt reached into his backpack, leaned down as if to tie his shoe, and took a swig of his Jim Beam.

"Easy there, buddy. You OK?" the biker said.

"Yeah. Just some hair of the dog. Tough night."

"OK. If you say so. Hey, my name is Shooter. What's yours?"

"Curt. Hey Shooter, nice to meet you. Did your mom give

you that name?"

"Ha, no. My battle buddies did. I was a sniper in Vietnam. Pretty good shot too. Were you military?

"Yes. I was Navy Special Warfare."

"You mean like a SEAL?"

"Yeah. Like that." Curt was growing frustrated at how many times he had to overcome others' doubts about his service.

"OK," Shooter chuckled. "If you say so."

With that, Curt stood from his stool and lifted his shirt over his head. "Well, if I wasn't a SEAL, I'm the biggest dumbass in the world for getting this tattoo." There, clearly on his chest over his heart, was the Navy Special Warfare badge, an eagle holding a trident.

"OK, OK, put your shirt on. You're gonna get thrown out of here." Shooter believed him now. And also knew it probably wasn't the wisest idea to upset such a guy.

Another voice spoke from behind the bar. "Hey sugar, you need to put that shirt back on, but I must say, ya look just fine without it." It was the waitress, wearing a name tag which read, 'Lucy.' She snickered after the comment, but it was clear she wouldn't stand for a half-naked man in her restaurant, no matter how attractive he was.

"Sorry, ma'am. I'm pulling it down now."

"Thanks, sugar. What you havin'?"

"Coffee and can I get your 2-egg platter?"

"Sure, sugar. You want some water with that? You look like you could use some."

"Yes please. Thanks." Curt took his seat again and handed over his menu to Lucy.

"So Curt, where you headed to?"

"Dunno. Kinda just on the move."

"OK. Do you have a home?" The concern in Shooter's voice was present. It was as if a caring old man was asking a young boy if he were lost.

Curt was taken aback by the question. Yes, of course, he had a home. But was it 'home' or was being 'homeless' his new home? Part of him didn't want to 'have' or 'be' home, so he lied. "Nope. Got no home."

"Sorry to hear that, buddy. If you want, I'm happy to give you a ride down to Key West. There's a good number of homeless there and many resources to care for you. Unfortunately, from Fort Lauderdale down to Miami, the police are instructed by politicians to 'keep the city clean.' You won't do well here."

Curt didn't need to think about Shooter's offer. He could again be on the move, and running was what he needed. "I'd be much obliged. Thanks."

The two ate their meals and chatted. Curt paid cash for both the meals. It was the least he could do. As they walked out, Shooter threw his leg over a 1990 Harley Davidson Fat Boy with saddlebags and a sissy bar. Over the sissy bar was Shooter's backpack. "Curt, tie your backpack on top of mine on the sissy bar. Sorry, I don't have a helmet for ya. You ready?"

As stupid as it was to get on a bike without a helmet, Curt didn't care. It was yet another way to take risk and feel alive. Curt jumped on and the two drove down A1A from Fort Lauderdale all the way to Key West. The ride would take half a day.

*****************************************

Just next to the WWII memorial on the path into Constitution Gardens Park, Don waited for Steve. The weather was nice, and he didn't mind the wait. It reminded him of old times. He was anxious and wanted to get back into the game. Finally, Steve walked up.

"Hey, Don. Good to see you."

"Yeah, you too, Steve. I hope you have good news for me."

"Unfortunately, the boss hasn't come up with any yet." Steve knew it wasn't what Don wanted to hear.

"Fuck. Come on, man. These guys sprung me from jail. I gotta give them something. They are serious players. Did you see the news about Thiessen?"

"Thiessen? Who's that?"

"He was the pilot we used for Nissassa that turned on us. He just had an unfortunate plane accident in Kosovo."

"I hadn't heard. Is he dead?"

"Not yet. But I'm certain he'll die soon."

"Was he on the plane with NATO Assistant Secretary Manzina?

"Yeah, I think so. Why?"

Steve's eyes opened in a bit of shock. "What the hell? Did the guys you work with sabotage that flight?"

Don paused. "Maybe? Frankly, I don't know for sure. Seriously, who cares?"

"Who cares? Reel it back in a bit, buddy. I understand your desire for payback, but you can't assassinate Senior NATO officials, even if they weren't your intended target."

Don thought about it. "Fair. But it wasn't me. I just need a mission."

"OK, look, I'll push the boss again."

"Great, thanks. Hey, can you do me a favor? Can you put out some pings on Curt Nover's phone? I'm trying to get a location. Here is his number."

"Sure. Too easy. I'll have something for you soon." They both said goodbye and separated. As they walked away, Steve pulled out his phone to turn it back on. As he pulled it out, he quickly realized the phone was on the whole time. *'Shit, gotta remember to turn these off,'* he thought. He then made a quick call to one of his staffers. "Hey, Steve here, remember that plane crash in Kosovo? I understand there was a U.S. Citizen on it. Can you get me an update on his status? Thanks. Goodbye."

## *Chapter Twenty*
# Blame Game Noise

Smitty awoke at 0500Hrs because of lingering jet lag issues. He ate breakfast and checked his messages. Allison had not found Curt but did receive a text from him. Smitty also wrote a quick note to Congressman Jack Donegan stating he had linked up with Erolld. After a shot of espresso and a quick workout in the hotel gym, Smitty waited in the lobby, sipping one of the best coffees he'd ever had in his life. Kosovo may have its issues, but they'd mastered coffee.

Around 0800Hrs, Erolld walked into the lobby. With Erolld were two U.S. Army officers, one a colonel and another a major. "Mr. Smith. Good morning. Please let me introduce our helper today. This is Colonel Mark Barlow, the U.S. Brigade Commander from Camp Bondsteel." Colonel Barlow was a grizzly, old Army officer who transitioned from the active duty into the national guard years ago. His home and family were in Arizona, but for Mark, home was wherever his brigade was.

They shook hands and exchanged formalities. "Hello gentlemen, please call me Smitty. Do you have any leads yet?"

The colonel spoke, "Smitty, please call me 'Buzz,' it's my nickname. This is Major Thad." The major nodded. Buzz continued, "Unfortunately, we only know one piece of questionable information. Per the filed flight plan in Belgrade, four people were onboard, but only three bodies were found by the Kosovo Security Force (KSF) who secured the crash site."

Smitty was intrigued. "OK, but what about the wreckage?"

Buzz continued, "The wreckage has been moved from the road to a large, abandoned aircraft hangar. That hangar is a cave in a mountain next to Adem Jashari airport, built during the Yugoslav times. As you can imagine, there are many people, KSF, NATO, Press, and others, in the hangar. I coordinated with the Commander of NATO KFOR as well as Lieutenant General Krasniqi, the KSF Commander, to get us access. If you're ready to go, we have a vehicle waiting outside."

Smitty was somewhat impressed at how much Erolld had coordinated in the past 24 hours. It was clear, things can happen fast in Kosovo if they need to, and if you have the right contacts. Smitty grabbed his backpack off the chair and followed the men out to the vehicle and drove away.

Twenty minutes later, the U.S. Military Humvee approached the Adam Jashari airport. They turned onto an old, abandoned taxiway that led from the airport to the nearest mountain. After 1000 yards, they were stopped at a fence by a KSF guard with a weapon. Colonel Barlow exited the vehicle and said a few words. After showing the sentry his identification, the KSF soldier jumped to attention, saluted, and then opened the gate. Colonel Barlow casually walked back to the Humvee and entered. "We're clear," he said to the driver. They transitioned through the gate, made a slight turn, and then were looking into the massive hangar carved into a mountain, described by Colonel Barlow. Smitty had never seen such a thing. The vehicle stopped, and the men exited.

Soon, they were approached by an Italian man wearing a very well-pressed and well-fitted military uniform. Colonel Barlow saluted as he approached.

"Major General Torres, good morning, sir." Buzz said.

"Buongiorno," the general replied. "Is this your guest?" It was clear the Italian general knew about Smitty, which meant the Italian government did as well. So much for a low profile.

"Yes, general, I'm Mark Smith, but folks call me Smitty. I thank you for letting me look around. Have you found anything?"

"We have found both engines, and we know at the time of landing, both engines were dead. Because of this, we are confident the issue was with the engines. I believe my team will find the problem soon." This overwhelming sense of confidence and optimism was a common trait among European Flag Officers. It was almost unbounding.

"Great, sir. Do you mind if we have a look around?"

"Not at all. Please." With that, the group separated. Erolld remained with the general, while Buzz grabbed Smitty's arm.

"Smitty, come with me." The two walked towards another man in a differently styled camouflage military uniform. His hair was a bit disheveled; he was smoking a cigarette, and he was clearly tired. It was obvious by the disposition of the surrounding others, he was their leader and revered.

"Lieutenant General Krasniqi, sir, good evening. This is Mr. Smith, the gentlemen that I told you about."

Lieutenant General Krasniqi extended his hand. "Mr. Smith, good evening. Welcome to Kosovo."

"Thank you, general. I appreciate the hospitality. Please call me Smitty."

"I understand you were here years before, helping us gain our freedom."

"Yes, sir, that's correct."

"I want to thank you for your support. Without you and America, we would not be where we are today. I also asked some of my fellow Kosovo Liberation Army soldiers about you. If what I heard is correct, you are a legend. Whatever you need, you have the full support of the KSF."

Buzz had no idea what Lieutenant General Krasniqi was referring to and did not wish to know. Perhaps later.

"Thank you, general. May I ask you about the conflicting news from Kosovo and Serbia? It seems each accuses the other nation of causing the accident. Is there any validity to either claim?"

General Krasniqi put out his cigarette. "Smitty, it is all bullshit. Balkan media has been broken for years. Journalists primarily make money for every click they get on the internet. They make money fomenting wild claims that stoke the anger of either Kosovars or Serbians. It's not just Kosovo. Serbia does it, too. Long ago, I attended the Military Academy in Belgrade when we were all Yugoslavia. My classmates were Serbians, Croats, Montenegrins, and Slovenians. We all know each other. Even though we fought Serbia through the 1990s, I have many former friends I served with in the Yugoslav Army. We still talk, albeit on unofficial channels. We all see the same thing from the media. We all know there is no evidence to support the press claims."

Smitty was refreshed to hear a Flag Officer speak so bluntly and clearly, but that was General Krasniqi. "Thank you, sir."

With that, General Krasniqi shouted something at one of his men, who ran up to them quickly and stood there. "Smitty, this is Berat. He will give you his number. Whatever you need, and whenever you need it, call him." Berat handed over his number.

"Again, thank you, general." Smitty and Buzz walked over towards the collected aircraft debris and started looking around.

From the wreckage, it was clear Buck tried to skid the aircraft onto the ground at a low angle of impact. The engines seemed to have been picked over and examined. They had not seized from an oil problem, nor did they show any catastrophic event which would have ripped them apart. Aside from being in a crash, they looked fine.

As they walked around, Smitty said to Buzz, "So, all we have is a missing body?"

"Seems so. It's crazy. The KSF has had over a day to perform a search and rescue of the crash site. Given it was a NATO flight, they've put over a hundred soldiers on the mission. There are no signs of a fourth body," Buzz replied.

"Great." Smitty replied. The group of them kept looking at the wreckage. *'There must be something,'* Smitty thought.

In the late afternoon, another man approached Colonel Barlow. "Hey Buzz, I think I have some info for you." The stranger was Mike Davis, another U.S. Military Officer assigned in Kosovo.

"Mike, hey. What's going on?" Buzz responded.

"Can you step over here?" Mike pulled Buzz away from the majority of folks towards a secluded corner. After 30 seconds, Colonel Barlow stopped Mike from speaking and brought Smitty into the discussion.

"Mike, this is the guest from the U.S., Smitty. Smitty, this is Mike Davis. Colonel Mike Davis, the U.S. Defense Attaché to Pristina. Mike, can you tell them what you have?"

"Smitty, hey. I heard you were coming. The Congressional military liaison office called a few days ago. Sorry I couldn't meet with you. I helped Congressman Donegan arrange Erolld. Hopefully, he has been of help. And I really hope this info helps. The Brussels field office for the U.S. Department of Transportation and FAA has sent our embassy an initial assessment of the black box. While the entire data isn't available, the only anomaly they have right now is significant problems being reported in electrical systems and then the box stopped recording before the crash."

"Thanks, Mike. I am not sure what that means, but at least another piece of info."

"Yes. I agree. Smitty, I was trained by the U.S. Air Force as a Safety Officer and have investigated crash sites for the military. I don't know this plane specifically, but I have about two hours of free time and can help you look through the wreckage if you want."

"I welcome the help, Colonel. Please join us." Smitty felt like they were getting closer. He had yet another piece of info, but what did it mean? He wasn't sure.

The men split up and walked around the hangar, examining the pieces. Fuselage, wires, charred tail sections, wing parts and more. It was like trying to find a needle in a haystack. After an hour, Mike stopped. He stared down at a piece of wing root that had ripped from the fuselage. Discretely, he took a picture of the wreckage piece. Next, he pulled out his phone, made a call, and put it away. Slowly, Mike walked over to Smitty and Buzz. He softly said, "Can you two come with me quietly?" The two followed slowly. The hope was not to alert the dozens of others examining pieces that a potential key part of the puzzle was found.

Mike stopped in front of a piece of wreckage. "If I'm not mistaken, the piece next to my foot is part of the fuselage, and this open area is part of the main electrical system. Notice the wires coming into and out of the box are in great shape or just slightly singed. But inside the box, the plastic coating is gone, and there are arc weld spots from where a short occurred. Also, the cover for the box is bent up and screws are missing. I don't think these screws removed themselves and they should have easily maintained structural integrity through the crash. The question is, did Buck have an emergency and try to get in here or did something else happen?"

Smitty leaned down to look at it.

"Please don't touch it," Mike said. "I have our Embassy Regional Security Officer (RSO) on his way over to try and get prints."

Smitty didn't know why, but his gut told him this was the problem, and Buck's accident was no accident.

"Buzz, why don't you and Smitty head back to the hotel. I'll stay here and wait for the RSO. All of us loitering will look suspicious. I'll pass the photo of the box to the FAA and if we can get a good print, the embassy will run it. Whatever we find, I will pass to you."

"Sounds good. Smitty, do you want to give Mike your number?"

"Yes, please. And thanks, Mike."

"No worries."

"Alright. I'll be in touch. Have a good night."

Erolld, Smitty, and Buzz loaded up into the Humvee and returned to the 'Four Points.' "Smitty, are you hungry?" Erolld asked.

"Tired and hungry. I was just going to grab room service."

"No need. I have reservations for us. It's a 2-minute walk from the hotel." Erolld smiled. Smitty did as well. 'Kosovar hospitality,' Smitty thought. 'It's over the top.'

They walked into Sarajeva Restaurant. It specialized in grilled meats with exceptional steaks. The smell inside the restaurant was wonderful. Smitty set his small backpack down on the floor, grabbed a seat and opened the menu, luckily in English. Every dish had a Balkan name except one. 'The Jeff Burger.' Smitty turned to Erolld. "The Jeff Burger?"

Erolld laughed, "Yes. Jeff is the name of a previous defense attaché here in Pristina. He was one of our favorites. The owner loved him and named a dish after him. The burger is good. It's like a bread bowl for chili, but filled with grilled sirloin steak, melted cheese, and onions. Believe it or not, it is the best seller here."

Smitty chuckled, "Nah, I think I'll eat some of the local fare." With that, a large bottle of red wine and grilled spicy peppers slathered in cheese, as well as other appetizers, started pouring onto the table before Smitty even had a chance to order. Grilled meats of all kinds except pork (Kosovar Albanians are Muslim), cheeses, veggies and freshly made bread. It was spectacular. Again, Kosovar hospitality.

During the meal, Erolld had placed a few calls. Nearing the end of dinner, the restaurant door opened, and a lone man walked in. Erolld waved him over to the table, and the man approached. "Smitty, I thought you may wish to meet someone while you are here."

Smitty set down his utensils, quickly wiped his face and hands, then stood. Erolld continued. "Smitty, this is Valton. Valton is the local Kosovar Albanian who pulled Mr. Thiessen from the burning wreckage." Erolld gave a full account of the details. He made Valton sound fearless, and frankly, he was.

Smitty reached out his hand. "Hello, Valton. It is truly an honor to meet you and thank you for what you did. You helped a very dear friend of mine. We don't know if he will survive, but I do know, without you, he would not have had that chance. Again, thanks."

"Mr. Smitty, sir. It is I who wish to thank you. Without you, your efforts years ago in Kosovo, and America's efforts, we would not be free. Erolld and I are friends and I begged him for the chance to meet you, just to say thank you."

Smitty was truly touched, and it was clear. Every word from Valton was from his heart. He reached down to his backpack, opened it and pulled out two items. He stood back up and said, "Valton, I have a few small gifts for you. The first is one of the patches from a dear friend of mine. He was assigned to the Army Special Forces, and it is one of his patches. On the patch, there are three letters, 'D.O.L.' They are an abbreviation of the Latin phrase, '*De Oppresso Liber*' or in English '*To Free the Oppressed.*' It is a phrase that many in the Green Beret Special Forces community use and it is what you did for my friend, Buck.

I want you to have it." Next, Smitty pulled out a shiny object. "Also, I want you to have this. It is the U.S. Navy's Special Warfare badge, worn by U.S. Navy SEALs. I want you to have it for the bravery and courage you displayed."

Valton was overwhelmed. He expected no gifts and, in his mind, freedom from the hell in which he lived under Slobodan Milosevic's rule was a debt he could never repay; even if he ran into 100 burning aircraft to save Americans. Valton had a small tear in his eye and emotion overtook him. He hugged Smitty. "Thank you, Mr. Smitty. Thank you. I am honored!"

"You're welcome, but again, it is I that must thank you. Would you like to join us?"

"Sir, that is a kind offer, but I must be going. It is growing late, and I must get back to my family. Thank you again."

Smitty sat down and Valton walked over to the kitchen. In a hearty voice, he happily yelled something to one of the cooks, clearly his friend, and immediately showed off his new Eagle and Trident badge. He was ever so proud. They talked for a while. Smitty turned his attention back to Erolld.

"Erolld, I'm a bit overwhelmed. Is this normal?"

"Smitty, the ethnic Albanians living in Kosovo love Americans. If they find any that fought for our freedom, they love them even more. Why do you think there is a 'Jeff Burger' on the menu here and be the best seller?" Erolld chuckled. "Most Kosovar Serbians feel completely the opposite. Right now, 95% of Kosovo is comprised of Albanians. The rest are Serbian or other minorities. However, up near Mitrovica, north of where your friend crashed, the percentages are reversed. That area is almost all ethnic Serb and very few, if any, Albanians. You are far more welcome down here than you would be up there."

"Good to know. Should we go up there to the crash site tomorrow?"

"We can, but I am not sure what you will find."

"OK, let me rephrase that. Are we safe up there?" Smitty wasn't asking out of fear, but rather preparation on how to set expectations while in the area.

"You are safe. Just because they may not like you doesn't mean they'll do anything."

"Got it. Hey, let's pay for the meal and get out of here."

"Smitty, we can go, but there will be no paying for the meal. The man Valton was speaking to is the owner. Your meal is settled."

"Valton paid for my meal?"

"I don't know. Maybe yes, maybe no. Maybe he told the owner about you and your military service here. Either way, no one will take your money here and if you try to make them, it will be an insult."

"Can I at least say thanks to the owner!?"

"Sure, come with me." Erolld led him to the owner, who shook Smitty's hand aggressively, both thanking each other. The owner then poured three small shot glasses of Rakia, a traditional Balkans schnapps that is far more potent than any most other schnapps you'd find around the world. They raised their glasses. Erolld and the owner shouted "Gëzuar!" and they all drank. The round of 'thank yous' passed one more time and finally Smitty and Erolld departed the restaurant.

Walking back to the hotel, Smitty spoke, "Hey, I thought you said Kosovo was predominantly Muslim. Why the alcohol?"

Erolld smiled, "Our Prime Minister, Ramush Haradinaj, often has said, 'We are Muslims, but we aren't very good Muslims.'" Erolld bellowed out a hearty laugh. It was one of his true trademarks. Smitty followed suit. They were getting close to the hotel. Smitty was looking forward to some well-deserved jet lag sleep.

As they turned to walk into the hotel, Colonel Davis was standing there looking for Smitty.

"Smitty. There you are. Let's go. Erolld, I need to take Smitty."

Erolld understood. "OK, Mike. Have a good evening." Erolld shook their hands and departed.

Smitty turned to Mike. "Wait, what's going on?"

"Smitty, we have something. Get in." An embassy vehicle sat idling outside the hotel. The two got in the car.

"Mike. What's going on? What do you have?"

"Smitty. In time. Let's get to the embassy." The 20-minute ride was agonizingly quiet. The vehicle pulled in and the two walked up to the Embassy. A Marine security guard saluted Mike and then checked Smitty's ID. He was quickly ushered in. After a few turns, they ended up in a small conference room. Inside were two other people, the Political Officer State Department official as well as the Regional Security Officer.

"Mr. Smith, welcome. We understand you are here on behalf of Congressman Donegan. Correct?"

"Yes."

"OK. We have some preliminary information for you but ask you treat it as classified, as you would when you were in the Navy."

"No problem. Go ahead."

"Sir, it appears the fingerprints on what we now know is the primary electrical distribution box belong to a woman named Katarina Stojanović. You claim you knew the pilot, Mr. Thiessen. Do you know this, Ms. Stojanović?"

"Never heard of her. Who is she?"

The RSO looked at him, paused, and responded, "We aren't sure."

Smitty's lack of sleep, a few drinks at dinner, and this wild goose chase had gotten the better of him. He took a deep breath. His demeanor turned confrontational. "Look, I'm sure you've run your traps on me. You know I'm a former SEAL. What you may not know is that I've worked in embassies and with many unique entities of our government. Please don't treat me like an idiot. If you run a fingerprint into a database and get a match in your system this fast, I am sure there is SOMETHING in the database about her. You'd have been wiser to tell me there was no match. Now, either say 'you can't share anymore' or tell me something else, but don't tell me you don't know."

The RSO was taken aback, but knew Smitty was right. He looked at Mike, who slightly nodded. He then looked at the State Department Political Officer, who also nodded.

"Sir, yes. OK. Ms. Katarina Stojanović appears to be an agent loosely affiliated with the Serbian government."

"An agent?"

"Yes, she has a history of being a honey trap and suspected of espionage activities.

Smitty's pulse quickened. *'It wasn't an accident,'* he thought to himself. Smitty knew that was all he needed from this trip to Kosovo. He had to get back to the U.S. He had to tell Allison, and he had to find Curt. They were all in danger. "Thanks. I appreciate your honesty. I need to get back to my hotel. I'll be flying out tomorrow."

"Smitty, if you want to stay and work this." Smitty cut off Mike.

"Colonel Davis, thanks, but no. I have your number and you have mine. I need to get back. This was no accident, which means my friends and I could be in trouble."

"I understand. I'll have the embassy motor pool take you back to your hotel. Good luck, Smitty." They all shook hands and Smitty got into the car. He pulled out his phone and texted Allison:

*"Allison – Buck's crash is looking less like an accident. I believe Buck was targeted. Watch your back. Update on Curt when you can."*

He got back to his hotel and packed. He would be on the ground in Kosovo for less than 48 hours, but danger lurked.

*****************************************

Back in D.C., another text message popped into Don's phone.

*"Seems your friend is in Key West, FL. Or at least his phone is... intermittently. Last solid ping was Atlanta. Key West could be an anomaly. Still working it, as well as other opportunities."*

Steve had at least delivered something.  Don was grateful.

## *Chapter Twenty-One*
# Leveraging Friends

Allison could take no more. She was going to find Curt. Hopping into her car, she drove to the only person she knew who could possibly solve the puzzle. After a half hour, she was in the Chicago suburbs near Midway airport. She pulled into the driveway of a ranch-style house, walked to the door and knocked. After a few seconds, a voice boomed from behind the door, "Who is it?"

"Frank. It's Allison! Allison Donley!"

The door cracked open enough to show the chain holding it from opening fully.

"Hey, Allison, you alone?"

"Yes, Frank. Please let me in. I need help!"

The door fully opened, and she entered. The place was a disaster. Empty pizza boxes and beer bottles littered the coffee table. The sofa had more stains than an infant's bib. It didn't matter to Allison. Frank was the best computer genius she knew. When she ran traps as a journalist, Frank had helped her gather info before. Frank operated in a gray area of legality, and that was OK with Allison.

"Frank, can you identify the origins of a text message for me? I need to know where someone is."

"A text message? I don't know. I can usually pull geo-tagged info from a photo, but not a text message. Was it between iPhones?"

"Yes."

"OK, let's go into my office." They walked over and entered another room in the house. It was cold and dark, with computer banks lining the wall. In the middle was a desk with three computer monitors on it, each with a few windows open and scrolling information. As filthy as the living room was, this was the opposite. It was immaculate. Frank took the phone and plugged it into the computer. Within seconds, he was looking at the protocol messaging of the iChat message. "Sorry, Allison.

There's no geo data here. Did the person send you a photo?"

Allison was crushed, and Frank could sense it. Tears started rolling down her face. "No."

"Hey, hey. Don't cry in here. I can't afford to get this stuff wet." Frank's efforts at humor were horrid. "You really need to know this location, don't you?"

"More than you realize. I know you tell me you never want to know the details, but this one is personal. He's family, and in trouble."

"OK. Hold on." Frank pulled Curt's number off the phone and then ran it into another open window on his computer screen. Within seconds, he had a set of geo coordinates. "Allison, I can't tell you where the text message was sent from, but I can tell you the last cell tower this phone solidly registered with was in Atlanta, Georgia."

"Atlanta?" Allison was stunned. It was much further than she expected. "Are you sure?"

"I am. And you don't want to know how."

"OK. Thanks, Frank." Allison reached into her purse to pull out her wallet.

"Is this really family?" Frank asked.

"Yes. It's perhaps the most important person in my life. He's my fiancé, and he's lost." The question and answer drove her again to tears.

Frank gently nudged her hand, holding a wallet, away. "Allison, no charge today. Good luck."

She hugged him. "Thank you, Frank."

He handed her a map with a cell tower and a set of lines that triangulated his location. "Here you go." She took the paper, he walked her out, and she started driving. To Atlanta. As she drove, she saw Smitty's message. She tried to call him, but the phone was off and immediately played the voice mail recording. Smitty was airborne, returning to the U.S. She left a message explaining everything.

Unfortunately, Frank's technology was good, but it wasn't as good as Steve's and the lead that Steve offered to Don would soon present challenges.

\*\*\*\*\*\*\*\*\*\*\*\*\*\*\*\*\*\*\*\*\*\*\*\*\*\*\*\*\*\*\*\*\*\*\*\*\*\*\*\*

Don's phone rang.  It was a call from 'caller unknown' number.  Normally, Don would ignore such calls, but given his recent contacts, he chose to answer.  "Hello, Don here."

"Good morning.  Nikola here.  I am hopeful you have good news for me."

"Well, yes, I do have some news.  Unfortunately, I don't have any business opportunities, but I do have a location on Nover."

"And where is he?"  Nikola ignored every other part of Don's message.

"According to our friends, his phone has been intermittent in Key West, FL."

"Listen to me carefully.  I will be in Key West by the end of the day.  So will you.  I'll pass further details later."

"How are you getting to Key West so fast?"

"I am in the U.S. currently."  Don was unaware, but Nikola had flown to New York the day prior.  It was part of the plan.

"Key West?  Really?  You want me to go to Key West?"  To Don, it made no sense.  How was he to work his contacts in the White House for a contract if he's running around Florida?

"At this point, it is no longer a want.  You 'will' go to Key West.  Do you understand?"

Don realized there was little chance to skirt this demand.  It was far wiser to play along.

"Sure, Nikola.  I look forward to it.  Can you tell me why?"

"Easy.  We took care of Buck.  It's your turn to show us you're committed to this relationship.  I will see you tonight."  The line went dead.

Don stood there for a minute, thinking, *'What just happened?'*

## *Chapter Twenty-Two*
# A Race to Key West

Smitty's flight back into Chicago touched down in the early afternoon. He'd been off the net for nearly 10 hours. He turned on his phone and checked the message from Allison and Ian. First, Ian popped in:

> *'Lungs stable now, but still on life support. Brain activity continues, but limited. No real update. Doctors are not optimistic. Won't move him to Walter Reed until stable.'*

It was time he talked to Allison. After listening to her entire message, Smitty called her.

"Allison. Where are you?"

"Hey, I've been driving since this morning. I am passing through Louisville now. Where are you?"

Smitty answered, "I just landed at O'Hare. Look, I need you to be careful. Don Denney's release and now Buck's crash, I am growing concerned we are being targeted."

"OK. I will be careful, but I don't think I've left much of a normal trail or followed normal patterns in the past 24 hours." Allison was right. If someone was trailing her, they'd likely be more confused than she was.

"Good. So, Curt's in Atlanta?"

"He sent me a text message, and according to a cell tower hit near that time, he was in Atlanta. It's the best I have to go on."

"OK. I'll book a flight to Atlanta and meet you there."

Allison paused. Another tear fell from her eye. "Thanks, Smitty. I'm losing it."

"Stay strong, Allison. There's a reason you and Curt are

together. He needs you. I know that. Keep fighting. I'll be there soon."

*************************************

Key West was warm, both day and night. Curt had been in the city now for over a day. He spent the evening with other homeless veterans on Simonton Beach. Every so often, the police would chase them away, but the homeless would slowly migrate back. With this group, Curt learned more stories and different plights the veterans faced. He also secured more whiskey and was drinking it like water. He'd pass out, failing to remember all of it once he awoke again.

The next morning, Curt's hangover was pounding, but it would soon be calmed by a strong Bloody Mary from Sloppy Joe's, which opened at 0900Hrs. Curt was already standing outside the bar at 0830Hrs, awaiting the opening. Eventually they'd start serving, and he downed his first drink as if it were water from an oasis. After his drink, Curt strolled south down Duval Street. He wanted to keep running. At the end of Duvall, he made a quick right onto South Street and then left onto Whitehead. A group of tourists were congregated around a large red object. Curt would go investigate.

In front of him stood a five- to six-foot-tall red cylindrical object, painted with horizontal stripes and text. *'Southern Most Point Continental United States. 90 Miles to Cuba.'* Curt stared at it. He'd run as far south as he could. *What next? Start swimming? Where to run now? Was that it?'* Facing the end of his trip was overwhelming, and in his mind, he wasn't done running. He sat down on the ground, opened his backpack and started drinking from the new bottle of Jack Daniels he'd bought off the Sloppy Joe's bartender. As he drank, his emotions swirled. He was free but confined by the sea. Happy, but sad because of Buck. Adorned, but lonely because of his running. Lucid from all the knowledge he'd gained, but dazed from all the drinking. He pulled out his phone. He missed Allison. After staring at it for 5 minutes, he turned it on. Once it registered onto the network, text and voice messages piled in. He ignored them all. He'd write a simple message to Allison:

*'I'm sorry. I love you.'*

He ensured it sent, then turned off his phone. Again, Allison saw the text and immediately tried to call. There was no use. She screamed in the car. She cried. She hated Curt for what he was putting her through. But she refused to give up on him. She kept driving.

Less than five minutes later, her phone rang. She grabbed it without looking. "CURT," she screamed.

"Allison? No, this is Frank."

"Sorry, Frank. I was expecting someone else."

"Yeah. I know. His phone was on again. He's now in Key West."

"KEY WEST? Are you sure?"

"Yes. It was a solid hit."

Allison slumped in her car seat. Atlanta was only a few hours away. Key West would be another 12 hours of driving.

"OK. Thanks, Frank. I owe ya."

"Good luck, Allison. Take care." Frank hung up, and Allison quickly dialed another number. Smitty answered.

"Smitty. Forget Atlanta. Curt's phone was active again. He's in Key West. Go there. You'll beat me, but I'll get there as fast as I can."

"Are you sure Curt has his iPhone, and this isn't a wild goose chase?"

"I don't know, but at the time his phone was on, I received his text saying he loved me."

"OK. We gotta assume it's him. Thanks for the call. I was just booking the Atlanta flight. I will reroute now. Drive safe." With that, Smitty began working a flight to Key West. He'd fly through Miami, then onto Key West, with a planned arrival of 2230Hrs. With tickets booked, he'd need to find a hotel.

## *Chapter Twenty-Three*
# Plotting Don's Revenge

The late afternoon weather in Key West was lovely. Warm, with a slight breeze moving through the streets. Nikola sat at a cozy table in front of the Mood Dog Café, just a block from Hemingway's historic house. While the next 24 hours would involve some intense work, he was currently enjoying himself; sipping on a mojito and watching the colorful roosters strut through the streets and sidewalks of the neighborhood.

As he sat there, Don would soon be approaching. They had coordinated their meeting place via text hours earlier. Don was currently checking into the hotel room that Nikola had reserved for him at the Signature Series Marriott, Saint Hotel Key West. The accommodations were immaculate, as they should be, for $800 a night. After checking in, it was a brief 10-minute walk to the Moon Dog Café.

"Good afternoon, Nikola. It's wonderful to see you again." Don said.

"Don, please join me. Would you like a drink?

Don sat down and responded, "Sure. How about a margarita?"

Nikola waved to the waiter and placed the order. "I presume your flight in was OK?"

"Yes, thank you. I didn't know you were in the U.S. What are you doing here?"

"It is all part of our plan," Nikola said, as if he were surprised Don wasn't knowledgeable about the plan. In reality, Don was unaware of the plan, and Nikola knew it. He wanted it that way.

"Uh… OK. I guess I missed the memo. Can you fill me in?"

"Sure," Nikola stared into Don's eyes. "Tonight, you are going to kill Dr. Nover." Nikola slowly took a sip of his mojito, then set it down.

Don didn't flinch. In the deepest recesses of his soul, he hated Curt, Smitty, Allison and Buck. His only hesitation was the timeline. "Tonight?"

"Yes. My sources know Nover is in the area and I have some of my men trying to locate him. I am sure within hours we will know where he is. As I understand, he quit his job and is on some sort of *'finding himself'* mission." Nikola reached down into a small briefcase and pulled out a plain white paper bag that looked as if it was procured from a pharmacy. He passed it over to Don, who peeked inside.

"The red one is first, the white one is second," Nikola said as Don opened the sack.

In the bag, Don saw two syringes, one red and one white. "OK. May I ask what they are?"

"Sure. The red one will quickly and partially incapacitate Dr. Nover. It can be injected anywhere. The white one is a lethal dose of heroin. As you may know, it needs to be intravenously injected; hence, the need to incapacitate Dr. Nover. I presume you can find and hit his vein, yes?"

From Don's time in the Army Special Forces, he had extensive training in dropping IV's as well as having to perform the task a few times in combat. "Yeah, that's not a problem."

Nikola's phone rang. He answered it in Serbian, "Da... Veoma dobre vesti.. Ostani na njemu." Nikola hung up the phone. Don understood none of the conversation.

"Good news. It seems my colleagues here have found Dr. Nover. He is loitering, drunk, somewhere near the southern most marker. I don't mean to tell you how to do your business, but I'd recommend you go find him, follow him, and at the right moment, provide him his medicine."

Don picked up his margarita and downed it in a single gulp. "Consider it done." Don could sense his welcome at Nikola's table was nearing expiration. He stood up, reached out to shake Nikola's hand, who reciprocated.

"Good luck, Don."

"Thanks." Don walked away, carrying his white bag.

## *Chapter Twenty-Four*
# The Smell of a Rat

The White House lawn was beautiful as workers decorated it in preparation for the annual Easter egg hunt. It was late afternoon on Thursday, a day prior to the event, and the President would be hosting a small gathering for key donors. Many of them had flown in from around the U.S. with their families; to provide a chance for their children to partake in one of the Executive Branch's oldest traditions.

Inside the White House, staff was putting the final touches on the cocktail reception. Steve awaited the President and First Lady at the bottom of the stairs in the lobby. The President was dressed in a traditional black suit, while his lovely wife looked stunning in a gorgeous soft pink spring dress. They floated down the steps as if on air.

"Good afternoon, Mr. President and Madam First Lady," Steve said in a fairly standard greeting.

"Hello, Steve," the First Lady replied. "Where is your wife? I still need to have her give me that jalapeno corn bread and chili recipe!"

Steve laughed. "Ma'am. She'll be here soon. If you wish, I can get it for you, too."

"Now Steve, I appreciate that, but she is much more fun to talk to. No disrespect, but it's a woman thing." The First Lady was wonderfully nice and could even make a small jab seem like a compliment.

"Yes, ma'am. Mr. President, the receiving line is formed, and all the preparations are in place."

"Excellent. Thanks, Steve. One thing, I received a quick note from Harry who's now sick and cannot come tomorrow. We need a replacement for him. Get me some ideas before you go to bed."

Harry was Harold Johnston, the Secretary of Education. The Easter egg hunt tomorrow was to have an education theme for the children. The White House rarely misses a chance to build narratives for such events.

"Yes, sir. Too easy." Steve led the President and First Lady into the reception area, stopping short so that the President would be the first to enter. Awaiting him was the start of an official reception line, being held back by a U.S. Air Force Major, decked out in her service dress uniform along with a Presidential Aide braid over her right shoulder. She would greet the guests, learn their names, and then pass them to the First Lady and President.

"Good afternoon, Mr. President and Ma'am. Are you ready to proceed?"

"Yes, Major. Thanks." The officer turned to the first guest, took their invitation (which had been checked at least five previous times by security and others), learned the names and performed as expected. The line moved at a snail's pace, each donor wanting not only the standard photo with the First Couple but also a chance to get their 30 second pitch on whatever issue they had paid for. Energy subsidies, agriculture policy, defense spending and other issues would all be discussed. Standing behind the President, taking notes, was Steve.

The line continued. Halfway through, the major took a card from the next guest and looked down at it, then up. "Good afternoon, Mr. Denney."

"Good afternoon, Major...." He looked down at her uniform name tag. "Buckhout."

She smiled, as few cared to even address the major in the line. Next, she turned to her right, "Ma'am, allow me to introduce Mr. Andrew Denney."

The First Lady reached out her hand, "Andy! So lovely to see you today! Where is your wife?"

"Madam First Lady, the pleasure is all mine. Unfortunately, Becky is under the weather. It appears to be going around."

"Yes! You're right! Harry, our Secretary of Education, called in sick and won't be here tomorrow. This bug seems to be a bad one!" The First Lady turned to her husband. "Honey! Look who's here! It's Andy!"

Andrew casually took one step to his left, now standing in

front of the President of the United States. "Mr. President. Great to see you again."

"Andy. The pleasure is all mine." They shook hands firmly, and the President leaned in for a slight hug. As he did, he said, "Andy, this thing with your son. Is it legit?"

In a quick response, "Sir, I wish I knew." It was all the President needed to hear. They separated, Andy turned to be between the two and a camera flash captured the moment.

The President turned to his Chief of Staff. "Steve, let's see if we can get Andy on the calendar for a lunch sometime soon."

Steve nodded and wrote it down. Both the President and Andrew knew the likelihood of such an event was less than 20%, but the gesture was nice. Andrew wrapped up his greeting and continued into the cocktail area. The White House wait staff was exceptional. He would have a drink of his choice and a plate of hors-d'oeuvres within seconds.

The line continued, many families bringing their children for a full family photo with the First Family. After a while, the reception area was packed with kids; many of them were bratty kids of wealthy and prominent families. It was more than Andrew could stomach. After finishing his first drink, he departed, choosing to skip the President's speech later in the event as well as the chance to socialize with others. He'd done what he needed to do.

As the receiving line ended, the President turned to Steve, who was prepared with the standard info.

"Sir, 143 guests. Key absences were the Fords and McCallisters. The largest donor coming in this weekend thus far was Branson, who pushed funds electronically."

"Ha, Gene McCallister. He's got more oil money than common sense," the President quipped. "Steve, thanks. One thing. Distance yourself from the Denney kid. Understand?"

"Got it, sir." Steve understood fully well the intent and gravity of that directive.

\*\*\*\*\*\*\*\*\*\*\*\*\*\*\*\*\*\*\*\*\*\*\*\*\*\*\*\*\*\*\*\*\*\*\*\*\*\*

Allison had been driving all day. It was afternoon, and she'd made it into Georgia, just past Chattanooga. Exhausted, her Powerade drinks were no longer keeping her awake. She would continue into Atlanta, then find a small roadside hotel to spend the night. If she were to start driving at 0500Hrs, she could be in Key West by 1800Hrs the next day. It wasn't great. But at least Smitty would be there before midnight.

## *Chapter Twenty-Five*
# Unrecognizable

Curt had sat near the Southern Most Point marker for most of the day. He drank the entire bottle of whiskey and was a wreck. There was nowhere to run. He'd met a few other homeless veterans around the area, but his inebriation was so severe that he could not even communicate. That even other homeless individuals wouldn't talk with him was telling. With Curt, however, it hadn't registered.

Curt slowly staggered from the marker to South Beach, a walk of no more than fifty yards. It took him nearly 10 minutes. His clothes tattered and full of stench. As he approached the beach, the manager intervened.

"Sir, I don't believe this beach is for you. I apologize, but I am going to have to ask you to leave."

Curt was in no shape to fight, but that didn't matter. "Your beach is too good for Doctor Curt Nover!?" Curt hollered out... then belched.

"Sir, please leave. You are clearly drunk, and we do not allow drinking on our beach."

"Well, that's perfect!" Curt replied. He fumbled around with his backpack and pulled out the empty fifth of whiskey. "I'm no longer drinking! See, it's empty." In Curt's state, he truly believed that was a solid argument.

The beach manager did not wish to escalate the issue, but held firm. "Sir, again, I am asking you to leave. If you do not, I will call the police, who will clearly arrest you for drunk and disorderly conduct. Please, let's not make a scene."

Curt stared at him. He was sure he could get past this problem. He again fumbled into his backpack and withdrew a handful of $100 bills. "Here. What will it cost for me to stay here?"

Most of the $100 bills remained in his hand. However, two fell to the ground. The beach manager was utterly stunned. He reached down, grabbed two of the $100 bills before they blew away. "Sir, I don't know who you are, but I don't think it's wise to flash around that amount of cash." He pushed Curt's hand back into his bag before too many other patrons, many who'd gathered to watch the confrontation, noticed how much money Curt had. Slowly, the beach manager walked Curt across the street to the Southernmost House Hotel.

As they entered the door, the hotel manager quickly ran out from behind his desk. "Brian! What are you doing!?" The hotel manager was at a loss as to why his friend would bring such a vagrant into an upscale hotel.

"Hey, Brian. Sorry. This guy was on my beach. He claims to be a doctor but is clearly on a bender. Look here." Brian helped Curt open his backpack, and the hotel manager saw the cash. "Can you get him a room and get him into it?"

"Sure." The manager quickly got a key, and the two helped Curt into a room, laying him on the bed. The manager took $300 cash for the room from the backpack.

Curt was now fading in and out of consciousness from blacking out. "Hey. Where am I?" Curt asked. "What are you doing?"

Brian spoke to him, "Buddy. You are at the Southernmost House Hotel. You have paid for a room for one night of $300 and I will ensure you get a receipt. I've been where you are, and I am now 5 years, 2 months and 21 days sober. I'll pray for you today. When you wake up, call me and we can have coffee. OK?"

Curt glared at him. He slurred his words. "I…. I aah… I appreshat your offer. But I assss-ure you, I don't need your help." As Curt said it, the room spun. Soon, it was spinning uncontrollably. Curt got up out of the bed and began vomiting in the toilet. The hotel manager took another $200 from the backpack. The housekeeper would get a worthy tip.

Once Curt was done vomiting, the two cleaned him up and put him back in bed. Curt's confrontational demeanor had vanished. He was done. Once in bed, they took off his shoes and tried to make him comfortable. The hotel manager found a wallet, opened it up to find an ID. He wrote down Curt's info on a sheet of paper. Brian found Curt's phone; it was dead. Brian pulled out the charging cord and plugged it in to a bathroom outlet. Once the phone began to charge and turned on, Brian set the phone to silent, in an effort to let Curt sleep.

Convinced Curt would be OK, Brian left his business card with a short note. The two departed and Curt was out.

Hours later, Curt awoke with another raging headache. He did not know where he was as he had blacked out for most of the time in the hotel. He found Brian's number and called it from the hotel room phone. "Hello? I found this number in my room."

"Curt. Hey, my name is Brian. How do you feel?"

"My head is killing me. Who are you?"

"I'm the manager of the beach across the street from where you are. You were extremely drunk and flashing cash around. I took you to the hotel, and we laid you down. The manager, a friend of mine, took $500 for your room tonight and will have a receipt for you in the morning. Look, I've been where you are. If you want to talk, I'm here and I know where you can get help."

Curt was slightly puzzled, but mostly embarrassed. "Yeah. Uh. Hey, thanks Brian. I really appreciate it. Where are you now? I want to give you some money."

"Curt, I don't need or want your money. I want you to be OK." Brian meant what he said.

"Yeah. OK. Me too. Thanks."

"By the way, the manager took one of your ID cards down to the lobby so he could check you in. I found your phone, plugged it in and started charging it in the bathroom. It's on silent so it didn't wake you. Also, you'll find all your money..."

Curt interrupted him. "You did WHAT!? Curt sprang from the bed and ran to the bathroom. There was his phone. There were over fifty text messages and dozens of missed calls. *'FUCK!'* he said to himself, unplugged it and turned it on airplane mode. His iPhone was lined to Allison's iTunes account, and she was savvy enough to use the 'Find My Phone' function. His location was blown. He missed her, but at this point, he had no desire to see her, or perhaps more accurately, let her see him in such a state.  He walked back to the hotel room phone and picked it up.

"Curt?  Curt, are you there?"

"Yeah, hey sorry.  Thanks for the help and everything.  I'll be in touch.  I got to go."  Curt hung up without saying goodbye. His mind was preoccupied.

## *Chapter Twenty-Six*
# A Funeral Fit for a King

The 30 national flags outside of NATO Headquarters flew at half-staff.  The headquarters was a newly built and an impressive building located just inside the ring of Brussels, Belgium.  Inside that notoriously highly trafficked beltway made the official address Rue Leopold III.  Today, the main lobby was solemn as two caskets stood next to each other, elevated and surrounded by flowers.  One was draped in a Spanish flag, the other displayed the Union Jack of the United Kingdom.  At each of the four corners of the two caskets, stood a NATO Honor Guard member.  It was comprised of military personnel from each of the NATO military commands.  Outside of these stone-faced, crisply uniformed professionals were a few concentric rings of seats.  Behind that, many people stood.  At the head of the caskets, stood a makeshift stage where NATO Supreme Allied Commander of Europe (SACEUR) General Walters and NATO Secretary General (SecGen) Luedtke sat motionless in oversized chairs.  SACEUR was a fill in as normally the NATO Chair of the Military Committee would perform such functions, however he was away in Halifax, Canada at a Security Forum.  The room was eerily quiet.

The commander of the Honor Guard ordered his detail to attention.  With perfect military precision, the team snapped their heels together and raised their rifles.  The place was silent.  Next, the Honor Guard commander belted out an order of parade rest.  Again, with precision, the rifle butts slammed to the ground in unison, as their feet separated.  The Honor Guard would stand like this for the next two hours, until relieved.

SACEUR slowly rose from his chair.  He was a U.S. Air Force Four-Star General, wearing his service dress uniform.  He walked to the podium, at a pace commensurate with the moment, and spoke.  His words were carefully chosen and to the trained listener, the following themes arose regarding Assistant

Secretary General of Operations Dan Manzina, and his staffer, Harry Davies. First, the two were successful at their job. Second, they would leave a huge void at the headquarters which would be challenging to fill. Third, they left behind wonderful families. Fourth, their mission, and more broadly, the NATO mission, was worthy and must continue. He finished his speech and stepped away. The speech was exceptional, however no one clapped.

Next, SecGen Luedtke walked to the podium and spoke. His speech, while offering different verbiage, echoed the same themes. To those paying attention, it was clear their speech writers had coordinated the talking points. It was also evident that neither would address the accident.

After speaking, both the NATO SecGen and SACEUR departed the stage. First, they walked up to the Ms. Manzina, who sat stoically with her three children and her mother. The two offered words of solace.

Next, they moved to Ms. Davies, who was quickly losing composure. It was all too much. She sat with both her parents and Harry's parents as they tried to console her. At four months pregnant, she could not stop wondering how on Earth she would be able to bring a child into this world alone. As SACEUR and the SecGen leaned in, her emotions took control. She sobbed violently. There was not a dry eye in the house. Her parents and in-laws pulled her close. The family hugged tightly. After a brief moment, she regained her composure. SecGen Luedtke and SACEUR walked by the caskets, followed by the Manzina and Davies families. After that, a line of NATO staff formed. The caskets would lie in state for the next two days to allow fellow staff members to pay their last respects. During that time, the NATO lobby would be a somber location, far from the life and noise it echoed with since it opened.

As Secretary Luedtke walked away, he turned to SACEUR and quietly said, "Do we have any more on the accident investigation?" A Norwegian, the NATO SecGen had read the NATO classified reports which addressed the oddity of four taking off but only three found at the wreckage. He'd also read the Norwegian classified reports that were deemed 'No Foreign,' (NOFORN) meaning they could only be read by other cleared Norwegians. Those reports had already determined the crash was the sabotage of a compromised electrical system.

SACEUR responded, "I read the NATO report yesterday regarding the issue of personnel onboard. It's strange." He, too, had also read the U.S. classified reports that were U.S. NOFORN. They not only had begun to consider it sabotage, but the information about Katarina's involvement was also in the report, which included a closed-circuit television (CCTV) still photo of her at the Brussels airport executive terminal, boarding the aircraft for Belgrade. The report also stated that, according to Serbian officials, the Belgrade VIP terminal's CCTV from that day was inoperable. While SACEUR had far more information, legally none of this could be shared with the NATO SecGen because of classification policies.

Secretary Luedtke responded, "Yes. But I feel there is more."

"I agree," said SACEUR. He was biting his tongue and could not take it much longer. As the senior military NATO war-fighting commander, one of his long-standing frustrations was a continued failure to share information across the command. Intelligence compartmentalizing within and under national caveats made doing business a key challenge for NATO. As the two were alone, SACEUR continued, "Sir, I have a gut feeling this was an act of sabotage, and since the plane took off from Belgrade, it is perhaps wise to start there. I've asked my staff to examine this possibility." Without either stating U.S. intelligence or divulging it, SACEUR had entered a gray area, the 'gut feeling.' He'd kept just enough wiggle room to protect himself. He hadn't made four-star general on just his looks.

"Yes. I think your assessment has merit," the NATO SecGen responded. "Please keep me informed." The two shook hands. As their discussion wrapped up, they had made it to the NATO Headquarters front doors where SACEUR's motorcade was waiting. He'd travel back to Mons, Belgium, where his command staff was located. After a brief goodbye, SACEUR entered the middle SUV.  The flashing lights turned on, and the vehicles pulled away.

*************************************

A few hundred miles away in the southwestern part of Germany, a hospital room remained eerily quiet except for a 'beep' that occurred nearly every second.  Next to a patient, a small monitor had been displaying a green line with a small amount of amplitude deviation.  For no real explainable reason, that line began to increase at far greater rates and with more regularity.  The patient was Buck, and his brain activity was increasing.  His brain swelling was subsiding.  An alert light flashed at the nurse's station.  Two scurried into the room to see this miracle.

Roughly fifteen minutes later, the doctor entered and begin assessing Buck.  His worst condition, the brain swelling, was now improving.  The broken bones in his legs, which had already been set and casted, were also healing, but these were far from life-threatening injuries.  Doctors still could not say when they planned to bring Buck out of his coma.  On the room's white board used by nurses, a Navy Petty Officer had written his cell phone number, requesting any updates in Buck's status.  After the doctor departed, the head nurse called the Petty Officer and relayed the good news.  That Petty Officer hung up his phone and relayed a text to his leadership, Ian, at Special Operations Command Europe (SOCEUR).  Ian immediately sent the same text to Smitty.  Buck wasn't out of the woods yet, but he was fighting.

## *Chapter Twenty-Seve*
# The Chat

Curt could no longer stay in the hotel. He had no idea where Allison or Smitty were, but he knew if it were him on the hunt, they'd be closing in fast. Shoving the complementary hotel water bottles into his backpack, Curt zipped it closed and left. Under normal circumstances, any sane human would have showered, cleaned up, ordered room service and relaxed. But with Curt's condition, much of that sounded like torture. He needed to be outside. Creature comforts were incongruent with the lifestyle he wanted or needed.

Curt stepped out onto the sidewalk and began walking back towards Duval Street. He had met the bartender at Sloppy Joe's and was hopeful he could grab a seat at the bar. It was getting close to 1700Hrs. The bars and restaurants would soon be filling up.

As he walked down Duval Street, he passed by Bert's Bar, a modern-day stomping ground for true Key Westers. A small place, street side, it was full of folks, which was a bad sign. Just a few more yards up the street, he looked into Sloppy Joe's. A band was playing live music, and the place was already packed. Turning the corner, Curt decided to try Captain Tony's which was slightly off Duval Street and was the old Sloppy Joe's Bar back in the day. Luckily, it was not too busy, and he could grab a seat at the bar.

Curt ordered a Dark and Stormy. The waiter looked at him for a bit, but given the low volume of clientele, he decided to serve Curt. Approximately ten minutes later, another gentleman walked into the bar, stood behind Curt and said, "Hey buddy, is this seat taken?"

Curt looked around at the stranger. "Nope. Help yourself."

The stranger thanked Curt, pulled out the stool, and sat down. The stranger was Don, and now Curt was sitting next to the man who would try to murder him. Curt only knew of Don from TV news reports about Nissassa. They'd never met. For whatever reason, most likely his current state, Curt failed to recognize him.

"What are ya drinking?" Don asked.

"Dark 'n' Stormy," Curt replied.

"Never heard of it. Any good?"

"Absolutely. It's ginger beer and dark rum. A great drink when surrounded by tropical waters."

"Great, I think I'll have one too. What's your name?"

"Curt. Curt Nover. And you? What's your name?"

Don had to think quickly. "My first name is Nikola, but my friends call me 'Nick.' Great to meet you, Curt." Don was almost certain the man he tailed from the hotel was Curt. Now, he was sure.

"So Curt, what brings to you to Key West? Are you on vacation like me?" Don's blood began to pump. The man sitting next to him had ruined his life, put him in jail and made the U.S. a less safe place. Revenge would be sweet tonight. He was anxious but needed to practice patience. The right time would come.

"Nah. Actually, I don't know what brought me, Nick. I had a job in Chicago and just walked away last week. I've slept in a handful of different cities with a bunch of homeless guys... I mostly gravitated to the military veterans. For some reason, their stories speak to my soul right now. It's really hard to explain."

Don was a bit taken aback by this. As a former Green Beret assigned to U.S. Army's 10th Special Forces Group, he too was a veteran and knew some of his colleagues had succumbed to homelessness. Sadly, for years, twenty-two veterans a day have committed suicide. The trend, disappointingly, continues. "Interesting," was the only word Don could muster as his emotions began to swell.

"Yeah. I think so, too. Crazy. You probably don't want to hear all this crap. Hey, you said you're on vacation. Where ya from?"

Don actually didn't want to give much more information to Curt than necessary, and also was truly interested in Curt's stories. "Hey, no, really, man. I'd like to hear more about your travels. It sounds interesting. I know some friends who are veterans. I bet they know guys like the ones you ran into. Can you tell me more?"

Curt smiled. For the past 24 hours, he'd been ignored and pushed away. Folks looked at him with disgust while he drank himself into a stupor at the Southern Most Point marker. He was refused entry onto the beach. Now, a fairly well-dressed tourist wanted to know what he'd learned. Curt took a long pull off his drink, finishing it and ordering another. "Well, Nick. The first thing I learned is everyone has a story. Each is unique. I'm not sold on this but if I were in charge of the VA right now, I'd stop trying to find cookie-cutter solutions to deal with veterans' issues and rather develop some sort of construct that is flexible enough to address a range of problem sets caused by unique reasons." It was far and away the most intellectual thing Curt had said in weeks, and after a few more Dark and Stormies, the chances of him meeting that level of intellectual thought again this evening would be zero.

"Yeah," Don said, "The VA truly has a challenge on their hands."

"I agree. But as a combat veteran, to me there is this yearning. A calling. It's a feeling I can't really explain. It's almost as if I NEED to be on the street. I need some level of exposure to risk. There's a strange comfort and perhaps a warped sense of safety in sleeping out in the open, lying near another combat warrior who defended this nation on some God-forsaken foreign shore." Curt paused…. "Ah… I'm sorry. That probably doesn't make much sense. Hell, until a week ago, I didn't understand and still struggle with the notion."

Actually, it made a world of sense to Don. "No, man. I think I kinda get it." Don wasn't being completely honest. He actually completely understood. Especially after his fight with his father, Don's mind drifted to his friends and colleagues of the U.S. Army's 10th Special Forces Group; many of whom had distanced themselves from him after the fall of Nissassa. "So, maybe it's kinda like having close friends you can count on?"

"Yeah, maybe. But I'm not sure that fully captures it. I mean no disrespect, but before I served, I had a number of close friends. I truly thought those relationships were strong until I served with my shipmates. Not only were the bonds with my shipmates stronger, but sadly when I came home, many of the ties I had with my childhood friends dissolved or diminished over time. It's strange."

Don took a slug of his drink, finishing it. He looked at the bartender and ordered two shots of tequila. "Hey man, that's pretty insightful stuff. Let me buy you a drink." Don needed to clear his head and remember why he was there. He'd kill Curt that night. This conversation was clouding his judgement. It needed to end, and it needed to end now.

The two slammed their tequila shots, and Curt ordered two more tequila shots and two more Dark and Stormies. Don spoke again. "So, Curt, enough of this deep stuff. Where did you grow up?"

Curt looked at Don. "Good question. Here, there, a bit of everywhere. I was a military brat when I was young. My granddad was a Navy pilot and shot down in Vietnam. His name is on the memorial in Washington D.C. I've seen it. My dad joined the Navy when I was born. We lived in Pensacola, Florida, Norfolk, Virginia, and Whidbey Island, Washington. When I was nine, my dad was killed off the West Coast in the Pacific during night carrier training. His EA-6B Prowler was cleared to land, but an S-3 Viking hadn't cleared the carrier deck landing zone. My dad's Prowler landed on top of the S-3."

"Hey, buddy. I'm sorry to hear that. Let's drink this tequila shot to your dad."

"I'd like that, man. Thanks. My dad was the greatest man I ever knew."

Don gritted his teeth. *'How nice it would be to have a noble father,'* he thought. "To your old man!" They drank.

"After Dad passed away, my mom wanted to move back close to her family, so we settled in the Chicagoland area. As a military widower, she used the Navy facilities there on Lake Michigan, so I always remained close to our Navy roots. I loved the Navy and was fairly certain I would join. I worked hard to get into the Naval Academy and then get commissioned. Once September 11th happened, I knew I had made the right decision. So, yeah. All over. Hey, I asked you before, where are you from? Not sure you told me."

"Yeah, sorry. I'm from Virginia. Down near Charlottesville." Don's answer was 50% accurate. Virginia was the truth. His town, however, was a lie.

"Wonderful country out there. I was only in Virginia for some training. I was mainly stationed out in California when I was stateside."

The drinks were beginning to have their effects, and Don had ordered yet another shot of tequila for good measure. After the shot, Don said, "Hey, I'm hungry. You wanna get out of here and grab a burger? I need something to soak up this booze."

Curt was hungry, and a burger sounded great. "Sure. Let me pay my tab."

"No, no worries, buddy. It's on me. Thanks for your service. I'd also like to buy you dinner if that's alright. Nothing fancy. How about some quick burgers from Wendy's up the street? After that, we can find another spot on the Duval crawl. That is, unless you have other plans."

"No, no plans. That actually sounds good. And thanks for picking up the tab. You're a really great guy." Don tried to ignore the compliment as he paid. It was clouding his judgement. The two got up and walked north up Duval Street. As far as Don was concerned, Curt had only minutes left to live.

## *Chapter Twenty-Eight*
# The Kingpin Update

Nikola spent a pleasant afternoon in Key West after his meeting with Don.  He strolled along the streets, took in some sights and enjoyed the tour of the Hemingway House.  From the fifty plus 'six-toed' cats to the story of the lawn fountain (which was originally the urinal from Sloppy Joe's Bar), he found Hemingway fascinating.

After the tour, he walked to Simonton Beach and grabbed a seat in Lagerhead's Bar at the small top table tucked away in the back.  After ordering his drink, he pulled out his phone and called Katarina.  The phone rang a few times, and she answered.  They spoke in Serbian.

"Hello?"

"Katarina, hello.  It's your brother, Nikola."

"Hey, good to hear from you.  How is your trip going?"  There was some slight trepidation in her voice.

"Actually, it is going just as planned.  Our friend is none the wiser about our efforts and tonight, the final hook will be set."

Katarina was pleased.  "Excellent news.  For me, though, this cannot move fast enough."

Nikola knew what she was talking about but chose to address her concern only tangentially.  "Patience, my dear.  We have waited for nearly two decades and are now very close.  As you know, dominoes must fall in sequence.  We should be grateful they are still falling."

"Yes.  You are correct."  Katarina accepted his explanation, but it wasn't fully satisfying.  "Have you reported our efforts upwards?"

"No.  That is my next phone call.  I am to call at four PM here, which is eleven PM at the Kremlin.  I should be going, I must prepare."

"OK.  Good luck tonight.  Please let me know how it goes."

They both said their goodbyes.  Nikola set down his iPhone and reached into his Bermuda shorts' pocket.  Inside was a small, cheap flip phone. He opened the battery case and removed the battery. On the inside of the phone, a SIM Card was held on by masking tape. Nikola pulled the SIM card from the tape and inserted it into the phone. After a few minutes, the phone lit up and was connected to the network. Only one number was programmed into the address book. It had no name associated with it. The number started with a +7 country code. It was Russia. Nikola hit the green SEND button, and the call processed through.

On the other end, a woman answered in thick Russian. "Hello. How may I help you?"

Nikola would respond in Russian as well. It was not his native tongue, but he spoke it well. "Hello. I have a teleconference appointment in two minutes with President Volkov."

"Are you Nikola Stojanović?"

"Yes, ma'am."

"Please hold." She replied.

Eventually, the other end of the phone clicked back to a live line. "Nikola, your party is on the line. Mr. President, Nikola is here." The receptionist disconnected herself from the line. Nikola was now speaking with the President of the Russian Federation.

"Nikola. I presume you have an update for me."

"Yes, Mr. President. Everything from my end is moving as planned. Should tonight go smoothly, the next few pieces should soon fall into place."

"Ah… Nikola, that is great to hear, but I do believe there are mutual desired events. Or do you no longer want your family's stolen assets back from Kosovo's possession?" President Volkov was providing a far from subtle reminder this was not just Russia's desire.

"You are correct, Mr. President. It is our grand plan. After tonight, I will go to D.C. and meet with your contacts. I believe there is more than enough information for us to move to the next phase of the operation."

"You've done good work. I'll receive further secure updates

through our embassy in D.C. I do appreciate your call, Nikola, and please tell your sister hello. She's completed impressive work for both our nations."

"I shall, Mr. President. Goodbye." Nikola ended the call, removed the SIM card, and bent the flip phone backwards on itself until it snapped in two. He threw one piece in the garbage can at the waiter's station in Lagerhead's Bar. He would carry the second one to his dinner location. Along the route, he'd casually drop the SIM card onto the sidewalk. It was just as he'd been trained.

Nikola arrived at the Wendy's Restaurant in the early evening. Before entering, he casually walked around the parking lot, discretely hiding a few GoPro cameras in the trees. After that, he continued inside, ordering a burger, fries and a Frosty, the standard fare for any Wendy's fan. After receiving his food, he grabbed a seat in a booth by the window. Nikola would have a front-row view for a show he did not wish to miss.

*************************************

The Miami International airport was bustling as Smitty awaited his next flight. Scrolling through his iPhone web browser, he was interrupted by an incoming text message that flashed at the top of his phone. It said:

> *'Smitty - Good News, brain activity is returning. Swelling shrinking. Broken legs are healing (Sorry, may have forgotten to bring this up, but given the other problems, I found sharing the broken legs to be pointless). Docs now considering when to reverse the induced coma. Will keep you updated. Congrats man. Seems the dude is a fighter.'*

Smitty couldn't believe it. He responded fast with,

> *'Fuck Yeah! Thanks Ian!'*

135

Ian shot back with a thumbs up emoji. Smitty was excited and all he wanted to do was tell Curt. *'God damn it, Curt. Where the fuck are you!?'* he thought to himself. He then dialed Allison. At least she would welcome the news.

Allison's phone rang; she picked it up on the first ring. "Smitty, where are you?"

"I'm still in Miami. My Key West flight is in a few hours. Where are you?"

"I'm about an hour north of Atlanta. I'm going to stop soon, but I really want to drive through."

"Allison, don't do anything stupid. We are going to find Curt. I'll be there late tonight and will call you in the AM. Hey. I do have good news. Buck's brain activity has increased."

"What!? Seriously?"

"Yes, just got an email from my SOCEUR buddy. Evidently, Buck has broken legs too, which we didn't know about. The docs are considering at what point they pull him out of the induced coma."

"Smitty! This is great! Curt will be over the moon! We have to tell him." Allison was praying for a positive report and hoped it would be the information that snapped Curt out of what she saw as a 'major funk.' Little did she understand the gravity of the situation.

"Allison, it is good news, but let's be cautious. I've had other buddies wounded in either Iraq or Afghanistan with similar challenges. When the induced coma was reversed, their response was not always what folks had hoped for."

"OK. You're right. But can we just be glad he's improving? Really, I'm hanging by a thread here."

She was right, and Smitty needed to give her hope. "Yes. He is improving and even I am getting excited about the opportunity to get a Buck bear hug again. You're doing great, Allison. Curt's lucky to have you."

"Yeah, well, when we find him, you better tell him that... and beat it into his ass. I can't take much more of this."

"Allison, I know, and I'm sorry... for myself and for Curt. Please don't forget, he's a great guy. One of a kind. He's just lost right now." It was all Smitty could say. Frankly, he'd seen other friends scared from war do far worse than what Curt was up to. Now, however, was not the time to share that info with Allison.

"OK, Smitty. I need to focus on the road. Call me first thing in the morning and let me know what your plan is to look for him."

"I will. Drive safe, Allison. Take care." Smitty swung his chair towards the bar at Miami International Airport, raised his hand and ordered another beer. His flight wouldn't leave for another few hours.

## Chapter Twenty-Nine
# The Confrontation II

As Craig and Kelly Hewlett stepped out of their house, Curt and Don walked towards the Wendy's on Duval Street.  Craig closed the door to their AirBnB.

"Where do you want to go first?" Kelly asked.  She knew Craig had done a minor bit of research on the city.

"I don't care what's first, but we need to make it to Sloppy Joe's and to Captain Tony's.  Sloppy Joe's is the historic Hemingway bar, but the truth is, it originally was located at where Captain Tony's is today.  So, we gotta drink at both."

Kelly smiled and sarcastically replied, "Darn."  Craig hugged her as they walked down Eaton Street.   In a hundred yards or so, they would turn onto Duval St.

Don and Curt had arrived outside Wendy's.  In the parking lot, Don said, "Hey, I gotta piss and I don't want to wait in that line.  I'm gonna take a leak over here by the dumpster."  The Wendy's toilet was notorious for being used by many non-patrons who strolled up and down the street with open containers.

He didn't have to wait long to see if Curt would take the bait.  "I'll join ya," Curt said, and the two stepped behind the dumpster.  They unzipped their pants.  Curt began to relieve himself while Don pulled the red syringe from his pocket and, in a swift move, jabbed Curt in the neck.  Don never asked Nikola what the drug was, he just presumed it would work.

In seconds Curt fell to the ground, still conscious but unable to control his muscles.  The drug had caused muscle/skeletal paralysis, but Curt's eyes remained open.  Don's chummily demeanor rapidly transitioned to that of a menacing killer.  "Good evening, Dr. Nover," Don said.  The look on his face was one that had not existed since his time at 10th Group.  "Forgive my deception, but my actual name is Don Denney.  Remember me?"

While Curt was groggy, he now recognized Don.  He couldn't

speak and although he tried to fight, it was pointless. Don set Curt down on the seat of his pants, propped against the dumpster. Once Curt was seated, he pulled out a short piece of rubber tubing and tied it around Curt's bicep. Curt strained to move, he tried to yell, he tried to scream. There was nothing he could do but watch.

Curt was motionless, eyes wide open and conscious. Horrifically, he'd witness his own murder. Don quickly put on rubber gloves and reached for the syringe of heroin. The well-worn shirt ripped easily, far beyond what was needed, now exposing Curt's bicep up to the surgical tubing. Tapping the arm bend at Curt's elbow, he found the vein quickly. On Curt's arm was a tattoo of an American flag. While Don had killed in combat, he'd never killed an American, especially a fellow veteran. His intensity for the kill faltered. He blinked a few times, trying to shake off the image of the flag. Curt just sat there, now softly moaning as if begging for his life.

Don took the needle and shoved it in Curt's arm just as he'd dropped many IV needles on fellow warfighters in combat. Those, however, were intended to save their lives, not take them. This time, it would be to kill. Don looked down as he pulled back the plunger and saw clear red blood. He'd hit the vein squarely. Next, he slowly injected the heroin into Curt's arm and watched Curt's eyes transition from utter fear to a glazy, hallucinogenic state.

Just then, he heard a voice call out, "Hey, you guys OK?" It was Craig Hewlett. Unknowingly, he and Kelly had just walked into a murder.

Don had been spotted. *'Fuck!,'* He thought. Don quickly pulled out the needle, untied the arm band and ripped off the gloves, shoving them all in his pocket. He turned to Craig and said, "Thank God someone is here! Please get help! I think this guy is overdosing! He's convulsing and unresponsive. I don't know, man. This is bad!"

Craig looked down. The man was right. Craig had seen a handful of overdose victims in his career. This was textbook. "Kelly!" He yelled. "Call 911 and get an ambulance! Probable overdose. Also, get the police!" Craig turned his attention to the tourist. "I'm an off-duty cop. I need your help to lay him down." Craig and the tourist laid Curt flat.

Don's heart raced. Of all the people to interrupt his efforts, a freaking off duty cop.

Kelly ran inside the Wendy's realizing the restaurant staff would have a better chance explaining the situation to the police. As she ran in, Nikola watched in an entertained fashion.

Don was scared. He kept looking around, trying to figure out when he could make a break for it. Then he saw the opportunity he needed. A Key West police car was entering the other end of the parking lot, near the drive through. Don yelled, "Hey! A cop car just drove in! I'm going to go get them!" Before Craig could respond, Don jumped to his feet and ran to the police car.

"Officers! Officers! There's a homeless man over there who appears to be overdosing!"

The patrol car stopped and the officer in the passenger seat jumped out, opened the trunk, and pulled out a small medic bag. The other grabbed the radio microphone. "Dispatch, Unit 27. Be advised, we have a med call, possible 10-85 at the corner of Duval and Eaton in the Wendy's parking lot. Request 10-41."

As the radio call was made, the officer with the medic bag arrived next to Curt and Craig. By now, Curt had stopped breathing. Craig administered CPR breaths as best he could, fighting through all the vomit and other secretions oozing out of the victim. To most, this would have been horrific. Craig, after so many years on the police force, was numb to it. Later, his mind would process it, much like a combat veteran. Curt's pulse was shallow and beginning to wane. The heroin was taking its toll. Between breaths, Craig looked up, "Officer, my name is Craig Hewlett. I'm an off-duty police officer from North Carolina."

"Got it. I'm Shawn. Keep him breathing, Craig. You're doing great. I'm breaking out our NARCAN. I need a minute." Craig had heard of NARCAN, but never seen it. In his small town, the need for overdose remedies was miniscule compared to big cities like Key West.

Shawn opened the NARCAN, and as Craig pulled away, he shoved it into the Curt's nose, administering one dose. "OK. Keep him breathing," Shawn told Craig.

Shawn's partner eventually made his way over after securing the patrol car and performing some minor crowd control. He scanned the area and found a black backpack laying near Curt. Holding it up, he asked the crowd, "Does this belong to anyone?" After thirty seconds of no response, he began to investigate the contents.

Shawn and Craig kept working. "Craig, just keep him breathing. Let me know if you need to swap out. If you're tired and we change out, have you ever administered NARCAN before?"

Craig kept breathing into the victim. Between breaths he said, "Administer it? Fuck, I don't even know how to spell it!" Police, much like military, seemed to have a strange habit of embracing humor at the oddest of times.

Shawn smiled. "OK. You keep going. I still have a pulse. If the first dose doesn't work, I can give him the second one after three minutes."

No sooner had Shawn stopped talking than Curt coughed. His eyes bulged wide open, then closed. He began to breathe on his own, but barely. He was despondent, uncommunicative, and lay there, but he was alive. Shawn's partner tilted his head down into the microphone on his chest. He notified dispatch of a probable successful use of NARCAN and queried as to the ambulance status. It would be there in minutes.

Continuing to rummage through the victims' belongings, he found a large amount of cash loosely stuffed in one of the pockets. His first thoughts were that this vagrant was likely on an All-Points Bulletin (APB) for petty theft. Later, he found a wallet. It was far nicer than any homeless person's wallet he'd seen. Opening it, there were many high-end credit cards and a few ID cards. Again, the officer presumed the wallet stolen.

He looked at the ID photo and then at Curt. Aside from the clean-cut photo image and the train wreck of a dirty, smelly vagrant, the faces appeared to match. It was all they had to go on.

Shawn looked up at his partner, who was holding the ID card. "You got a name?"

"Possibly," he responded. "If this is our guy, the ID says he's a doctor in Chicago. His name is Curt Nover."

## *Chapter Thirty*
# No Regrets?

Now two blocks away from the Wendy's parking lot, Don stopped walking at an accelerated pace and slowed. He reached into his pocket and pulled out the syringe of heroin. Only half of the dose had made it into Curt's arm. Standing alone in a quiet residential area of Key West, he shoved the remaining heroin out onto a flower bed, bent the needle and threw it, along with the other paraphernalia, into a private citizen's street trash can. Don was freaking out. He couldn't go back, longed to know what had happened. A world of emotions poured over him. Part of him wanted Nover dead. Another part wanted to be removed from this nightmare. Entering the hotel, he went to his room.

Don needed to talk. He needed to call someone. First, Don tried calling Nikola. Inside the Wendy's, Nikola's phone rang. He picked it up off the table while watching the commotion outside. Nikola recognized the number, hit ignore, and set his phone back down. Now was not the time to talk to Don. Perhaps later. Nikola sent the call to voicemail. Don's message was frantic, as he desperately requested a call back.

Don looked at his watch. It was not that late. He decided to call Steve. Back in D.C., Steve's phone rang in the kitchen while he was helping his wife with the dishes. He looked at the number and, remembering what the President had told him, he too ignored the call. Steve's wife was puzzled. "Hey, isn't that your work phone? Don't you have to get that?"

"Not tonight, sweetheart. Not tonight." Steve replied, kissing her on the forehead.

For a second time, Don's call was met with a voicemail recording. Again, he left a brief message, this time simply saying he was checking in, trying to conceal the anxiety in his voice, then hung up.

Who else could he call? He couldn't think of anyone. Don turned on the hotel room TV; curious if there would be news of his exploits.  Clearly it was too early for this, but Don was not thinking rationally, and he would again be forced to wait.

'*Mom*!' He thought.  Don dialed his mom, Becky.  The phone rang.  "Hello, Don!  Great to hear from you."  She was always so pleased when he called.  In her mind, it was too rare of an occurrence.

"Hey, Mom.  How are you?"  She didn't sense the terror in his voice.  Even if it was there, she never did.

"Oh, I'm good.  Your father and I just finished a lovely Beef Stroganoff dinner.  I overcooked the noodles a bit, but your father said they were just fine.  I'll do better next time."  Frankly, she could have talked about needlepoint, and it wouldn't have mattered.  Don just needed to hear a voice... her voice... any voice.

"That's great, mom.  I wish I was there.  I'm sure I would have loved it."  Don looked down and raised his hand to look at it.  It shook as he was still trying to calm himself.

"Yes.  Now Don, are you and your father done with your little spat?  I'm sure he'd love to talk to you."

Before Don could say anything, his mother passed the phone to Andrew.  "Hello Son.  How are you?"

His father's voice was too much.  He lost it.  "Hey Dad."  His hand now shook uncontrollably.  "Dad..."  Don began sobbing.

Andrew took the phone from the dining room into the study.  "OK, son, relax.  What's going on?"

"Dad, I think I may be in trouble."

"Oh.  Come on.  It can't be that bad.  It's not like you killed anyone."

Don didn't reply.  The silence lasted for what felt like an eternity.

"Don."  Andrew paused.  "What did you do?"

Andrew could hear Don breathing erratically on the line.  His son had killed before, but within the legal constraints of the Laws of Armed Conflict.  Don still didn't talk.

"Don.  Did you kill someone?"

"I.... I think so."

While Andrew understood killing sometimes needed to take

place, he was far from accepting that the murderer could be his son; other than in combat, of course.

"You did what!?"

"Dad. I don't know. Maybe I did. I'm scared."

Andrew's blood boiled. "God Damn it, son! I told you! I TOLD YOU!" Andrew paused. "Fuck, son. This time, you need to learn your own lesson. I told you not to come to me with your next problem and I meant it. And instead of you listening, you bring me the fucking whale of all problems. Jesus! You need to figure this out." Andrew hung up. Don was alone. He fell to the floor of his hotel room.

*****************************************

The Wendy's parking lot was packed as the ambulance pulled out. Curt was alive, but barely. The NARCAN was working, but given the paralyzing drug as well as the alcohol in Curt's system, he was far from out of the woods.

As he was being transported, the ambulance forwarded his vitals. While one paramedic watched over Curt, the other rifled through his belongings, looking for a medical bracelet or any other information. His Cook County Hospital Identification card was the closest they could come. The ambulance also forwarded that to the Emergency Room.

The receptionist in the Lower Keys Medical Center Emergency Room quickly googled the number for the Cook County Hospital and called. Once connected, she asked if Curt worked there. Upon confirmation, she shared his current medical predicament. The receptionist was placed on hold for a brief moment, then another person answered, "Hello, you have Dr. Nover there and he did what?"

"Ma'am, he's overdosed on heroin. Who am I speaking with?"

"My name is Wanda. I'm the charge nurse in our E.R. I think you have the wrong guy. The Dr. Nover I know would never do that."

"Ma'am, I don't know what to say, but if it is your Dr. Nover, are there any medical conditions we need to know about?"

"Well, that boy is fit as they come, but he does take medication for some stuff he witnessed in the war."

"Ok, thanks. Does he have insurance?"

Wanda knew that Curt was in the process of being fired from the hospital, but she also knew that the process took time. "Yes, his insurance is through our hospital. Hold on, I'll get you his policy number." With a few clicks of the computer, Wanda had the number and read it out to the receptionist.

"Thanks for your help."

"Sure thing. Please call us and let us know if there are any errors or updates. I still don't think it is our Dr. Nover." Wanda hung up the phone, then paused. She and Curt had been friends for a very long time; ever since he first served at Cook County as a student. She took out her phone and called Allison. The phone rang, and Allison answered.

"Ms. Allison, good evening, ma'am. Sorry to bother you. This is Wanda from Cook County hospital; I work with Dr. Nover."

"No bother, Wanda. Yes, I remember you. Please, just call me Allison. What can I do for you?" Allison had just woken in a roadside hotel along the highway.

"Ma'am, I'm from the South. Sorry, 'Ms.' is just something I gotta do. Anyway, I just got a call that Dr. Nover is being admitted to the Lower Keys Medical Center Emergency Room."

"Jesus! He *is* in Key West!" Allison knew where he was. The clues were now coming together.

A bit confused by Allison's happiness and excitement, Wanda continued, "Yes, ma'am, but he's being admitted for a heroin overdose."

Allison's heart sank. She didn't know what to think, and her excitement faded rapidly.

"Wanda, are you sure?"

"That's the same thing I asked. It don't seem right. They say it was him."

"Thanks. Did they say anything else?"

"No, ma'am. I can text you their number after we hang up. I

was kinda hoping this wasn't our Dr. Nover and there was some mixup. Kinda sounds like he is in trouble. I'm gonna pray for him tonight, Ms. Allison."

"I can't be certain it's Curt, but the latest news I had was him being in Key West. Please do send me the number and I'll keep you posted. I will be in Key West tomorrow."

"Yes, ma'am. You have a good night." They hung up. Allison tried to call Smitty, but his phone was off during the flight to Key West. She hung up and sent a text *'CALL ME ASAP!'* Allison tried to sleep, but it was pointless. She tossed, turned, cried, and stared at the ceiling. The love of her life was broken, and she was hundreds of miles away from helping fix him. Unbeknownst to her and Smitty, the two were merely just a few hours too late from stopping the attempted murder of Curt. Had they known, it would have likely only hurt more.

*****************************************

The crowd outside Wendy's dissipated and the dinner rush subsided. Nikola strolled out of the restaurant and casually into the parking lot by the dumpsters, acting like any other curious onlooker. When not being observed, he nonchalantly removed the GoPro cameras from the trees. He placed them in his pocket, turning onto Duval Street, soaking in the nightlife. It worked, just as planned. Duval Street was alive. It was festive, loud, and full of energy. From Nikola's perspective, it could not have been a more perfect night. As he strolled along, he pulled out his phone and sent Don a text.

*'Good job tonight. Fly home. I'll be in touch.'*

Don saw the text come in. He had contact with someone. Validation! A response! Actual contact! Thank God. It was going to be OK. Don grabbed a few beers from the hotel room fridge and drank them. He kept telling himself everything was going to be fine. It's all gonna be alright.

*****************************************

The commuter aircraft landed at Key West airport and Smitty's phone immediately displayed Allison's message. He did as instructed and called Allison. She was in bed, but far from sleeping.

"Smitty! They have Curt," she yelled into the phone as soon as she saw it was him calling.

"Hold on. Who has Curt? Where?"

"He's at the Lower Keys Hospital. They admitted him with a drug overdose."

"Drug overdose? Are you sure?"

"Yes, I think so. Wanda, his nurse from Chicago, called me. She said heroin. Please, can you go?"

"Yes," Smitty acknowledged. "I'll go there as soon as I get my rental car."

"Perfect. Please call me when you find out anything."

"I will, but you need to get some sleep."

"I can't sleep. Please. Call me. No matter what time," Allison asked.

"OK. I will." Smitty hung up, signed for his rental car, and drove straight to the hospital. After a few engagements with hospital staff who tried to explain visiting hours were over, he found Curt's room. Inside, Curt was sleeping, hooked up to several contraptions. Before he spoke to the head nurse, he called Allison. "Hey, I'm here and it's him. I'll stay until you get here. We have him."

"THANK GOD," Allison felt a wave of relief wash across her body.

"Now, please get some sleep. Now that we have Curt, we don't need to lose you to a car accident."

"OK. I will. I promise. Thank you, Smitty. Thank you."

Smitty hung up the phone and found the night shift nurse.

"Ma'am, I am friends with... er, uh, family with the guy in room 302. Can you tell me what happened?"

"Sir, it's after visiting hours. You'll need to leave."

"Yeah, I've gotten that a lot tonight. Sorry, can you please tell me your name?"

"Sure, I am Nurse Welch. Who are you?"

"I'm Mark Smith. Ma'am, I realize it is after hours and I don't mean to be a pain, but here is the deal. The man in there is a doctor from Chicago. Over the past few weeks, he's had a horrible and traumatic experience. The best man for his wedding just had an aircraft accident and is clinging to life, and then your patient quit his job. He broke communications with everyone and has been on the run. If you don't let me stay here and watch him, as soon as he wakes, he will be gone, and I'll need to start tracking him again. His escape will be on you, not me."

The nurse looked at her charts on Curt. Smitty's info regarding Chicago and Curt's profession checked out. "Mr. Smith. I appreciate your concern, but I don't believe your friend is going to magically get up and walk out of this hospital."

Smitty thought, '*Lady, you don't know Curt*,' but realized that was likely not going to get him any closer to his goal of staying overnight. Instead, Smitty responded, "Can you please tell me why you think that?"

"Sure. He came in with enough heroin in his system to kill a horse. If the police didn't administer NARCAN when they did, he'd be dead. As it stands now, his body is still trying to process out the drug. His liver is also barely functioning. While his vital organs are working and keeping him alive, he's going to be out for at least a day, if not two."

"So, he's in a coma, too?"

"Excuse me, what do you mean by 'too?'"

"Sorry. His best man is in a coma in Germany."

"I think I've said enough. Perhaps it's better if you speak to the doctor tomorrow."

"OK. Thanks, but may I ask a favor? Is there any place I can stay here at the hospital? Perhaps a chapel? A dining area? My friend's fiancé is literally on her way now, driving from Chicago, and I promised her I'd not leave his side until she arrives."

Nurse Welch looked around to see if anyone was watching, which was really pointless given there was no one else on the floor other than sleeping patients. "OK. Come with me." She led Smitty back into Curt's room, opened a standing wardrobe, and pulled out a blanket and pillow. "You can stay in here on this chair that folds into a recliner, but please be quiet. There is a bathroom over there. Don't leave out of here until tomorrow. I'm on shift all the way until morning. Got it?"

"Yes, ma'am. Thank you for your help. I really appreciate it."

"Sure. Have a good night." They said goodbye and Nurse Welch departed.

Smitty was alone with Curt for the first time in weeks. It had felt like months. He looked down at Curt, grabbed his hand. The nursing staff had tried to clean it, but it still showed signs of being dirty and weathered. *'What hell have you gone through, my friend,'* Smitty thought? He wasn't much of a praying man. For several combat veterans who've seen unimaginable atrocities, the concepts of God and religion seemed impossible. Smitty squeezed Curt's hand and whispered, "Come on, buddy. The only easy day was yesterday." It was a motto that served as their common bond, a statement often uttered among SEALs. Smitty sat down on the recliner next to the bed, pulled the blanket over himself, and slept.

## *Chapter Thirty-One*
# Daybreak Over Key West

As the sun rose over the U.S.'s southernmost city, Curt, Smitty, Don, and Nikola all lay in their respective beds, all within a five-mile radius, tied together by a woven storyline but clearly on different teams.

Nikola opened his hotel room door to find coffee and breakfast placed neatly outside his hotel room on a lovely cart. It would be another beautiful day and he'd pack for a flight to Washington's Reagan National Airport. The local *Key West Citizen* newspaper accompanied his breakfast and Nikola was drawn to a story on page three. A concise and hastily written article about last night's event had made the paper. There were few details provided in the report - details Nikola already knew, but also that the victim was in critical condition and still alive. Of course, too many other readers, the article's speculation that the victim may be a somewhat prominent doctor in Chicago would be the article's juiciest part.

Allison was already awake and driving south on I-75. She soon transitioned onto the Florida Turnpike, which would lead her to Highway 1 and Key Largo, the entrance to the Keys. At this pace, shed be in Key West soon. As she drove, she recalled her promise to Wanda. Allison picked up the phone and called.

"Wanda, it's Allison, good morning. I hope I am not waking you."

"Naw, you ain't waking me, Ms. Allison. Couldn't sleep. I think I know what happened. Some strung out druggie in Key West stole Curt's shit?" That was the narrative Wanda had built in her mind.

"I wish that were true, Wanda, but unfortunately it is Curt." The line was silent.

"Wanda? Are you still there?"

Allison could hear Wanda softly sob. "Aww, damn. I loved working with him. Now he's gone and screwed it all up. This Is all just too close to home for me."

"Wanda, he's still alive, and that's important."

"Yes. At least he is." Wanda emphasized the word 'he.'

Allison was confused. "I'm sorry. I don't understand."

Wanda took a deep breath. "Ms. Allison. I love working with Curt for many reasons. Perhaps the most significant one is that he reminds me of my ex-husband. He also served in the military. He, too, was very focused and dedicated to making the world right. He showed ever so slight signs of PTSD in his daily life. And he too tried to commit suicide. Unfortunately, my Clarence succeeded." Wanda's sobbing grew more intense.

Allison was stunned. Amid her crisis, she'd never suspected such a thing from a colleague as close as Wanda. "Wanda, I'm sorry. When did this happen?"

"Six years ago. I never stop thinking about it. I can't think about another relationship. Being around Curt to me is nearly just as important as it is to you. Please don't let him go."

Allison was even more determined to save Curt. "I won't. I'll be there later today and can share more with you."

Wanda's sobbing began to dissipate. "Yeah. OK. I know. I'm sorry. I'm making this about me, and I shouldn't. I haven't known any doctor that ever kept his medical license after a drug addiction. I don't know if I'll ever work with him again."

Allison knew that was correct, but right now, that wasn't the focus.

"Let's take one step at a time. I'll call you later. OK?"

"Sure. But when you see Curt, you smack him a hard one for me. OK?

Allison smiled. You just had to know Wanda and her southern ways to appreciate that comment. "Yes, Ms. Wanda. I will. Goodbye." The two hung up, and Allison kept driving.

*************************************

Don's bedside alarm clock rang, but he was far from asleep. He'd been staring at it for hours. His bags were packed, and he'd booked the first flight out of Key West. Don no longer wanted to be anywhere in that city. Robotically, he showered, dressed, checked out, and took a cab to the airport. Once there, he finally relaxed enough to have a coffee. Above the coffee vendor, the local morning news blared out of a TV. A reporter in front of Wendy's restaurant was dramatically recounting the incidents of the night prior. The scene cut to a brief interview with Craig Hewlett, the man who, with the help of another anonymous Good Samaritan, potentially saved the homeless man's life who, sadly, had overdosed on heroin. Craig and the police were looking for this Good Samaritan to both thank him and question him. That Good Samaritan was ironically, Don. *'Another important reason to get the hell out of this city,'* Don thought. Frustrated that Curt remained among the living, Don knew there was no one else to blame but himself, as he reflected on the remaining fluid in the needle. He'd failed to complete the task perfectly. Don's mind raced:

> *What would happen when Curt awoke?*
> *He was paralyzed, but was he truly conscious?*
> *Would he remember?*
> *Should I go back and finish the job?*
> *What does Nikola think? Is he upset?*
> *Will Nikola and his contacts fix the botched hit?*

Void of answers, Don's anxiety and loneliness grew more and more intense. He had to get back to D.C. Pulling out his phone; he called Steve. Steve again ignored the call, which would eventually transition to voicemail. This time, Don left a longer message. He may have tried to hide the desperation in his voice, but at this point, that was quite impossible. Based on the discussion with his father last night, there would be no more calling dear old dad. Don was an adult now, technically he had been one for quite a while. This time, however, the shadow of his father no longer blanketed him with protection. He was exposed to the full force of life.

*****************************************

The hospital room door swung open and Smitty was startled as the morning shift nurse entered. "Good morning," he said, as he wiped the sleepers from his eyes.

"Good morning. Has your friend joined us among the living yet?"

"Nope. He's still asleep."

"OK. Well, he has a breakfast coming. Clearly, he won't eat it. Would you like it?"

"Sure. Thanks." Smitty was starving. Even hospital food sounded good.

The nurse departed and left Smitty alone with Curt. Bored and now awake, he looked at his phone and realized he'd slept through a text update on Buck.

> *"Smitty - Your patient is progressing, but I will no longer be able to give you updates. Admin has requested a stateside medevac back to Walter Reed. Once there, a team of professionals will try to bring him out of the coma. He departs tomorrow morning and arrives that afternoon, your time." – Ian"*

Smitty fired back a quick thank you text then stared down at his iPhone, opening the calendar. He swiped to 'tomorrow' and at the top of the screen it said, "Easter Sunday." *'Jesus,'* he thought, *'It's freakin' Easter already.'* Someone needed to be there when Buck woke up. Smitty knew full well Buck had no close family. He'd lived in Europe and Africa for so many years that his parents and siblings, while friendly, were far from the kind who'd drop everything for him. Frankly, Smitty had a strong suspicion few even knew about his accident and coma.

Smitty called Allison, and she answered, "Hey, Allison. How are you progressing?"

"Morning, Smitty. I'm in Florida, well south of Orlando now. I'm guessing about four more hours."

"OK. When you get here, I gotta go. Just got word Landstuhl Medical in Germany is air evacuating Buck to Walter Reed. Once there, they plan to try and bring him out of his coma. I wanna be there."

"I understand. If this whole thing with Curt didn't exist, I know both of us would want to be there, too. I promise, I'll get there as quick as possible, but please don't leave Curt until I get there."

"I won't. You have my word." Smitty knew how important this was. To suggest otherwise would be counter to their friendship.

"OK. I'm going to stop and grab another coffee. I'll talk to you later."

"Coffee sounds like a freaking winner. I'll join you, just a couple hundred miles away. Drive safe, Allison. Goodbye." They hung up. Smitty exited the room and walked towards the nursing station, planning to inquire where a decent cup of coffee could be found.

A cute nurse, somewhat flirting with Smitty, directed him to a small kiosk down the hall that sold coffee and some other morning eats. He thanked her, oblivious to the flirt, and bought some coffee; then returned to the room. Curt's vital signs were strong, but he was still asleep, with no noticeable physical movement. Smitty would remain until Allison's arrival.

An A319 Airbus was on short final to Reagan National Airport, Washington, D.C. On it was Don, who would grab his bags and rush home via the underground Metro subway system. He rode it past the Pentagon, over the Potomac River, and then into D.C. He'd continue on the Metro until he was near his apartment, then jump off and ride the escalator back up to the surface world.

Once above ground in the heart of D.C., Don just stopped. He stared around the familiar scenery, but any passerby would swear it was his first time soaking in the surroundings. After a few minutes, he started walking. He entered his apartment, dropped his bags, and stripped naked. He was safe now and his pace of effort slowed. Don entered the shower and stood there under the spray until the hot water heater had emptied. He would have stayed an hour longer if the heater would have cooperated. Drying off and putting on some clothes, Don laid down on his sofa, firing off a quick text again to Steve:

*'Hey. Wanted to wish you a Happy Easter. Looking forward to linking up and learning what options may exist.'*

Steve immediately saw the text and responded.

*'Happy Easter to you as well. Still nothing from the boss. Not sure he's ready to restart the effort. Let's link back up in May.'*

The message could not have been more poorly received, but Don knew there was no point in responding or escalating. Steve was his only source and harming that relationship would destroy everything he worked for with Nikola. He rolled over on the sofa and closed his eyes. Tomorrow would be Easter dinner with his family. Perhaps that would take his mind off of Key West, even if the thought of time with his father was miserable.

\*\*\*\*\*\*\*\*\*\*\*\*\*\*\*\*\*\*\*\*\*\*\*\*\*\*\*\*\*\*\*\*\*\*\*\*\*\*\*

Allison finally arrived in Key West and ran into Curt's room. It was almost too much to believe he'd be there. As she entered, Smitty sat in the chair, packed and ready to catch a flight to D.C.

"Allison!" Smitty shouted. She ran over and hugged him as if he were Curt, not wanting to let go.

"Smitty. Thank you SO much for finding him." As she hugged Smitty with her head on his shoulder, she looked down at Curt. He was so peaceful. Motionless and almost angelic. Yet she knew inside, he was struggling in a life-or-death fight.

They separated. "Curt's status hasn't changed, but his vitals and some other stats have improved. I told the nurse out at the station about you. She's set it up so you can remain past visiting hours as well as set out a fresh towel and toiletries. There's a shower in the bathroom. You'll be fine."

"You coordinated all this?" Allison was grateful, but somewhat surprised. This wasn't really Smitty's modus operandi. Smitty was more the type to require coordination, not provide it.

"What do you mean?" Smitty offered back slightly defensively. "I was just talking to the nurse about you. She offered all this stuff. I didn't ask for anything."

"Smitty. So, some nurse was just talking to you and offered all this stuff without you asking. Is she married? Did you at least ask for her phone number?"

"No, why?"

"Man, I love you, but it's clear why you're single. I tell you what. When you walk out, why don't you look to see if she's married or engaged? If not, ask for her phone number?"

"Nah. I gotta go. Look, serious stuff is going on. If Buck wakes up, I need to be there."

Allison understood. "OK. Get outta here. I love you, and thanks again."

"No worries. Happy to do it. When Curt wakes up, gut punch him for me." Smitty ignored Allison's 'I love you' comment. Humorously, asking Allison to gut punch Curt was an easier reply than to tell Curt or Allison he loved them.

Smitty grabbed his gear, hugged Allison again, and squeezed Curt's hand one last time. With that, he departed the room. Allison smiled as she could see him stop at the nurse's station and say goodbye to his new nurse friend. 'Good boy, Smitty,' she thought. Allison then turned back to Curt, leaned over, and kissed him on the forehead. Softly she whispered, "Curt. Please wake up. I'm here now. Please wake up. I can't make it without you." Her lips fell back onto his head and remained there as tears leaked from her eyes.

"He's your fiancé, isn't he?" It was the cute nurse from the nurse's station standing in the doorway.

Allison wiped her eyes quickly. "Yes. Yes, he is. Do you have any more information?"

"You should speak to the doctor. I can get him if you wish. But I can say Dr. Nover has put up an impressive fight."

"Yes, he seems to thrive in conflict and struggle."

"Is there anything I can get you?" the nurse asked.

"No, thank you. Uh, hey sorry, what's your name?"

"Jennifer. Jennifer McPeek. I believe your name is Allison. Allison Donley, right?"

"Yes. You seem to know a lot. Did Smitty tell you that?"

"You mean Mark? Yes. He told me you'd be here."

Allison smiled. "Can I ask you, did Smitty... I mean, Mark, ask for your phone number when he left?"

Clearly disappointed, Jennifer said, "No. Is he single?" It was clear she'd have welcomed the inquiry.

"Yes, he's single, but stubborn as a mule and about as obtuse to flirting and romance as they come. Would it make you happy if I took your number and shared it with him?"

Jennifer's eyes lit up. "Sure. That would be great."

"OK. But I'm gonna warn you right now. Dating former military guys comes with a whole unique set of challenges."

"Oh, I know. My dad was Navy. I'm a military brat. I've dated my share of military. And you're right. They're very different from a non-military guy, but in many ways, far better."

Allison was struggling to find the 'better' part, but at the present moment, chose to nod in agreement. "Jennifer, I think I am going to take a shower and try to clean up. If the doctor comes around, could you please let him know I'm here, and I'd like to speak with him?

"Sure. And here is my number." Jennifer handed a small piece of paper over.

The number was handwritten with her name and a small heart. Allison presumed the heart was meant for Smitty, not her... then again, in today's America, who knew? "Thanks," she said.

"No problem." Jennifer replied as she departed the room.

Allison looked down at Curt. She mouthed, *"Come on Curt. Show me the 'better' Jennifer referred to. I need to see it."*

Allison cleaned up and passed out in the chair next to Curt's bed. She was exhausted but was with her love. As challenging as the last few days were, it was the only place she wanted to be.

# *Chapter Thirty-Two*
# 1 Corinthians 15:4

Easter daybreak over Washington D.C. was beautiful. Churches across D.C., Northern Virginia, and Southern Maryland were packed with believers, all wearing their best spring attire. Don was in his apartment, preparing to depart for his parents' house. The night prior, he couldn't sleep and took an oxycodone left over from an old back injury. Knowing the day would be nearly as challenging as the night, Don took another one. It wouldn't help much. The pain he experienced was mental, not physical. He just wanted it to go away and stay away. Hopping in his car, he headed out to his childhood home.

\*\*\*\*\*\*\*\*\*\*\*\*\*\*\*\*\*\*\*\*\*\*\*\*\*\*\*\*\*\*\*\*\*\*\*\*\*\*\*\*

On Capitol Hill, in a cute brick row home, Smitty woke up to the wonderful feeling of two kids laughing, screaming, and jumping around downstairs. He threw on some clothes and proceeded to the kitchen, greeted by Congressman Jack Donegan and his wife Bonnie.

"Good morning, Smitty! Happy Easter!" Bonnie said. She stood up and grabbed a fresh cup of coffee for him.

"Good morning. Hey, thanks for letting me crash here. The hotels were packed for the holiday."

"Mark, if you didn't stay with us, I would have been furious. The kids love you." Bonnie would hear none of his quibbling about staying.

With that, two rug rats ran from the living room into the kitchen, "Uncle Mark, Uncle Mark!" They grabbed his legs, pulled on his shirt. Smitty wasn't their biological uncle, but clearly, to them, it didn't matter.

Smitty reached down and picked up their daughter, Lina, throwing her towards the ceiling. "Look how BIG you are now!"

Lina giggled and screamed as if she was scared. It was a

ruse. She trusted Uncle Mark with all her being. Smitty set her down and looked at Jack's son, Jack Jr. "And YOU! Come here!" Jack Jr. smiled and ran with all the speed he could muster into the living room straight at Smitty. He was still at the age where gaining speed was fun. Stopping, however, remained a challenge. Jack Jr. smashed into Smitty's knees. Smitty grabbed his arms and flipped him upside down in a singular swift motion.

Jack Jr. laughed hysterically. "Uncle! Uncle! Hahahaha!"

Smitty set him on the ground, unscathed.

"Kids. OK, who wants pancakes?" Bonnie asked.

The two screamed with excitement and grabbed seats at the kitchen table. The kids sat down, and Jack Senior entered the room.

"Smitty, come with me. We'll go into the living room." Jack led the way, and the two headed out.

"So, what's going on?" Jack asked.

Smitty filled him in regarding Buck and Curt. Jack had followed both stories loosely. Smitty just filled in the gaps.

"I meant to thank you for getting Buck into Landstuhl and then Walter Reed. Without that, there is a good chance he wouldn't be alive." Smitty was sincere and right.

"Don't mention it. Buck was AFSOC (Air Force Special Operations Command). He qualified for veteran medical care; I just expedited the paperwork with the help of Admiral Hersey." Jack smiled at Smitty. They both knew that traditional approval for such paperwork could have taken months and arrived well after grass grew on Buck's gravesite.

"Smitty, I did receive an intel brief about the crash. There's growing belief there was sabotage. I spoke to Erolld, my Kosovar buddy, and he said you may have found something too?"

"Yeah. Apologies for not getting to you sooner. I'd say someone wanted him to crash. Two issues. First, there is still a missing person who took off from Belgrade, but they never found the body. According to the declared ICAO filed flight plan, there was a woman onboard. I don't know if she just walked away or what. Second, the Embassy shared that they pulled fingerprints of a Serbian operative female from the electrical panel that had screws missing and was open. I am presuming it's likely the same woman."

"Yes. That's what I heard as well. And Curt? Did he really O.D. on Heroin?"

"That's what they say. Some Good Samaritan found Curt, but now, no one can find the guy." Smitty shared this info with Jack framed in a sense of frustration.

"OK. I am going on a morning news show in an hour. I need to get ready. Make yourself comfortable and take Bonnie's car to Walter Reed. She won't need it until Tuesday. She'll use my car and I'll walk to the Capitol. It will do me good."

"Wow. Thanks. Are you sure?"

"Yes. Absolutely." Jack got up, went to the kitchen, hugged the kids, kissed Bonnie, then ran upstairs to prepare for his interview. It would revolve around national security and threats to the U.S., far from an Easter Morning topic.

Smitty waited a bit, then also walked into the kitchen. He spent about a half hour with the kids, eating breakfast and playing. Buck's aircraft would not arrive at Andrews Air Force Base, Maryland, until 1400Hrs, so there was plenty of time to waste.

*****************************************

In Key West, Allison managed to move Curt far enough over so that she could share the bed with him. He was warm and his body was firm. It was all she had, and she was going to take every second of it. A new nurse entered with a breakfast tray; it wasn't Jennifer. She was young and most likely a new hire since she was working the Easter Morning shift. "Ma'am, you can't be in bed with the patient." She was also still very clear on the rules.

"Yes. OK. Sorry." Allison saw no point in arguing. She began to get up and pushed down on Curt's chest.

Softly, Curt muttered... "Don't go."

The nurse dropped the tray as if she'd heard a ghost. Allison laid back down, and it would take far more than that tiny nurse and a dumb hospital policy to convince her to get off of Curt.

The nurse ran to her station and paged the doctor.

"Curt! Curt! Baby!! It's me! Talk to me."

Curt's eyes flickered. "Al... Allison?"

"Yes, baby!"

"Allison." Curt was coming around.  When he understood it was her, he relaxed again.  He was safe.

The nurse came back in and began scribbling down all the vitals and information she could from the machines, preparing for the doctor's questions.

Curt was waking up.  Allison fired off a text to Smitty:

*'He has risen!'*

Smitty replied:

*'Yes, Happy Easter to you too, but I'm not much of a religious guy.'*

Allison responded:

*'No! You idiot! Not Jesus! CURT! He's still groggy and can't talk, but he's awake!'*

Smitty pumped his fist when he read the text.  Curt was coming around.  Perhaps God does exist.  It was an Easter miracle.

*****************************************

The Denney house was in a full festive nature.  Don's parents hosted the entire family, which included Don's siblings and their children.  With seventeen in attendance, the house was chaos.  Don made small talk with his siblings, many of whom were still befuddled by his freedom and the dropped Nissassa charges.  Each discussion he had was awkward and uncomfortable, a fact not lost on Don.  Eventually, Don was face to face with his father in the kitchen as he reached for another beer.

"Hello, Don."  His father's best greeting to a son on Easter.

"Yeah.  You too."  The coldness in both their voices demonstrated no intention to de-escalate the tension.

 "Look.  You don't want to be here as much as I don't want you here.  Let's do both of us a favor.  You leave and I'll explain to your mother you were sick."

Don just smiled as he stared into his father's eyes, lifted his beer to his lips and drank.  Behind Andrew, Don's mother stood there, horrified at the words she just heard from her husband.  "Andrew!  Why would you say that!?"

Andrew was caught, but doubled down.  "Stay out of this, Becky," he said.  "Don, your failures are tarnishing my name and the achievements of your siblings.  You continually make poor choices.  That MUST remedy itself.  Instead of spending the day with us, perhaps it is best to spend it alone and reflect."

Don's brothers and sisters stood outside the kitchen, staring at each other.  They were speechless.  Don again raised his beer.  He finished it, wiped his face with his sleeve, and leaned into his father's ear to whisper his answer.  The kitchen was silent, and Don forcefully pushed out a belch that would make a saloon whore blush.  With that, he set down his empty beer, walked over and kissed his mom, and left.

On the way back to his apartment, Don called Steve.  Not only did the President recommend distance, but it was also Easter.  Steve had no intention of answering.  Don followed the call up with a quick text message:

 'Steve- Sorry about contacting you on a holiday, but really need to chat.  Please call.'

Steve didn't respond.  The silence began to infuriate Don.  As he drove, his blood pressure climbed at the same pace as the speedometer.  Flying down the George Washington Parkway,

Don again dialed Steve. Again, no answer. Passing cars, he looked through recent calls and tried Nikola.

Sitting in a gorgeous room at the Willard Hotel, Nikola's phone rang. Much like Steve, Nikola had no interest in speaking with Don. Actions were put in place and their orchestration was critical.

Once again. Don tried Steve. Again. No answer. He was enraged.

*****************************************

The C-17 landed at Andrews Air Force Base like the other dozen or so every day. An ambulance waited, lights flashing, and doors open as Buck was rolled off the plane into the patient compartment. Within an hour, they would be at Walter Reed Medical Center with some of the best head trauma doctors in the world standing by. Along with them, Smitty waited by the Emergency Room entrance.

The normally packed highways of the National Capital Region were barren because of the Easter holiday. The ambulance arrived, and the doors swung open. There, for the first time since Chicago, Smitty saw his friend. The head was shaved, and fresh stitches surrounded the crown of his head where they'd made room for the brain swelling.

As the attendees wheeled him past Smitty, they moved in an expeditious fashion. Smitty just watched them pass. One of the attendees, in an attempt to not hit Smitty, pushed the gurney too far to the left and slammed it into the wall. As he did, the gurney immediately stopped. A collective gasp among the staff filled the air.

From the bed, Buck let out a soft moan of pain. The hospital staff froze and simultaneously looked down.

"He moaned!" Smitty yelled. "Did you hear that? He moaned!"

Smitty was quickly whisked away, and the doctors began talking. Buck had made progress.

Smitty waited for a few hours and was eventually

approached by a doctor.

"I understand you are a friend of the patient?"

"Yes, Doctor. How is he?"

"Actually, better than we could have imagined. He hasn't spoken words, but his moaning is a strong indication that he's feeling pain at least somewhere in his body. We've sedated him a bit to reduce the pain. Would you like to see him?"

"Very much so. Can we go now?"

"Sure." The doctor led Smitty to the room. Smitty grabbed the chair next to the bed and sat there. He leaned over to Buck and said, *"Alright fucker. Curt came around. Your turn now."* It was a bit of wishful thinking. Buck would not come around that day, but his condition had far improved. Smitty grabbed his hand.

*****************************************

Don drove his car into the parking garage and went up to his apartment. He walked in, threw down his keys, and proceeded straight for a beer. As he rummaged around inside the fridge, a familiar voice called out. "Hello, Don."

Don turned around and immediately saw Nikola standing in his kitchen with two sizeable men, one on each side.

"Nikola, what are you doing here? Why didn't you answer my call?" It was very confusing. Part of Don was angered by Nikola's unscheduled entry, and another half was happy to see someone.

"Don. I don't have much time. Come with me." The two walked into the living room. The walls were covered with black and white photos of Don talking to Steve, Don injecting Curt with heroin, Don talking to Nikola. On the kitchen table was a computer that was looping video of many of those same events, as well as scrolling all the text messages between Steve and Don. Nikola bent down and turned up the volume on the computer. There were snippets of Don talking to Steve, trying to set up mercenary hits as well as discussions that clearly implicated the President.

"Don, listen carefully. I want you to share this computer with Steve. My associates and I wish for a meeting with him tomorrow. Should that not happen, all of this will become public from a clone computer we have."

Don's anger got the best of him. He'd been had, and the hood was set... deep. Don lunged at Nikola. Before he even came close; however, both of Nikola's henchmen crushed him to the ground, then provided a few more 'incentive punches' for good measure. Nikola and his party retreated out of the apartment. Don lay there, alone. The world was closing in on him fast. Don again tried to call Steve. There would be no answer. Don took another oxycodone, and drank a beer while sitting on his floor, listening to the loop of discussions between Steve and him.

Closing Nikola's computer and opening his own, Don finally got up and began drafting up a document. He printed it and neatly signed at the bottom. He placed his newly created letter, along with some other items, in an envelope, addressed and stamped it. With that part of his task complete, Don loaded up Nikola's computer into an old gym bag he'd had for years, stashed away in his bedroom. He walked down to his condo's parking garage, stopping at a U.S. parcel box, and dropped the envelope in the chute.

Don drove across D.C. towards Georgetown. It was later in the evening and the sun was setting. The streets were mostly empty as he sought out parking on a treelined residential street. Grabbing the bag, Don walked roughly fifty yards down the sidewalk, stopping in front of a beautiful white and black historic two-story row home. He began yelling. "STEVE! STEVE YOU FUCKER! GUESS WHAT BUDDY! WE'RE FUCKED.... WE! ARE! FUCKED!" He laughed and repeated the message.

Inside, Steve heard the yelling and rushed to the door. He swung it open to find Don standing in front of his house, holding a Glock 9mm semi-automatic handgun to his head.

"Why are you ignoring me? Did you hear me? We are fucked. I've been checkmated by some freaking Eastern Bloc oligarch who's fifteen feet up my ass and you can't even answer my calls? Jesus. Now, I can't get rid of him. Steve, he's gonna take everyone down. Me, you, the President."

The severity of this event was not lost on Steve. But whatever it was, Steve believed it was certainly survivable. Don had no such hope. Calmly, Steve spoke. "Don. Listen to me. Put the gun away. What are you doing? I'm sorry I didn't get to your calls. I assure you; it was nothing personal. I work for the President. Come on, man. I'm just always really busy. I'm not ignoring you. Look, we can get through this. I'm the fucking Chief of Staff to the most powerful man in the world, for Christ's sake!"

"Buddy. When you see what they've got, you could be the Chief of Staff to God. It wouldn't matter." Don then said, "Do me a favor."

At this point, Steve would do anything. "Sure. Anything."

"Tell my father... fuck you, Dad."

With that, Don swung the gun from the side of his temple towards his face, rotating it so the trigger guard and butt of the weapon faced upward. The gun was upside down. Don placed the barrel in his mouth, tightly closed his eyes, winced, and pulled the trigger. The gun fired. Don had bitten down on the barrel so hard that his lower two front teeth were shattered as the gun's slide recoiled and the front sights smashed into the back of his teeth. Dental issues wouldn't matter, however. Don would no longer require the use of his teeth. His body fell, lifeless, as a large section of his bone, skin and hair exploded out the back of the crown of his skull. If he wasn't dead when he hit the ground, he would be soon thereafter.

Steve charged as soon as Don began rotating the gun to his mouth, screaming Don's name. There was no chance he'd arrive in time. It was D.C. and with the sound of gunshots, unique things happened. Some porch lights along the street turned on. Others turned off and blinds were closed. Steve grabbed Don's bag and quickly put it in the house, then ran back out.

The police would soon arrive. They would find Steve on his knees next to Don. Holding his hand. After a while, Steve was questioned. They asked if he knew the next of kin. Steve passed along Andrew's contact information. *'It should be the police that tell him,'* Steve thought. He had no desire to share such news.

The coroner took away the body.

Steve did not call the President, but he did open Don's bag. In it were many photos of them together. He also watched the computer videos, listened to the audio files, and read the text messages. Don was partially right. It was very damning. In the bag was also a handwritten note from Don:

> *'Here is your contact. +381 649 2354. You have 24 hours. Don't forget the message for my father.'*

The number was Nikola's. Steve lamented how he'd present this to the President the next morning.

On Easter, of all days. Curt and Buck appeared to distance themselves from the grips of death while Don greeted it with open arms. It was unbelievable.

## *Chapter Thirty-Three*
# Monday Blues

Curt was waking up in the Key West hospital. He had no pain, and his memory was returning. Next to him, in the hospital chair, slept his fiancé. She was a woman that he knew he had just hurt more than she ever deserved and that she'd likely ever be able to forgive. As soon as she woke, Curt knew it would be a struggle just to look at her. He was embarrassed. He'd run from the only woman who loved him. He didn't even say goodbye. He didn't check-in with her, nor did he try to ease her concern.

Curt's discomfort was overwhelming. A large portion of him wished to start running again. But where? He'd just run to the nation's border and still it wasn't far enough. Would there ever be a 'far enough?' He stared at her for over an hour. What would he say to her when she awoke? More importantly, what would she say? He had no desire to receive a lecture, no matter how deserved it was.

\*\*\*\*\*\*\*\*\*\*\*\*\*\*\*\*\*\*\*\*\*\*\*\*\*\*\*\*\*\*\*\*\*\*\*\*\*\*\*\*\*

During the morning White House briefings, Steve had not told the President about the previous night's events. How could he? Steve sent a text message to the number:

*'I understand you wish to meet. I am Don's colleague.'*

Steve waited for a response. There was nothing immediate and work was piling up. Steve would have to check his phone again later. As he walked into the Oval Office, Steve carried the files for the day and said, "Good morning, Mr. President."

"Good morning, Steve."

"Sir, here are your files for today's meetings. Decision briefs are on the bottom; should you choose to review or act upon them."

"Thanks, Steve. How are you doing?"

"I'm fine, sir. Why do you ask?"

"Well, according to the news, as well as my morning intelligence read out, your house was the site of a shooting that involved a fatality. I also understand you witnessed the shooting. I'd think something like that could affect you. More importantly, the fact that the name of the victim is the son of one of my largest donors also leads me to believe your failure to start with that information today means you're hiding something."

His decision not to tell the President was an ill-conceived plan. "Yes, sir. I just didn't want to trouble you."

"Steve, I appreciate that. But as we both know, I would learn of this soon enough."

"Yes, sir. OK. Don was trapped in an espionage sting. I don't know by whom or what they want, but I have seen the files and photos they have. It's fairly damning."

"OK. Bring them to me and set them in my bottom right drawer. I'll review them in my private quarters."

"Yes, sir."

"Have you attempted to make contact with our little blackmailer?" The tone in the President's voice demonstrated he was far less concerned about the events than Steve was.

"Yes. I sent him a text and am awaiting a response."

"Good. Let's allow this vile rat to emerge from the shadows. Thanks, Steve, and please, hide nothing from me again. Now, onto today's events. Who's my first meeting with?"

The President's nature was calming to Steve. He communicated the next event and then welcomed in the guest.

*****************************************

The medical staff at Walter Reed was elated. Buck's brain activity was increasing, and the swelling in his head was dissipating  He was responding well to an assortment of tests, to include pain & tickling in all his extremities. Buck was coming around and Smitty was there, watching it all unfold. Buck's tests for the morning were complete. He lay on his room gurney while Smitty sat there, watching the morning news. A noise caught Smitty's attention, and it was Buck's hand, moving.

"Buck. Hey, buddy. It's me, Smitty. You there?"

Buck's eyes tried to open, and he struggled to turn his head towards the noise. The face was blurry, to the point of nonrecognition. Buck finally slurred out a word. "Smitty?"

Smitty was overjoyed and wanted to scream his response, but under the circumstances, took a far more reserved, yet excited tone. "Yes! Yes, Buck, it's me."

Buck felt Smitty's hand. It was strong, just as he'd remembered it from all the handshakes and bear hugs. In Smitty's company, Buck knew he was safe. He relaxed, or at least tried to. "What happened?"

"Buck, you were in a plane crash. In Kosovo. You were the only survivor. Do you remember anything?"

Buck did not. "What? No. A crash? Is my airplane OK?"

Smitty didn't have the heart to tell him at this moment. "Buck, dude, you've been through hell. Seriously, we can have this discussion later. Tell me. How do you feel?" Smitty tried to change the subject, and as miserable as Buck felt, it worked.

"My fuckin' head feels like it's stuck in an elephant's ass that's undergoing the strongest constipation contractions in recorded history."

With that singular phrase, he knew Buck was back. Maybe not out of the woods, but Buck was back. "Can I get you anything? How are your legs and arms?"

"My arms feel heavy. My legs ache. Hey, where's the morphine drip? What hospital am I in, anyway? Is this one of those VA hospitals that's skimping on the good drugs?" Buck was gaining more and more consciousness.

"Walter Reed."

"Walter Reed? How the hell did I get in here? I'm not active duty anymore."

"No, you're not. But Congressman Donegan pulled a few strings."

"Who is he?"

"A former SEAL. Curt and I knew him from our time in the military. We were worried about you."

"Smitty. Buddy. You know me. I'm a survivor."

"Maybe, but to be fair, you haven't told Curt or I where you have all the money from Akjoujt stashed, so until then, we couldn't take a chance with you in any hospital." Smitty was referring to the windfall of cash that Smitty received for his part in taking down Nissassa.

Buck's face cracked a grin.

"Fuck you, asshole."

A female voice from the other direction emerged, "Excuse me!" It was the floor nurse. "Sir, you are damn near death's front door. You keep cussin' like that, St. Peter is NEVER gonna let you in! You understand me?"

Buck couldn't swing his head all the way to make eye contact. He stared at the ceiling and said, "Lady, I'm holding an American Express Platinum Plus membership into hell. If you think a few F bombs are gonna change that, I got some really bad news for ya."

"Well, maybe so, but it's never too late to ask forgiveness. Now, I see you're awake. I'm going to have the doctor come in soon. While you're conscious, and at least ornery enough to swear, will you sign a form stating this other gentleman can act on your behalf should something happen while you are unconscious again?" She was referring to Smitty.

Delaying his response to the nurse, Buck tried to turn and look at Smitty as best he could. Somberly, he said, "Smitty, tell the truth. Are you really after the cash?"

Smitty's eyes popped opened in shock. It was just a joke. He was surprised Buck could even imagine it was real. "No! No, Buck. Buddy, it was a joke."

Buck tried again to turn his head but couldn't manage eye contact with the nurse. "No. I won't sign it. Can I give that authorization to someone else? I need someone who wants to keep me alive. To this guy, I'm better off dead. I won't sign it."

Smitty was floored. Obviously, the accident did something

to Buck's thought processes and logic patterns.

"No! Buck! Seriously. I'm here for YOU!" Smitty was slightly freaking out.

Buck slowly turned his head towards Smitty, then moved his eyes the remaining way until they locked onto Smitty's, "Gotcha, buddy." His smile turned to sincerity. "Hey... thanks for being here. I really appreciate it. I don't know anyone else who'd come, or that I'd want. It means the world to me."

Smitty was still reeling from the practical joke. "Yeah, well, keep up the deadpan sarcasm, and I'm leaving!" He paused and grabbed Buck's arm. "Anytime brother. Anytime."

"Yes, Nurse, I'll sign it. Can you get me some more drugs, though? My head and legs are throbbing."

The nurse placed a document in front of Buck, which he signed without reading. "You can have that discussion with the doctor." It was clear Buck would receive no more 'good' drugs until his chat with the doc.

"Buddy. I'm staying until you walk out of here. Seriously, Buck, try to get some sleep."

"OK. I will. Thanks again, man." Buck was safe.

"All good, buddy. All good."

\*\*\*\*\*\*\*\*\*\*\*\*\*\*\*\*\*\*\*\*\*\*\*\*\*\*\*\*\*\*\*\*\*\*\*\*\*\*\*\*\*

Curt watched as Allison began waking up. All he wanted to do was run like hell. He didn't though. There was no place left to run. Allison's eyes saw Curt looking at her. She groggily sprung from the hospital room recliner and grabbed him. "Curt!" She screamed. "My God! You're OK." She cried. Her heart raced. Allison's arms wrapped around him as he lay in bed. "I love you so much!"

Curt was confused. In his mind, he was certain Allison's waking would spark a confrontation. Instead, she professed her love, and he hadn't even yet apologized, something he fully well knew she deserved. Now, his desire to flee vanished. He wanted nothing more than to be held by the one person he loved most in life. His arms raised and slowly embraced her.

Tears fell from his eyes and rolled down his cheek. "I'm…. I'm sorry." He could barely mouth the words. It hurt so.

Allison slowly pulled back and wiped the tears from her eyes. "Curt, I accept your apology, and I promise I am no longer angry." She held him. "I just want to understand why?"

Curt thought about it. "Baby, I am grateful for your forgiveness, but I don't think you can understand."

"Please. After all this, please, let me at least try."

"OK. Back in Chicago, I snapped. Everything that was under control changed in a split second. Buck was dying. The hospital leadership was a joke, and I could do nothing to change either. For years, my military training conditioned me for combat. If I was out manned and outgunned, it's wiser to withdraw, regroup, and fight another day, than stay and likely die. So, I did that. I fled. Not from you, and not to hurt you, but to survive, for me to survive."

Curt took a break. Allison wasn't fond of the answer, but was desperately trying to understand. "OK. Is that it?"

"As I ran, I began to feel a peacefulness I hadn't felt for a long time. I was around others like me. I was around others who'd slept out under stars in combat, with nothing to protect them but the one who was manning the watch - a brother who swore to protect me and vice versa. It's hard to explain how sleeping under an overpass in Atlanta is comforting, but it was. I also learned of other's plights. Their weaknesses, their strengths, their vices, fears. Allison, there are so many homeless veterans."

Allison tried to smile as she grabbed Curt's hand. It was at that point she knew Smitty would have been the one to fully understand Curt's rationale. She would not understand today, nor would she likely be able to make sense of it for years to come, if ever.

"Baby. I'm sorry. I never meant to hurt you. I know, I could have called countless times, but I was…" Curt caught himself. He was hung up on the next word. "I was afraid. Afraid you'd tell me you were leaving me, and we were done. And as much as I knew then and I know now, that is a possibility, I was in no condition to hear it while I ran. It would have crushed me. I know not all of this makes sense, but do you at least understand that?"

"Yes, Curt. I understand that. But know this. I love you. And yes, I was livid. I cursed your name over and over. But I am not leaving you. You are my knight in shining armor. Yes, you might have some chinks, dents, and holes in your armor, but as long as you're willing to work on them, I'm here. Can you promise me you'll get help?"

Curt didn't need to hesitate. "Yes. I promise."

"For everything," Allison said. Pausing, she continued, "Even the heroin addiction."

"Heroin? I've never done heroin!"

The reaction was one Allison had anticipated. Denial was a common response.

'Heroin?' Curt thought. What the hell? I never... Then the cobwebs cleared. He began to recall what had happened. Becoming agitated and excited, he screamed, "Don! Don did this! I remember now! He tried to kill me!" The machines next to Curt worked themselves into a frenzy, lights were blinking, buzzers and alarms were blaring. Within seconds, nurses came running in.

"Sir! Calm down! Calm down!"

"It was an attempted murder!"

The nurses had seen enough heroin addicts' physical antics when Jonesing from withdrawal. In a locked drawer, one pulled a syringe and injected it into Curt's arm. The drug was methadone, a heroin substitute to ween off addicts. Within seconds, he'd be calm.

"Curt, this won't hurt. The Doc will be here soon. Please relax."

"But!" Curt tried to get out of bed, but it was too late. He felt the drug blanketing over his body. "But..." Curt calmed down and before falling asleep, looked Allison in the eyes again. "I love you. Please get the police." With that, he was asleep again.

Allison wouldn't let him down. She'd find an officer

somewhere and be back. But first, she called Smitty and relayed the good news. The discussion was comical, in that both tried to relay their respective story first. Finally, they both slowed down and were able to finish. Towards the end, Allison finally said, "Smitty, one last thing. Curt said he never took heroin and that some guy named 'Don' injected it into him in an attempt to kill him. Does that make any sense?"

"Don, huh? Did he give a last name?"

"Not that I recall." Allison was correct. Curt didn't relay a family name.

"I'll have to think about it. Doesn't ring a bell. Let's catch up later today or tomorrow if more news breaks."

"OK. Thanks, Smitty. Goodbye." They hung up.

Smitty's eyebrows began to pin down against his eyes. He knew exactly who Don was. From an earlier discussion with Curt, Smitty knew it could only be one guy, Don Denney. Smitty was still friends with Don on Facebook and quickly searched to see if Don had made any recent posts. There was no activity. He also searched across various social media platforms to see if there were any new 'Don Denney' accounts. Again, nothing. Finally, Smitty searched for Don Denney on Twitter, trying to find new profiles. With that search, Smitty hit the jackpot. There were no new profiles; however, there were a growing number of tweets linked to the 'unknown victim' of a D.C. residence suicide to an individual named Donald Denney. Smitty had a lead, albeit a dead one. *'Rest in Peace, a-hole,'* he thought to himself.

*******************************************

Via her 'channels,' Katarina learned of Don's demise. She immediately dialed her brother, Nikola, furious the plan was ruined.

"Nikola! Did you hear? Our asset is lost!"

Nikola was sitting alone at a table for two, out front of Anbar Restaurant. Anbar is a great little Balkan bistro, on 'Restaurant Row,' 8th Street Southeast near Eastern Market in D.C. Nikola was missing his native food and Anbar was the perfect place to get his fix.

He responded to her in Serbian. "Katarina, good to hear from you. Look. You mustn't worry. It isn't healthy. I have everything under control. Yes, you are correct. There was a minor miscalculation, but fortunately, it seems it has placed us in a position to deal directly at a higher level. So, it's worked out to our advantage. Don served his purpose. Just another stupid fucking American. Katarina, I must go. Please, do not worry." He hung up.

At the table next to Nikola was a tourist couple from Arkansas. They overheard the conversation and Rose, the wife, couldn't help herself. "Excuse me... Excuse me, sir. Was that Russian? We've never heard someone speak Russian before. It's so interesting!"

Nikola humored her interest, "Yes. Yes, it was." What ignorance, he thought, in Serbian. She wouldn't even know where Serbia was on a map, so trying to explain would be pointless.

"That is really fascinating! Can you say something else?"

"Sure." Nikola rattled off something, and the only discernable word to her was something about America.

"Oh!! What does that mean?" Rose asked quizzically.

"It means, '*I love America*,'" Nikola said. It didn't. It actually translated to, '*Stupid fucking American*.'

## *Chapter Thirty-Four*
# Days to Recover

The healing process for Curt and Buck was progressing well. A few days had passed. Both were regaining cognitive skills, but each still faced challenges. Buck would be in leg casts for a while and Curt was experiencing slight heroin withdrawals as well as struggling to find the right PTSD medication that would balance his infliction. The good news was Allison and the medical staff now believed Curt was not a heroin addict and, in fact, Don had really tried to kill him. Key West police, now with a description of Don, were able to confirm the two were drinking at Captain Tony's on Duval Street. Closed Caption Television confirmed both walked from there to Wendy's. Don's untimely death somewhat cleaned up the case from the perspective of the Key West Police and District Attorney. It was extremely difficult to prosecute a dead man for attempted murder. However, some investigative entities back in D.C. were still quite interested in Don Denney's activities.

Two federal agents knocked on a door of a large Virginia mansion. It was the home of Andrew and Becky Denney. Becky opened the door wearing a robe. She also had not done her hair or makeup, something she rarely did before Don's death. "Hello, may I help you?"

The two, as if choreographed, showed their badges, "Ma'am, I'm Agent Bozarth. This is Agent Myers. We are with the FBI. May we come in?" Both in suits, black sunglasses, and emotionless faces. If the FBI had a mold, they were it. It was highly likely they were never asked for a closer look at their identification cards and badges.

"Yes. Of course." With that, Becky backed away and let the two gentlemen in.

"Ma'am, is your husband home, or are you alone?"

"It's just me. Andrew is out for work right now. I think he is in D.C. somewhere."

"OK. That's fine. I realize now is a difficult time, but we

were curious if you would allow us to ask some questions about your son."

"No, I don't mind. He was a good boy. I am happy to talk about him. I want the world to know about how great of a young man he was. I can't talk about him enough." She sat down with a box of tissues next to her.

"Yes. Of course. Ma'am, was your son in Florida anytime recently?"

"Well, I am not sure. How long ago?"

"Last week?"

"No, I do not know. If he was, I don't know about it. Of course, I didn't get much chance to talk to him during Easter. Andrew and he had a fight as soon as Don arrived, and he just left. It was... It was the last time I saw him. And I didn't even get to hug him goodbye." She began to sob. As if on cue, one agent handed her a tissue.

"Ma'am. Do you know what your husband and son were fighting over?"

"No. I don't. They were always arguing about something."

"OK. Is there anything else you can tell us that may be of interest?"

"No. Nothing. My son graduated from West Point. He was a great soldier and a great son. I don't know why he would do this." She cried some more. The situation became uncomfortable for all, and the agents would soon leave.

Back at the White House, a social event was underway, organized by the State Department. While the Christian Easter had been the week prior, the Orthodox Easter was approaching the next Sunday. With a political push to promote the diversity of the U.S., the White House would host a small gathering of nations that had a predominance of Orthodox followers such as Greece, Serbia, and Russia, to name a few. The event would include ambassadors and prominent national level religious figures from within the U.S.

As the guests gathered, Steve checked his phone again. He'd written Nikola three times, and there was no answer. Steve began to fear the information would explode in the media, putting the White House in a reactive position. This was exactly why Nikola waited. Finally, a message came in.

*'Meet me at Old Ebbitt Grill in 15 minutes. Don't be late. Leave your phone behind.'*

The timing could not have been worse. Steve walked into the President's private residence as he prepared to meet his Orthodox guests. "Mr. President, our thorn has finally responded. He's asked me to meet him at Old Ebbitt in 15 minutes."

"Good... good. What are you waiting for? Don't worry about me. This is a simple event. Go. Now. And come back directly to tell me what he wants."

Steve nodded and left. He walked out of the Eastern White House gates and crossed 15th Street. He would arrive precisely on time. Steve, as the White House Chief of Staff, was well known within D.C. circles, especially to restaurant wait staff. A hostess looked at him. "Mr. Lewis?" She was quizzical, not sure if it was him.

"Yes, please call me Steve."

"Yes, sure." She gushed. Power in D.C. was and will always remain sexy.

"Steve, please come with me. Your party is in the back bar."

He followed her and immediately knew which bar she was referring to. Old Ebbitt has four themed bars inside the restaurant, one waterfowl hunting, one big game hunting, one a raw bar and one a poker room. His blackmailer would be found in the latter. The poker room bar was stunning. Behind the bar hung an oversized nude female painting. On the ceiling was similar décor. The booths had extremely high backs and at midafternoon after the lunch rush; the place was nearly empty. Steve approached to find Nikola sitting there, calm as could be, with a drink in front of him. Two muscular men stood at the bar, directly across from the booth. They were clearly with Nikola. As Steve approached, one took a quick scan of Steve with a handheld electronic device designed to sense out electrical equipment that could transmit, record, or receive. The device remained silent, and the thug nodded to Nikola. Steve had followed the rules. Steve was clean.

"Mr. Lewis, how great it is to make your acquaintance."

Steve had been trained by the best to be polite to even the most egregious of assholes. "You too, sir, although I don't believe I've caught your name."

"My name is Nikola. Please sit."

The hostess asked if they'd need anything and before departing, Nikola insisted she bring Steve a matching drink.

"I believe Don shared with you the information package we gave him."

"Yes. I've seen it. Is that all of it?"

"All of it? Please, Mr. Lewis. I think there is more than enough there. Clear ties between the White House and Nissassa, the fact that Don's charges were dropped."

Steve interrupted. "We had nothing to do with that."

Nikola took a deep breath. "Of course you didn't. I did that. But, to the rest of the world, with all our evidence, it won't matter. You will be accused, if not legally, certainly in the court of public opinion. May I continue?" It was a rhetorical question. "Your 'loose cannon,' Don, also attempted to murder the one man who uncovered the Nissassa operation. Let's not play stupid."

"OK. Shelving the discussion of your evidence. What do you want?"

Nikola took a long drink. As he did, Steve's drink arrived. The waitress departed, and Nikola responded. "In a few weeks to a month, Serbia will mass forces on the ABL with the so-called region of Kosovo. The U.S. will take no action. Further, Serbia will then invade and reclaim its land, which is predominately settled by our ethnic Serbians north of the Ibar River."

"You're crazy. You know we can't do that."

"Oh, but you will. Additionally, you will use diplomatic pressures to ensure no other NATO nation interferes with Serbia's mission. No weapon sales, no force build-ups, no airpower support. Nothing."

Steve sat back and almost laughed aloud. *'Who does this joker think he is, placing demands on the President,'* he thought. "The U.S. can neither predict nor control the actions of independent nations. Look. It would be far easier for me to pay you cash. I can't speak for the President, but I am fairly certain he won't go for the plan. Sure, your information will damage him and possibly make our reelection effort more challenging, but he'll survive any impeachment. Can we negotiate money?"

"Mr. Lewis. Please. Do not insult my intelligence. The U.S. has been controlling countless nations around the globe for decades. As for your counteroffer, I appreciate it. But money is not my desire. You've heard my request. Please let me know by Monday, following the Orthodox Easter." Nikola finished his drink and gestured at his two bodyguards.

Steve realized his welcome was over. And frankly, he didn't want to stay one second longer than he had to. *'Nikola is freaking crazy,'* he thought, as he walked back to the White House. There is no chance the President would go for such a plan.

Back in the White House, the President was ending his address to his Orthodox guests and was mingling with them individually. He eventually made his way to Russian Ambassador Tarlov. He was a pudgy man, full of himself, and at most times, full of vodka. "Mr. President. Thank you very much for your kind invitation and for the United States' recognition of the Orthodox Easter."

"Ambassador Tarlov, you are most welcome. I thank you for coming. As you know, when our nations fail to maintain dialogue, it disheartens me. We must try to keep the lines of communication open."

"Mr. President, I agree! Oh. I nearly forgot. I have a video you must see. It is my granddaughter trying to skate this past winter in D.C."

"I'd love to see it," the President said. With that, Ambassador Tarlov pushed some buttons on his phone, opened a video and then turned the screen towards the President. Immediately, the President realized the video was not the

Ambassador's granddaughter. It was the President's mistress, bent over the President's bed in the White House master bedroom. It was a grueling thirty-five second clip that the President rapidly recognized.

"Out of discretion, I've turned down the volume, Mr. President," the Ambassador said while smiling. He continued. "Today, your Chief of Staff will come back with a proposal. I suggest you follow it, or this video could fall into the wrong hands. Good day, sir."

Ambassador Tarlov walked away. The President stood still for a moment, then continued greeting other guests, as if nothing had happened. It was a rare gift shared by only the best politicians. The event would be over soon enough, and he then could talk to Steve.

After the event, the President retired to his private quarters. In the bedroom, his wife sat, reading a book. "How did the event go?"

"Oh, it was fine. Nothing special." He leaned over and kissed her on the forehead, softly. She cooed and felt the warmth of his love. "I am going to go back down to the Oval Office and try to catch up on some paperwork. I may be back up late tonight. Please don't wait up and get some good sleep. I love you."

"I love you, too." She said.

The President pulled away from her and walked over towards the dresser. A small stuffed teddy bear that he'd not seen before sat there with a lovely red, white, and blue bow around his neck. He picked it up and knew. Slowly, he carried it out of the room and threw it away. It really didn't matter, though. The damage was done.

The President went back down to the Oval Office. Steve was in the West Wing, working on other projects. His phone rang. It was the President's secretary, requesting his presence. Steve dropped everything.

"Mr. President, you wanted to see me?"

"Yes, Steve. I'm curious. How was your meeting today?"

Steve relayed the events in great detail. The President

didn't flinch. "Sir, I told him his request was ludicrous. He was unmoved."

"Interesting..." The President hesitated, as if truly digesting the request. "Perhaps... Perhaps it is not as ludicrous as you think. The Kosovo conflict has continued for decades. It's just another endless war our nation is immersed in."

"Mr. President. Are you considering allowing this to happen? The information they have. It's not great, but it's survivable."

"No, Steve. I'm not suggesting we follow Mr. Nikola's plan as he laid out. I am suggesting we try to finalize the problem between Serbia and Kosovo before the conflict."

Steve began to see the President's vision. "Sir, I like the premise, but for decades, diplomats from around the globe have attempted to quell Balkan tensions. I'm not optimistic we can resolve this in less than a month."

"Steve. You miss the point. Imagine this. The U.S. leads one last massive diplomatic push to solve the problem. If we succeed, great. If we don't succeed, we message that Kosovar leadership scuttled our efforts and they have no one to blame for the conflict but themselves. Once that narrative is planted, the Serbian invasion is merely a logical 'next step' to Kosovo's stubborn behavior."

Steve understood the premise but wasn't as open to the notion of conflict as the President. "Got it, sir. Shall I prioritize this issue?"

"Please. I want a meeting with Secretary Baker tomorrow first thing."

"Yes, Mr. President."

"Thanks, Steve. I appreciate your help on this." The President never shared his meeting with Ambassador Tarlov. He'd not share it with anyone.

*****************************************

Buck was sitting up in his bed. He was accompanied by Smitty and two federal agents. As Buck shared what happened, he grew more and more animated. Nurses closely monitoring the machines attached to him, which were transmitting out his vitals to the main nurse station.

"I don't know what happened to her. The last thing I remember, Natalie jumped from the airplane. I saw her legs go out the cargo door. I think maybe she may have gotten scared and jumped. You gotta find her. She's important to me. Please." His animation was beginning to cause pain, both physically and mentally.

Smitty sat silently next to his friend. Now was not the time or place for him to share his knowledge of Natalie. Smitty also wanted to hear how much the federal agents would share.

One of the agents spoke. "Mr. Thiessen. We asked the Belgrade authorities for a copy of the video from their VIP terminal CCTV as well as in and around the airport so we could get an image of Natalie. We were told that every single camera in the area was either inoperable, or the video failed to record. Frankly, that's one hell of a coincidence. After that, we reached out to authorities in other locations such as Brussels and Vienna. They've sent us the following images. Is this Natalie?" He handed a photo to Buck.

"Yes! That's her! Where is she?! Is she OK?! She must be worried sick!"

The agents looked at each other, then at Smitty. All three knew what was going on, as well as 'who' Natalie really was. Explaining it to Buck would be difficult.

"Mr. Thiessen. What I am going to tell you now won't be pleasant, but you need to know. Natalie Brandstetter isn't who you think she is. Her actual name is Katarina Stojanović. She also is a known asset for Serbian intelligence, with potential ties to Russian intelligence as well." The men handed over dozens of other photos of Natalie.

Buck looked through the photos. He was crushed. He looked at Smitty. After roughly twenty seconds, Buck's sadness turned to anger and rage. How could he fall for such a plot? All the military training about espionage, especially within the special operations community. How could he let his guard down? *'That fucking bitch. I'll kill her,'* he thought to himself. Soon, the medical monitoring devices next to him began to blink, beep and ping. Two nurses ran in.

"Gentlemen, you'll need to leave now." She began trying to comfort Buck.

"Mr. Thiessen. It's OK. You aren't the first and won't be the last. We have what we need for now. Try to get some rest. Perhaps when you calm down, we can discuss this further. Here is my card." The agent handed a business card over. Smitty took it for Buck, who was breathing deeply as if he were about ready to throw a roundhouse at the wall.

"Buck," Smitty said. "Buddy. You're gonna have to calm down. Look. You got played. I get it. You're pissed. But you're still alive, and karma has a way of working things out. Please. Ease up or the nurses are gonna knock you out again with a shot."

"Fuck. Smitty... I really liked her."

"Ha. OF COURSE you did. She'd have been a shitty honeypot if you didn't like her. Dude. That's how the game works. She literally does everything she can to make you like her. You could have farted on her head, and she would have told you how romantic it was. Relax, buddy. Let me tell you a story." Smitty rattled off a story about another Special Ops buddy who fell prey to a honey trap. Of course, a traditional 'honey trap' involves an attractive spy preying on an unsuspecting person, only to extort the individual later. Honey traps involving attempted murder were a bit beyond the normal constructs. As Smitty finished the story of his friend, in the end, the situation was recoverable. His friend kept his career, and entities within the U.S. government dispatched the honey trap. 'Dispatched' of course, being the polite term for actions a bit too distasteful to articulate among some of the government's elite circles.

Buck had physically calmed, but he was far from being at peace mentally. He would beat himself up for days over his lapse in judgement.

# *Chapter Thirty-Five*
# Saturday Meeting

Secretary Baker was unaware as to why the President wished to meet on a Saturday morning, but she knew that at her level, weekends don't exist.  She and her staff unsuccessfully attempted to pry any information about the meeting from Steve.  No secretary level member was comfortable entering a meeting with the President uninformed and unprepared.

"Ah, Marleen, please come in," the President said.  "Apologies for cutting into your weekend."  A common yet empty phrase uttered across D.C. every weekend.

"Good morning, Mr. President. I welcome the meeting.  Think nothing of it."  Secretary Baker was actually being honest.  At her level, any chance, at any time, for a one on one with the President was welcome.  Marleen may not be prepared for the President's topic, but she was extremely prepared with her own agenda items should the chance present itself.

The two sat down, and the President relayed his idea and desire for a massive diplomatic push to resolve the Balkan tensions between Serbia and Kosovo.  While the news was unexpected, Secretary Baker was receptive, if not excited.

"Mr. President. I do welcome your idea; however, I must confess, this will take a very serious lift.  We will need resources as well as support, and buy-in from allies."

"Marleen.  This has shifted to be my number one issue.  You will have all the resources you require."  The President intentionally looked at Steve, who nodded.  It was part of the show and Marlene was an attentive audience.  She didn't miss a thing.  "Also, I will personally call our allies. I can't imagine they'd welcome another few decades of sending troops to Kosovo to keep the peace."

"Yes, Mr. President.  But I must ask.  Why the dramatic shift on Kosovo right now?  Has something transpired to bring this issue to the forefront?

"Marleen, I confess, I fear that Serbia and Russia are

considering some sort of action this spring. I don't have anything definitive, but both the Serbian and Russian delegation at my Orthodox Easter event acted strangely. Of course, you were there. I don't know if you noticed anything."

Marleen was there, but had not noticed anything peculiar. That said, she wasn't about to question the President's impressions. "Sir, I concur. OK. My staff will start on this immediately."

"Marleen. One last thing. I realize Serbia remains indignant regarding the 1999 war and their loss of territory. Perhaps, as a way to incentivize Serbia, we could reconsider our position on the current border. Perhaps there is merit in moving it south so that the ethnic Serbians in the northern part of Kosovo could again fall under Serbian control. I'm willing to consider giving some land back to Serbia if it will settle the dispute and have them recognize Kosovo. Do you understand?

Secretary Baker looked at the President with a face of concurrence; however, inside her head, she questioned if he'd lost his mind. "Mr. President, of course, every option should be on the table, but the U.S.'s long-standing position has been a multiethnic solution is the only viable option. This shift from current policy is quite substantial and..."

The President cut her off. "Marleen. I know the policy. It's my policy. I'm the President. I know what our position was. Yes, it's a dramatic shift, but let's both drop the diplomatic bullshit. The current policy isn't working. It's been decades. We both know Serbia and Russia are just waiting out the full erosion of our NATO footprint as our allies grow weary of continued and costly deployments. The day KFOR fully withdraws is the day that ALL of Kosovo will again fall to Serbia. Should that happen, the U.S. and the West lose. I won't stand for that. This new proposition at least salvages some of Kosovo. It also gives Serbia, Russia and the West some semblance of a 'win.'"

Everything the President said was true and Marleen knew it. She also knew there would be serious pushback from invested allies as well as career State Department staff who'd worked for decades to mature a multiethnic Kosovo. No matter. This was the President's directive, and in her mind, the State Department had the lead on the executive branch's top issue. "Sir, my immediate plan will be to summon the Serbian and Kosovar Ambassadors to explain the U.S.'s intent for an immediate diplomatic resolution. From there, I will travel to Belgrade and Pristina to meet with Presidents and Prime Ministers. I will also send your Chief of Staff a list of allies to call along with recommended talking points. Hearing from you directly on this matter will be critical to a successful engagement strategy. From there, we can evaluate progress and set out a plan for further actions."

"Marleen, that sounds perfect. Thanks." The President stood up, as did Secretary Baker. They shook hands and the State Department team departed with their boss. Steve and the President looked at each other.

"Steve, at your next meeting with Mr. Nikola, please relay the details of this meeting. Let's see if it interests him."

\*\*\*\*\*\*\*\*\*\*\*\*\*\*\*\*\*\*\*\*\*\*\*\*\*\*\*\*\*\*\*\*\*\*\*\*\*\*\*\*

Across the ocean, Serbian President Sokol was in a meeting with local Belgrade businessmen as his secretary burst into the office. The surname 'Sokol,' was a strong Serbian name, meaning 'Hawk' in English. He had long served the people of Serbia; exceptional at playing Serbia as a non-aligned state, much like Marshal Tito, ensuring his nation remained in the middle of the constant West versus East political struggles.

It was Saturday afternoon, and perhaps closer to a social gathering in a Westerner's eyes. They were drinking slivovitz, a traditionally local plum brandy, laughing and talking about things unrelated to work. She interrupted, speaking in Serbian, "Mr. President, my apologies. There is an urgent phone call for you."

President Sokol kindly asked his guests to step outside his office and directed his secretary to transfer the call to his desk. As the guests departed, the President gazed out his office window onto the city of Belgrade below. It was beautiful. Soon, the phone rang, and he picked it up. The line was his secure phone, heavily encrypted, with only a few others able to call it. He answered in Serbian.

"President Sokol."

In Russian, the voice replied, "Aleksandar. Greetings from Moscow." It was Russian President Vladimir Volkov. President Volkov had also served for many years in the government with a strong Russian name, translating to 'Wolf.' Years before, he was an operative in the Soviet KGB. He had parlayed the skills and networks garnered from that career into a successful political life.

Aleksandar immediately switched from Serbian to Russian. "Mr. President. It is great to hear from you. To what do I owe this fortunate call to?"

"Aleksandar, for years, Russia has promised you will again have so called Kosovo back under a Serbian flag. Well, the time has come. I encourage you to prepare your troops for a movement south."

The message was welcome, but far from exciting. Russia's promise was stale with age, and President Sokol was already aware of Nikola's efforts. Regardless, President Sokol was diplomatic in his response. "Mr. President, this is great news. May I ask when all of this will transpire, and do I have confirmation from you that Russia will provide support for this?"

President Volkov expected both questions. "Of course. Our forces, together, will be moving into so called Kosovo in roughly a month. Perhaps sooner. I have dispatched three of my best military planners to Belgrade. They will meet with your defense ministry officials to craft an invasion plan."

Immediately, Aleksandar was impressed. Russia's promises were now backed by substance, activity, action. Previously, most of Russia's promises were verbal hot air, never containing plans or dates. Volkov's current message contained both. "Mr. President, I will notify my staff. Your planners will be our special guests and most welcome. Thank you for this."

"Aleksandar, you are welcome. But we must be in very close cooperation on this. And you must also realize, the first stage of the plan is to move only to the Ibar River.  All of so-called Kosovo will eventually fall, but for now, we just take back a piece."

Sokol was still elated there would be some action on Kosovo. His popularity in the polls was waning, and he needed a boost. For decades, he'd always been able to saber rattle about Kosovo to gain five or ten percentage points when needed, but the Serbian people had grown disillusioned over these tactics, realizing the saber rattling never materialized into anything of substance.  "Yes, Mr. President.  I understand.  Thank you." They both said farewells and hung up.  President Sokol summoned his Defense Minister and in person relayed the message.  Within days, the Serbian Army would be exercising and honing their skill sets for war.

## *Chapter Thirty-Six*
# Striking a Deal

By Monday morning, Secretary Baker was already churning hard on the Serbia-Kosovo diplomatic efforts.  On Sunday, she'd eaten lunch with the Kosovar Ambassador and then dinner with the Serbian Ambassador, both setting the stage for potential trilateral engagements.  She was certain diplomatic cables were flying through the night from D.C. back to Pristina and Belgrade.

A note from Secretary Baker's aide to Steve highlighted these events.  Steve read the text as he walked past the White House secretary into the Oval Office.  "Good morning, Mr. President."

"Good morning, Steve.  How did you sleep?"  It was a question rarely asked, but under current circumstances, wasn't without merit.

"Good, sir.  Thanks for asking.  Here are your prep packages for today's events and decision briefs on the bottom.  Also, Secretary Baker has already met with both Ambassadors."

"Thanks, Steve.  That's great news.  Any readout?"

"No, sir.  Not yet."

"Fine… OK, for our schedule today.  Who's first?"

"Sir, Attorney General Erwin Reese is here for his update."

"Great, send him in."

The meeting with the attorney general progressed smoothly. A few prominent cases were discussed, and of course, the President listened intently, even though he'd received a read ahead briefing the night before.  It was the standard.

The President was pleased with Reese as his AG pick, a former Senator from Massachusetts.  As the meeting wrapped up, AG Reese said, "Mr. President, there is one more thing.  It's a bit early in the investigation, but given the implications, I wanted to make you aware."

The President was intrigued.  "Of course, Erwin.  Please, continue."

"I am not sure if you recall, but a contracted private aircraft carrying NATO senior personnel crashed in Kosovo."

"Yes, I recall. Horrible event."

"I agree, sir. Well, we have pieced together some of those events which now lead us to believe it was sabotage by the Serbian government. We have identified a Serbian intelligence agent involved in the event." As he spoke, he handed over photos of Katarina and Nikola. Steve also received a copy of the photos. When Steve saw Nikola, his face turned white, and he tried to control his eyes from bulging too much. He stared at the President as if he wanted to scream out.

The AG continued. "What is perhaps interesting is, this man, Nikola Stojanović, is currently in the U.S. Further, we have evidence he was recently with Don Denney in Key West, just prior to Mr. Denney's suicide." Before the AG had made his last comment, Attorney General Reese turned and looked at Steve, attempting to judge his reaction. As the words left his mouth, Steve sighed. Other than that, there was nothing else to discern.

The AG was done. Both the President and Steve looked at the photos, intrigued, as if they'd never seen these people, or knew of their intents. "This is interesting stuff. Do you have anything else?"

AG Reese responded, "Unfortunately, Mr. President, we do not. The Serbian government is not cooperating in our investigation, and we've gotten as much as we can from witness reports."

"I see," said the President.

"Sir, I am aware the Denney family has close personal ties to the White House, which is why I bring this to you now. I also want you to know I have placed extra agents on this case. I'm certain you agree that Mr. and Mrs. Denney deserve closure on their son's death."

In principle, the President agreed that the Denneys, a prominent D.C. family that sat atop the party's donation list, deserved closure. In reality, the last thing the President wanted was more agents working on this case. "Yes. Well, Erwin, I greatly appreciate that. I have already spoken with Andy, Don's father. It was a difficult discussion. Tough stuff, burying a child.

I think Andy and his wife are somewhat at peace with this and trying to move forward. Let's be careful with what we share. No point rattling bones unless we are certain."

He continued, "Don and Andy were always at each other's throats. It was a strained relationship and Andy now thinks he may have just pushed too hard. He's really beating himself up over it. Because of that, I'm inclined to believe Don's meeting with this Nikola character is perhaps just a coincidence. I don't know, of course. I tell you what, though, I have directed Marleen to take on a top-level effort to resolve the Serbia-Kosovo conflict within the next month. I'll talk to her about Serbia's help with this. Perhaps we can get them to become a bit more cooperative. I don't know this Nikola, but if he is an oligarch tied to the Serbian leadership, I hope we don't undermine Marleen's efforts."

The President continued, subtly trying to shift topics. "Erwin, do you have any update on the fentanyl trafficking into the Norfolk port?"

The question caught the AG off-guard. "Nothing I can brief today, Mr. President. Why do you ask?"

"Oh, nothing. The Virginia governor is getting heat on the issue, and I was hoping to pass him an update or perhaps even secure a large drug bust to help him. Just curious. Nothing more."

Steve didn't flinch, but knew there was no such discussion with the Virginia governor. He also knew exactly what the President was doing. Gently, the President suggested an exposure of Nikola could undermine a massive State Department effort, and then threw the AG another bone to go chase down, hopefully with extra agents. It was delivered brilliantly. But far from brilliantly enough to trip up Attorney General Erwin Reese. Erwin now knew he was onto something with the Denney suicide. He also knew he'd now have to play it extremely well and chase down something for the Virginia Governor. Or at least feign an effort.

The political savvy of the President always impressed AG Reese. In a single breath, the President had nonverbally recommended a slow down to an investigation, but he'd also offered another solution. Should he ever be accused of interfering in an ongoing FBI investigation, he could easily dismiss the accusations.

"Yes, Mr. President. You're right. I'd hate to waste scarce assets on an issue we will eventually solve at a time that could undermine a greater good. Let's see what Secretary Baker can do. Until then, we will hold off from increasing agents on this case."

"Great. I agree." The President stood up, as did AG Reese and Steve. They all shook hands, and the AG departed. As he walked down the White House halls, he placed a phone call to his staff. And with that, the FBI's energies on the Denney case would drop by nearly 50%. The ways of D.C.

Steve looked down at his phone. A text had come in from Nikola. It was the day they were to meet.

> 'Steve - Shall we meet at your common spot with Don? 10AM. Just like old times. Same rules, no electronics. ~N'

Realizing Nikola was aware of Steve and Don's 'secret' meeting location caused a slight gritting of Steve's teeth. *'What else did he know,'* Steve thought. No matter. Steve and the President had a solid way forward. "Mr. President, it appears I now have an appointment with Nikola."

"Great. Please go. Send in one of your staff as a note taker for my next few meetings. I'll catch you up when you return. Good luck, Steve."

Steve proceeded into the area of the WWII memorial. Nikola, with his two 'far from incognito' henchmen, stood along the edge of the reflecting pond, staring towards the Lincoln Memorial.

Steve walked up, but before he got too close, the bodyguards intervened. One pulled a scanner from his pocket as a snub-nosed Uzi submachine gun flashed from under his coat. Steve immediately realized these guys were serious. Guns in

D.C. were illegal, at least for law-abiding citizens.

"Good morning, Steve. I am confident you will bring me good news."

"Nikola. I have good news. The President has taken significant steps over the weekend and just today set conditions for a diplomatic resolution to your issue. This could happen as quickly as a month and involve no military action."

Nikola stared at Steve for a while. He then finally spoke. "Perhaps I did not make myself clear on what will exactly happen."

Nikola's pushback was not unexpected. Steve continued explaining exactly what steps were taken, as well as the path forward.

The Serbian blood within Nikola began to boil. "You do not understand. That is not the deal. If you think I am fucking around, please try me."

"No, Nikola. I don't believe you're fucking around. But I do believe you'd want to avoid war. This is best for everyone, don't you think?"

"Steve. What ever gave you the impression I wished to avoid war?" Nikola smiled, then nodded to his henchmen, and one of them placed a call. Steve did not know what was happening, but it wasn't the most comfortable he'd felt given the weapons. "Steve. Clearly, we do not have an agreement. You will call your President now. You will tell him this, so listen carefully. My two friends and I will come to the White House, now, to meet the President, or we will go to the Russian Embassy and speak with Ambassador Tarlov. The choice belongs to the President." Nikola, should he experience any pushback, was advised to make such a threat. In reality, he did not know why, nor did he know what Ambassador Tarnov possessed.

"Nikola, the President is a busy man. I don't think you..."

"Call him." Nikola's tone rode on a knife's edge. The two bodyguards moved closer and handed Steve a phone. It was already ringing to the White House switchboard.

"White House communications office. How may I help

you?"

"Hello, this is Steve Lewis. Please get me Sandy, the and tell her I need to speak to POTUS immediately."

The White House communications office received thousands of calls a day, but she immediately recognized Steve's voice. "Yes, Mr. Lewis. Please stand by."

Steve sat on hold for a bit.

Finally, the President picked up. "Steve, are you OK?"

"Yes, Mr. President." Steve relayed the demand.

"That's crazy. There's no need to involve the Russians. OK, bring them to the White House." The President had little appetite for Nikola to meet Ambassador Tarlov.

Steve was shocked. "Sir, are you sure?"

"Yes." The President was clear. Steve hung up and handed the phone back to the bodyguard. They all walked to 17th Street, which passed in front of the WWII Memorial. A large black SUV waited. After piling in, the vehicle drove to the White House.

As it approached the gate, Steve jumped out and spoke to the guard. Security protocols had hastily been coordinated with the guards. The vehicle was stopped. No matter who was in it, the vehicle would not enter without a pre-announced arrival. Steve and Nikola would be forced to exit the vehicle at the gate and walk up the driveway.

The doors of the vehicle opened, Nikola was searched, Steve waited, and then they were both escorted up the drive by Secret Service to the Oval Office. Once there, the two walked directly into an office with an extremely rare, waiting President.

Nikola walked towards him with his hand extended. "Mr. President, it is an honor to make your acquaintance."

"Yes, well, I wish I could say the same." The President didn't offer his hand. His response was rude and delivered with such political nuance, it was almost a cute joke. They both sat. "It appears you were not pleased with my offer that Steve relayed."

"Unfortunately, sir, no. I am not."

"Steve, can you leave the room?" Steve's eyes popped wide open. He was at a loss for words.

"But. Uh?"

"It's OK, Steve. Please." Steve stepped out and Nikola remained. "Please tell me what it is you disapprove of. I have laid out the plans for Serbia to regain the northern portion of Kosovo."

"Yes, but your plan involves a peaceful solution."

The President was taken aback. "Of course. It avoids bloodshed. On both sides."

"Mr. President. Please don't insult me. Your 'diplomatic' effort would be roughly the tenth 'big push' for resolution, when all previous nine failed, both Republican and Democrat." Nikola paused and adjusted himself on the comfortable sofa. "Why is it that the U.S., the Ottomans, the Austrians, and many others all believed they could understand, or better yet, control the Balkans? Pens, paper, words, handshakes, or certificates with golden seals... None of these will ever resolve issues where I come from. You realize, in the Balkans, strength and conflict solves issues. Forgive my bluntness, but bloodshed is a necessary part of the process for what I seek. To me and many other Serbians, we long to battle the Albanians in a fair fight, without interference. No U.S. fighter or bomber aircraft. No Special Forces. No Navy. No Army. Simply, us versus them." Nikola stared at the President. He was as serious as he could be.

The President thought for a while. Open conflict was not a part of his political platform. He'd long leaned more towards being a dove than a hawk. "OK, Nikola. I understand. You realize, though, for you to have your war, I must give the appearance of exhausting all diplomatic options."

Nikola thought about it. The President was right. "I see your point. But while this happens, there must be no buildup of U.S. or NATO forces in the region."

"Agree. I won't let that happen. Nikola, may I ask, why are you doing this? What have you to gain?"

"Mr. President, I'd suggest that is none of your concern, but because of your gracious invitation into the Oval Office, I will share." Nikola was feeling emboldened and powerful. "Years ago, my family owned a mine in the region of so-called northern Kosovo. Under Yugoslav communism, it was taken from my family.  After the fall of communism, we tried desperately to reacquire the mine, but as soon as the war with the Albanians began, there was no chance.  The mine fell into the hands of the Kosovo government, which for decades, has left it unused.  My father sat by and watched many prominent families across Russia, Serbia and other former Warsaw Pact nations become powerful oligarchs after the fall of communism.  Many of these were his friends.  But not our family.  My father died despising the Albanians who deprived us of our fortune.  I promised him I would regain our mine and enact his revenge."

The President listened intently.  The concept of revenge in the Serbia was far from surprising.  In fact, revenge across the Balkans was nearly a full-contact professional sport, making Alexander Dumas' *Count of Monte Cristo*, a novel thick with revenge, read like a boring love story.  There was no chance to assuage Nikola from his position, but at least the President now knew his motivation.  "OK.  Nikola, I understand.  Do we have an agreement on our way forward now?"

"Yes, Mr. President."

"Good.  From now on, however, you meet with Steve.  You've taken substantial risk coming here."

"I understand.  But I disagree.  It is you who took a substantial risk allowing me to enter.  However, under the circumstances, you had little choice.  Good day, Mr. President."  Nikola, escorted by Steve, returned to his SUV still waiting outside the gated entry and drove off.

After ensuring Nikola was off the White House grounds, Steve stormed back into the Oval Office, fuming.  After a few minutes, the President was able to calm him, and then shared the details of their discussion.  The threat of exposure was quelled.  At least for the time being.

\*\*\*\*\*\*\*\*\*\*\*\*\*\*\*\*\*\*\*\*\*\*\*\*\*\*\*\*\*\*\*\*\*\*\*\*\*\*

Deep inside the Pentagon, the European desk officer, working in the National Military Command Center (NMCC), received a routine email on his classified system.  It was an intelligence report stating the Serbian military was mobilizing in substantial numbers, with the presumed intent to take part in a 'no notice' exercise. While not critically alarming, the report did note that such a scenario had never been seen before. Flagging the email, the desk officer pushed it forward to his watch officer. Tomorrow, it would be rolled into a briefing for all flag officers across the Joint Staff as well as the service chiefs.

Over in the State Department's Truman Building, the same intelligence report was being disseminated across the top floor. It eventually made its way to Secretary Baker. As she read it, she thought, *'Damn him. The President knows something, but how?'*

\*\*\*\*\*\*\*\*\*\*\*\*\*\*\*\*\*\*\*\*\*\*\*\*\*\*\*\*\*\*\*\*\*\*\*\*\*\*\*\*\*\*\*\*

In Key West, Curt was finally being discharged from the hospital. He and Allison would drive back to Chicago and face the fallout of his actions together. It was a long drive, broken into a few days. They both avoided the discussion of how Curt hurt and scared Allison. Being locked in a car for such a discussion was not advisable. Curt spoke, however. He talked about all the homeless veterans he'd met. Allison couldn't help but hear the passion in Curt's voice. He reiterated their stories, their struggles. It truly intrigued him. Her biggest concern, perhaps, was that he openly considered inviting all of them to their condo for Christmas. They finally made it back to Chicago, calling and telling Smitty they were back. Smitty was still with Buck, however. It would be a few more days until his release.

## *Chapter Thirty-Seven*
# The Build Up

Military training ranges across Serbia were experiencing more activity than they'd seen in years. Mechanics were repairing every available military vehicle as logistics officers were given blank checks to build up supplies. It would not take long for whispers across Serbia for the citizens to realize something was afoot. The underlying chatter across both Serbia and Kosovo would amplify over the next few weeks. Frankly, this was to be expected. Once Secretary Baker flagged high-level efforts seeking a diplomatic resolution, it was commonplace for each nation's posturing. The goal, as always, was to take steps that would garner the best outcome. In the Balkans, that meant demonstrations of force, bowed up chests, and threats.

Senior leaders across the U.S. Defense Department, U.S. European Command and NATO were busy digesting intelligence briefs, all reporting increasing Serbian military activities along with speculating future intent. To this point, however, no nation had undertaken activities in response to Serbia. All stood by, taking a 'wait and see' approach as to any U.S. reaction. None would come.

Inside the White House, the National Security Council (NSC) was set to convene. Serbia's activities had finally grown to a level of concern that the issue would be included in the meeting's topics. A polished Army intelligence officer provided an exceptional and concise briefing about the ongoing activity. He took questions, then remained silent as the NSC members began to discuss the topic.

To begin, Secretary of Defense John Gerzema, well prepared by his staff and the Service Chiefs, provided a strategic-level array of potential courses of action. As he spoke, the President cut him off.

"John, thanks. I have no doubt our military is not only well positioned but also extremely capable of dealing with Serbia, should it come to that." The President then shifted his attention away from John and more towards the entire table. "But I am not ready to consider any military activity on this. A week ago, I spoke with Secretary Baker about Kosovo and Serbia. We've undertaken a strong campaign to secure a diplomatic solution, and I don't want any of your activity to undermine that effort." Turning back to John, he said, "Do you understand?"

"Yes, Mr. President." Secretary Gerzema's, as well as the entire NSC's orders, were clear.

"Marleen, can you please update everyone on your recent progress?"

"Of course, Mr. President. To date, we've met with both the Serbian and Kosovar Ambassadors and have bilateral and trilateral meetings scheduled in the next few weeks. Our analysts believe Serbia's military activity is merely posturing, and if I am correct, I believe Greg concurs." She was referring to Director of National Intelligence Greg Cromwell. Everyone's head in the room spun towards DNI Greg Cromwell, who silently nodded. Marleen continued, "I agree with the President that any military activity could undermine our efforts."

The rest of the room remained silent. "So, State Department has the lead on Serbia and will keep us informed," the President said. "Good." The President then looked at the administrator of U.S. Agency for International Development (USAID). "That reminds me, Sam. After the meeting, I'd like to talk to you."

"Of course, Mr. President."

The remainder of the NSC meeting was standard protocol. Few, if any, actions were approved, but many sidebar meetings would take place outside the conference room after the meeting. It was one of the few places secretary level members had a chance to meet and discuss issues face to face. As those impromptu meetings took place, Sam Austin and the President remained in the room. "Sam, I'd like you to look into something for me. I had dinner with an old friend a few days ago. He told me that in northern Kosovo, there is an old run down mine."

"Yes. You're correct, sir. I actually was briefed on it a few days ago. Our staff is attempting to prepare Secretary Baker for her pending trip to the region. The name, I believe, is Trepca Mine."

"Good! Glad to hear my friend wasn't crazy! Anyway, he said the mine is in horrible shape, and that got me to thinking. Is there any USAID program that could rehabilitate it? Perhaps this too can be a benefit to the region and inject an economic boost."

"I can look into that, Mr. President. But from our initial look, this place will need a ton of work. No matter, however. We can run a full assessment and likely have something in a few months. Should it be acceptable, we can probably have some sort of funding in a year."

"Yes. Great, but is there any way to reduce that timeline?"

"Sir, as you know, we need to run not only an economic assessment but also look at second, third, and fourth order effects of the mine on the community. That will also need to be evaluated by our environmental impact study group to ensure the mine is operating in an environmentally friendly manner. I can perhaps reduce the funding flow down to nine months if we truly prioritize it."

The President was done with the polite dialogue. "Sam, look. I need incentives now. We are really going after a last solution in the Balkans. To date, for decades, nothing has worked. Help me help Secretary Baker. Find me some quick money to rehabilitate even a portion of the mine."

Sam Austin was a political appointee and was quickly reminded of his position. Everything he'd relayed to the President truly was how USAID works. Somehow, though, he'd be forced to find fast money. "Yes, sir. I will do what I can."

"Thank you. I knew I could count on you." They walked out past the squabbling and deal making of others in the lobby. Eventually, the President made it back to his office.

As Secretary of Defense Gerzema's helicopter lifted off from the White House, he sent a quick text message to the Chairman of the Joint Chiefs, Admiral Hershey, who was traveling at the time and unable to attend the NSC:

*'Squirts, maintain status quo on SRB.  Will back brief later.'*

The Admiral winced at the casual use of his old call sign by a seasoned politician and then exhaled deeply at the expected, yet unhelpful political guidance on Serbia.

\*\*\*\*\*\*\*\*\*\*\*\*\*\*\*\*\*\*\*\*\*\*\*\*\*\*\*\*\*\*\*\*\*\*\*\*\*\*\*\*\*\*\*

It was cold in Chicago.  The wind off Lake Michigan was so biting it could freeze a person from the inside out.  A knock at the door of Curt's condo startled both he and Allison, who were curled up on the sofa, relaxing and trying to reconnect.

Allison got up and opened the door.

"Hey, sexy!" Smitty said as he jumped out to hug her.

"Smitty!"  She hugged him and, as she did, she noticed Buck standing behind him.  His head was bandaged up and his legs were in braces.  He stood there on crutches.

"Buck!" she yelled, pushing Smitty aside and rushing to help Buck.

"Allison.  Aren't you a sight for sore eyes?"  Buck's comment was void of his usual humor.  He was far more serious than normal.

From the other room, Curt heard the discussion and rushed to the door.  "Smitty!  Buck!  No way!"

"Yeah.  I convinced Walter Reed to let Buck go.  I told them you'd take care of him, and he'd stay here.  Not to mention, I REALLY need to get back to work."  Smitty had been gone for roughly two weeks.  It was more time than he had saved up for vacation, but his boss was former military and very understanding... to a point.

"Yeah, yeah.  Screw you, buddy!  You just wanted to dump me off because caring for a cripple just ain't your thing," Buck said, half telling the truth and half trying to find his way back into his humor, and being himself.

Curt and Smitty helped Buck into the condo.  They seated

him on the sofa, trying to make him comfortable as Allison brought him something to drink. "Buck, relax. Here is some Coke."

"Coke?" Buck said quizzically,

"Oh, I'm sorry. Did you want Diet Coke or something else?"

"No. Coke is fine, but it's kinda only half of the drink. Where's the rum, whiskey, vodka?" And with that, Buck's humor was emerging.

Smitty spoke up, "Buck, with all the meds you're on, I'd suggest just Coke is perhaps a solid decision."

"Good to see you doing fine, Buck." Curt just laughed. "Maybe you can share some of your meds. As it turns out, I am on administrative leave from the hospital, prescribed methadone, and labeled a recovering heroin addict."

"Curt, stop. We both know that's going to be resolved. You were attacked." Allison would not let him begin to spiral down the road of depression.

"True, but you and I both know dead men tell no tales." He was referring to Don Denney's suicide. "They can't interview Denney after he installed that new air vent in his skull."

Smitty added, "Yeah, what's going on with the investigation?"

"Sadly, very little," Curt said dejectedly. "Certainly, it's a suicide, but questionable since it took place in front of the Chief of Staff's residence. FBI won't talk to me. I asked Jack to see if he could get any info. So far, nothing."

Buck knew the feeling. "Yeah, well, at least your issue is localized in the U.S. I need to get back to Europe and track down that bitch that tried to kill me."

"Slow your roll, big fella. Smitty says you're in my care and you aren't going anywhere. Neither is she. Let's get you fully healthy. Then I'll go help you find her. That's a promise." Curt was right. Buck was in no condition to go anywhere.

"What is quite strange," Allison lamented, "is two back-to-back murder attempts against you both with no ties? And they were right after Don's release."

She was right, and they all knew it. Smitty responded, "After years in Special Forces, I've learned that genuine coincidences are about as rare as unicorns."

Buck tried to adjust himself on the sofa to get comfortable and banged his leg against the coffee table. "Ouch! Fuck a duck!" He screamed.

"OK, none of us are Magnum P.I., and it's clear Buck needs some sleep." Allison had taken the lead. "Smitty, thanks for bringing him. I'll get the spare room made up. Curt, you need to go to your medical appointment. Smitty, you're welcome to stay."

"Nah, I gotta get home, get back to work, and grovel to keep my job. Thanks for taking Buck. He's a handful." Smitty said.

"Yeah, I'll walk you out," Curt replied. "I gotta go see my shrink."

"CURT!" Allison said. "You, as a doctor, should know better. If you don't take psychologists seriously, this treatment will not help."

Curt and Smitty had their coats on and were walking out. "Baby, I do take them seriously. I just say that to annoy you. Love ya!" Smitty and Curt smiled as the door closed.

*****************************************

An overcast day with chilly rain blanketed Arlington National Cemetery. Don Denney's funeral was held with all the requisite military honors, a 21-gun salute, a trumpet in the distance playing taps, and an honor guard to lay him to rest. Attendees, however, were far outnumbered by the military Honor Guard. Becky, Don's mom, was certain the weather was to blame. Andrew, his father, knew differently and was infuriated. None of the politicians he'd donated to were present. None of his business partners. None of Don's military friends, all of whom had distanced themselves after his Nissassa-associated arrest. Andrew steamed. He would never attribute Don's suicide to his parenting, but he also would not just sit quietly while his Special Forces veteran son was lowered into Arlington's sacred ground nearly alone. Someone would pay.

## *Chapter Thirty-Eight*
# Holding the Line

In Serbia, brigades and battalions were returning from their training ranges. But instead of returning home, the garrisons further mobilized. War reserve stocks were being replenished or filled to levels not seen since the late 1990s. The actions of Serbia had now drawn the attention of NATO SecGen Luedtke, who began making press statements as well as social media postings openly questioning the intent of Serbia. All of this, however, had little impact on Serbia, nor did much of the rest of the world take notice. To the world, there were a good number of reasons why Serbia was undertaking such actions, and most of them did not involve precursors for war.

On the Pentagon's third floor, in the 'E' ring, Admiral Hershey entered his meeting with Secretary Gerzema and took a seat. "Mr. Secretary. At some point, NATO or the U.S. will need to undertake some sort of response with respect to Serbia. There are many options available. We could stage a rapid response exercise in Albania, Montenegro, or Croatia as a show of force. We could sail a naval carrier group into the Adriatic Sea, or we could increase flight operations out of Aviano Air Base and other locations across Europe. My best professional advice to you and the President is that leaving Serbia's build up unchecked is a very poor decision."

"Admiral, I take your point and I clearly understand the options you laid out. I discussed this recently one-on-one with the President, and he's adamant we take no military action. Let's look at any preparations we can undertake stateside that would not tip our hand or undermine Secretary Baker's efforts."

"Sir, I can do that, and to a large degree, already have. But Kosovo is about the size of Georgia. If conflict breaks out, Kosovo would be gone before we could even get close to responding. Additionally, the NATO forces in Kosovo number roughly two thousand. They are a peacekeeping force, not a fighting force. Protecting them should be a priority."

"Squirts, I get it. But this is not our call. It is the President's. And he clearly has information we do not."

The Chairman of the Joint Chiefs was growing irritated. Every intelligence briefing he'd received over the past week since the NSC meeting assessed Serbia was going to take some sort of action. "Mr. Secretary, we would be wise to try and either see this problem through the same prism as the President or find a way to change his mind." The Admiral stood up, walked away, headed out to his helicopter waiting on the Pentagon helipad. He'd discuss nothing else with the Secretary, sending a clear message Serbia was becoming a top priority.

From the moment Secretary Gerzema was appointed, there was friction between the two. Secretary Gerzema was far too political for the Admiral's liking and would often prioritize political perspective over security. That pressure would grow just as the tensions in the Balkans continued to rise.

The Chairman jumped in his helicopter. It would be a thirty-minute flight to the Patuxent River Testing Range in Maryland. As Admiral Hershey flew and watched the scenery below, his temper began to cool. He was looking forward to his next event where he, other senior flag officers, congressional members and a host of students from National Defense University would attend a new weapons demonstration by Raytheon. Their new 'Raytheon HEL' (High Energy Laser) would be shooting down a drone in mere seconds. Powerful lasers were not new technology. They had been around for years. The problem had always been operationalizing the capability for combat. Rumor was Raytheon had found a way to integrate a military grade laser onto a vehicle the size of a jeep and operationalize it as a viable fighting vehicle on the battlefield.

The helicopter landed, and Admiral Hershey joined a waiting crowd in the viewing stand. After a few words from the Raytheon public relations announcer, the HEL rolled out in front of the stand. It could seat two up front. The back, or bed of the vehicle, held the power generation boxes, computers. Nested on top was an optical ball with what appeared to be electro optic and infrared tracking lenses, and a much larger lens that was most likely the laser. Next to the viewing stand, a large screen was showing a medium-sized drone flying at a distance that was not specified for security classification reasons. The two operators were given a tactical radio call, stating roughly where their target was as well as a cleared to fire order. The two operators fired up the generators, the ball rose out of the carriage rack, rapidly spun to the correct azimuth. A few 'clunk, clunk, clunk,' sounds were all that was heard other than the hum of generators. The laser was not visible to the naked eye. There was no gun recoil or 'booms.' Nothing happened that would normally be associated with firing kinetic weapons. As the 'clunks' occurred, the video screen showed the drone skin glow then catch fire. Immediately, the air vehicle spun out of control and crashed. To no one's surprise, the event was a success.

After the demonstration, Raytheon hosted a small reception, and experts stood by to answer questions. Many of the National Defense University students rushed the Raytheon engineers and operational experts, trying to learn as much about the weapon as possible. Admiral Hershey stood at a well decorated high top bar table, speaking with Raytheon VP of Energy Weapons Development Aaron Kraft. The discussion was far more friendly than merely work related. The VP was retired Navy Vice Admiral Aaron Kraft who attended the Naval Academy with Admiral Hershey. It was the ways of the U.S. Defense Industry. The two caught up on their respective families, a bit about mutual friends and a quick discussion about how Navy Football might perform this coming year. As the two spoke, Congressman Jack Donegan approached their table.

"Squirts. How goes it?" Jack said.

"Jack. Hey, good to see you. Things are good. Great demo, huh?"

"Yes. Now I just have to find money in the budget when you want to buy five hundred of them." They both laughed. Admiral Kraft joined in, awkwardly. "Hey, on a serious note, are you ramping up for Serbia?"

"Jack, you know I can't say an..."

Jack cut off the Admiral mid-sentence. "Squirts. Yeah, yeah.

Look. Our sources say the President is sitting idle while it's clear Serbia is mobilizing. While I commend his diplomatic initiatives, I think it's foolhardy to take no measured military action. Can you do a paratrooper exercise with the Army bubbas out of Italy into Croatia? Something?"

The Admiral shared Congressman Donegan's frustration. "Jack. Right now, we are on a hold, and you know the rules on civilian control of the military. If you want the President to change his mind, it is far wiser to approach this via political channels than coming directly to me." Chairman Hershey was correct.

"Yeah. You're right. I just wish there was something. I'm concerned."

"Off the record... So am I." They shook hands and parted.

* * * * * * * * * * * * * * * * * * * * * * * * * * * * * * * * * * * * *

Andrew Denney stood in Don's apartment as a professional moving company was clearing it out. Boxes from the kitchen were loaded into a truck. The dining room table stood sideways, disassembled against the wall. Two large movers leaned down to pick up the sofa. It was leather and somewhat heavy. As they began walking it out, a white sheet of paper was exposed, sitting on the floor previously under the sofa, along with all the dust bunnies and stale potato chips. Andrew walked over and picked it up. On the other side, a black-and-white photo of Don and Steve, clearly taken at a distance and discretely. Andrew was confused. He'd known about Steve and Don's previous dealings on Nissassa, but why such a photo? Did the White House try to blackmail Don, or vice versa? Was there someone else? It didn't make sense.

"Hey, how much longer are you guys gonna be packing out?" Andrew asked.

"About a few hours, sir." The lead mover responded.

"OK. I need to go. Lock up when you're done and bring the forms to my office. My secretary will sign them. Thanks." Andrew didn't wait for a response. He exited the condo and stepped out of the building. Reaching into his pocket, he pulled out a cell phone. It wasn't his, but rather Don's that he'd gotten with his other effects. Andrew was growing more convinced that the small Samsung held secrets he needed to know.

Andrew took the phone to the most tech savvy person he knew. Within minutes, the phone was hacked and opened. Andrew paid the hacker, changed the pin, and walked out. As Andrew sat in the car, he scrolled through the phone, in a way reliving the last few days of Don's life. Thing began to come into focus. Andrew's blood boiled. Everything was clear. It was true, Don had attempted to kill Curt. It was also clear the White House had stifled any investigation. Andrew knew, if he could learn all this in five minutes from Don's phone, a team of FBI agents clearly should have been able to discover it. Andrew found the phone number for "Nikola." He tried to call it, but the number was disconnected. Whoever Nikola was, Andrew believed he held the key. Andrew took out his own phone and called home. "Hey honey, do you still have the business card from the FBI agents?"

"Why, yes? What's wrong?"

"Oh, nothing. Can you ask them to come to the house? I'd like to get an update on their investigation."

"Sure. Are you coming home soon?"

"Yes, dear. I'll be home within the next few hours." Andrew had never grown comfortable committing to when he would be home.

Mrs. Denney said, "OK. I love you."

Andrew hung up.

\*\*\*\*\*\*\*\*\*\*\*\*\*\*\*\*\*\*\*\*\*\*\*\*\*\*\*\*\*\*\*\*\*\*\*\*\*\*\*\*

"Mr. President, NATO Secretary General Anton Luedtke is on the line," Steve said as they both sat in the Oval Office. Joining them was Secretary Baker and Secretary Gerzema.

"Secretary Luedtke, sir, good morning. You are on with the President of the United States," Steve said into the speakerphone.

The President jumped in. "Mr. Secretary, good to hear from you."

"Mr. President, yes. I've been looking forward to our discussion. I hope you've been well."

"Yes, yes. Everything is great here. But I'm certain you didn't schedule this meeting for such things. What's on your mind, Mr. Secretary?"

"Sir, I've been in close coordination with your ambassador to NATO and I confess, I and many of the NATO nations are not aligned with the U.S. position on Serbia."

"Yes, Anton. I'm aware. I think though there is perhaps a bit too much concern being levied. Some in our intelligence community believe much of this is just Serbia posturing to get the best diplomatic outcome they can." Both the Defense and State Department Secretaries looked at each other. Technically, the President was correct. There were 'some' who believed this, but they were far from the majority.

"Yes, Mr. President, I'm aware of such reports as well, but as NATO, we have a serious problem. The NATO forces in Kosovo under Major General Torres at KFOR roughly number 2000. They have no heavy equipment, no artillery, and no tanks. They've been in such a permissive peacetime posture for so long that many do not carry weapons or ammunition. Should Serbia continue to demonstrate a force buildup, some of the NATO force contributing nations will only grow more vocal. They've made clear that either KFOR needs to be beefed up by the U.S. or their force contribution may be withdrawn. That said, it is clear they all intend for the U.S. to lead in this effort."

"Secretary Luedtke, let me be clear. I have no intent to alter the U.S. force posture in Kosovo, nor do I support any other nation increasing or decreasing forces in the region. Should any take such actions and undermine our collective effort, there will be repercussions. Do I make myself clear?"

Anton had done all he could. The message was clear. "Yes, Mr. President. If I am understanding correctly, you expect I relay your intent to our allies."

"Yes. Please. And I thank you for your commitment to the

alliance. I know it is difficult, but I believe all this will blow over. I also believe we are very close to a final diplomatic solution. Anton, I'm 'all-in' on this diplomatic push. I'll be furious if one of our NATO allies steps out of line and takes some military posture response, which undermines this." The President took a deep breath and calmed. "Let's not make too much of the current Serbian posturing. We've both been around long enough to know this is something they've done in the past. Perhaps not to this level, but to be clear, they could be undertaking such a significant force build up because they know this is the last one."

"I do hope you are correct." Secretary General Luedtke's comment lacked any hope.

"I will be. You'll see. I must go, Anton. Please take care." The line was disconnected. The President looked at his two Secretaries. "So, how do you think that went?"

They both sat there, silent for a few seconds. Finally, Secretary Baker spoke, "Mr. President. I am very grateful you have such faith in our diplomatic effort, but I confess, there are some in State that believe even a modest show of U.S. military posturing would not be unwarranted."

Both the President and the Secretary of Defense were a bit surprised. It's rare for State Department officials openly endorse escalatory military response. The President then looked at the Secretary of Defense. "And you, John?"

"Sir, the Chairman and I have advised for a regional no-notice exercise in either Germany or Italy or a carrier strike group port call in Croatia or Montenegro. We stand by those recommendations."

"I thank both of you for such frank input. But listen. Every previous diplomatic effort in the region has failed because one of these damn countries tries to jockey way too hard for an advantage at the last minute. That advantage pushed the other side away from the table. This time, I won't flinch, and neither will you. When we have a diplomatic solution to show the world, we will be right."

The two were again reaffirmed in their orders. Secretary Baker spoke up. "Mr. President, I am clear as to your intent. But

I must say, our Embassy in Pristina has sent cables reporting the Kosovo Security Force are matching the Serb build up. There has been no movement of forces yet, but training efforts have increased, as have munitions stockpiles and logistical preparations."

"Please relay to Embassy Pristina to do everything they can to quell the Kosovo response. Tell them I will speak personally with the President and the Prime Minister if I have to. I will tell them the nation that doesn't act like a bully going into the agreement stands a far better chance of getting the better deal in the end." Countless examples in history would suggest the President's comments were completely false, but at the time, it didn't matter. The message would be relayed to the Pristina Embassy. The meeting adjourned, and not one attendee left with a good feeling.

\*\*\*\*\*\*\*\*\*\*\*\*\*\*\*\*\*\*\*\*\*\*\*\*\*\*\*\*\*\*\*\*\*\*\*\*\*\*\*\*

Three senior Russian military strategists were working day and night deep in the basement of the recently constructed Serbian Ministry of Defense. The old one was destroyed by NATO in the 1999 war. The three Russians crafted a plan that would concentrate massive military forces in the mountains north of the Administrative Boundary Line (ABL). The Kopaonik mountain range stretched across southern Serbia into northern Kosovo. Once the buildup began, it would take three days to mass forces into a formation ready to press into northern Kosovo. Soon, Serbian forces would start to move from their bases into the mountains. In true Russian fashion, military operations were important, but overshadowed by the information campaign. The morning headline out of Belgrade read:

*Serbians in the so-called region of Northern Kosovo being beaten and killed by Albanians.*

In the article, Serbian President Sokol made clear it was Serbia's responsibility to protect and care for Serbians all around the world. "Much in the way Russia, our closest ally, takes seriously it's responsibility to care for all Russians. We too must protect our citizens wherever they may be. I strongly encourage the Albanians south of us to immediately change their behavior or we will act." While the article incited and energized the Serbian population, it was nearly void of any obvious examples of such activity. The allegations were completely false, but it didn't matter. The hatred in the region over the past two decades had grown to where everyone had enough 'examples' in their minds to validate the news. Serbians wanted to believe it.

\*\*\*\*\*\*\*\*\*\*\*\*\*\*\*\*\*\*\*\*\*\*\*\*\*\*\*\*\*\*\*\*\*\*\*\*\*\*\*\*

Nikola read the paper sitting under the sun's warmth at his favorite Belgrade coffee shop, The Russian Tsar. He smiled. His plan was working without a hitch.

## Chapter Thirty-Nine
# The Enemy of My Enemy

"Gentlemen, I thank you for taking the time to meet," Andrew said to Agents Bozarth and Myers. "I'd like to see if you've learned anything about my son's death or his involvement with this issue in Key West."

"Mr. Denney, it is our pleasure to meet with you," Agent Bozarth said. "We made a bit of progress, but to be clear, this is an ongoing investigation, and we really can't say much."

"Agents, come with me," Andrew said. The three stood up and walked into his study. "You see this wall? I have a photo with every President for the past thirty-five years. Here you can see them dining in my house. Here, my wife and I are spending the night in the Lincoln Bedroom at the White House. Drop the horse shit. Yes, it's an ongoing investigation, but what are you going to do? Dig up my son and arrest him?" Andrew led them back to the living room, and they all sat down.

The agents knew he was right. Finally, Agent Myers spoke. "Sir, do you know a man by the name of Nikola Stojanović?"

Andrew absolutely knew the name Nikola from Don's phone, but denied it. "Nope. Not that I can recall. Why?"

"Sir, we have indications this man was close to your son before the..." Agent Myers paused. "The death."

"Interesting. Becky, do you know this man?"

"No. I've never heard of him."

Agent Bozarth pulled out a photo of Nikola and placed it on the coffee table in front of the Denneys. "Here is his photo. Do you recognize him?"

Both said no, but now Andrew had a full name and photo. His plan was working. "This Nikola guy. Do you know why my son was with him?"

"Not yet, sir. We actually were making substantial progress on the case, with a host of agents assisting, and then one day many of them were redirected to another priority case. It was strange. This case was one of our top efforts. Then, in a day, it was at the bottom."

"Interesting," Andrew said. He was fairly certain he knew why, but threw out a completely bogus answer. "Perhaps it was because my son was already dead."

"Maybe, sir. One other question. If you don't know Nikola, do you know his sister Katarina?" They placed her photo down in front of the Denneys, just like before. Again, neither had seen her.

"No. Who is she? Was she a friend of Don's?" Andrew asked. Trying to gain as much information as possible.

Agent Bozarth smiled, "Sir, I hope not. She's a known Serbian - Russian agent living in Belgrade."

"Oh my," Becky said, "Do you have indications Don was associating with her, too?"

"No, ma'am. We don't. But..." The two agents looked at each other as if they shouldn't share anything further.

"Please tell us," Becky implored. "I can't sleep. I need some closure. Please. I beg you."

"Ma'am, OK. We have indications your son, along with Nikola, attempted to murder a Doctor Curt Nover, one of the individuals who uncovered your son's involvement with Nissassa. What's of interest is that another member of that group also suffered a near fatal plane crash and there is a possibility this woman is linked to that attempted murder. And finally, it appears Nikola and Katarina are siblings."

It wasn't the information that was going to soothe Becky Denney. She burst into tears. Andrew stood up and escorted the agents to the door. "Gentlemen, I thank you for your help. Look, I know many of Don's friends. Why don't you leave those photos with me, and I'll ask around."

"Sir, we aren't supposed to..."

"Yeah. I know. But you yourself said you've lost much of your help. Let me do this."

Reluctantly, the agents left the photos, said goodbye and departed. Andrew now had a lead. His son's death would not be in vain.

\*\*\*\*\*\*\*\*\*\*\*\*\*\*\*\*\*\*\*\*\*\*\*\*\*\*\*\*\*\*\*\*\*\*\*\*\*\*\*\*\*\*

Breaking news out of Europe rustled most of the senior decision makers out of bed the next morning. Austria announced it would be immediately withdrawing its 300+ forces from Kosovo, which were part of the NATO KFOR peacekeeping structure. The action caught Washington by surprise because U.S. Embassy Vienna had not been informed of the decision prior to public announcement. For a few hours, the news grew from a smolder into a fire. With the six-hour time difference between D.C. and Vienna, by the time Washington woke, this troop withdrawal was a five-alarm fire.

To deal with the crisis, the White House Chief of Staff called a video conference with State Department, Defense Department and Joint Staff. It would be the first event of the day. Communications officers across each of the locales scrambled to load the correct Video Conference inputs over the JWICS system and ensure it was secured to the level of top secret.

"Good morning, team," Steve said from the White House Situation Room. "If all agree, could we start with Marleen? Marleen, what do you have?"

"Good morning, Steve. It appears the stories about Austria pulling forces are accurate, and they may not be the only nation. Others are signaling a similar course of action. Most if not all of our allies are uncomfortable about the Serbian military build up and they also express an uneasiness about President Sokol."

"OK. Thanks, Marleen. John, what's your take?"

"Steve, Marleen is correct. I'm getting flooded with questions from allied defense ministers if the U.S. posture in Kosovo will increase. Also, getting similar queries from the defense attachés in D.C."

"Thanks, John. Admiral Hershey, anything to add?"

Admiral Hershey took a deep breath. "Steve. If we remain

on this trajectory, we will end up with one U.S. light brigade at Camp Bondsteel south of Pristina, approximately 600 U.S. personnel, alone. We will likely be abandoned by our allies regarding Kosovo. While we have F-16s at Aviano Air Base in Italy, the Italians maintain control over much of our flight operations, and it's possible they will impede our operations should conflict break out." He took a breath. "Sir, I truly applaud the efforts of Madam Secretary of State, and as a man who's fought more than I care to admit, I pray her diplomatic solution is successful. But failing to take any action at this point is analogous to signing a death warrant for Kosovo, a nation the U.S. and the west fought for decades to establish."

After the Admiral spoke, it was as if Steve's video was frozen. He didn't move. Steve was trying to evaluate all the comments through the President's lens. In his heart, he knew every input he received was accurate. But it could not outweigh the information Nikola shared. He just needed to find a way to twist the narrative. "OK. I truly appreciate everyone's input. Marleen, please ask our ambassadors in allied nations to make every effort that will ensure all our allies maintain existing force structures in Kosovo. There can be no change. John, please take the same tack with your defense minister colleagues. Let's see if we can incentivize them with foreign military sales or offering training opportunities later in the year. I will relay all of your comments to the President later this morning and get back to you if there is any change." It was the best Steve could offer. All the participants on the video conference noticed that he'd offered no response to Chairman Hershey. They all said goodbye. Admiral Hershey was angered but maintained military bearing as if he didn't have a care in the world.

*************************************

Since returning home, Smitty had been working doubles at U.S. Steel, trying to make up for the time he missed. His job wasn't all that difficult, and he was grateful to have an understanding, former military boss. As Smitty sat at his desk, the mill's mail delivery kid plopped down a stack of envelopes in front of him. Smitty had just finished drafting up the security shift schedules for the next few weeks and started digging into the mail.

Most of the envelopes were advertisements from security firms, technology firms promising systems to cut costs and make security even safer and a large amount of junk mail. One after the other, they would end up in the trash. The next envelope, however, was plain white and had no return address. No matter, Smitty just assumed it was a company that was so amateur, they'd simply forgot. He opened it and a single 8x10 black-and-white photo slid out. It was Katarina. On the photo was a singular sticky note that said,

*'Is this Mr. Thiessen's girlfriend?*
*703-555-8930'*

Smitty looked at the image closely, but didn't really need to. He knew it was her. Someone was messing with him, but who?

Smitty dialed the number on the sticky note. A man answered. "Hello?"

Smitty responded. "This is Smitty. You have my attention."

"Mr. Smith. I believe you received your package. My name is Andrew. Andrew Denney. I am Don's father."

"Mr. Denney. If you're Don's father, I have no interest in speaking with you. Just tell me where you got that photo."

"Mark. You'd be wise to hear me out. Let me be clear. First, I had nothing to do with Don's attempt on Dr. Nover's life. Second, the people who put him up to that are the same ones that tried to kill Mr. Thiessen. I personally believe they are also responsible for pushing my son to commit suicide. While we may not be friends, I was hopeful we would have a common enemy and thus could communicate. Perhaps I was wrong. Good day." Andrew hung up the phone.

"Hello?" Smitty said. "Hey! Hello?" There was no response. Smitty looked at his cell phone and saw the call was disconnected. Smitty sat in his office, holding his cell phone. He had few options. He dialed the number again. "Mr. Denney. OK. I'm listening."

The two spoke for the better part of an hour, well into the afternoon. By the end of the conversation, Smitty had sympathy for Mr. Denney, and more importantly, he had a lead on Nikola and Katarina.

*****************************************

The day was winding to a close in D.C. Admiral Hershey headed towards his motorcade SUV just outside the Pentagon 'River Entrance' with plans to transit to his government quarters on Fort Myer. A familiar secret service officer held open the back driver side door. It was the Admiral's preferred seat. From both Iraq and Afghanistan, he'd grown uncomfortable on the passenger side of the vehicle. It was the side which suffered the most fatalities due to IED explosions. While the likelihood of an IED in Washington D.C. was slim, he'd take no changes.

As he entered the car, a sealed envelope sat alone on the back seat. Admiral Hershey leaned forward and asked his driver, "Hey, where did the envelope come from?"

"Admiral, it was brought over from the White House. A gentleman gave it to your lead security detail, saying it was from Steve Lewis, the President's Chief of Staff. We were going to bring it to your desk, but you were going to be in the car soon. We did a scratch and sniff on it, sir. It's safe." Scratch and sniff were the unofficial terms for chemical, explosive and biowarfare testing.

While unorthodox, it was not uncommon for such deliveries, as long as they were checked out. Given the morning video conference, Chairman Hershey was confident the envelope would provide clarity from Steve on the President's position. As he opened it, a handwritten letter stated:

> "Admiral,
> This is not from Steve Lewis. My name is Andrew Denney. Yes, my son was a senior official in the Nissassa

*operations. I'm that Andrew Denney. I'll get straight to the point. I believe the President is being extorted by Serbian and or Russian oligarchs acting on behalf of their respective nations. Ironically, because of my son's involvement is how I've come to learn of the President's dilemma. Take a look at the pictures included. I can explain it all if you wish to meet. I will be standing in front of the Marine Corps Memorial in a brown trench coat. Alone. Tonight, at 7 PM. For our nation, I hope you choose to meet."*

Admiral Hershey looked at the photos. Along with Nikola and Katarina, there were images of email and text exchanges with Steve and with Nikola tied to a number from Serbia.

The Admiral looked at his watch. The time was 1905Hrs. He was already late if he wished to meet Mr. Denney, but it was only three minutes away. "Driver. Change of plans. Please take me to the Marine Corps Memorial." He turned to his aide, who was riding with him. "Call my wife. Tell her I will be late for dinner."

## *Chapter Forty*
# The Stalemate Dance

It was midday in Belgrade. Nikola and Katarina were finishing lunch and basking in pleasant imaginations of their future. Local newspapers were filled with charged rhetoric and jabs between the Serbian and Kosovar leaders, just as Nikola had envisioned.

"Katarina," he said. "Look at the streets of Belgrade. Once again, they are full of life. People are energized."

Katarina was far more pessimistic than her brother. "Yes. But will this just be one of the other dozen build ups to regaining Kosovo? Forgive me if I don't share your optimism, but the Serbian people have been promised for years that Kosovo would one day return under the control of Belgrade, only to have their hopes dashed time and time again."

"You will see. This time will be different. Trepca mine will be ours and our family will once again thrive." As he spoke, a text message buzzed into his phone on the table. He looked at it and smiled. "It appears the White House wishes to speak with me again," he said to Katarina as he answered.

Nikola called the number. Steve saw the incoming number originating from Serbia and answered, "Nikola, good morning." It was 0700Hrs in D.C.

"Good afternoon, Steve. I am just finishing lunch. What can I do for you?"

"Well, Nikola, I think I have some wonderful news for you."

"I'm listening." Nikola was skeptical.

"I can't explain everything as we are on an open line, but we have confirmation that one of our governmental organizations called USAID has secured $1.5 million dollars for the refurbishment of Trepca mine."

"That is wonderful news. You must relay to your President that I am very grateful."

"I'll do that, and I'm sure he'll be happy to hear you're

pleased, but there's more. Currently, our diplomats in Belgrade and Pristina are working to have the ownership of the mine transferred back to Serbia, where we believe, based on your contacts, it would be handed to you."

"I understand. And let me guess. In return for all this, you'd like my help at deescalating the current tensions. Am I correct?"

"Yes, that would be welcome. And part of the deal." There was far more Steve wished to say, but there was no way to speak on a secure network with Nikola.

"Steve, please tell your President I appreciate his offer, but as I told him, the western ways will not work in this part of the world. Diplomatic agreements and documents that transfer land are virtually as worthless as the paper they are written on. In the Balkans, it almost always takes blood to gain treasure."

"Nikola, please be reasonable. Right now, the President is under extreme pressure, much of which you can't even begin to understand. If this were simply a Serbia and Kosovo issue, it would be far less problematic. This escapade is threatening the core of the NATO alliance and has the potential to spark wider conflict in the region. Is that what you want?"

"Steve, I told you what I want. Your perceived ramifications are not my concern. They are yours. Again. I appreciate your offer, but I must decline. Please give my best wishes to the President." Nikola hung up the phone, failing to wait for Steve's response.

Steve looked down at the desk speakerphone and heard the line go dead. He looked up across the table, into the eyes of the President, who'd been listening to the conversation.

"Well, that's unfortunate," the President muttered.

"Sir, I can try again."

"No. There's little use. Steve, can you leave me for a minute? I'd like to collect my thoughts."

"Yes, sir. Right away." Steve departed the Oval Office. The President stood, staring out the window into the Rose Garden.

Silently, he prayed to God for a way out of this mess.

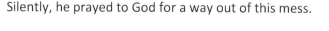

Back in Belgrade, Nikola was writing a text message in Serbian.

*Just heard from the White House. This was their message...*
*'Please stop. You are tearing apart the NATO alliance.'*
*It is just as you wished.*

The message was received on President Sokol's phone. He smiled and said aloud, "Vladimir will be pleased." Without delay, he forwarded the message. For years, Russia's key objective in Europe had been to undermine and erode the NATO alliance. Nikola's plan clearly had unintended beneficial aspects for Russia as well.

**\* \* \* \* \* \* \* \* \* \* \* \* \* \* \* \* \* \* \* \* \* \* \* \* \* \* \* \* \* \* \* \* \* \* \* \* \***

The Chairman's motorcade slowed to a full stop in front of the Marine Corps Memorial. It was early evening, and the lights of the memorial filled the sky as they reflected off the men who bravely climbed Mount Suribachi on Iwo Jima to hoist the American flag. It was stunning, and a favorite of many tourists to D.C., especially current and former Marines. Tonight, however, was bitterly cold, with only a smattering of onlookers.

Admiral Hershey exited his vehicle and walked towards the monument. He quickly spotted Andrew. He was facing the memorial, looking up at it. Admiral Hershey approached him slowly from behind, stopping roughly ten yards alongside him. The two were both looking up at the beauty of the sculpture.

"It's an amazing sight, isn't it, Admiral?" Andrew knew his guest had arrived. The flashing red and blue lights of the motorcade gave it away. As he spoke, his warm breath condensed against the cold air.

"Yes. Yes, it is, Mr. Denney. Look, I am a very busy man, and

I can tell you, this is highly irregular. What can I do for you?"

Andrew Denney looked down at the ground with a slight grin of exasperation. "Sir, frankly, I don't think you can do much for me. Perhaps the better question is, what can I do for you?"

Admiral Hershey was confused. "Please. Humor me and explain."

"Well, if my logic is correct, you are in command of the world's greatest military, and yet you can do nothing to stop the Balkans from devolving into war. To me, that sounds like quite the dilemma."

"Mr. Denney. You are only partially correct. I advise the President. He commands them. I do not decide where and with whom we engage in battle."

"True. Our laws deny you that ability. That falls on our elected officials. But as I have mentioned in the information I shared, that decision maker has been compromised."

Admiral Hershey walked closer to Andrew. They were now standing face to face. "Mr. Denney, are you in any way suggesting we surface the notion our President is unfit to lead?"

"Heavens, no," Andrew laughed. "Even if I thought he was unfit, any 25th Amendment vote would take months, if not years. The Balkans do not have that kind of time." Andrew paused, then continued again. "Frankly, all of Kosovo might again be speaking Serbian before that vote." He smiled at his own joke.

"OK. What do you suggest?"

"Sir, you are the Chairman of the Joint Chiefs. You occupy the head of the highest non-political office in the military. I've shown you why the President refuses to act in Kosovo. I am hoping you can find a way to, shall we say, 'manage' that directive."

The Admiral was stunned. "Mr. Denney. You've done nothing of the sort. Your information was interesting, but far from compelling."

Over the next half hour, Andrew Denney shared everything. He shared his son's cell phone. He shared his conversation with Smitty, who Chairman Hershey held in high regards ever since he stood up and exposed Nissassa. By the time Andrew finished, there was little doubt left in the Admiral's mind. That said, he was still just an admiral. "Sir, I serve at the pleasure of the President. Civilian control of our military is the bedrock of our constitution. I have no intention of starting a coup, nor do I have any intention to disobey orders from my leaders."

"Admiral, I understand your plight. I do. But thousands of Kosovars and Serbians will be killed in the next month. You face a far greater ethical dilemma than your oath, one that I personally could not stomach."

"I respectfully disagree. The dilemma is not my burden to bear. It is that of the President."

"OK, Admiral. Let me ask you this. If the President were not currently being blackmailed, do you believe he would have remained idle through this Serbian build up?" Andrew's question stung. "If your answer is 'no,' and you are the only one in the chain of command who both knows of the extortion and does nothing, upon whom does the actual burden fall?"

Admiral Hershey digested Andrew's comments as if they were a bitter pill. "I'm not saying I agree with you, but I take your point. I need to speak with the Secretary of Defense about this."

"That would be foolish. The Secretary of Defense is a politically appointed position. His loyalties are to the President just like every secretary before him." Andrew was correct. Secretary Gerzema had been a U.S. senator, serving in the shadow of the President for years. Both being congressmen, then senators, but the President leading the way. During the last primary election, Secretary of Defense Gerzema ran against the President but dropped out after someone leaked information that he'd had an affair while married to his first wife years ago. While the leak was never identified, Secretary Gerzema always presumed it was the President's political campaign. Such was the way of U.S. politics.

Andrew continued. "Let me ask you. In your meetings with the President regarding Serbia, how much push back have you seen from Secretary Gerzema? If the answer is little to none, do you have any faith that bringing this information to him will change his position?"

Admiral Hershey was frustrated with Andrew. Not because of his arrogant nature, but because he was right. "Mr. Denney, let me ask you. What do you care of this?"

"Oh, Admiral. I care greatly. To begin with, the man who's blackmailing the President is who I believe drove my son to kill himself. Don may have pulled the trigger, but I know he killed my son. That man led Don down the path, then left him alone in a dark place with no options. Secondly," Andrew began to choke up a bit, "This was the highest award my son received." Andrew lifted his hand and opened his palm. In it was a Silver Star with a 'V' device for combat valor. "He was awarded this fighting for the freedom of Kosovo. As long as Kosovo remains free, this medal means something to me, and I know my son's sacrifices were not in vain. Should that country cease to exist, to me, so does the meaning of this medal."

"Mr. Denney, even if I wanted to send forces to Kosovo, I never could. The oversight in the Office of Secretary of Defense and other safeguards in place would expose any and all efforts I could undertake."

"Maybe. You can't send in forces. But you are a wise man. And I'm sure options exist. Nissassa, the private mercenary group my son worked for, didn't just 'hatch' out of thin air. Look, I know you and I see things differently about Nissassa, my son's company. I am not here to argue their merits or their faults. While Nissassa no longer exists, one of their previous employees who designed and ran operations remains a free citizen. To be blunt, you know him. Smitty. Mark Smith, a former SEAL. I just spoke to him and he shared what he knows of Katarina and Buck." It was true. Smitty was the one who exposed Nissassa to the Admiral. "I'm sure as a naval officer, the thoughts of mercenaries and mutinies are taboo lore, but the world has modernized. Many nations are already using such private firms, with success. I likely need not tell you about all the Russian mercenary companies."

There was little chance Admiral Hershey was going to agree to sponsoring a mercenary effort at that time and place.

Andrew had made his pitch. "Admiral. For our nation, I pray our Lord gives you the guidance you need." Andrew didn't turn to shake the Admiral's hand. Instead, he walked up to the base of the Marine Corps Memorial and placed Don's Silver Star on the ground next to some flowers left earlier by another admiring tourist. Then, he sauntered down the hill towards the Potomac. Admiral Hershey watched. Andrew walked for roughly fifteen minutes, strolling along the riverbank on the walking path. No vehicle in sight. He was a man with nothing but time; a rarity in D.C.

## *Chapter Forty-One*
# Forward, March

The sunrise over Serbia was stunning. It was the 1$^{st}$ of May, a national holiday celebrated across most European nations as 'May Day,' in honor of laborers. Serbians were enjoying their morning coffees and breakfasts with family when the news interrupted their normal broadcasts.

Local TV channels displayed video of Serbian military vehicles rolling out of garrisons from multiple installations, all of them heading south. The vehicles did not travel on highways, but rather drove in small unit columns along local country roads, through village after village.

As news spread, Serbians stood in front of their houses, watching the roads, hoping to see their military in action. Horribly kept secrets about the mobilization flew across the communities and within an hour, the routes for each convoy were widely known. As Serbians heard the vehicles approaching, they rushed out onto the streets to meet and greet them, as if these were some sort of pop-up parades, cheering when the soldiers drove past. The news cycle fed upon itself. The original story of vehicles on the move morphed into a story about the crowds. More news spread across Serbia and as the columns traveled further south, the size and scope of the crowds crescendoed into near mobs. It was exactly the scene President Sokol desired. He watched the TV and thought, *'Never question Serbia's mastery of strategic messaging and owning the narrative,'* a lesson they'd learned well from their instructor, Russia.

Serbian news did not remain local for long. Soon, it was broadcast across the Balkans, Europe and the rest of the world. National capitals energized, defense ministries buzzed, and NATO Headquarters in Brussels called an emergency meeting. There were a few problems, however. Many ambassadors were away for the holiday, called back for the emergency session. Once the meeting started, one attendee all the NATO

Ambassadors wanted to hear from failed to show.

While Serbia is not a NATO ally, it has been a 'partner for peace' for years, and thus provides a liaison diplomatic officer for coordination. That liaison officer's seat, however, remained empty through the meeting. In fact, he never even showed up to the headquarters that day. It was, after all, a national holiday, which always served as a perfect diplomatic excuse.

Beyond NATO Headquarters, Prime Ministers and Presidents from across Europe were forced to work, summoning Serbian Ambassadors to explain their nation's ongoing military actions. However, all the Serbian embassies were closed, in observance of May Day. Again, it was a convenient excuse, and each Serbian Ambassador had been given explicit instructions to turn off their phone for the holiday, enjoy the time off and take no official meetings. Days ago, that cable with orders from Belgrade seemed odd. Given the morning news, every Serbian Ambassador around the globe now understood, smiled, and inhaled their cigarettes, while tucked away into local watering holes scattered around the continent.

At Kosovo's Camp Film City, NATO KFOR Headquarters, Major General Torres called a no-notice meeting with his staff. Even that was challenging. The meeting evolved into a finger pointing contest. Every subordinate commander from different nations looked to the general for answers, as he looked to them for information. His worst fears would soon be validated as an 'unofficial' notification made its way to his office. Other nations would begin to pull their forces out. The next nation to depart was Greece. It was a fairly easy departure for that nation, as their drive home would only be a few hours through North Macedonia, then onto Greek soil. The Greek departure from KFOR would set off similar warning bells, whistles and alarms that the Austrian departure did, but in the end, diplomatic channels could neither stop the departure nor take any substantive actions to fix the problem.

After holding his meeting at NATO KFOR Headquarters, Major General Torres picked up his 'red' phone. It was a phone that had only two connections. His and the other in the office of the Serbian Chief of Defense. The phone rang and after nearly a minute, the phone was answered by Lieutenant General Peter Bojović.

"Major General Torres, good morning to you and happy May Day."

"Yes, good morning, Lieutenant General Bojović. I presume you've seen the news today. It appears your military is on the move."

"Oh. Yes. That. It is nothing. I assure you. Our President asked if we could drive some of our vehicles out of the garrison through some cities. Think of it like... a military parade."

"Peter, I'd love to think of your military movement as a parade, but most parades use all the cardinal directions on a compass. All your parades are headed south. And you've spent the past few weeks training and fortifying your stockades. I don't believe those would be required events for a parade."

"You are correct. But you are misunderstanding. It is springtime, and our soldiers, like many other nations, grew fat in the winter. The recent pleasant weather provided an opportunity to help them get in better shape. As for my supplies, I was fortunate our government found some money and we could replenish many of the things we've needed for a long time. As a fellow general, I am sure you can appreciate that."

General Torres was frustrated. All Lieutenant General Bojović's answers were rational but were clearly lies. All possessed obvious undertones of deception. It was, however, pointless to press him. As the discussion drew to an end, both generals agreed to keep in contact. Major General Torres reiterated his concern and Lieutenant General Bojović again restated there was no cause for alarm.

As they hung up, General Torres lamented the discussion. *'What did he expect? Was Peter just going to come out and tell him he was preparing for an invasion?'*

\*\*\*\*\*\*\*\*\*\*\*\*\*\*\*\*\*\*\*\*\*\*\*\*\*\*\*\*\*\*\*\*\*\*\*\*\*\*\*\*\*\*

Curt and Allison awoke to the sound of Buck singing in the kitchen. Loudly.

Curt rolled over in bed, facing Allison. "Man, I love that guy. But he's gotta go."

"I love him, too. And I agree. Hey, doesn't he have a medical appointment today?"

"Yeah. That reminds me, we've gotta go." Curt jumped out of bed and made his way to the kitchen. Naked.

"Good morning, Buck."

Buck turned around to offer his morning greeting, "Good mor... Holy hell! Dude! Why the fuck are you naked in your kitchen!? Put some clothes on!"

"Buck! Why are you singing in my kitchen? I'll make you a deal. You stop singing in the morning and I'll stop being naked... in my own kitchen."

"Deal, boss. But if this is some sort of Adam and Eve thing, when does Eve come out naked?"

Allison overheard the comment from the hallway. "Buck! Keep dreaming, big guy."

Buck and Curt smiled as Curt threw on a pair of running shorts and grabbed coffee. "Let's get ready to go to the hospital. You've got some important tests."

"Ready when you are, Adam." Buck laughed aloud at his ridiculously stupid joke.

In the hospital, Buck was subjected to myriad tests for his head as well as a few X-rays of his legs. Everything was healing nicely. The only question Buck kept asking was when he could be medically cleared to fly again. It was his true passion, and he missed it dearly. Unfortunately, today would not be that day, but luckily for him, one of his leg casts would be removed, and he'd be given an air cast. The other leg had suffered a compound fracture and would need longer to heal.

After the medical tests, Curt treated Buck to a meal at one of his favorite places to eat in downtown Chicago, the Serbian Village Restaurant. It was renowned for having some of the best meats and authentic Serbian cuisine. For carnivores, Balkan food was tailor made. In most parts, it was the land vegetables forgot. Buck and Curt pulled up chairs at the bar and ordered some beers.

"Hey, thanks for going with me to the hospital and caring for me while I've been laid up."

"No worries, buddy. It's not like I'm missing work." Curt took a swig of beer. The comment was not offered as a joke, nor did Buck take it that way.

"Yeah. Hey, any news on your medical review? Did they indicate when you may be reinstated?"

"Buck, I don't think I'm going back into medical practice."

"Whoa, boss. What? You love taking care of people. What gives?"

"Buck, did you notice anything in the hospital? Most of the staff ignored me. They looked the other way. They made physical efforts to avoid me, so they didn't have to talk to me. I may as well be a leper in that place."

Buck hadn't noticed, but in retrospect, he realized Curt was correct. It was his place of work, yet few actually spoke with him. It was quite depressing.

Two elderly gentlemen joined them at the bar. Buck looked up at the TV, hoping to change the subject. "Hey, looks like Serbia is gearing up for a party."

Curt looked up, too. "Yeah, the existence of Kosovo will be short-lived if Belgrade has its way."

One of the elderly men spoke. "They ain't gonna do nothing. Sokol is a coward and a coke head. I grew up in Yugoslavia and left under a miserable life of communism."

The other gentleman next to him just nodded his head and drank his beer.

"Wow. What part of Yugoslavia did you live in?" Curt asked.

"Novi Sad. Name's Milos." the gentleman said. He stuck out

his hand. "My buddy's name is Zoran. Don't mind him. He's always grumpy."

Curt shook his hand, "Hey Milos, I'm Curt, this is Buck."

"Nice to meet ya." He raised his glass, and they toasted together. Before anyone drank, Buck stopped him. "Hey! Don't we have to look each other in the eye?"

Curt was puzzled and Milos grinned. "Buck, have you been to Serbia?" Milos asked.

"Briefly, but I also dated a chick from there."

"Superstitions are things of legend in Serbia. I don't believe in them, one of the reasons I live in the U.S. You dated a Serbian chick? Wow. You're brave. They're ruthless."

Curt slowly turned towards Buck with a fat smirk on his face. Buck raised his hand and flipped Curt the bird.

Curt turned back towards Milos. "They're really that superstitious still?"

"Oh yes. Here in the U.S. if a black cat crosses your path, it's bad luck. In Serbia, just seeing a black cat is bad luck." Milos paused and then began to laugh. "I remember one time, my mom scrubbed the floor for two days straight after my grandmother, her mother-in-law, came to visit."

"Why? Did your grandmother spill something?"

"No. Serbians believe that if you scrub the floor after an unwanted guest, they'll never return. It was her hope to never see my grandmother again." They laughed, loudly.

"Mind if I ask what religion you are?" Curt inquired.

"No issues. Serbian Orthodox. Why?"

"I've seen many of your churches here in Chicago and in Northwest Indiana. They are stunningly beautiful."

"Yes. Our churches are beautiful, and we may believe in different ways than American Christians, but we all believe in God. And that's good."

Buck had felt somewhat left out of the conversation, and in an abrupt if not rude way, he said, "Hey, if Serbians are superstitious, do they also believe in ghosts?"

Both Curt and Milos turned and looked at him. It was a strange question indeed. "Excuse my friend. He's about as loveable as a bear, but at times shares the same intellectual capacity."

Buck didn't argue.

"It's no problem. Yes, kind of. To Serbians, it's more about vampires. That and superstitions."

Curt wanted to change the subject back to something substantive. "Milos, why do you think the current force buildup is a bluff by President Sokol?"

"Simple answer. Sokol was the spokesperson or something like that under Milosevic during the war. And if you recall, Milosevic was the one the U.S. and NATO destroyed in 1999. Sokol knows quite well what will happen if he goes into Kosovo and picks a war with the west. He will suffer the same fate as Milosevic, who died in jail. It's all part of a grand campaign to continue to get Serbians to vote for him. Just look." Milos pointed at the TV. "Look at the Serbians greeting the soldiers in the streets, waving flags, kissing them on the cheek. Hell, you'd think Serbia already won the damn war."

Curt sensed Milos was getting a bit irritated. "Do you miss Serbia?"

"I miss the people. Serbians are some of the greatest people on the earth. They are fun. They love life. They care for one and another. Sure, perhaps they hold grudges longer than others, but that can be said of other nations, too. Our food is amazing. And if a Serb makes a promise, you can bet your life he will keep it."

Zoran again nodded and grumbled something in agreement as he took another swig of beer. As the four watched more of the news from Serbia, the door of the restaurant was opened by a family coming to eat. As they entered, the last in failed to close the door. Zoran leaned back from the bar and yelled, "Promaja! Promaja!"

Milos just started laughing. "Ignore my friend. It seems he may have brought some superstitions with him. 'Promaja' is the Serbian word for 'cold wind.' There is a belief that a draft or chilly draft will cause illness if not death. Anytime someone leaves the bar door open, he begins his rant." The three chuckled at the old man. Zoran just nodded and drank his beer.

Milos kept looking up at the TV. "It breaks my heart. It really does. Whenever Sokol's poll numbers are low, he ratchets up the war rhetoric with Kosovo or other neighbors. As soon as he does, my fellow countrymen rally to his side, forgetting they are hungry, thirsty and poor or worse, willing to suffer in such poverty for the nation's greater good. It's the same old routine."

"I'm sorry. It must be tough. But didn't President Sokol and Russian operatives try to instigate a coup in Montenegro a few years ago?" Curt asked. "That's far from just hot wind and rhetoric."

"Yes. And who suffered because of it? The Serbian people. Serbians in the Balkans may be blindly loyal to Sokol, but make no mistake, they are not blind to everything. They see the economic advances in Croatia, Slovenia, and Montenegro, all neighbors of Serbia and at one time unified with Serbia under Yugoslavia. Many Serbians, however, don't really see Yugoslavia as a former communist conglomeration of regions. In their mind, Yugoslavia was a Serbian Empire. As the empire crumbled and nations broke away, many believed it was just a matter of time for those nations to eventually come crawling back. Not only did that not happen, but now the neighboring countries are prospering, they are in NATO, and some are in the European Union. Citizens in those nations have more opportunity and a better quality of life than Serbians. Frustrated, Serbians see this, but their anger and resentment are the underlying reasons that they refuse to even consider joining NATO. In some crazy world, they believe they'll get revenge for the 1999 bombing campaign. Until then, they'll take few, if any, steps to join the European Union or NATO because they feel they should be accepted as they are."

"They sound like they are very proud people." Curt said.

"They are. And to a degree, they have a right to be. Serbians have a rich heritage. But some things they do still make me shake my head. For example, every June, dozens of Serbians, most of them members of the Night Wolves motorcycle group, ride south into Kosovo to a place just two miles north of Pristina. At that location, they celebrate the Battle of Kosovo from the year 1389, where Serbians fought against the Ottomans."

Buck seemed puzzled. "Milos, that's not strange. Every nation has war memorials to celebrate their victories in battle."

"Yes, Buck. But in this battle, the Serbians were crushed by the Ottomans. They celebrate a loss."

"OK, yeah. That's kinda strange."

"Maybe to you, but not to them. It's been decades since the bombing of Belgrade in 1999. It wasn't until recently that the government began to rebuild the Ministry of Defense. They just left it there as a symbol. Daily, Serbians would drive by and see the massive bombed out sections of the building. Shattered windows, twisted rebar, massive damage. It was crazy."

"A symbol of what? That building had more holes in it than Swiss cheese by the end of the war." Curt said.

"True, but you miss the point. The narrative in Belgrade was always that the West was coming to defeat the nation. While we all know that's utter nonsense, Serbians in Serbia believe it. In their mind, Serbia won the war. The nation didn't fall to the aggressors. That building was a symbol of Serbia holding off the aggressors." They all took another drink of beer and the pause in the conversation offered a chance for the waitress to serve their food. It was fabulous.

As Curt and Buck settled their bill, Curt reached out his hand. "Milos, it was a pleasure sharing lunch with you and Zoran. Thanks for your insights today. It was absolutely interesting."

"Anytime." Milos shook his hand, and Buck's hand, then he said, "Go Cubs!" Zoran again grunted something in support. Buck and Curt responded in unison, "Go Cubs!" and walked out into the street.

"Man, that's some weird stuff. Celebrating a war loss?" Buck said.

"Eh. We have a memorial to Vietnam and one for Pearl Harbor. It's not the strangest shit I've seen in cultures. It's hard to judge people unless you walk in their shoes. Most places I've been, the people are truly great. It's shitty leaders and wealthy assholes that tend to ruin it."

"True." Buck said. They just kept walking.

\*\*\*\*\*\*\*\*\*\*\*\*\*\*\*\*\*\*\*\*\*\*\*\*\*\*\*\*\*\*\*\*\*\*\*\*\*\*\*\*

In the Pentagon, Chairman Hershey and other flag officers were fielding calls from their colleagues and counterparts in allied nations. Intel reports were one thing, but when the tanks and armored personnel carriers are moving on international news, it's a whole different ballgame. The Greek departure from NATO KFOR was alarming. U.S. leaders in both the Defense and State Departments were concerned more nations would follow. Chairman Hershey left his office and walked into the Secretary of Defense's office.

"Mr. Secretary. We need to talk."

"Yes, I presumed you'd come by, and before you start, let's remind ourselves of the President's intent."

"Sir, I am well aware of the President's intent. It's that very intent that has us in the position we are currently in, quite frankly." Admiral Hershey did not mince words.

"OK. What's on your mind?"

"Mr. Secretary, I do not wish to disrupt Secretary Baker's diplomatic efforts, but can we at least put some of our U.S. based units on alert? Current spin up time for most units is over three days. I'd like to put some units on a 48-hour or even a 24-hour tether. It would all be done quietly, and there will be no movement of forces or supplies without your express approval."

Secretary Gerzema thought about it for a while. He realized he had to find a way to calm down Chairman Hershey, and this seemed like an easy do. Putting units on alert did not overtly disobey the President. He was OK with it. "Admiral, yes. Please put the units of your choosing on a 48-hour alert posture, but the alert posture is to be classified SECRET, and not even one can of bean soup moves towards Europe without my approval."

"Thank you, sir. But you realize, we have ongoing

commitments to our European allies. We have cargo flights in and out of Europe daily. Should we continue those or turn them off? I would offer, if we turn them off, we would make a bad situation worse."

"Yes, you're right. Cargo aircraft that are undertaking pre-planned missions can continue to transit in and out of Europe."

"Thanks, Mr. Secretary. I appreciate your time." Admiral Hershey walked away and returned to his office. As he walked in, he told his aide, "Get me Jack Donegan on the line. Now."

A few minutes passed and Congressman Donegan was on the phone, being patched into Chairman Hershey's office.

"Jack. Squirts here."

"Yes, Admiral. What's up?" Jack was surprised. He rarely received calls from Chairman Hershey.

"Nothing. And that's the problem."

"I see. What can I do for you, then?"

"That guy you brought me about the Iranian assassination attempt? Do you still have his contact?"

"Smitty? Sure. But why?"

"It's better if you don't ask. Can you have him in D.C. by tomorrow? I need to talk to him privately."

"I'll do what I can."

"Thanks. Keep me informed."

Admiral Hershey leaned back in his oversized chair. He was about to make a deal with the devil.

## Chapter Forty-Two
# Goliath's David

As the steel mill noise churned in the background, Smitty entered his office just as the phone rang.

"Smitty! Jack here! How are you doing?"

"Jack? Donegan? Shit! Great to hear from ya. I'm great. Trying to get caught back up with work. Hey, not sure if I told you, I have a lead on the chick on Buck's airplane."

"Yeah, that's great. Hey, I got a big favor to ask." Smitty was a bit stunned. Jack clearly should have cared more about Buck. Whatever he was about to ask, it must be extremely important.

"OK. Yeah. What do you got?"

"I need you to fly to D.C. tomorrow."

"Jack, I can't, I'm about two weeks in the hole on vacation days as it is. Trying to square away Curt and Buck nearly cost me my job. There is no chance I am getting off work anytime soon. Maybe we can do it later?"

"Smitty, it's not me asking. Admiral Hershey is requesting to meet you."

"Admiral Hershey? The Chairman of the Joint Chiefs of Staff?"

"Yes. That one." Jack replied.

"Well, fuck. Hey, are you at your desk?"

"Yes. Why?"

"OK, stay there. And tell your staffer to patch through a call from Tommy. Tommy Taylor."

Jack tried to say OK, but before he could, the line went dead. Back at U.S. Steel, Smitty walked into his boss' office. "Hey, Tommy, you got a minute?"

"Sure, Smitty. What's up?"

"I was wondering if you could ring this number. Congressman Jack Donegan is waiting for you to call him."

"Quit busting my balls and get back to work."

"Sir, I'm not joking. Look. I'll dial." Smitty picked up the phone and switched it to the speaker. Tommy watched. Nervously.

"Congressman Donegan's office."

"Yes… um… my name is, uh, Tommy Taylor. Is the congressman expecting my call? This is Tommy Taylor." Tommy was so scared, he said his name twice without realizing it.

"Yes, Mr. Taylor. Please stand by."

He was dumbfounded. "Dude. Who's on the other end of the line? This is some freaking elaborate prank and I'm gonna beat your…."

"Congressman Donegan here. Mr. Taylor, are you there?"

Tommy froze. He'd seen Jack do interviews on TV and the voices matched. If this was a prank, Smitty had gone to some amazing great lengths to make it happen. "Uh, yes Mr. Congressman. Tommy here."

Smitty took the phone from Jack's hand and clicked the speakerphone button. "Hey Jack, you're on speaker phone. Smitty here. I'm wondering if you can relay to Tommy what you just asked me."

With that, Jack explained the situation to Tommy. As the conversation continued, Tommy realized it was not a prank, but absolutely real.

"Yes, Mr. Congressman. Yes. I can spare him for a day."

"Hey Tommy. You were military as well, correct?"

"Yes, sir. I was Navy enlisted. A bunch of sea time. Took an IED in Afghanistan, but we killed the bastards."

"Awesome. Hey, I know you probably hear it a lot, but I want to thank you. Not just for your service, but your sacrifice. Time from your wife, your kids. Missed holidays. And having to endure through some of war's most ugly moments."

Tommy was touched. Yes, he'd heard countless people thank him for his service, but he'd never had one like that.

"Thank you, Congressman. It was my honor."

Jack hung up and Smitty looked at Tommy. "Hey, thanks for letting me go."

"Anytime, but I have a feeling this won't be a one-day trip."

"No, you're probably right."

"Look, I have a deal for you, Smitty."

"Sure, what is it?"  Smitty was excited to learn about this new offer.

Without batting an eye, Tommy said, "You're fired."

"What?!  That's a 'deal?'"  Smitty's excitement just vanished.

"Yes.  Hear me out.  If I fire you, you'll pull unemployment pay for the next few months.  Look, we love you here, but this isn't for you.  I see you in your office sometimes and you may as well be a caged and chained lion.  Go do what you love.  Just find a way to get paid for it after 90 days."

Tommy was right.  Smitty shook his hand, then man-hugged him.  "Thanks, Tommy.  I won't forget this."

"How could ya?  No one ever forgets getting fired.  Just try not to curse me as the asshole boss who shit canned ya."

They both said their goodbyes.  Smitty walked out of U.S. Steel for the last time, but more important things awaited him.

He dialed a number on his phone.  "Curt, guess what?"

"Hmm... You're in a massage parlor and just noticed the masseuse's Adam's apple?"  Curt put the phone on speaker to ensure Buck, in the other room, could hear Smitty's response to his witty comment.

"Ha.  Fuck you.  No.  Jack just called me.  Admiral Hershey wants to meet me tomorrow."

"That's nuts.  Seriously?"

"Yup.  I was wondering if you wanted to tag along?"

"Smitty, I'd love to, but I gotta take care of Buck."

Buck screamed, "I don't need to be cared for like a fucking cripple anymore!  Please, Smitty, take him!"

Allison, who was on the other sofa, then spoke up, "Uh... do I get a say in this?"

Curt looked at both of them.  Without saying a word, Allison, Buck, and Smitty all knew the right place for Curt was to be with

Smitty in D.C. Allison and Buck nodded. Curt turned and said, "Smitty, book two tickets. I'll see you at O'Hare tomorrow."

\*\*\*\*\*\*\*\*\*\*\*\*\*\*\*\*\*\*\*\*\*\*\*\*\*\*\*\*\*\*\*\*\*\*\*\*\*\*\*\*\*

Across the U.S. military, units were being placed on a 48-hour alert window. Army units were quietly mobilizing their gear onto pallets, ready for deployment. Air Force assets were palletizing critical supplies, ready for a movement. Navy ships, already at sea in the Atlantic Ocean, began plotting out courses on charts to move towards the Adriatic Sea, should the orders come down. U.S. EUCOM (United States European Command) Headquarters in Stuttgart, Germany, had planners furiously trying to come up with the best deployment plans due to recently established time constraints. Such events were always a crazy staff war. Each service lead advocated relentlessly that their service's assets must be first into the country. With DoD's limited movement capacity, the fights often became heated. Worth noting, the theater command staffs routinely held peace time planning sessions, which would culminate with the approval of the four-star commander. Those planning sessions thoroughly ironed out lucid and orderly deployment process. Somehow, however, during crisis, nearly every staff officer forgot about the shelved plans (except those that put in the blood, sweat and tears to craft it). If the command wished, these plans easily could serve as a blueprint for any actual operational build up. Rarely was that the case. The staff officers would spend countless hours, each advocating for either land, air, or sea assets. Sleepless nights, high-level meetings… it was chaos. Ironically, in the end, the solution often ended up being roughly 90% similar to the methodically planned out shelved deployment schedule.  Such were the ways of the military.

\*\*\*\*\*\*\*\*\*\*\*\*\*\*\*\*\*\*\*\*\*\*\*\*\*\*\*\*\*\*\*\*\*\*\*\*\*\*\*\*

President Sokol sat on hold for 15 minutes, waiting for the other party to pick up the phone.  Finally, a voice spoke up in Russian.  "Aleksandar, Hello?" It was Vladimir Volkov on the line.

"Hello, Mr. President." Aleksandar responded.

"I see things are progressing well."

"Yes," Sokol replied.  "I have been watching our intelligence reports.  Kosovo is building up their forces south of the Ibar River, approximately 20 kilometers south of the ABL."

"Yes, I am familiar with the Ibar River.  I would not worry too much.  Kosovo is in a tough position.  Should they cross north of that river, they would be in violation of U.N. Security Council Resolution 1244.  China, Venezuela, Cuba and I are all ready to call an emergency session of the U.N. Security Council to protest.  I would tend to believe Kosovo's leaders realize this.  They are nearly all alone now.  NATO is dwindling away, and the U.S. is not rushing to their aid.  I hope it is as entertaining for you as it is for me."

"Yes, Mr. President.  It is.  I will keep monitoring the Kosovo Security Force."

"Good.  On another topic, which is a bit more sensitive.  I have decided this operation will be completed solely by your nation.  You will not receive Russian soldiers to assist.  I can send some equipment, but that would be it."

Aleksandar was speechless.  "Sir, that was not our deal.  You had promised at least one brigade."

"Yes, I know.  But Aleksandar, be realistic.  The so-called Kosovo Security Force numbers under 3,000 troops.  They are only trained in humanitarian disaster relief.  Kosovo may be able to get another 2,000 of the former Kosovo Liberation Army.  You have three times that number, you have heavy equipment, and you will be seizing land that is predominately owned by ethnic Serbians, unguarded by Kosovo's Forces. Surely, your military is capable enough for such a task. Not to mention, when Serbia accomplishes this victory on their own, it will again demonstrate the might of Serbia."

Volkov was right. Not only did Serbia have superior numbers and firepower, they also would march into unguarded territory. Per UNSCR 1244, north of the Ibar River was a 'neutral zone' in which Kosovo could not have forces. By the time Serbia crossed the ABL, invading to the south, Kosovo could only muster a few hundred or maybe a thousand soldiers, which would be positioned south of the Ibar River. Further, it would be a significant challenge, both physically and politically, for the KSF to move north across the Ibar River, through predominantly ethnic Serb (albeit Kosovo) inhabited villages. "Yes, Mr. President. I understand. It is unfortunate, but we will continue with the plan alone."

"Aleksandar, you should make a greater effort to choose your words more carefully. You are not alone. You've explained in great detail your anger and frustration about the U.S. and NATO involvement in the Kosovo War. I'm giving you a chance to engage the Albanians in so called Kosovo one on one, with no external assistance from either side, yours or theirs. Should you prevail, and you will, there will be no nation that can protest based on external influence and support."

Again, Volkov was correct. "Yes, Mr. President, I apologize for the words I chose. Russian is not my first language."

"No worries, Aleksandar. Perhaps in a few years." Volkov's comment, said in jest, was not really a joke. Over the decades, Russia had made great strides converting sections of Georgia, Moldova, and Ukraine into Russian Federation 'annexed' territories.

As Sokol digested Volkov's bitter humor, he reflected. Perhaps it actually might be better to NOT have Russian troops bedding down and fighting in Serbia, as they may never leave. "Yes, Mr. President. Perhaps."

"Aleksandar, when do you plan to attack?"

"I've spoken with Chief of Defense General Bojović. He believes we can have forces in place in eight days for the attack. He will establish a makeshift command headquarters at Kopaonik Ski Resort hotel, on our side of the ABL. The ski season is over, and there is ample space for a headquarters and the required space to preposition the multiple brigades."

"Good. I wish you luck. Let's keep in touch. General Bojović has passed along a list of supplies and weaponry to our defense ministry that he requires. I am in the process of approving it. You should have a cargo plane full of gifts within three days."

"Thank you, Mr. President. I appreciate it."

"You are very welcome. Take care, Aleksandar." The President hung up.

\*\*\*\*\*\*\*\*\*\*\*\*\*\*\*\*\*\*\*\*\*\*\*\*\*\*\*\*\*\*\*\*\*\*\*\*\*\*\*\*

In Pristina, things were spiraling into chaos. Protests erupted outside the U.S. Embassy. Ironically, just weeks before, a poll taken among Kosovo residents had showed a 90% approval rating regarding the local Kosovo sentiment towards the U.S. That number fell to 15% in a similar poll taken the day prior. For decades, the Kosovars loved America and Americans. They erected a statue of Bill Clinton, named roads after famous politicians, diplomats and generals. Their gratitude towards the U.S. was unwavering until a week ago. In the Balkans, emotions can change quickly. Love can instantly transition to anger. It was one of the less desirable character traits common to the region.

Inside the Kosovo President's office, the U.S. Ambassador was engaged in a difficult conversation.

"President Gashi, I understand you're concerned about the Serbian build up. Frankly, so is the rest of the world to include the U.S. But, I would ask you to see past that and look at the deal on the table negotiated by Secretary Baker. Kosovo and Serbia have a genuine chance of lasting peace if you would just approve the deal."

President Gashi listened carefully. He paused for a moment,

then responded, "Mr. Ambassador, let's be very clear. For Kosovo to agree to this deal, I need the parliament to approve it. Our parliament is elected by the people. Should parliament members vote to approve this deal now in the face of an impending Serbian invasion, they would all appear weak. None of them would be re-elected. It is not in our nature to back down and run. We do not cower because of threats. If America wants us to sign the agreement, tell Serbia to put their toys away and act like adults. As for this 'concern' you mention, I am not so certain I believe the U.S. is concerned. If they are, it appears they have a strange way of showing it."

The Ambassador had no remaining maneuver space with nothing to offer in the way of hard security for Kosovo. No additional combat aircraft, troops, or equipment, and he was doing everything he could to keep as much of NATO KFOR in Kosovo, which was now dominated by U.S. soldiers. "I can assure you, my counterpart in Belgrade is doing everything he can to encourage President Sokol to return the vehicles and personnel to garrisons. But to be clear, you are doing the same thing Serbia is. General Krasniqi has mobilized and prepared many of your forces for conflict. It is difficult for the U.S. to ask Serbia to de-escalate while you are mirroring their build up."

"Mr. Ambassador, our 'build up' is in response to Serbia. There's no comparison. Forgive us if we don't act like the U.S. and just sit idle, doing nothing." His words rang true, then he continued. "Not to mention, Serbia has tanks and armored personnel carriers. We have armored Humvees and others that are equipped to respond to a humanitarian crisis. The latter were gifts from the U.S. In retrospect, perhaps the U.S. could have done more to prepare the Kosovo Forces for war, rather than disasters." The President paused for effect, then continued. "Mr. Ambassador, I must go. I thank you for your time. I am passing your staff a list of immediate weapons requests I received from General Krasniqi. He has also passed this list onto Defense Attaché Colonel Davis. The vast majority of weapons on there are defensive and designed to stop an invasion or at least mitigate it. Given the current nature of our relationship, I am hopeful these can be here soon. Good day." The President rose as a sign for the Ambassador to leave.

The Ambassador rose as well, taking the list. "Yes. I will forward this to State Department at once. I can make no promises, but I understand why you are making such a request, and I support that." It was interesting verbiage. The Ambassador supported the purpose of the request, not the request itself. He was a well-seasoned diplomat. The two shook hands, and the Ambassador departed.

Across town in the Kosovo Defense Ministry building, Colonel Davis was meeting with Lieutenant General Krasniqi. The discussion was similar to the one in the President's office, but far more military in nature.

"General, I understand your plight, but as of now, there are no plans for the U.S. to engage militarily."

"Mike, that is bullshit. Have you relayed my requests to the Secretary of Defense and to the Chairman of the Joint Chiefs?"

"Yes, General Krasniqi. Daily... sometimes hourly. The Pentagon fully understands the situation. Secretary Gerzema and Admiral Hershey are talking multiple times a day with NATO and other senior leaders throughout Europe. Additionally, they've spoken to their Russian counterparts, encouraging Russia to talk sense into Serbia. You may think the U.S. is doing nothing, but you'd be wrong, general."

The general got up from his sofa and opened the curtains to a window. "I'd be wrong? Please show me what the U.S. is doing." Outside the window stood the newly completed U.S. Embassy Pristina, across the road from the Ministry of Defense. General Krasniqi's point was valid. The embassy was silent. "I see nothing. Do you? In war, talk is nothing. That is what the U.S. is doing. Other than talk, I see nothing."

"General," Colonel Davis took a deep breath. "I've explained what the U.S. is doing. Perhaps I should share what we are not doing. The U.S. has not, nor have they even made mention, that they are evacuating the Embassy. The U.S. has not, nor have they made mention, that they are reducing or withdrawing the U.S. Brigade at Camp Bondsteel assigned to KFOR."

General Krasniqi could sense Colonel Davis' frustration. He knew he was treading on thin ice and had perhaps crossed a line. The U.S. may not be acting as General Krasniqi wished, but should he do anything to permanently burn a bridge, there was no other nation that would help. He'd gotten his point across and backed off. "Yes. Mike. You are right. But at current estimates, there are around 10,000 Serbian forces out of garrison on the move. That is a third of their entire Army."

"Yes, sir. I know. And I will do everything I can to share the U.S. intelligence on those forces that I am allowed to. I must speak with Colonel Barlow. If I learn of anything else, I'll call."

"Thank you, colonel. I remain hopeful your nation wakes up."

"Yes, sir. I am sure you do." Colonel Davis departed the Ministry. That meeting would not rank among his favorite events in his military career.

\*\*\*\*\*\*\*\*\*\*\*\*\*\*\*\*\*\*\*\*\*\*\*\*\*\*\*\*\*\*\*\*\*\*\*\*\*\*\*\*

Empty the day prior, the Kopaonik Ski Resort parking lot was rapidly filling up with Serbian military staff vehicles. As if they were mafia mob bosses, the military officers walked into the hotel lodge demanding to speak with the manager. After a brief exchange of words and a significant amount of cash, a good portion of the lodge would belong to the Serbian army. Conference rooms were converted into command posts, the parking lots were cordoned off to separate military vehicles from the other guests. The lower ski runs were prepared to bed down multiple brigades.

Overlooking the ski lodge was a large white globe that looked like a massive golf ball. Inside of that ball was a gigantic air surveillance radar which provided air coverage for most of southern Serbia and Kosovo. Power and data cables were run up the mountain and plugged directly into the radar. A hard-wired air defense radar would soon be the 'eyes' of the Serbian military. And tied to the 'teeth' of a few SA-6 surface-to-air missile systems. Protecting ground assets from air attack was a key lesson learned in 1999. There'd be no desire to re-learn it again.

A few hours later in the day, Lieutenant General Bojović arrived in his staff car. He walked around the hotel as if he owned it, checking on all the different rooms being established as a headquarters. He was escorted by Major General Dučić, the officer Lieutenant General Bojović handpicked to lead the attack on Kosovo. Major General Dučić was a true-blue collar military officer, burly, a bit of a drinker, and not much for politically correct policies. He was perfect. If there was ever an officer who fell into the category of, 'Break Open in Time of War,' it was Major General Dučić. After their walk, the two sat down for a briefing in which the logistics officer and the operations officer provided detailed information on where the arriving units would bed down. Multiple trees had already been downed to create space for some units already present. Further cutting would be required, but everything was on track. The chart with all the units hung in the hotel's main conference room. It identified not only the pre-positioning of units but also the unit designators, the radio callsigns of the units, and the individual names of the command sections. It would be relentlessly referenced as more and more units piled into the Kopaonik area.

## Chapter Forty-Three
# This Meeting Didn't Happen

Smitty and Curt's plane touched down at Reagan National Airport as scheduled. A gentleman in a black suit and sunglasses stood with a sign, awaiting them. They grabbed their bags and proceeded to a black armored SUV. Inside, there was a well-dressed gentleman with a discrete earpiece and a large radio in the center console. Smitty and Curt got in and the car sped away. In less than 10 minutes, the two were waved onto Fort Myer and then another cordon of security which guarded "Generals Row," a set of houses that the four-star service chiefs occupied along with Chairman Hershey. The vehicle stopped outside the Chairman's house, and the front doors swung open in unison with the front occupants opening the back doors. Smitty and Curt exited. The professional display was impressive.

Standing in front of the house was Admiral Hershey, wearing khaki pants and a Hawaiian shirt. "Boys! It's great to see ya! Come on in and get a drink!"

The two looked at each other, grabbed their bags, and walked into the house. Once inside, they were ushered into the admiral's private study. It was just the three of them. "Gentlemen, give me your phones." The two handed them over and the Admiral took the phones out of the room, walked back in and closed the door.

"Please sit. Thank you for coming."

"Sir, it's an honor, but I confess, I am not sure what you need."

"Smitty, it's good to see you again. Frankly, I don't know either." The Admiral was clearly uncomfortable. "I am sure both of you have seen the news regarding Serbia. Well, it is clear to me and the Secretary of Defense that the President is hell-bent to take no action."

Curt spoke up. "Wow. I would not have seen that coming."

"Yes, neither did I." Admiral Hershey continued. "I have come to learn from a source that the reason for this is the

President is…" the Admiral needed to choose his words carefully, "… he is under, shall we say, 'undue influence' forcing him to take no action."

Smitty and Curt looked at each other. "Is he being blackmailed or something?"

"I didn't say that." It was as close as the two would get the Admiral to confess the fact. "I have tried everything and exhausted every avenue to persuade him, but there is no chance. He's even being pressured by his own party. Hell, one of his closest allies in Congress is from a New York District that gets 80% of its political campaign funding from ethnic Albanians and Kosovars. He's furious, as are his constituents. Bottom line is, the President won't budge."

Smitty spoke up. "Unbelievable. God, our nation's politics suck."

"I won't disagree with that, but there's no time for such a discussion. This issue, though, is why I needed to see you. Smitty, I'd like to talk to you about Nissassa. I want to know. Did you believe you were doing good for the world?"

Smitty was uneasy with the discussion. Through all the fallout, he agreed to plead guilty to a very low charge with only a very loose parole as punishment. "Sir, I admit, at first it made sense. But I realized it was wrong."

"Well, son, I admit, I too, for a long time, have believed it was wrong. But I think I've stumbled into a situation in which it may be the 'least wrong' option of many wrong options."

"Admiral, are you considering some effort to re-energize Nissassa?"

"Hell, no," Admiral Hershey said. "My orders are clear on this. I can take no U.S. military action in Europe beyond current ongoing missions as well as planned air cargo movement. I am curious, though. What would be the smallest size civilian unit you and Curt could lead to thwart an impending invasion?" There it was. It even hurt for the Admiral to suggest. It was insubordination of the highest order. Should he be found out, it wouldn't simply be removal from office. Admiral Hershey was wading into criminal actions according to the Uniformed Code of

Military Justice and possible jail time. He felt a sharp pain in his side from the stress.

Curt had enough. "Admiral, we aren't your guys. Sorry. It's perhaps best we don't ever discuss this conversation any further or ever again."

"Dr. Nover... slow down. I confess, I dislike this idea any more than you. But let's be candid. I have a question for you. If the President was not under influence, do you believe he would take the same course of action on Kosovo?" It was the same rationale Andrew Denney had used.

"No, sir. I don't. The U.S. has spilled too much blood, spent too much treasure and risked too much diplomatic standing for Kosovo."

"Exactly. And if we are the only ones who know of this pressure and do nothing?"

Curt was beginning to understand. Frankly, he wished he didn't know about the President's potential problems. It would just be easier. Now, Curt faced trying to decide which course of action would be the least shitty. "OK, but why not just expose the President? Why not come forward with the evidence?"

"Son, Presidents on both sides of the aisle have been implicated if not impeached for such things. But the political haggling and circus show will take months even if it comes to pass. Hell, Clinton was actually impeached and remained in office. We are about a week away from an invasion. There would be no point. Also, we only have enough evidence to suggest the President's impropriety. If I were to raise the issue, I'd be fired, the President would suffer only minor political damage, and Kosovo would still be invaded."

Smitty was rubbing his chin, thinking. He was not even in the same ethical ballpark as Curt. His mind was already trying to come up with a brilliant way to stop the Serbian attack. "Admiral, I'm in."

Curt swung his head as if it was on a rubber band. "What!? Seriously? Did you not learn anything from Nissassa?"

"Curt, buddy. Yes, I did. But the Admiral's points are correct. There literally is no other option than to let Kosovo fall.

Is that what you want?"

Curt's blood pressure rose. He didn't know how to respond. The ethical dilemma raged in his head. *'How can I condone, and worse, participate in, the very thing that I risked my life to expose as wrong?* Nissassa *was an illegal mercenary organization, yet here I am... potentially doing the same thing. I left the military to stop fighting. And yet here I am again.'* Curt would find no easy answers. "Admiral. I don't know if I can support this, but I'll offer my help to Smitty in trying to craft an operation that has a potential for success."

At that moment, it was the best Admiral Hershey would get. "I appreciate that, son. I do. Trust me, this is just as hard on me mentally as it is for you. There's a car out front. It's yours for the time you're in D.C. Passes for the two of you to get onto Fort McNair are on the dashboard. On that post, there is a small group of National War College students waiting at National Defense University. They are under the impression they are doing a strategic training exercise regarding Special Operations against a massive 'force imbalance.' Anything else you need will be at your disposal. But let's be clear. These are the rules. One, I can give you no military kinetic force structures. Two, conflict and/or killing must be minimal if not erased. And three, the only military assets available are cargo aircraft into and out of theater."

Smitty was in heaven. He was again planning Special Operations missions. "Got it. Hey, Admiral, one last question. Why are you in khakis and a Hawaiian shirt?"

"Because, according to the Fort Myer visitor log, you two are my nephews visiting from out of town. I am trying to cover all my tracks, as I hope you do, too."

The two smiled. Smitty couldn't help himself. "Awe. Thanks Uncle Squirts." Curt tried to stifle his laugh, pivoting his head away.

Admiral Hershey was partially amused, but refused to acknowledge the joke. "Get to fucking work. I pray the two of you can come up with something." With that, they jumped in the car and drove across the Potomac River and into Southeast

D.C. towards Fort McNair.

*****************************************

Evening fell on Kosovo, and as it did, a small convoy of military vehicles staged just outside of Pristina. Unannounced, the Romanian contingency to KFOR was mobilizing for the redeployment home. They would leave without telling anyone. This was not surprising. Romania shared a very long border with Serbia. The last thing Romanian leadership wanted to do was create a scenario where Romanian soldiers fighting to defend Kosovo could be used as leverage to escalate an even greater conflict between Serbia and Romania. The contingent wasn't large, only fifty-four personnel, but the diplomatic signals hurt far worse than the military strength. Another NATO nation was abandoning its commitment. In KFOR, the larger contingents remained. Italy, who held the command position, the U.S., Turkey, and Hungary. Of those, Hungary, like Romania, shared a border with Serbia and should things further escalate, they too would probably pull their forces.

News of the Romanian departure broke quickly in Kosovo before the vehicles had a chance to move. Hundreds of Kosovars rushed to the convoy. Some waved Romanian and NATO flags, begging them to stay. Others, angered by the news, cursed them, threw bottles of water, rocks and other objects at the vehicles. The Kosovo Police did the best they could to hold back the protestors, but deep in their hearts, they were with the protesters. *'What if Serbia invades? Will the Kosovo police still have jobs? Or worse, will they still have their lives?'* The questions had merit, based on some atrocities associated with the conflicts of the 1990s between the two nations.

## Chapter Forty-Four
# Channeling Mao

The Serbian buildup progressed as scheduled. More trees were being cleared, vehicles and forces continued to flow in. Assets were being staged and sleeping quarters for the soldiers were being erected. Only the most senior officers would stay in the ski lodge. There were not enough beds for every soldier, and frankly, it would have cost the Serbian government too much. The Serbian military, while powerful in the region, was far from flush with cash and did not have unlimited resources.

Additional air defense systems were being moved into and around the area. Communications checks between units were underway. Given the size of the force structure and the expected rapid pace they would move into Kosovo, the Serbian military leadership made the decision that wireless VHF/UHF radios would be the primary means of communication. There was no time to run land lines across the rugged terrain, and it would be pointless given the anticipated departure in just days. Plus, there was little need for the secrecy provided by wired communications. The parade of forces mobilizing on May Day eliminated the opportunity for secrecy and surprise.

On Fort McNair, Smitty and Curt pulled into a parking slot just outside the U.S. National War College. The building sat on the waterfront plot of land where the Potomac and Anacostia rivers converged. It was a spectacular building; with all the stature and dignity one would expect from an institution that cranked out the top flag officers for the strongest military the world has ever seen.

Inside, the two were directed into the General Colin Powell Library, where a team of five students waited. They were uncertain as to the day's assignment but pleased it didn't involve another lecture or another 300 pages of reading. All had signed nondisclosure agreements, which was odd, but it mattered little. They all held Top Secret clearances for years.

What was perhaps unfortunate was that in the Pentagon,

many professional and highly strategic planning cells existed in spades. The Air Force had an office called 'Checkmate' with some of the best and brightest. Other services had similar organizations, and the Joint Staff had their operations and planning cell. Any of these would have been exceptional assets to leverage, but under the circumstances, they were all nonstarters. Should the Secretary of Defense get wind of the plan, Admiral Hershey's career would be over. National War College provided the perfect guise of being a 'training event' designed to address a real-world event. The War College was so far removed from the Pentagon and the Office of the Secretary of Defense, no one would ever learn of the task.

Smitty and Curt presented the challenge as laid out by Chairman Hershey (not mentioning he had anything to do with it), and a chart was placed onto a large table. The simple answers were all quickly dispensed, as not possible.

*"Why not simply use air power? The F-16s from Aviano Air Base, Italy, could easily handle this."*

*"Why not load up paratroopers from Camp Ederle, Italy and jump them into northern Kosovo as defense?"*

*"Why not position a naval expeditionary strike group in the Adriatic and fire a few Tomahawk missiles into the Serbian strong holds?"*

All were met with the same answers. "There can be no use of kinetic force."

The team of planners continued to chew on the problem until one officer, Lieutenant Colonel Philip 'Monk' Baylis, looked at the problem and he chomped on an apple and said, "Mao."

The room got quiet, and they all turned towards him. Curt responded, "Excuse me?"

"Mao. Mao Tse Tung. It's perhaps the only way under the ridiculous and, frankly, unrealistic limitations you've placed on us." Monk still believed the effort was an academic drill.

Smitty and Curt had obviously heard of Mao, but they weren't clear as to what Monk was referring. "OK, go on."

"Think about it. In the lead up to the Chinese Revolution, Mao and his merry men were heavily outnumbered and outgunned. Still, his strategy took down an entire government. He and his rag tag units would strike villages at night, raid them and instill fear into the local's minds. Eventually, his efforts drove the Chinese citizens into absolute fear, as they began to question the government's ability to protect them. Next thing you know, boom... a rebellion... or revolution. Tomato, tamahto. In your scenario, it's impossible to attack the Serbian soldiers from a force-on-force construct, but if you find a way to make them wish not to fight, you may have a chance. It's a long shot, no doubt. Clearly, the center of gravity for your best shot at success is the minds of the Serbian foot soldiers."

Smitty and Curt looked at each other. "Excuse me, Lieutenant Colonel Baylis, is it?" They could see his rank and name from his uniform. "What's your first name?" Curt said.

"Friends call me Monk. Monk Baylis." Curt could see from Monk's patches he'd attended the U.S. Air Force Weapons School. It was a school to create the 'best of the best' and the 'instructor's instructor.' Often compared to the Navy's Top Gun, it was clearly an unfair comparison. Top Gun is a six-week program. Weapons School is a six-month program and far more advanced. It remains a common argument between Air Force and Navy. *'This guy probably thinks they'll make a cool movie about that Air Force school someday too,* Curt thought.

"Monk, perhaps you didn't hear me? We can't attack."

"No, sir, that's not what you said. You said you can't kinetically attack. Bombs on skulls or bullets on bones are just a mere few ways to compel others to your will. There are many ways to influence someone. I agree, bullets and bombs tend to have the best and most immediate outcomes, but there are clearly other, shall I say, less violent means. For the past decade, I have studied intelligence through the eyes of information operations. There's a host of assets you can use: cyber warfare, psychological warfare, electronic warfare, etc. Since the U.S. has a metric shit ton of H.E. (high explosive) as well as high-tech assets to deliver them, our military often overlooks and sometimes just ignores other capabilities. In your planning exercise, these types of warfare would work, but I should note, any desire to use them also should include an extreme amount of precise planning."

Smitty was intrigued. "Have you done planning for these kinds of operations?"

"Yes, sir. Numerous times. But to understand how to do this is difficult to explain to someone who's been trained all their lives to break down doors and kill people. Let me try." Monk turned and pointed at one of his classmates and asked Smitty a question. "My classmate over there is hypothetically charging you and you want him to stop. Where would you shoot him?" His classmate wasn't particularly pleased with the question, but played along.

Smitty answered, "Two to the chest, one to the head."

"Right. But not the knee, or forearm, etc. And you know this, because you've been trained. Now, Todd is charging you again. Before he gets within arm's reach and without touching him, shooting him, stabbing him or any form of violence, what would you do to compel him to stop?"

Smitty and Curt looked at each other. "Can I bribe him?" Curt said.

"Sure. But do you know if he's bribable?"

"Can I yell at him?" Smitty asked.

"Sure, but do you even know if he's deaf? My point is, there is perhaps an argument to be made that the U.S. military has become overly reliant on swinging the 'big stick' because, well frankly, it can. There's very little need for finesse in war when a B-52 drops over eighty 500lb bombs. Why should U.S. warfighters try to even appreciate the teachings of Sun Tzu when they have such immense capabilities at their disposal? I always chuckle when someone rattles off Sun's principle of *Know your enemy and know yourself and you shall be victorious in 100 battles.'* Yes, I know *'a 500lb bomb will kill him'* is the usual response. Simply put, we've become exceptional at understanding the physical vulnerabilities of our enemies because we are a nation with the luxury of nearly unlimited kinetic sticks. We suck at understanding them mentally."

Curt and Smitty knew they'd found the right guy.

Monk wasn't smitten or full of himself. He was merely being matter of fact. His last comment sealed it for Curt and Smitty. He said. "I don't know where the quote came from, but I've always found it valuable. *'Only when a mosquito lands on one's testicles do they embrace the notion of solving problems without violence.'* Funny, but true."

They looked at each other and silently nodded. "Monk, can you please take us to your instructor?"

"Sure." Monk walked them out of the library and down the stairs. In one of the small corridors, Monk led them into a small office. It had a desk, probably, but it was hard to tell given the enormous number of books stacked on it.

Monk spoke to the apparently empty office. "Doctor Kuehl. These guys wish to speak with you."

A head popped up from behind the books. "May I help you?"

"Yes. My name is Curt, and this is Mark. We were sent here by the Chairman of the Joint Chiefs to lead a small tabletop training exercise. Is this your student?"

"Hi. I'm Dr. Dan Kuehl. Nice to meet you. Yes! That's Monk. He's one of my best. Did he pull another practical joke? I'm sorry. Monk is sometimes too smart for his own good and..."

"No, sir, it's nothing like that. We'd like to take him for a few days to help us with a project. It is all legitimate and you can reach out to Chairman Hershey's office to verify it."

"No. No need. I heard about the tabletop exercise and was thrilled Monk was considered to take part. Please take him. I will ensure his workload doesn't get too out of hand while he's gone."

"Perfect. Thanks." Smitty turned to Monk. "Dude, get your things and meet us in the car out front."

"Got it." Monk went back to gather his things, then met them in the car. As they drove across the Potomac, Monk would learn that the exercise story was a façade and there truly was a real-world planning effort. Monk called his wife Carrie, and said he'd be delayed. She was the wife of a military officer. She didn't even ask why.

For the next twenty-four hours, the three would not sleep, and craft a plan from the den of the Chairman of the Joint Chief's house. It was far from perfect, but given the limitations, it would be their best shot. Mrs. Hershey kept bringing them cookies and drinks. She had no idea what they were doing, but was elated to have guests in the house. With all the tight security associated around the Chairman's residence, she rarely had visitors.

The next day, Admiral Hershey returned home to his study, prepared for an operational briefing. Monk led the brief, answered all the questions. Chairman Hershey was not overwhelmingly excited about the plan. How could he be? A handful of folks versus nearly one third of the Serbian army? Unfortunately, he also realized it was likely his best shot, and the plan met his intent…. for the most part. There would be more risk required than he'd like, and he'd need to find a way to deploy some assets to theater. But his risk was far less than that which would be undertaken by Curt and Smitty.

"OK. Let's do it," the Admiral said. "Pack your things. The two of you are heading to Pristina. Lieutenant Colonel Baylis, look at me." Admiral Hershey paused. "You will go to Fort Bragg as you briefed, but if you mention a word of this to anyone, so help me God, you will be dining on Thai baboon toe jam through a fucking straw for the rest of your life. Do you understand?"

"Yes, Admiral, got it. But I'm a student at National Defense University right now, so… I'm not sure if that's much of a threat." The order was clear but unnecessary, and Monk's joke clearly pointed that out. He would never talk.

"Admiral, there is one thing. Once we are done with the op, Curt and I have some unfinished business in Serbia to tend to."

The Admiral didn't ask, and under the circumstances, he didn't want to know. "Fine, but if you get caught, you know the rule. None of this was sanctioned by the U.S. I don't know you. You don't know me. Understand?"

They both looked at Chairman Hershey and in unison said, "Yes, sir."

With that, Admiral Hershey ordered his aide to draft

deployment orders that would be needed to support the mission. One would go to Davis Monthan Air Force Base in Arizona and the other to the Air National Guard in Harrisburg, Pennsylvania. Within an hour, the messages were dispatched. Neither unit knew exactly what it would be doing, but they knew their aircraft would be 'wheels up' in less than 48 hours.

\*\*\*\*\*\*\*\*\*\*\*\*\*\*\*\*\*\*\*\*\*\*\*\*\*\*\*\*\*\*\*\*\*\*\*\*\*\*\*

Later that day, Smitty placed a phone call. "Mr. Denney. Smitty here. It looks like I may have an opportunity that will interest you."

"Yes, I'm listening."

"I need a favor...." Smitty continued to explain his request. It was a significant 'asker.' Once he finished, Andrew Denney would agree.

## *Chapter Forty-Five*
# Covering My Six

Curt called back to Allison. It had been over a day since they'd last spoken. "Hey, baby. How are you?"

"Curt! Yeah! Thanks for calling! I miss you! When are you coming home?"

"Well, that's what I'm calling to discuss. Smitty and I have one more night here in D.C., then it looks like we are off on an adventure."

"What? Please tell me you're kidding."

"I wish I were, but I have to do this…. Or, actually, I guess Smitty has to do this, and I can't let him go alone."

"Promise me it won't be dangerous."

"I promise. It will be a walk in the park, but I won't be able to call that much. Hey, baby. For this trip, I really could use your help."

"Sure. Anything, baby. What do you need?"

"Great. So, I gave your number to a guy called 'Monk.' He's going to ask you to push out some news and social media at specific times. Please do it. I realize some of it may not make sense, and the journalist in you will want to investigate the merits of the information, but I beg you. Please, just push it out and try to get others to amplify it."

"Curt, I'll do my best, but can you tell me more? Am I putting my credibility on the line? I've worked really hard to get where I am and gain the trust of my peers. I can't just throw that away."

"I understand that. Can you at least hear him out and consider doing what he asks? He's a brilliant guy. You'd like him."

"OK, baby. I promise to at least listen."

"Sweetheart. I love you. I'll check in again when I can. OK?"

"I love you too, Curt. Sweet dreams."

Back in the Chicago condo, Buck had overheard the phone call and knew just from hearing one side what was going on.

He'd be there to care for Allison. Curt knew it too and was grateful. Curt and Smitty tucked in for the night at the Pentagon City Ritz-Carlton. Their adventure would soon begin.

\*\*\*\*\*\*\*\*\*\*\*\*\*\*\*\*\*\*\*\*\*\*\*\*\*\*\*\*\*\*\*\*\*\*\*\*\*\*\*\*

That night, the Admiral had requested a video teleconference (VTC) with SOCOM Commander, General Glenn Etcher. Both would execute the conference from their private residences, one in D.C. and the other at MacDill Air Force Base near Tampa. Both opened their secure laptops and Admiral Hershey began the protocols to make the connection. It took approximately 30 seconds until the connection was made because of the immense security protocols. General Etcher was sitting at his home office desk in his Air Force uniform.

Admiral Hershey was also at his desk, wearing a golf shirt, with a bottle of whiskey in view of the camera and a glass already poured. Three fingers over ice.

"Admiral Hershey. Sir, are you OK?"

"Glenn, to be honest, I am not sure. Are you alone in your room?"

"Yes, Squirts. Just me. What's up?"

"Glenn, I've tried my damnedest to advise the President of Kosovo. He's not going to take any action."

"I'm aware. I read your readouts. Tough stuff. I agree with your assessment, for what it matters."

"Thanks, Glenn. That means a lot." Admiral Hershey paused. It was so long it was nearly awkward. "Glenn, do you remember back in 2012 when the Benghazi incident happened?"

"Of course, sir."

"Yes… I believe you and I were freshly pinned one star flag officers at the time. We both attended Capstone flag officer school together."

"Yup. That was a great time."

"I remember, specifically, you and I sitting in a hotel bar

during one of the travel events. We may have had a bit more than our share to drink. And during that, we both boasted that if there was anything in our power, those four Americans, to include the Ambassador, would be alive today."

"Admiral, I remember that conversation as if it was yesterday. And I meant what I said."

"Glenn, I was hoping you'd say that." Chairman Hershey took a huge swig of whiskey, downing the glass. "Glenn, what I am about to tell you, I have not told any other military member. Frankly, it could get me fired, and at the end, if you believe that I should be, you'd have every right to take up that action. I am hoping, though, that you not only understand, but support me."

"Sir, I am listening, and I think I know where you're going with this. I'm here for you, admiral."

With that, Admiral Hershey told General Etcher everything. General Etcher didn't think twice. He would support the effort.

"Sir, count me in. I am going to dedicate one officer to this task from my unit. He won't know why he's doing what he's doing, just that he's supporting a mission."

"Glenn, I can't thank you enough. I believe in my heart this is right."

"Sir, so do I. Get some rest. We have work to do." They both signed off. Admiral Hershey poured another full glass of whiskey and drank it in a singular gulp. Rage was growing in him. Insubordination was something he'd never stand for in any of his commands, yet here he was, performing that vile act from the highest military position in the land. Admiral Hershey wound up his arm and threw the glass against his office wall. It smashed into an old photo of him and his classmates from the Naval Academy. Both the glass and picture frame shattered, falling to the ground. While he believed he was making the right decision, he'd struggle with the ethical aspect. It tore at him more than words could describe.

\*\*\*\*\*\*\*\*\*\*\*\*\*\*\*\*\*\*\*\*\*\*\*\*\*\*\*\*\*\*\*\*\*\*\*\*\*\*\*

The next morning, General Etcher walked into his office and

asked his staff to fetch Lieutenant Colonel Rob 'Moose' Smith from the commander's action group (CAG). The general settled in, poured some coffee, and sat at his conference table. Within minutes, Moose knocked at the door, standing there with the general's front office executive officer.

"Moose, Good morning. Come on in." The general looked at his executive officer. "Knocker, no need to be in this one. I'd like this meeting to be four eyes" (a military term for just two people in the meeting). Knocker acknowledged, exited the room and closed the door.

"Moose, sit down. How are you doing?"

"Great, general. Julie and the kids are enjoying Tampa. Things couldn't be better."

"Great. Good to hear. What are you working on right now?"

"Well, sir. The SOCOM Commanders Conference is about a month away and we are pulling together returned invites, tracking RSVPs, arranging hotel rooms, working visas for foreign commanders. The usual stuff."

"OK. I need you to stop that. I have a task for you, and it will be the only thing you work on until I tell you to stop. Do you understand?"

Moose was already salivating. He, like many at SOCOM, had spent most of his career planning and performing combat operations. Now, at the twilight of his career, he was sequestered to a military staff position, anchored to a desk. It was excruciatingly painful. Whatever the general had in mind, it had to be better than arranging a stupid conference. "Yes, sir. You can count on me."

The general pulled out a single piece of paper. It was on SOCOM letterhead and read:

*Memorandum for Record*
*Subject: EC-130 Movement*

*Lieutenant Colonel Robert Smith is authorized to act on my
behalf, making all decisions, to include but not exclude
movement, funding and support for 1xEC-130H and
1xEC0130J. Due to the sensitive nature of this mission, any
and all questions that he cannot answer will be directed to
me personally.*

The letter was signed by General Etcher. "Moose, this is a
critically important mission we are supporting in utter secrecy.
Orders for their movement have been sent to the bases, but
that's it." The general continued to explain the intent for these
aircraft, careful not to explain Curt and Smitty's roles in the
mission. In the special ops world, the full picture of an operation
was known to but a very few for two reasons: First, to protect
the other entities involved in the mission, and secondly to limit
the beatings one would receive, should they be captured.

"Sir, I got it." Moose jumped up from the table and was
ready to go.

"Moose. Again. The chain of command is you to me. There
is no one in between. That is the only copy of the letter I crafted
about this issue. Do not lose it. Finally, I need you to use
delicacy with some offices. That letter does not mean you get to
be a bull in a China shop…. Or a Moose."

"Got it, Boss. I'm on it."

Within hours, Moose had coordinated with SOCOM
accounting. MFP-11 funds (special operations funding) had
been funneled into the units in Arizona and Pennsylvania. In
addition, message traffic was sent, which placed them under
SOCOM authorities. In those messages were clear instructions.
From a classified perspective, each unit would get their
directives once in theater. None of the other squadron officers
or even commanders would know the actual mission.

Their unclassified cover mission was to support ongoing
NATO efforts at identifying illegal immigrants trying to gain

access to Italy via boats in the Adriatic. With that, one EC-130H Compass Call and one EC-130J Commando Solo, each with a full crew plus an additional flight crew for extended operations, prepared for a departure to Aviano Air Base, Italy. Within 24 hours, both aircraft would be airborne with air refueling planned along the way. The trip would take roughly 16 hours. After some rest at Aviano Air Base, they would be ready to operate in a day or so.

## *Chapter Forty-Six*
# Setting the Chess Board

Curt threw on some running clothes and stepped out of his hotel. He'd arose before the sun and had an appointment to keep. The air was cool, and he started his run at a brisk pace, trying to warm up. There was little traffic as he crossed Army Navy Drive, then running under Interstate 395 through a tunnel that connected to the Pentagon's south parking. From there, he ran along the edge of Arlington National Cemetery on his left and the Pentagon on his right. The lights from the Pentagon's 9/11 Memorial shined bright up into the sky. As he passed the Pentagon and traversed over Columbia Pike Road, the lights of the Air Force Memorial lit up its three silver spires as they climbed into the sky. After a few minutes, most lights were behind him, and he was running along the Potomac. The air was crisp, and his legs felt a great burn. The endorphins were flowing. It was times like this he felt the best. Curt turned onto Memorial Bridge, now running straight towards the back of the Lincoln Memorial across the Potomac River. The blending of morning sun and manmade flood lights onto the memorial was magnificent. The Georgetown rowing teams were passing under Memorial Bridge as he ran. Once at the Lincoln Memorial, he turned to the left and continued towards the Vietnam Memorial. There were only a handful of visitors at that early hour and one lone park ranger, observing the tourists. Curt slowed down to a walk once he was close. He pushed the button on his stopwatch, halting his training time. Slowly, he walked along the black stone wall inscribed with 58,281 names. As he walked, he gently dragged his hand over the polished black marble; his fingers bouncing in and out of the carved names. He stopped in front of plate W10 and raised his hand to line 35. Scrolling over, he found the name he was looking for and the subject of his appointment, LCDR EUGENE W NOVER. Curt rested his hand over the name. He paused and looked down at the ground, closing his eyes. He whispered to the wall, "Good to see you again, Grandpaw. I miss ya. Hopefully, I'm still makin' yap round. The only easy day was yesterday." After a few minutes, Curt pushed his body away from the wall, started his stopwatch and continued running, as if re-energized. He'd jog another three miles, along the Reflecting Pond, past the World War II Memorial, by the Tidal Basin and the Jefferson Memorial, then crossing back over the Potomac on the I-395 Bridge leading to the Ritz-Carlton. It was a great start to the day. For the remaining portion until his flight, he and Smitty would do everything they could to learn about Serbia. The terrain, culture, food, drink, fears, dreams, aspirations, history and mindsets of the people he'd be soon engaging.

Roughly 100 miles away from Curt, a single EC-130J Commando Solo in Pennsylvania spun up its engines on the Harrisburg Airfield ramp. Spring flowers had begun to bloom, and the pilots took note that colors were finally back on the ground as the aircraft climbed out on departure. The navigator set a course for Goose Bay, Canada, where they would rendezvous with the first KC-135 tanker. Another KC-135 would meet them off the coast of Scotland. Should anything happen, Goose Bay, Canada and Shannon, Ireland were two of the primary divert airfields. Approximately three hours later in Tucson, an EC-130H Compass Call would follow a similar routine, taking off in the early AM. Their flight path, however, would take them first to Bangor, Maine, where they would refuel on the ground. After refueling, the crew would again take off and also meet a KC-135 over the Atlantic Ocean. The aircraft was equipped with a second flight crew, enabling them to continue through a longer duty day. If the winds were favorable, they would make Aviano Air Base, Italy, in fifteen hours.

Back in the Pentagon, Admiral Hershey had put the wheels in motion, and there was no turning back. In his morning staff huddle, he asked his secretary to cancel his existing lunch plans and reach out to retired Vice Admiral Kraft, the Vice President of technology development at Raytheon. His secretary would do as requested. Chairman Hershey knew the meeting would take place unless Vice Admiral Kraft was either dead or in a coma.

When the Chairman of the Joint Chiefs asked to meet the defense industry, the answer was never, 'no thanks.' Within minutes, lunch was confirmed.

The Admiral made every effort to continue with his normal duties. No matter how much his mind would stray to think about the ongoing operation, he had to maintain a presence and projection that he knew nothing, and everything was business as usual. At the end of the morning huddle, he stopped his vice chairman's before he could leave the room.

"General McKinley, can you stay back for a minute?"

"Certainly, admiral."

The room cleared, and the two were alone. "Pete, look. I'll be blunt. I'm worried about Kosovo. Can you do me a favor? I think I have lost some of my credibility with the West Wing. Can you try to go over there today and see if you can get any traction to craft some sort of, at this point, haphazard response?"

"Admiral, I am completely aligned with you on Kosovo. I'll clear my calendar and see what I can do."

"Great. Pete, I appreciate it. I know it's a big ask. Good luck." General McKinley departed. To a degree, Admiral Hershey was doing everything to craft his alibis.

\*\*\*\*\*\*\*\*\*\*\*\*\*\*\*\*\*\*\*\*\*\*\*\*\*\*\*\*\*\*\*\*\*\*\*\*\*\*\*\*

Around 1000Hrs, there was a knock at the door of the 4th Psychological Operations Group, on Fort Bragg, North Carolina. A unit that is a part of 1st Special Forces Command. As they opened the door, Monk stood there in his U.S. Air Force uniform. The unit's mission was to conduct psychological warfare operations. As part of the 1st Special Forces Command, his visit had been pre-coordinated by Moose. Monk was whisked into the building and a small team awaited his direction. Over the next half hour, Monk would provide extremely specific details as to what was needed. With the massive workload, there was no time to waste.

\*\*\*\*\*\*\*\*\*\*\*\*\*\*\*\*\*\*\*\*\*\*\*\*\*\*\*\*\*\*\*\*\*\*\*\*\*\*\*\*

After a few meetings and 'chopping' on a few staff packages (a military term for reviewing, coordinating, or signing a staff packet), the admiral would be departing for lunch. His secretary pre-coordinated his motorcade and as he departed out the river entrance doors, his vehicles were waiting, passenger door open and security establishing a perimeter.

The vehicles traveled to the Army Navy Country Club, just a mile from the Pentagon. It was a private club, members only, and crawling with military industrial complex folk. The admiral pulled up and retired Vice Admiral Kraft stood waiting for Admiral Hershey. "Squirts! Great to see you! Thanks for the invitation."

Admiral Hershey shook Vice Admiral Kraft's hand, "Aaron, no. Thank you for meeting on such short notice." The two entered the club restaurant and sat down. Lunch was served, and they had engaged in a significant amount of small talk. Well, most of it was small talk, but Aaron couldn't help himself and asked questions about Raytheon projects as well as competitors. Under normal circumstances, such questions would irritate the Chairman to no end, but he had a favor to ask, so he grit his teeth and pleasantly answered.

As dessert was served, Aaron said, "So, Squirts, I'm going to presume you didn't invite me here on a few hours' notice just to catch up. What's up?"

"You're correct, Aaron. I need a favor. I wanted to tell you that I was impressed with your High Energy Laser (HEL) demo last week."

"Great! I'm glad to hear it. We've spent a great deal of time on HEL, and it's already prepped to move into Operational Test and Evaluation from the development stage."

"Well, before you do that. I am wondering if you can release it to the DoD for a few weeks, starting today or tomorrow. We'd like to look at it."

It wasn't unusual for the DoD to inspect future potential weapon systems. It was, however, strange for the Chairman to ask for it to be within 24 hours. Aaron didn't know how to respond. "Uh, Squirts. Yes, we can absolutely let you look at it, but today? Tomorrow? Where is it going, Wright-Patterson? Edwards?" Aaron named a few of the expected testing locations within the military.

"Aaron, look. I can't tell you where it's going, and I can't tell you what it's going to do. My ask is simple. I want your HEL for a week or two, with one technician that will sign a SOCOM NDA."

The last two acronyms gave it away. It was clear Chairman Hershey wanted the vehicle for a Special Operations mission and whatever it was used for, it would never be known to Raytheon. "Admiral, I... Uh. Look, I can't make that decision, and this is going to take time."

"OK. Never mind. This meeting didn't happen." Admiral Hershey stood up and began to leave the room.

"Hey Squirts, wait."

"Wait for what? Buddy, when you were in the Navy, you were fearless. You were one of our best F-18 pilots and flew so hard you bent wings on those damn jets. Now that you're in a suit, you're about as impotent as a eunuch." The admiral paused. "Where are your fucking balls?"

Aaron did not appreciate the dress down, but he also knew it was warranted. "Alright. You can have it tomorrow. One week. I'll give you the lead engineer. Whatever you do, it cannot be attributable to Raytheon."

Admiral Hershey smiled. "Aaron... it felt good, didn't it?" The admiral played his cards perfect. "Can you have it at the Andrews Air Force Base main gate tomorrow by 10AM?"

"Done. But you're buying the fucking meal." They both smiled and shook hands. Admiral Hershey had secured yet another piece of the puzzle.

As Chairman Hershey got into his car, a text message arrived from General Etcher.

*"Moose is your guy. 703-555-0847"*

The admiral immediately dialed the number. "Lieutenant Colonel Smith," the receiving party answered.

"Moose?"

"Yup, who is this?" Moose didn't recognize the voice or phone number.

"Moose, it's Admiral Hershey."

"*Thee* Admiral Hershey??? As in 'The Chairman?'"

"Yes. The same. I understand you are working a special mission for your boss."

"Correct, admiral."

"OK. Have a cargo aircraft on Andrews AFB tomorrow ready to take a payload to Pristina, Kosovo. Cargo is a vehicle the size of a personal passenger SUV and one PAX (Passenger). Got it?"

"Yes, admiral. I'll make it happen."

"Good. Take care." Admiral Hershey hung up.

Moose sat frozen at his desk. He just spoke with the freaking Chairman of the Joint Chiefs of Staff. Such things rarely happened to lieutenant colonels. He jumped up from his desk and marched down to the mobility and air movement section of SOCOM. After a quick discussion and a coordination effort with the Tanker Airlift Control Center (TACC) on Scott Air Force Base, a C-17 crew would be at Andrews and ready to move the HEL and its lead engineer.

As afternoon approached, Smitty and Curt prepared for their flight. The standard commercial flights across the Atlantic from Washington, D.C. all departed in the late afternoon, flying through the night. The two former SOF operators checked in at Dulles with nothing more than a few changes of clothes, most of which they'd just purchased at the Pentagon City Mall. Other items they would require for the mission would be provided upon arrival in Kosovo. They cleared security and customs, then sat in the Austrian Air lounge for 45 minutes. Eventually, their boarding was called. Within an hour, the aircraft would be on its way. The next morning, when they'd land in Vienna, two different EC-130 airframes would be on the Aviano Air Base ramp and their crews would be resting and recovering from the long flight and circadian rhythm issues associated with the time change.

\*\*\*\*\*\*\*\*\*\*\*\*\*\*\*\*\*\*\*\*\*\*\*\*\*\*\*\*\*\*\*\*\*\*\*\*\*\*\*\*

The Italian Ambassador had his orders. At NATO Headquarters in Brussels, he requested an Article 6 meeting of the North Atlantic Council, requiring the presence of all Ambassadors and the SecGen. This obsolete clause, following the well-known Article 5 'Mutual Defense' clause, was included back in 1949 for those with extra-territorial holdings. Italy was leveraging the UK's and France's reliance on Article 6 to ensure the Italian troops in Kosovo, supporting the KFOR mission, would be protected by the ENTIRE alliance. In actuality, it was a bogus excuse for a meeting, but had the desired effect, a mandatory high-level meeting.

Other nations feared Italy would consider relinquishing the command of KFOR and withdrawing their forces in the next 48 hours. Rumor swirled. Lawyers and analysts at NATO Headquarters realized this could be the pressure release valve that eliminated KFOR... or even worse, the entire NATO alliance.

## Chapter Forty-Seven
# Time Waits for No One

"General Bojović! Good morning, sir," a Serbian voice boomed over a loudspeaker.

"Good morning, Major General Dučić. Go ahead."

"Sir, regarding the pre-strike force posture. Currently, we have 70% of the required forces in place. We hope to have all assets in the vicinity over the next 48 hours. Once everything is in position, we will hold a mass briefing, tabletop exercise, and then, on your order, commence the operation. I believe we will be ready in three days."

The general digested the information. "And the soldiers. Are they ready to fight? What are you having them do while waiting for the operation? They must not get soft."

"No, sir. We are running them, conducting small unit drills and pushing hard on tactical communications and connectivity. As you directed, we have shut down wireless cellular 3g, 4g and other networks in the area. We know all too well soldiers can compromise efforts on the internet and social medial, jeopardizing the mission. The soldiers are not happy about this, but such is far easier to deal with than the alternative." Major General Dučić was correct. "The lessons learned from our Russian comrades about soldiers posting information are well understood. And there is perhaps no greater danger than an idle soldier with access to social media."

"Good. Please keep me informed."

\*\*\*\*\*\*\*\*\*\*\*\*\*\*\*\*\*\*\*\*\*\*\*\*\*\*\*\*\*\*\*\*\*\*\*\*\*\*

The 31st Mission Support Group on Aviano Air Base, Italy, worked overtime to bed down the two EC-130s that arrived overnight. They would secure hotel rooms for all the aircrew as well as fuel and service the aircraft. The 31st Security Forces Squadron would set up a cordon around the aircraft with a manned entry control point. No one other than aircrew were to enter or exit the cordon except for those that were specifically under aircrew escort.

As the base began to come alive for the workday, one aircrew member from the EC-130J Commando Solo entered the 31st Operations Group Sensitive Compartmented Information Facility, a top-secret vault, and established communications with both his home unit and the 4th Psychological Operations Group. Once communications were established, the aircrew member returned to the hotel and would try to get a bit more sleep.

Further south in Pristina, Curt and Smitty landed and processed through customs. As they exited the controlled area of the Adem Jashari airport, Colonel Mike Davis called out, recognizing Smitty. "Hey, Smitty! Smitty!"

Curt turned towards Smitty. "You know him?"

"Yeah, he's the defense attaché."

"Colonel... Uh..." Smitty had forgotten his name.

"Davis. No worries. How was your flight?"

"Good. How did you know we were coming?" Curt was confused. If this was to be a covert operation, it appeared more and more were aware of it.

"I received a phone call from a guy named Moose at SOCOM. I was asked, well, ordered to take the two of you to Camp Bondsteel and outfit you with specific gear. As I was instructed by Moose, I have told no one about your arrival, and I am driving alone, even ditching my driver."

Colonel Davis' words were a bit more reassuring to Curt... and Smitty. They entered his car and began driving. As with normal covert operations, there were very little communications in the vehicle.

The defense attaché's up armored white Land Cruiser with diplomatic plates entered the Bondsteel main entry control point. As the vehicle flashed it's headlights, both guard arm gates arose in unison and the guards lowered their weapons. Smitty and Curt tilted their heads down with baseball caps on, realizing there were likely Closed-Circuit TV cameras at the gate. They didn't wish to be identified

Colonel Davis drove onto the base and pulled into what

appeared to be an abandoned shack. He parked the vehicle, turned off the engine and said, "OK, wait here."

Mike ran into the building and after five minutes, an Army major walked out of the facility, looking down and walking the other direction. A minute later, Mike waved the two into the building. Inside, the room was clean, and a matching set of gear greeted the two former SOF operatives. Curt and Smitty were both former SEALS, but they'd appreciate what Colonel Davis, an Air Force Officer had assembled with the help of an Army logistician. The two picked up two sets of chest rigs with plate carriers and all the toys. It was obvious that Mike had either Amazon'ed some Cryo gear or worked with Special Operations Command Europe to weasel some good stuff. The PVS-31A night vision googles were as modern as the two could expect, seeing as they were not assigned to tier one units or even back in their old SOF outfits. The two Glock 19s reminded them of their old rigs and were equipped with Trijicon sights, index finger-activated visible lasers, and were neatly packed in Safariland holsters. While the drop leg version would not be helpful for this mission, Curt and Smitty quickly tucked the concealed holster into their waistbands.

Next, the two picked up their M4 carbines. While both men recalled the original SOPMOD heavy barrel version, the new models acquired by Mike were impressive, providing ample room for add-ons to include the tried-and-true Harris bipod, standard Surefire white tactical light, an Aimpoint, and the PEQ 15 aiming laser for night operations. The weapons and body armor coupled with gloves, climbing gear and other niceties were a welcome sight for both Curt and Smitty.

They loaded everything into waterproof Mountain Hardware duffels and threw the large sacks into the back of the Land Cruiser.

Colonel Davis made a quick phone call and hung up. Within minutes, they were at the Bondsteel firing range. The facility was empty, just as Mike had coordinated. "Grab your weapons. Let's dial 'em in."

The two grabbed their long guns. After shooting about a

hundred rounds, they were happy with their respective weapons.

"OK. From what I understand, I have done everything you need. Is that correct?" Mike was willing to do more if required.

"Yes. This is great. What's the plan for our bed down?"

"I have reservations for you at the Sheraton Four Points in Pristina. It's a U.S. based hotel chain and you'll not stand out there. Additionally, your escort, 'John Doe,' will be there as well. As I understand, a vehicle will be provided for you by tomorrow morning. I'll call the hotel when your package arrives."

"Perfect. Thanks, Colonel Davis. We really appreciate the help." Curt was pleased with the service, and somewhat missed the world of military special operations.

"No worries. Here's my number. Don't hesitate to call. Use the hotel room phone. Your cell phones, as you likely know, have a shelf life. They are brand new, with new sim cards, but once you make your first call, the clock begins to tick on their remaining life."

Mike drove to the hotel and dropped them off. John Doe was already at the hotel. His real name would never be disclosed, but for the mission, he was Nick Petrović, an ethnic Serb living in Kosovo and would serve as a critical link in the mission, as well as preparing them in mission planning. It would take days to explain and rehearse. His Serbian and English were both perfect and for years he'd been on the U.S. Government's payroll. He was the perfect guy for the job.

Before departing, Mike looked at Curt and said, "Hey, I got this from a guy who calls himself Monk. Two envelopes. First one he said open now, the second one he asked you to open on D-Day... whatever that means." Curt took the envelopes and opened the first. Inside, it said:

> *Never forget this quote from Sun Tzu. 'Great results can be achieved with small forces.'*
> *v/r*
> *Monk*

Mike departed the hotel. He still had much to do for the day. Italy's pending withdraw from KFOR would tie him up well into the night, answering questions back to D.C. and to the U.S. European Command (EUCOM)

\* \* \* \* \* \* \* \* \* \* \* \* \* \* \* \* \* \* \* \* \* \* \* \* \* \* \* \* \* \* \* \* \* \* \* \* \* \* \* \*

Outside the main gate of Andrews, a desert brown open cabin jeep style vehicle was parked. In the passenger seat, Vice Admiral Aaron Kraft sat, occasionally glancing at his watch. After a few minutes, an Air Force blue sedan approached and a captain in a flight suit exited the vehicle. "Are you Admiral Kraft?"

"Yes. Who are you?"

"My callsign is Skip. Is this the vehicle that's being transported?"

"Yes. This is the...."

"Admiral, sorry to cut you off. I don't care what it is or what it does. Who is flying with the vehicle?"

Aaron pointed at an elderly man sitting in the vehicle. He was heavyset, with a long white beard. "He is."

"Cool. Buddy, you look like Jerry Garcia."

The man grinned. "I get that a lot. Name is Edward."

"OK, Edward, follow my vehicle onto the base. Admiral, thanks for your help." It was clear the captain had no intent of entertaining any of Aaron's questions, nor signing for the vehicle. Skip got in his car and began driving. Edward put the HEL in gear and followed close behind. Neither stopped at the gate and they continued straight towards the flight line. There, a security forces airman stopped Skip's vehicle. After a thirty-second exchange, Skip began moving onto the flight line, and the airman waved Edward through. Three hundred yards in front of them was a C-17 with its ramp and door open. As they got closer, a loadmaster raised his hands, pointing at Edward. The HEL came to a stop, and the loadmaster approached. "Hey. How ya doing? How much this thing weigh?"

"About 2300 lbs."

"Good. Is it hazardous?" The loadmaster queried.

Edward grinned. "Only when it's on."

"Great. Let's try to keep it off for the ride. Thanks." The loadmaster walked towards the front of the HEL and began guiding it up into the C-17's cargo area. Once cleanly onboard, the C-17's ramp and doors began to close. Within the next hour, the aircraft would be en route to Pristina, requiring only one KC-135 air refueling. The plan was still coming together.

*****************************************

In Brussels, the Italian Ambassador pressed the microphone button in front of him and addressed the North Atlantic Council. Every ambassador was seated, even the 'back bencher' seats were filled. His speech was not allowed to be public, but he'd reiterate the speech to the press afterwards. While everyone knew the reason for the speech, the Ambassador dedicated the first thirty minutes rehashing all Italy had done to help Kosovo. Clearly, he was highlighting these positives, hoping they would outweigh the negative news about their abandoning KFOR. After the laundry list of positive, he dropped the bomb. Within 24 hours, all Italian forces would be out of Kosovo, and the command position would be relinquished to whomever NATO wished to designate. As the audience gasped, the Ambassador paused, then moved onto his next point. For the next five minutes, the Ambassador railed the United States, blaming the nation for a failure of leadership. He diplomatically lamented that if the U.S. would have stepped up with a response weeks ago, the NATO alliance would not be falling apart. Further, while Italy wished to 'stand up' to Serbian aggression, it could not do this alone, nor would it do so without the support of U.S. Forces.

In both Belgrade and Moscow, senior political leaders relished the Ambassador's speech. For years, a key Russian strategy was to erode and fracture the NATO alliance. Today, the NATO alliance was crumbling right before their eyes.

## Chapter Forty-Eight
# D Minus 3

The luxury Mercedes SUV transitioned south through Kopaonik National Forest, passing hundreds if not thousands of Serbian military vehicles. Nikola stared out the backseat window, smiling happily. The car approached the customs checkpoint on the Administrative Boundary Line with Kosovo. There would be little problem for him to pass. Both the Serbian and Kosovar customs officers were ethnic Serbian. The car continued south into Mitrovica. It would arrive within twenty minutes. Once there, Nikola told the driver to pull into the empty Trepca mine parking lot.

Both Nikola and Katarina exited the Mercedes as the driver remained in the car. Ironically, they stared at the abandoned mine as if they were looking at a winning lottery ticket. Nearly all windows were either cracked or completely shattered out of the facilities. The mineral conveyor belts were so dilapidated they were dangerous. The ground, soaked through from chemicals that had seeped from leaky containers, was a health hazard. Trepca mine was an eyesore to everyone else who looked at it, but to Nikola and Katarina, it was one of the most beautiful sites in the world.

Nikola spoke to her in Serbian, "Soon, Katarina. Very soon."

She was anxious. Having wealth and a comfortable life was everything she'd dreamed of. It meant no longer working as an agent in the world of espionage, sacrificing her morals, body, and more for her country. "I pray you are correct, Nikola."

"Oh, there's little need to pray. This will soon be ours, and we are the only ones who know of its full value." Nikola was correct. Trepca had been abandoned for so long, the worlds' mineral demands had shifted. The Stojanović family were the only ones aware of the significant lithium deposits in the mine. Decades ago, lithium's value had been decent, but other minerals were in greater demand, and drew a far better price. Now, many companies were scrambling for lithium supplies as the world was shifting to sustainable energy systems such as electric vehicles. The need far outpaced supply. Globally, there were investors, speculators and venture capitalists attempting to open new lithium mines, but any output would be years away. Trepca could be harvesting within months and drawing a premium on the mineral.

"Our meeting with Tesla officials will be in a month. If everything plays out as I believe it will, we will have a contract for $15 to $25 billion for the first ten years. Given their car factory in Berlin, we will be the closest supplier. If not Tesla, then BMW or VW. It doesn't matter. Our family name will once again be placed next to the other famous oligarchs of Serbia."

Katarina reached out to her brother and gently hugged him, as if he'd saved her from a life she begged to escape. "Brother, I so want to believe you, but it has been so long. And you have sacrificed everything our family had to make this happen. If we fail, it's all over."

Nikola wanted to hear none of this. "It will not fail. It cannot fail. I have thought through everything. This will be ours." They stood there for just a while longer, staring fondly.

After their admiring gaze, the Mercedes pulled away, stopping at a local restaurant. They would eat some exceptional Serbian food, both of them filling their bellies for under fifteen euros. Mitrovica would soon be their home again, something they remembered fondly from their childhood.

South of Mitrovica, the Kosovo government could no longer stand by. Politically, demands for increased NATO assistance rang out from the President, Prime Minister and numerous other politicians. It was perhaps the first time Kosovar politicians from across the spectrum were aligned on an issue. In the past few years, Kosovo politics had, at times, resembled a circus. Once, politicians set off tear gas in parliament in an effort to impede votes. This, along with other events, served for entertaining television but did nothing to serve the people. Today, however, there'd be one singular political voice from Kosovo; something western diplomats were refreshingly pleased with. Unfortunately, there would be little they could do.

NATO Headquarters held yet another emergency North Atlantic Council meeting in Brussels. U.S. Embassy NATO had worked hard to garner advocacy among some allied nations, but far from all. While the U.S. and others preached support for the diplomatic solution, Croatia, Slovenia, Montenegro, and Albania, all Balkan nations, sternly argued for a military response to the unchecked Serbian build up. When the Albanian Ambassador took the microphone to address the council, another surprise dropped. Albania had mobilized its military and would be deploying forces under a bilateral agreement with Kosovo, external to any NATO agreement (or, more appropriately, disagreement).

Albania's announcement had crossed a red line directed by the White House to the U.S. NATO Embassy. After the Albanian Ambassador had finished speaking, the U.S. chair took the floor, and in the politest diplomatic way, scolded Albania for undermining the diplomatic solution.

After addressing the security council, the embassy would send a flash message back to Washington, D.C. In under two hours, Secretary of State Baker would summon the Albanian Ambassador to the U.S. Their meeting would be a one-way discussion, reminding Albania of the multiple bilateral defense partnerships it shared with the U.S. (the vast majority funded via the U.S. government). It was diplomacy. There was no overt threat. There didn't need to be one.

Later that day in Tirana, the discussion between the President of Albania and Kosovo would be difficult. Counter to earlier claims, there would be no Albanian forces deploying. Albania was backing down. The news broke in Kosovo. It would sting the Kosovar citizens. Kosovo was well over 90% ethnic Albanian. It was as if Kosovo's closest relative had just slammed the door in their face.

\*\*\*\*\*\*\*\*\*\*\*\*\*\*\*\*\*\*\*\*\*\*\*\*\*\*\*\*\*\*\*\*\*\*\*\*\*\*\*\*\*\*

As diplomacy efforts were unraveling across the region, the covert pseudo-military operation crafted by Monk was underway. The EC-130J Commando Solo and EC-130H Compass Call aircrew arrived onto Aviano Air Base after a few good nights of sleep. They'd receive intelligence briefings titled "D Minus 3;" meaning it was three days prior to the significant military action associated with this operation, which would be D-Day. Coincidentally, it was also the day intelligence analysts expected Serbia to launch their offensive into Kosovo. How the intelligence community knew this was not asked. Somehow, such things were always quite accurate.

At the end of the crew briefing on Aviano Air Base, a sealed briefcase was handed over to the Commando Solo crew. Inside was data critical to their mission. It was also the result of hundreds of man hours back at Fort Bragg under the direction of Monk in the 4th Psychological Operations Group.

The time was 1700Hrs local in Italy and most of the Aviano Air Base had shut down for the day. On the air base ramp, the Commando Solo aircrew performed pre-flight checks on the plane while a few hundred yards away, the 31st Fighter Wing Commander stood in front of a Public Affairs camera, being interviewed. He'd be explaining the mission for the recently bedded down C-130s to the local public. The interview would play well with the local Italians as they welcomed any help to deal with their ongoing refugee challenges. The notion that C-130s with special sensor systems could help spot vessels moving refugees across the Adriatic made perfect sense to the Italians and the rest of Europe.

As the interview was wrapping up, one of the visiting C-130 airframes began cranking their number three engine in accordance with the 'Starting Engines Checklist.' Eventually, all four engines would be loudly churning out that distinct sound of a Hercules Turbo Prop hum. To C-130 aircrew around the globe, it was known as 'The four fans of freedom' and sounded like a symphony.

The interview grew challenging because of the aircraft noise, and it would come to an end. Throughout the event, television cameras were only fixed on the Wing Commander, with an empty hangar in the background. The Air Force had some

Operational Security (OPSEC) concerns with local television crews directly filming the aircraft, something local media desperately wished to do. Base public affairs eased that situation by promising to provide Air Force approved file footage of the aircraft for their segments. An hour later, she kept her promise and forwarded the video. It was, however, not a Commando Solo but rather an HC-130 Combat King aircraft; another heavily modified U.S. Air Force C-130 specifically designed to do search and rescue. A simple mistake and to the vast majority of the public, there'd be little way to tell the difference between the two.

Once the Commando Solo was airborne, the lead operator opened the brief case he received back in the Aviano intelligence vault. Contained within was a pre-recorded multi hour audio tape. Playing that singular audio tape would be the entire mission for the night. An email note affixed to the audio tape said,

*'D Minus 3. On station time 1915Hrs. Transmit time 1930Hrs. Good Luck! Monk.'*


The flight crew loaded their waypoints into the flight computer. The flight path would put them over the middle of the Adriatic Sea, flying northeast and southwest between the Italian and Croatian/Montenegrin coasts in a racetrack pattern. To air traffic controllers or others monitoring the flight path, the cover story of observing refugee operations was perfect. It would take a few hours to get established into their operating area and at 1930Hrs, the mission crew fired up the amplifiers and transmitters. The Mission Crew Commander transmitted to SOCOM on the secure satellite communications (SATCOM) radio, "Chariot, Psycho. Music on." The audio was going out live. Moose was monitoring the discrete SATCOM frequency and replied, "Chariot copies."

Later that evening, back at Aviano Air Base, the Compass Call would take off. Their mission flight profile would mirror a standard C-130 cargo flight route. The aircraft would fly east over Slovenia, into Hungarian airspace, then turn south. The flight path would take it through Romanian and Bulgarian airspace, flying south, paralleling Serbia's eastern border towards North Macedonia.

As the aircraft flew along the Serbian border, the crew monitored the electromagnetic spectrum (EMS) environment. Given the altitude, it would not be difficult to openly observe transmissions within Serbian borders to include all those units performing radio checks. Intercepting open air transmissions in the EMS was completely legal under international law. The aircraft was doing absolutely nothing wrong. During this part of the mission, the crew would jot down notes. It was dull work, but it was critical to ensure the next few days would be a success.

Nearing North Macedonia, the aircraft would descend for its scheduled landing into Skopje. Once on the ramp, the engines would let out one last whine, then slow their windmilling until they stopped. While refueling, a crew member would hand over a small package to the U.S. Defense Attaché assigned to Skopje. To the general public that was aware of the landing, the package contained time sensitive information that could not be mailed, or so the story was relayed. To the very few aware of the Special Operation, there was nothing in the package and the landing was a feint; other than requiring fuel.

On the other side of Serbia, over the Adriatic, the Commando Solo continued its mission. From a military perspective, it was quite boring. The aircraft transmitting a pre-recorded tape that played culturally popular Serbian music, Serbian disk jockey discussions and very limited commercials. Popular music would likely quickly garner listeners to the radio station. Over the next few hours, however, the disk jockey's discussions would slowly and ever so subtly transition. They'd lament the impending military offensive. Was it worth it? How many lives would be lost? What value was Kosovo other than another region that would take Serbian tax revenue away from 'real' Serbians? Each of these messages gently placed in between great songs and other content.

Across the Kopaonik area, Serbian soldiers cleaned their

weapons, played cards, or wrote letters home. As they did, many listened to the radio as cellular and Wi-Fi signals were shut down. Radio was the only form of entertainment. The Command Solo messages would not sway a single soldier to question the war effort. They weren't intended to. The mission for the day was just to plant a seed. Many thought, '*What do these DJs know?*' as they drank beers, played cards, smoked cigarettes and bragged about their future heroic efforts. The music was pleasant, though, so they kept listening. Later in the night, however, psychological studies suggested the messages would weigh on the soldiers as they slept alone.

As Commando Solo flew its prescribed route over the Adriatic, another U.S. military aircraft, callsign Reach 77, was passing west to east directly into the Balkans. The aircraft was a large C-17, which had departed hours earlier from Andrews Air Force Base, Maryland. Reach 77 flew over Albania and started a decent into Pristina's Adem Jashari International Airport. The landing was uneventful, and the aircraft taxied to the NATO ramp where many pallets ready for transport waited to be onloaded. Most were full of supplies from the nations vacating their KFOR commitment.

After stopping, the cargo ramp and door slowly opened. Inside was the Raytheon HEL. However, the 'Raytheon' label affixed to each side was scratched off and replaced with big labels that said BAE, short for British Aerospace and Engineering. At the wheel of the HEL was Edward, or as he'd be referred to, Jerry Garcia. Slowly, he drove off the C-17 onto the ramp. A NATO Logistics Officer from Germany stood aft of the C-17 with a clipboard alongside the C-17 load master aircrew member.

"Sir," said the German major, "I have no information on my manifest regarding an inbound vehicle. What is this?"

The load master, Senior Airman Mark Costello, was a youthful and energetic man. His callsign was 'Elvis' for obvious reasons. Elvis asked the German officer to stand by as he retrieved the aircraft commander. Minutes later, as Jerry Garcia and the German officer sat there, awkwardly looking at each other, the aircraft commander arrived. He was the same young captain that acquired the HEL from retired Admiral Kraft. "Hey, I understand there is a problem?"

"Yes, I have no paperwork to support the offload of this vehicle." The German officer was firm, as they all are.

"God damn it! I knew we should have never taken this thing," the aircraft commander announced. "Shit. Well, I guess we will have to load it back up." He looked at Jerry. "Jerry, turn around and put it back on."

The German officer, proud of himself for adhering to the rules, turned again to the captain. "Captain, great. Now, for the rest of your load, I have these pallets ready for your manifest." It was true, the German major's paperwork was perfect, and the pallets were prepared perfectly.

The captain looked at him, puzzled. "Uh? Yeah. I can't take any of that stuff. This vehicle is screwing us. It is a very sensitive testing device to fine tune radar systems. Because of that sensitivity issue, the shipping instructions clearly state it must fly alone. No other cargo." The aircraft commander perfectly delivered the pitch he was given back at Andrews Air Force Base.

The German logistics officer froze. He looked at the other side of the ramp at his massive logistic backlog of outbound pallets. It was growing by the day. He'd already confidently told his leadership a C-17 today would be able to take twenty pallets of gear. Now, that wasn't going to happen. Flexibility and adaptation were still traits uncommon in the German military.

The aircraft commander spoke again. "Hey, before we go too crazy. Lemme check something." He opened his phone. "I have a local contact for this thing. His name is Colonel Mike Davis and I believe he is the U.S. defense attaché assigned to Pristina. Should I call him?"

"Yes. Please." The German was elated to hear there may be a way out of the mess.

"Colonel Davis, hey sir, I am the C-17 pilot, captain ...." The rest of the conversation was irrelevant. Colonel Davis was sitting inside the NATO VIP room at the airport awaiting the call. He'd be on the ramp in five minutes.

The German logistics officer, like many other NATO

personalities, knew Colonel Davis. There were only two defense attachés permanently assigned to Kosovo: one from the U.S. and one from Turkey. Other nations had attachés assigned to Skopje, Belgrade, and even as far away as Vienna, that, while also accredited to Kosovo, would only spend a few days every quarter in the country. They were also accredited to other nations, making their jobs extremely complex and challenging.

After a quick signature on a fudged logistics movement manifest, Mike Davis would jump into the passenger seat of the HEL and ride away with Jerry Garcia. The two would drive directly to the Sheraton, where Curt, Smitty, and Nick were planning and rehearsing for their operation. The ride would be far from pleasurable. The vehicle cabin was still open air like a Jeep and the chilly spring air burned on Mike's face. Jerry just drove along as if it was 70 degrees and sunny out. Once at the Sheraton, Jerry drove the vehicle into the underground parking lot of the Marigona Sheraton. Mike coordinated Jerry's hotel room, and he was soon checked in. The two grabbed a seat at the hotel bar and waited for Curt, Smitty, and Nick to come down. After a brief introduction, Mike departed. For the remainder of the night and into the next few days, Curt, Smitty, Nick and Jerry would discuss in detail the operational capabilities and procedures for the HEL as well as rehearse and re-rehearse the plan. It would need to be perfect. There was no time to waste.

The last piece of the day's mission was the EC-130H Compass Call departing Skopje airfield. After filling up, the specially modified C-130 took off and climbed out. Along its return route to Hungary, it would again monitor the Serbian signal environment along the eastern border. The crew again making notes and preparing for the next day.

Once back at Papa Air Base, Hungary, where NATO beds down half a dozen C-17 cargo airplanes, the EC-130H Compass Call would bed down for the night.

As the plane taxied to a halt and the doors opened, roughly ten aircrew members exited, far more than what a normal C-130 would require. This, along with the strange wiring array on the back vertical and horizontal stabilizer, began to raise suspicion from a senior member of the Hungarian Air Force, Colonel László Szatmári. He was a sharp officer and had attended the U.S. Air War College at Maxwell Air Force Base, in Montgomery, Alabama, as a foreign exchange officer two years prior. His English was near perfect and his ambitions, as well as his chances for promotion in the Hungarian Air Force, were strong.

After a short amount of time, the EC-130H mission crew commander, Major Bacon, approached. "Good evening! Thanks for the chance to rest our old girl here tonight. We really appreciate it."

"Yes, Major. Hello. I am Colonel Szatmári. Hungary welcomes you."

"Colonel, sir, hello. Please call me 'Bits.'"

"Sure…. Bits. Your aircraft appears to be different from a normal C-130."

Major Bacon looked at the colonel confusingly. "What do you mean?"

"Well, you have more than four aircrew, which would be normal for a C-130, and you have wires and such hanging off the back of the aircraft. This is not normal."

"Oh! That crap. Yeah, if I had my way, you could just take it off the aircraft and keep it. So, you are familiar with C-130s?"

"Somewhat." The colonel responded.

"Good. That will make this easier. Let me explain. This is an older model, a C-130, an 'H' model. The U.S. Air Force has upgraded their C-130 fleet, now purchasing 'J' models. Those have very different engines. For example, it has a six-blade propeller versus the four-blade propeller you see on our aircraft. Unfortunately, the new 'J' model aircraft are quite expensive, and our Air Force cannot buy as many as we'd like, so we are now investigating what option exists to upgrade older aircraft with the new engines. The wires you see here are designed to produce an extra amount of drag, which will be compiled into test data required for the cost benefit analysis. The hope is this real world data matches that which was computer generated in modeling as well as just flying aircraft locally around the U.S.

The other aircrew you saw pile out of our aircraft are folks monitoring the testing. I'm very sorry. I didn't think it would be an issue. Oh, I forgot. I have a small gift from my commander for you. Here is one of our unit coins."

The explanation was far more than the colonel wanted. And it was also far from the truth, but to a degree, believable. The colonel reached out his hand. "Many thanks for this coin. I appreciate it. No, no. No worries. Just very interesting. I had never seen such a contraption." The colonel was also pleased he would have some information to share with his ministry that the U.S. Air Force was considering an upgrade of older C-130s to use the newer 'J' model engine.

"Great. Well, we are going to gas up and then seal the aircraft. If I understand correctly, we are authorized to bed down here for tonight and tomorrow. And one of our crew will be able to stay here on the ramp with security?"

"Yes, your nation is NATO. You are always welcome here." The colonel meant that. Hungary was quite happy to be part of the NATO alliance. They also enjoyed a significant revenue boost because of the collective C-17 operations on Papa Air Base Operations.

As they spoke, a few U.S. Air Force security forces, nicknamed 'Defenders,' assigned to Papa Air Base, set up floodlights and a red rope cordon around the aircraft. They'd watch it through the night.

With that, everything was set. The crew loaded onto a bus which drove them to Hotel Villa Classica in downtown Papa. They'd soon be asleep, resting for tomorrow's mission.

\*\*\*\*\*\*\*\*\*\*\*\*\*\*\*\*\*\*\*\*\*\*\*\*\*\*\*\*\*\*\*\*\*\*\*\*\*\*\*

Back in the United States, the issue of Kosovo was becoming more and more of a concern for Steve. As the White House calendar of events came to a close for the day, Steve and the President were alone.

"Mr. President. May I speak with you for a moment?"

"Sure, Steve. What's on your mind?"

"Well, sir. Serbia for one. This whole thing is out of control. I understand the issue with Nikola, but this is just crazy. Politically, you can easily survive if he goes public with what he has." Based on what Steve knew, that was true. But the publicity about the President's mistress would be political suicide.

"Steve. I appreciate your concern, but we are too far into this now. Let's see how it plays out."

"Frankly, sir, that's what worries me. Nikola stated Serbia would stop at the Ibar River. But the forces that are massed could easily take all of Kosovo well before there was any response."

The President knew Steve was right. He sat there for a minute. "Steve, where are the Balkans?"

"Excuse me, sir?"

"What continent?"

"Sir, is this a trick question? It's Europe?"

"Yes. Correct. And in history, the Balkans were part of the Ottoman Empire, part of the Austrian-Hungarian Empire, part of Yugoslavia... I could continue. As this buildup of Serbian forces began, only one nation so far has offered to bolster troops and step in."

"Yes. But I fail to see your point."

"My point is, that if a potential conflict in the Balkans is not important to the power nations of Europe, why should it be important to the U.S?

"Sir? It's important because some nations argue NATO's involvement in 1999 in the region was in conflict with the United Nations Security Council because of Russia's veto. The U.S. sacrificed significant diplomatic..."

The President cut him off. "Yes. I know. And I do not require a history lesson, Steve. And I could point out far more, and arguably 'more recent,' examples of Russia's failures to follow legally binding treaties, international law and United Nations guidance. What else do you have?"

Steve rightly sensed he was going to make no headway with the President. "Yes, sir. I understand."

"Kosovo has had well over a decade and a half to get their act together. The U.S. cannot wait forever. Nor can many of her strongest allies in the region. The clock has stopped ticking, and the buzzer is ringing."

"OK sir, should I start formulating your comments and actions, post invasion?"

The President was relieved. His closest confidant was giving in. "Yes, Steve. Now that would be something productive with your time. There will be many moving pieces after Serbia invades. Press comments as well as communications with other NATO nations. I'd welcome you to start thinking through those chess moves. Thanks."

Steve nodded and departed the Oval Office. The President stared out at the rose garden. *'There was no other answer,'* he kept telling himself. Much like other recent Presidents, his narcissism overrode any sense of responsibility for the loss and deaths he was about to cause.

\*\*\*\*\*\*\*\*\*\*\*\*\*\*\*\*\*\*\*\*\*\*\*\*\*\*\*\*\*\*\*\*\*\*\*\*\*\*\*\*

Moose had heard from all those who owed him an end of day report: Defense Attachés in Kosovo and North Macedonia and contacts on Aviano Air Base and Fort Bragg. D minus 3 was successful, and the operation was not exposed. Moose pulled out his cell phone and texted,

*'D-3 complete, as fragged.'*

In Arlington, Virginia, on Fort Myers, Admiral Hershey sat in his study. His iPhone buzzed. He set down his glass of scotch and looked at Moose's message. There'd be no reply. At the same time, General Etcher, the SOCOM Commander, also viewed the message. The three, along with Monk, were perhaps the only ones outside the Balkans with the full picture.

Tomorrow, however, would be another day, and far harder to execute under the cover of secrecy.

## *Chapter Forty-Nine*
# D Minus 2

The sunrise over Belgrade was spectacular. Low-hanging clouds painted the sky with hues of red, purple, orange and colors in between. The city was abuzz with the anticipation of another conflict with Kosovo. Serbians across the country were stocking up on food and other supplies. Many of the older Serbians who lived through the war of 1999 remembered running out of goods and supplies. They weren't the only ones.

In Kosovo, the hoarding was far worse, as Kosovo would likely be where the conflict took place. Grocery store shelves were empty, hardware stores were selling out of wood, truckloads of lignite coal were only dumping loads at residents that could pay 'top euro.' Politicians were trying to downplay the chaos, which was impossible. For years, Kosovo's mainstream media had become profitable by promoting fear, uncertainty, and doubt. Over the past week, revenues were never better. The concern across Kosovo was palpable, and the media danced in profits of reporting it.

A small meeting was convened in Kosovo's Presidential offices. President Gashi, Prime Minister Haradinaj and the 'Quint' sat around a large room. The 'Quint' was the nickname of the five 'western & like-minded' ambassadors assigned to Kosovo from the nations of Germany, Italy, the UK, France and the U.S.

A large sense of tension filled the room. After a few minutes of sidebar discussions taking place, the President of Kosovo tapped the table. The room fell silent. "Ladies and Gentlemen. I thank you for coming on such short notice. As we've discussed, I am fearful of Serbia's imminent invasion and am curious what your nations will provide in the way of support."

The Quint Ambassadors gazed at each other, waiting for someone to speak. The U.S. Ambassador was given specific instructions to await a response from the other nations. He said nothing, yet it was clear. Many in the room were hoping he'd be the first to speak.

Finally, the German Ambassador spoke. "Mr. President. Before we take a fatalist attitude, can you tell us if there is any progress in the diplomatic front regarding the Kosovo & Serbian agreement?"

"Mr. Ambassador, I wish there was, but I cannot get our parliament to agree. They would rather go to war than agree with the terms."

The UK Ambassador jumped in. "President Gashi, I realize in Kosovo there is a strong pride, and perhaps a false sense of strength juxtaposed the Serbian military, but you realize there is no western support at this time? Do you believe the Kosovar people understand this?"

"Yes, Madam Ambassador." The President wasn't receptive to her question. The President had fought years ago with the Kosovo Liberation Army and was quite aware of the cost of war, as was much of Kosovo. "We are not ignorant to war. For nearly a decade, we fought alone against Serbia. It wasn't until 1999 when the west joined the fight." Gashi's answer wasn't just filled with pride, but also much truth. Kosovo's hero, Adem Jashari, had fought for years with the resistance against Serbia until one day when the Serbian Army surrounded his entire family in their home. After Jashari's multiple refusals to surrender, on 7 March 1998, the Serbian army unloaded thousands of rounds into his house of all different size calibers, to include artillery. Miraculously, there was one survivor; a small girl who was placed inside the oven for protection. To date, that house stands as a memorial and the reason the Pristina Airport is named after Adem.

The French Ambassador interjected, "Mr. President, I understand the desire to fight, but that desire must be weighed against the cost."

"Mr. Ambassador, I completely agree. As my colleague, the Prime Minister and I see it, Kosovo must either pay diplomatically or with blood. To us, however, the diplomatic cost is greater, and it is one our people will not accept. Because of this, it will be blood. So, I ask you all again, what will your nations provide to help defend our nation?"

Each ambassador in the Quint offered nothing other than they would forward the question to their respective capitals for a response. It was clear no nation had given any option for military support. The meeting would end with little accomplished, other than Kosovo demonstrating its strong desire to fight.

The main road from Pristina to Mitrovica was quickly becoming a parking lot for the Kosovo Security Force (KSF) military vehicles. Hotels along the road were filling up with KSF soldiers, and the conference rooms were turned into makeshift command posts. It was the same road where Buck had his horrible accident, the skid marks of his landing as well as the scorch from the flames still scarred the road.

While the unproductive meeting in Kosovo ended, a speech was about to be delivered in Brussels at NATO Headquarters. U.S. Secretary of State Marleen Baker had flown in from Washington and would be addressing all the ambassadors, discussing the ongoing diplomatic solution between Serbia and Kosovo.

"Mr. Secretary General, Ambassadors, and colleagues. It is my esteemed honor to address you today regarding what is perhaps one of the most pivotal moments in European history. I confess up front, I have no solution yet, but I am confident we are close, and that crisis can be averted."

It was all the room needed to hear. While the speech continued for the next twenty minutes, pointing out the concerns of each side as well as the 'offerings' of each, a deal was no closer than it was the week prior. In private negotiations between Secretary Baker and President Sokol, there was no movement. Sokol knew quite well he had Northern Kosovo sealed up through Nikola's deal. The only interest he had was something greater than this, and that was a deal neither Kosovo nor the unknowing Secretary of State was willing to negotiate.

Secretary Baker ended her speech with a notification that the President of the United States would be speaking with President Sokol and President Gashi the following day, imploring both to find common ground. It was the best news she could offer and yet, it was nothing.

On this afternoon, similar to the D minus 3, the Commando Solo aircrew departed their Italian hotels and headed for Aviano Air Base. The copilot grabbed a weather briefing while other crew members performed their specific functions. And again, another large, sealed brief case was handed to the mission crew commander. On the top is said, *'Mission D-2. Happy Hunting. Monk.'* It was a product of the 4th Psychological Operations, under the direction of Lieutenant Colonel Baylis.

The entire crew stepped to the aircraft and strapped in. It was roughly 1900Hrs when they lifted off the runway heading for the Adriatic Sea. Their flight profile would remain the same as the previous night. The mission, however, would change drastically. The EC-130J lumbered slowly into the sunset.

In Papa, a similar scene took place. The EC-130H aircrew stepped to their plane as well. Once there, they too strapped in and would take off at approximately 2030Hrs. They would fly toward Skopje again, pass along an empty 'important package' and then return. The mission was categorized as a cargo movement, but the only cargo onboard would be electrons, millions of them.

*****************************************

Back in the U.S., Monk placed his first call to Allison. "Ms. Donley?"

"Yes. Who is this?"

"My name is Monk."

"Yes, Monk, Curt said you'd call. What can I do for you?"

"Tonight, there are going to be some, shall we say, fireworks, in Serbia. Information about this will probably surface first on social media, most likely Twitter. It would be extremely helpful to Curt and all of us if you could retweet or share any and all you find worthy of pushing."

"Monk, I understand. Can you tell me if these are real social media posts or are they fake?"

"Ms. Donley, I can't predict the future, but I believe much of what you see on social media tonight will be very real. How it's interpreted... well, I'd offer you should judge for yourself."

She could no longer hold back the question she really wanted to ask. "Will Curt be safe?"

"Curt? Heavens, yes. He's nowhere near what's about to happen."

Allison was relieved. "OK, Monk. I'll do my best and also make some calls to others with large social media followings once it starts."

"Perfect. I appreciate it. And by the way, I'll be calling again later. Please keep your phone on."

"You got it." The two hung up.

# Chapter Fifty
# Under Attack?

Much like the previous nights, Serbian soldiers in the Kopaonik region sat around, smoking cigarettes, drinking beer while playing cards and other table games. They were just awaiting orders. Those on duty tested their equipment, cleaned their weapons and grew bored waiting. It was standard for militaries around the world. *'Hurry up and wait'* was a phrase nearly every soldier, sailor, airman or marine lived out, no matter the nation.

Miles away, up in the air over the Adriatic, the Commando Solo crew calibrated their transmitters away from traditional FM radio station frequencies onto the frequency used by the Serbian forces positioned in Kopaonik. Once tuned, the Mission Crew Commander transmitted on SATCOM, "Chariot, Psycho. Music On."

Again, Moose, back at SOCOM replied, "Chariot Copies."

Shortly after those transmissions, the Compass Call Mission Crew Commander transmitted, "Chariot, Vampire. On Station. Buzzer On."

Moose replied with another, "Copy."

Inside the Kopaonik Ski Resort where the Serbian Army established its command post, a young major sat at the main desk, playing with the cord of his radio microphone. A massive tactical military radio sat in front of him. The speaker remained silent other than low-level background static, much like it had been all day other than the two or three radio checks across all the units. Subordinate to the command post, younger officers sat out by their battalion's and company's vehicles, manning the watch.

Unexpectedly, the radio cracked to life, and in Serbian, a voice cried out, "WE ARE UNDER ATTACK! WE ARE UNDER ATTACK! Bombs are falling on us!"

With that, every radio operator jumped to life. They quickly alerted leadership, and the major at the command post sent a runner to get Division Commander Major General Nate Dučić.

Another transmission cut in, "WE'RE HIT! WE'RE HIT! SEND MEDICS TO WOLF UNIT 2-32!" In the background of the transmission, explosions could be heard. The soldier transmitting sounded scared for his life.

Quickly, the command post dispatched a combat medical unit and then ordered each unit to check in with any damage or casualties.

Flood lights fired up, horns and sirens blared. Serbian soldiers were rustled from their tents. They all grabbed their gear and headed to their vehicles. The notion that Serbia would fall under a preemptive attack was never planned for, or even considered. The soldiers had not crafted any fallout shelters. The Serbian military was exposed.

Major General Dučić arrived in the command post, demanding an update. After a one-minute update, he grabbed another radio. It was a radio relay system that could reach back to the Ministry of Defense in Belgrade. How could airplanes be bombing him without someone noticing their approach?

"Belgrade Ministry, this is Wolf Six. Belgrade Ministry, this is Wolf Six. Come in!"

There was no response. He would try the transmission again. After waiting, he threw the radio handset onto the desk. He pulled out his cell phone and would call his boss. As he hit SEND on his phone, he noticed there was no signal. He raised his phone up and tried to hit send again; then remembered he had ordered all cellular networks turned off. There was no signal, and there would be no way to communicate with Belgrade, other than landline. The EC-130H Compass Call and its electronic attack capabilities would deny communications between Kopaonik and Belgrade as it slowly lumbered along the eastern Serbian border.

As Major General Dučić stood there, another announcement cracked over the tactical radio, "THEY'RE OVERHEAD NOW! NOW! SHOOT! FOR GOD'S SAKE SHOOT!"

Although it was far from the correct military protocol or discipline, many soldiers raised their rifles and began firing into the air. Covers were already being removed over large artillery guns and had pointed their barrels skyward, shooting at the aircraft lights of commercial aircraft that were openly and legally flying above Serbia, thankfully at altitudes far higher than the artillery could reach.

As gun fire erupted across the bed down locations, others joined in. The Major General looked at his air defense officer in the command post. "WHAT THE FUCK IS UP THERE?"

After taking a big gulp and looking at his screen, the air defense officer said, "Sir, I don't see anything. The radar is clean."

Nate Dučić looked at the command post radio operator. "God damn it! Tell everyone to cease firing!" The order was relayed over the radio and silence again fell across the Kopaonik valley.

The air defense officer sent out engineers to check the radar. They walked the entire cable all the way up to the Kopaonik radar facility. It was fine, and since the radar was modern, it should have easily identified any aircraft on an inbound attack. The engineers reported back to the air defense officer. The radar was reporting accurately.

Fifteen minutes after the start of the show, both EC-130s transitioned to 'Music off' and 'Cease Buzzer,' the traditional codewords for halting transmissions. Each Serbian company, battalion and brigade would report in it had no casualties with minimal damage. The damage, ironically, was caused by their own rounds falling back down to earth. Additionally, the wireless radio relay radio system magically began working again.

"Wolf Six (the callsign for Major General Dučić), this is Belgrade. What is going on down there? We have multiple reports from villagers about gunfire and social media is full of video of your anti-aircraft artillery shooting skyward?"

"Belgrade! Where were you!? I couldn't get through! Did you have any indications of aircraft overhead? Who was shooting at us?"

"Wolf Six. Who is shooting at you?? We want to know who YOU are shooting at! We have no unidentified aircraft in your sector. What are you talking about?"

For the next hour, Belgrade and Kopaonik would try to figure out what happened. As they did, social media, mainly Twitter and Facebook, flooded with posts from Serbia and Kosovo stating everything from an attack had begun, to U.S. stealth fighters had once again begun bombing Serbia, just like 1999. Capitals across Europe, North America and Asia were reporting gunfire, but no one could gain an understanding of what had actually happened. Sun Tzu's 'Fog of War' had yet again proved itself a true tenant of warfare.

During that first hour, Allison and her social media army saw the Twitter activity, as predicted. She thought to herself, *'Damn, Monk. This shit looks as real as it gets.'* Reposting, retweeting and sharing, all of them sent out the activities of southern Serbia for the world to see.

The KSF would not wait. Upon hearing the news of shots fired in the north, soldiers began pouring into vehicles and preparing to drive north. The only problem was, per UNSCR 1244, KSF members were not authorized north of the Ibar River without KFOR escort. And currently, the only KFOR forces remaining were mainly U.S. and Turkish, both of which were extremely hesitant to face over 10,000 Serbian soldiers rushing south.

In a KFOR Blackhawk helicopter, Colonel Mark Barlow, the U.S. KFOR Brigade and Bondsteel Base Commander hastily flew north to the front of the KSF column of vehicles. Mark had assumed command of the entire KFOR, given the Italian's withdrawal. It was his show. By the time they overflew the lead KSF vehicle, it was only two miles south of the Ibar River. Mark ordered the pilot to land on the highway in front of the lead vehicle and the pilot complied. Once on the ground, Colonel Barlow jumped out of the helicopter and, with the best swagger he could muster, he walked towards the stopped KSF convoy. Standing in front of the convoy was Lieutenant General Krasniqi, frustrated.

"General Krasniqi, stop this shit now. I'm in no mood to start World War III."

The general sat there, puffing on his cigarette. "Buzz, your helicopter is in my way."

"General, I'm not screwing around. Turn around!" With that, Mark's cell phone rang. It was his boss, the U.S. Ambassador to Kosovo. He relayed credible sources confirmed Serbian forces had NOT moved south across the ABL. Kosovo was not (yet) under attack. "Ambassador, that's great news. I'm standing here with Lieutenant General Krasniqi. Perhaps you could repeat that." Buzz handed the phone to LTG Krasniqi. After a few moments, Lieutenant General Krasniqi hung up. "General. Turn around! There is no attack, not tonight anyway. Call your President now! You know my nation has far better intelligence than yours."

The general looked at him. He paused, then placed the call to President Gashi, who'd already been in contact with the U.S. Ambassador. Buzz was correct.

In Albanian, the general said, "Thank you, Mr. President." It was the only thing Buzz could translate. The general then turned to Mark. "OK, Buzz. Today, you win. But I warn you. If your helicopter tries to stop me again, I'll shoot it. I'm more than grateful for everything your nation has done for Kosovo thus far, but I will not let America stand in the way of me defending what I and my Kosovo Liberation Army colleagues fought and died for."

Mark stared at him. It was not the time to get in a pissing match with the commander of the KSF, but a threat to shoot down a Blackhawk could not go unaddressed. "General. I'd strongly recommend you chose your future words carefully. MY helicopters defend YOUR land. Shoot one, and the rest are gone. Remember. We're on the same fucking team. As for returning your convoy South, thank you, general." Mark turned around, not waiting for an answer. The convoy would turn around, and that was the tactical victory Mark desired. He walked back to the helicopter. He boarded it and flew back to Bondsteel. Crisis was averted, at least for today.

\*\*\*\*\*\*\*\*\*\*\*\*\*\*\*\*\*\*\*\*\*\*\*\*\*\*\*\*\*\*\*\*\*\*\*\*\*\*\*\*

One and a half hours later, the EC-130H Compass Call was flying north out of Skopje after its quick stop, while the EC-130J Commando Solo lumbered slowly over the Adriatic.  At the pre-planned and coordinated time, they both made their respective SATCOM calls to Moose, '*Music on*' and '*Buzzer on.*'  With that, a second communications attack took place.  First it was the Commando Solo.

The Serbian tactical radio again cracked to life.  "WE BEG YOU DO NOT ATTACK.  WE ARE YOUR DEAD RELATIVES OF THE LAST WAR."  The command post radio operator had enough and demanded to know who made the last transmission.  After a minute or two, the Commando Solo started reciting a list of Serbian soldier's names killed in action during the 1999 war, many of the fathers and grandfathers of the current soldiers.  The names stung.

Major General Dučić had enough.  He directed the communications officer for all units to 'Chattermark,' or switch to the backup frequency.  The comm officer did as instructed.  After transmitting, the command post communication's officer dialed in a new frequency, then began radio checks to ensure all units had made the transition.  The entire evolution took roughly ten minutes, with near nonstop transmissions by the units onto the backup frequency.  Eventually, all units had checked in.

During the previous day, the EC-130H Compass Call had monitored a Chattermark practice drill by the Serbian units, making both EC-130s fully aware of the backup frequency.  Their effort to 'run and hide' would prove to be all for naught.

The Serbian radios remained silent for roughly five minutes, enough time for the EC-130J Command Solo to adjust their tuners and amplifies to the new frequency.  Once dialed in, the Commando Solo started broadcasting again.  "YOU THINK YOU CAN CHANGE FREQUENCIES FROM THE DEAD?  YOU CAN NOT.  NOW LISTEN TO OUR DEATHS AND LEARN."  Over the next 15 minutes, screams, moans, cursing, and more could be heard on the radio.  A majority of the Serbian soldiers listened in on the radio.  '*It is all bullshit,*' many of them thought.  '*This can't be real.'* But Major General Dučić was losing it, and some damage had been incurred in the night, all from falling Serbian artillery that was shot into the air. As the command post tried to communicate with Belgrade, Compass Call again denied the link. Throughout the second communications attack, the brigades in Kopaonik would be alone. Isolated.

The last transmission from the Commando Solo stated, "GO HOME TO YOUR FAMILIES OR TOMORROW YOU WILL SUFFER FROM OUR HANDS, IN THE NAME OF THE SERBIAN ORTHODOX CHURCH AND ALL THINGS HOLY. THE DEVIL WILL DESTROY YOUR VEHICLES. YOUR FORESTS WILL RAGE IN FLAMES."

The radio was quiet. Wolf Six, Major General Dučić, was so angry that his veins pulsed from the temples of his forehead. He immediately called a meeting of his battalion commanders. The meeting would last for hours as he demanded to know which unit made such transmissions. None of the commanders knew. After the meeting, the commander took control of the tactical radio microphone. "This is Wolf Six. I do not know who made the transmissions tonight, but whoever you are, we will find you. You are either a vile Albanian or a traitor to Serbia, and not worth your own life. You will be killed unless you turn yourself in immediately." To be fair, the general was smart enough to know the Albanians or Kosovars were not capable of pulling something like this off. He merely said it to plant a seed in his soldier's minds.

Slowly, the floodlights around Kopaonik dimmed, and the tension faded. The fear, however, did not. No one would turn themselves in that night. Later, two C-130s would land at Aviano Air Base and Papa Air Base, respectively.

In the wee hours of the night, the Major General would communicate directly with General Bojović, the Serbian Chief of Defense.

"General. You must maintain order and discipline. Everything will be OK. While we don't know what happened, the most likely explanation is the U.S. sent stealth fighters over to scare you. They may have dropped tiny bombs or something. We don't know. That said, you must blame someone, anyone, for these transmissions. Find your weakest soldier and publicly shame him. Make the others believe you. We will work to identify the source of the problems."

Major General Nate Dučić called in his executive officer. He asked who the weakest soldier was. A name surfaced. The next morning, he'd be an innocent victim.

\*\*\*\*\*\*\*\*\*\*\*\*\*\*\*\*\*\*\*\*\*\*\*\*\*\*\*\*\*\*\*\*\*\*\*\*\*\*\*

Late into the night, Curt, Smitty, Nick and Jerry Garcia sat in the Sheraton lobby bar, watching the news about the Serbian military activity. Smitty and Curt smiled at each other. The plan was working. Jerry did not know what was happening, but presumed it was good. He didn't want to know anymore.

\*\*\*\*\*\*\*\*\*\*\*\*\*\*\*\*\*\*\*\*\*\*\*\*\*\*\*\*\*\*\*\*\*\*\*\*\*\*\*

At the end of the day in D.C., another text from Moose came through from Tampa.

*'D-2 complete, as fragged.'*

Both Admiral Hershey and General Etcher read the text. For them, tomorrow would be a challenge. U.S. intelligence assets throughout the U.S. Government would scramble to figure out where the erroneous transmission emerged from. If the intel world could definitively find the right answer, the Chairman's and SOCOM Commander's days would be numbered.

\*\*\*\*\*\*\*\*\*\*\*\*\*\*\*\*\*\*\*\*\*\*\*\*\*\*\*\*\*\*\*\*\*\*\*\*\*\*\*

Monk would place his second call to Allison. "Ms. Donley, Monk here."

"Hey Monk, please call me Allison. Ms. Donley is my mom."

"Sure, Allison. I can't talk long, but I sent you a photo before calling. Did you get it?"

"Yes. I think so. It has some text on it that says it's an F-117 in the boneyard?"

"Yes."

"OK, but I don't understand. There is no plane. Just three wheels on the ground and a step ladder standing straight up but leaning on nothing."

"Yup. That's the picture. It's a joke meme. The F-117 is a stealth fighter that has limited capability to be seen by radar. It's also the aircraft that Serbia shot down in 1999. The joke is that the aircraft is there, in the photo, but invisible."

"Oh. OK. I get it." Allison understood the meme, just not why Monk sent it.

"Allison. If you're willing, I'd like for you to send that photo out in a tweet with verbiage like *'Is it possible the stealth fighters may not really be in mothballs?'*"

"Monk, that's not really true though, right? The U.S. Air Force retired the stealth fighter years ago."

"You are correct. But the words I suggested for you can be interpreted a few ways. Some will see it as a joke, especially those who know the aircraft is retired. Those folks will reply as such." Monk paused and then continued. "Some who wish to believe the U.S. may have flown stealth aircraft over southern Serbia will believe it, whether that narrative is supported by facts or not. They too will retweet it. Finally, some will point out the U.S. still flies B-2s."

"Monk! Did the U.S. fly B-2 Bombers over Serbia tonight!?"

Monk grinned, but Allison couldn't see it. He wouldn't answer her question. "Thanks."

Allison was confused. "Thanks? Thanks for what?"

"For proving my point. Other than my mention of B-2 bombers, you possess no evidence they flew over Serbia. But you have no better answer as to what happened, and that narrative seemed both convenient and possible."

"Well played." Allison had never met Monk, but she liked him. The way he explained what had just happened was as if instructing and teaching in a kind fashion. There wasn't a hint of arrogance. "But I noticed you didn't answer my question. Did B-2's fly over Serbia?"

Monk paused and said, "I have to go. But I'll say this. If you think that is possible and wish to offer it up on social media, I, Curt and others would very much welcome it. Have a good night, Allison, and thanks again for your help. It's been instrumental." Monk hung up.

'*I gotta meet this guy,*' was all Allison could think. She tweeted out the F-117 meme and also delicately offered that 'something' happened in Serbia and clearly no radars intercepted it. Could it have been a B-2 Bomber? Both tweets spread like wildfire. Her colleagues she'd contacted prior to the events in Kopaonik were certain Allison had inside news given her validated prediction. Anything she posted about this would be grabbed by multiple mainstream media and other news outlets. Many of Allison's friends were journalists like her. Somehow, she had inside info about the previous events. Many watched her social media closely, if not sending her direct texts. She'd answer them all, just as Monk had instructed.

# Chapter Fifty-One
# D Minus 1

0700Hrs rolled around the next morning in Kopaonik. Companies, battalions and brigades funneled up their morning situation reports. Photos of some minor damage were highlighted by eager company grade officers, trying to validate that 'something' had attacked them. Later in the report, less popular information was buried. There was a desertion rate of 10% across the force structure, roughly 1,000 men and women. Major General Ducić ordered the 'presumed' guilty member be brought to him. He also demanded a commander's formation. Thousands would form, and the poor Serbian soldier was beaten... mercilessly. When he could no longer stand, military police drug him away. Major General Ducić then addressed the formation. Some knew the soldier was innocent, others didn't but speculated... silently, of course. As for those who deserted, they would be found and receive the same treatment as the poor soldier. All of those that remained and stood in front of Major General Ducić were glad they'd stayed. It was one thing to fear ghosts and superstitions, it was another to fear living major generals.

From the overall operation perspective, today was D-1. Curt, Smitty, Nick and Jerry would become the main act. As the sun rose, they departed the Pristina Sheraton en route to Skopje and then onto Kopaonik. They'd drive straight into the eye of the hurricane, riding in two vehicles. The HEL and a Land Rover SUV, two personnel in each.

Crossing the border into North Macedonia was uneventful. But in under an hour, they'd be crossing into Serbia and that border would prove challenging.

As they approached, Nick sat in the driver's seat of the SUV. Once at the border control point, he handed his and Curt's passports over. Nick's passport was North Macedonian, and Curt's was British.

"What is your intent in Serbia?" The border official asked.

Due to the previous night's escapades, the increased security was not unsuspected.

In Serbian, Nick replied. "Yeah, we are running up to Kopaonik. The crazy jeep looking vehicle behind us is a radar calibration device. Belgrade demanded it immediately, given some press reporting U.S. stealth aircraft were flying over Serbia unseen last night. With this device calibrating the Kopaonik radar, we can hopefully catch those fuckers and shoot down another stealth fighter like we did in 1999."

The border guard said, "OK, wait here." He turned and walked to the guard post. Within a minute, he emerged with three other border guards. With Curt in one vehicle and Smitty in the other, they simultaneously and slowly reached down along their sides, lifting the bottoms of their shirts which concealed their sidearms. Both were concerned. They hadn't even entered Serbia and worried the plan was already compromised.

Two of the other border guards jumped into a parked patrol car, backed it out and turning on the lights.

The border guard who previously spoke with returned the passports. "Glad you are here. Follow that vehicle, they will escort you to Kopaonik." Nick's delivery was not only good, it was brilliant. The two vehicles would be welcomed into Serbia, with a police escort to their objective. *'Nicely done, Monk,'* Curt thought to himself. Headlines splashed across Belgrade, Pristina, the wider Balkans and Europe, news media sensationalized the previous night's events, contemplating the likelihood of Stealth aircraft over Serbia. What else could it have been? They speculated.

As the border officials drove towards Kopaonik, the only complaint was from Smitty, who was getting windburned from the cold air and excessive pace set by the Serbian police escort. No matter... They were in Serbia. Step one, complete.

Nearing Kopaonik, the team observed a massive number of Serbian forces. The Serbian vehicle in front of them slowed and then stopped. Talking to one soldier who was manning a perimeter check point, the Serbian customs officer proudly announced he was the one escorting a critical asset to help the military. The customs police car began driving again, and the three vehicles had penetrated the outer cordon driving straight into the hotel parking lot.

Curt and his team stopped their vehicles then waved at the customs officials, thanking him for the escort as he drove away, back towards the border. Nick got out of the SUV and walked into the command post.

"Hello?" He said in Serbian.

A guard stopped him, "Who are you?" as he raised his AK-47 assault rifle.

"Hey, whoa! I am here with the team to fix the radar!"

The guard, a low-level soldier, did not have Nick on the visitor list, but sent his colleague onto the command post floor. Eventually, a captain in charge of air defense emerged.

"Yes, can I help you?"

"I hope so. I'm leading the team that was sent here to fine tune the radar up on the hill. You can see we have a specialized vehicle from BAE SYSTEMS which uses GPS and lasers to tighten target acquisition and mitigate Doppler notch issues." Nick pointed out at the HEL.

The captain had not heard about the upgrade from his superiors, but after yesterday's tongue-lashing the air defense officer received, he was not going to question any help. "OK, give me a minute to get my jacket and I will ride with you."

Nick stood there and waited. The five of them all took both cars up the hill to the large golf ball looking radar dome. Smitty entered the facility and once inside, he opened a laptop. He'd practiced for days to speak with a British accent, having BBC news run in the background of his hotel. "OK, mate. Computer's up. Let's work the quadrant angles."

"Righty." Curt's response. Also, trying to be a Brit. Curt returned to the HEL. He and Jerry drove it approximately 100 meters directly north of the radar and raised the laser ball, pointing it at the radar. Curt and Smitty spoke on a walkie talkie, both looking at their respective screens. The words were in English and few at the site could understand. After covering the cardinal direction of north, the same thing was done south, east and west. Next, Curt took the HEL approximately a half mile away, again raising the radar ball at the radar. None of these activities did anything to fix a radar that wasn't actually broken to begin with.

The air defense officer, in Serbian, asked Nick what was happening. Nick turned to Smitty and translated the question. "What are you doing now?"

"Right now, we are trying to measure the amount of side lobe and back lobe leakage, and if possible, we will try to mitigate it via software updates. If we can reduce side and back lobe loss, then the main lobe becomes stronger, giving the radar a better chance to acquire the target."

Nick looked at Smitty as if he had three heads. Apparently, Smitty had done his homework, and while impressive, the entire story was bullshit. Nick relayed it to the air defense officer, who was amazed at the HEL's fictitious capabilities. Over the next two hours, Nick, Smitty, Curt, and Jerry would continue to perform extremely detailed radar calibrating. By the end, absolutely no improvement had been made on the Kopaonik radar's ability.

It was 1300Hrs, and the team was done for the day. It was lunchtime, and they all headed back down the mountain, deciding to leave the HEL on top of the mountain, in the event the stealth aircraft returned that night.

The air defense officer was so pleased with the efforts, he personally coordinated hotel rooms for the team, then offered to buy them lunch in the hotel restaurant. They all sat down, and through Nick's translation, engaged in small talk.

As they spoke, the room fell quiet, and everyone turned. Major General Dučić, a towering and stocky man, walked into the room. He was the type of leader who just commanded respect from his stature. Smitty and Curt looked down into their plates. Jerry sat there fascinated with the entire scene, completely oblivious to the danger he was in.

"Major General Dučić, sir! General!" the air defense officer called out.

Major General Dučić stopped. "Yes, captain," he said in Serbian.

Responding in his native tongue, the captain said, "I wanted to let you know the team that's here to calibrate the air surveillance radar on the hill is complete and spent hours getting it just right."

Major General Dučić had heard nothing of the team's arrival, but communications with Belgrade had already proved unreliable. Their presence was a surprise, but so were many other things. It was not without merit someone would be trying to adjust the main surveillance radar for southern Serbia. Additionally, his air defense officer was escorting them. They obviously were doing goodness for the Serbian military.

In Serbian, the Major General said, "Gentlemen, welcome, and thank you for your help. Last night was fucking chaos. I must go, but again, I appreciate your help." Nick translated the message and the other three just nodded in appreciation of the kind words. As the Major General walked away, Curt couldn't help but think, *'If he believes last night was fucking chaos, he's in for all out madness, tonight.'*

After lunch, the four retired to their rooms. Smitty, still carrying the laptop, told the air defense officer he and Curt would likely need to go up to the radar that evening. Atmospheric conditions such as fluctuations in the ionosphere could affect radar performance, and they'd need to look at it again after dusk. The air defense officer nodded, completely understanding, and said he'd coordinate their movement if needed. It was all too easy.

\*\*\*\*\*\*\*\*\*\*\*\*\*\*\*\*\*\*\*\*\*\*\*\*\*\*\*\*\*\*\*\*\*\*\*\*\*\*\*\*\*

Earlier in the day, both the U.S. embassies in Pristina and Skopje held their morning round table meeting with senior staff. Both Ambassadors could not understand what happened the night before and were desperate for answers. In Pristina, the meeting ended, and everyone stood up to depart.

The Ambassador called out, "Hey Mike, can you come to my

office with me?"

"Of course, Ambassador."

The two walked from the conference room to the Ambassador's office. It would only be the two of them.

"Mike, do you have any idea what happened last night?"

"Sir, I don't." Mike was telling the truth. He had not been read into the covert operation and had no knowledge of the C-130 efforts. He did, however, know that Curt, Smitty, and the gang departed Kosovo that morning. Moose had done an excellent job compartmentalizing each slice of the mission.

"OK. Let me ask you this. Is there an ongoing special operations mission in Kosovo that you haven't shared with me?"

"Sir, there is not an operation here. I escorted a team a few days ago, but they departed Kosovo this morning into North Macedonia. I don't know any more, but for these guys to cause the havoc from last night. That's a stretch."

"Thanks, Mike. I appreciate it. Can you do me a favor? I'd like to you reach out to SOCOM. I want to be read into this team's mission."

"OK, sir. I'll contact them when they are awake. They are in Tampa, so it will probably be later this afternoon."

"I got it. OK. I need to go meet with the Kosovar leadership and beg them to agree with Serbian demands. Wish me luck," the Ambassador said, realizing his efforts would most likely fail.

"Sir, sometimes I'm glad you do what you do, and I do what I do. I do not envy your position, given the past few days."

"Thanks, Mike. I am not too enviable of my current position either." Mike departed the Ambassador's office. He'd reach out to Moose, who would immediately reply to Mike's email request as 'acknowledged,' but he'd slow roll any read in for the Ambassador until it was too late.

In Skopje, things didn't go as well. That Ambassador asked similar questions; however, on the Skopje airfield ramp, the past two days had been a heavily modified EC-130H that had been actively transmitting into Serbia the night prior.

"Ambassador, yes, there is a SOF mission ongoing, but even I don't have the full story."

"OK. I want you to bring me the aircraft commander today when they land."

"Sir, I can't do that without disrupting the mission. There is no way to bring him here, get him back and allow the aircraft to depart in their schedule takeoff window." The defense attaché was correct, though the answer would be a weak one in the eyes of any state department employee.

The Ambassador did not want to disrupt a mission, no matter how much he wanted to know. "Colonel, you need to look me in the eye. Do you know if that mission had anything to do with last night's issues?"

"Sir, I do not. I know the aircraft flew back and forth to Papa Air Base in Hungary, and to the best of my knowledge, never entered Serbian airspace. Frankly, it would be nearly impossible for a C-130 to enter Serbian airspace undetected." Everything the defense attaché said was true.

The Ambassador paused and rubbed his chin. "Call SOCOM. I want to be read into this mission." It was the same demand as Embassy Pristina, which would also be slow rolled by Moose back in Tampa.

*************************************

The sun crested over the East Coast as morning raised its head. Both Admiral Hershey and General Etcher walked into their respective morning briefings, curious if the intelligence agencies could uncover their plot. Concerningly, they came close. The briefing officials reported it was possible that the transmissions emerged from Montenegro on one side and from Romania on the other side of Serbia. How they arrived at this information would not be shared, nor would leaders ask. While the agencies got that part right (the two aircraft were physically in the airspace of those respective nations), the intel assessment drastically diverged from reality. Senior intel analysts speculated that Montenegrin assets performed such actions in retaliation for Serbia's failed coup attempt on Montenegro back in 2016. As for Romania, officials believed this was a token effort to demonstrate loyalty to NATO, or to try to disrupt any Serbian invasion.  Clearly, both were wrong.  Both Admiral Hershey and General Etcher were safe for another day.

## Chapter Fifty-Two
# D-Day

As the sun set on the Balkans, apprehension and anxiety filled the Serbian forces in Kopaonik. If they could just get through this night, they'd be invading Kosovo the next day. Commanders reassured the soldiers nothing was wrong. A standing order came down. There'd be no alcohol drinking this night, and all were to get to bed early. Many soldiers had private talks with the Serbian Orthodox priests who were walking through the camps, trying to calm the masses. Talking with priests the day prior to a major offensive was not uncommon; however, the priests were surprised to learn many of the soldier's questions revolved around how the dead could talk to the living, rather than questions related to combat.

Other soldiers were taking matters into their own hands, performing superstitious rituals passed down through their families. They just needed to get through one more night.

Darkness set on Kopaonik. This night, it would be darker than most with no moon. Belgrade war planners had scheduled the invasion to take place on a day which would transition to full darkness, allowing Serbian forces to bed down at night in locations across Kosovo, using the darkness to mask their locations. They gruffly dismissed how vulnerable the darkness would make their forces, which were all packed into a small valley. *'Who would attack Serbian forces in Serbia?'* they thought.

As the team sat in their hotel room, Curt opened the second envelope from Monk. It said:

*Best of luck today.*

*Last Sun Tzu quote for you. 'To win one hundred victories in one hundred battles is not the acme of skill. To subdue the enemy without fighting is the acme of skill.'*

*Fight like warriors.*

*v/r*
*Monk*

Curt passed the letter around to the team. Smitty was the last to read it, and said, "Don't ya find it somewhat humorous that we are placing all our faith in a guy named 'Monk' who keeps quoting a famed historic Chinese philosopher and warrior?" They all laughed. Smitty lit the paper on fire and threw it in a metal trashcan.

All four stood up and shook hands one last time. It was a serious moment. Smitty and Curt grabbed their bag full of gear. They walked out of the hotel and drove the SUV up to the HEL. Once there, they threw their bags in, put on night vision goggles and fired up the vehicle, slowly driving in the darkness away from the radar, positioning on a cliff crest. Kopaonik, being a ski resort in the winter, had cleanly cut ski paths down the mountain, which provided a clear line of sight onto many of the staged vehicles, tents, and support entities. Curt and Smitty stopped the HEL pointing it straight at the forces, and raised the laser ball. A display in front of the passenger seat of the HEL with a targeting lens and electric optic night vision imaging could clearly zoom in on a 2 ft x 2 ft target from farther than most people could imagine. Smitty sat there watching the screen, Curt exited the vehicle, cross carrying his M4. He moved discretely, roughly fifty meters away, into a nearby tree line and found some concealment to provide Smitty some over-watch coverage. The two had earpieces and discrete boom mics affixed to their top of the line Special Ops radio systems. Comms were checked and verified.

For the third and final night, the EC-130J Commando Solo flew off the coast of Croatia and Montenegro over the Adriatic. At 2115Hrs, the Mission Crew Commander reported 'Music On.' Seconds later, the EC-130H reported 'Buzzer On.' The four massive generators on the Commando Solo's turbo fan jet engines directed energy into the transmitters. Within milliseconds, the Serbian radio nets received the broadcast. "WE WARNED YOU! NEVER FORGET, YOUR FATHERS AND GRANDFATHERS TAKE THIS ACTION OUT OF LOVE."

The message played over and over. Major General Dučić sat in the command post, ready for tonight's shenanigans. He jumped on the radio net. "Who the fuck are you? We will destroy Kosovo!" He ordered the operations officer to turn on the floodlights around the camp and sent officers to scan vehicles and find whoever was transmitting. Within seconds, flood lights blanketed the large formation. Officers searched frantically to find who was making the transmissions. They would find no one.

Approximately one mile away, Smitty saw the encampment lights come on. That was his cue. He warmed up the laser, locking it on the rear tire of a support truck sitting in a row of vehicles.

No one was near him, but Curt was on the radio. Smitty said, "Showtime!" and fired the laser. The laser made a 'clunk, clunk, clunk' sound and within seconds, the tire heated up and popped. Making a somewhat loud 'boom.' Serbian soldiers in the area scrambled, wondering if incoming fire hit the vehicle. They would never see the laser beam as it operated well outside the visible light spectrum. Seconds later, Smitty locked upon another vehicle tire and fired the laser. BOOM, the tire exploded. "Oh, that truck is toast!" he said into his boom mic.

Curt just listened and smiled. Not one Serbian soldier was near, nor did any suspect them. The plan Monk laid out was working perfectly. As Curt listened to Smitty babble like a child on his first trip to Disney, he couldn't help but reflect on the range of emotions in combat or conflict. There is fear, anger, sadness, confusion and so many more that fall on the negative side of traditional emotions. But there is also excitement, satisfaction, accomplishment, and even humor.

"Hey Curt," Smitty transmitted over his radio. "Who was that freakin' guy in Guardians of the Galaxy?"

"You mean Chris Pratt?"

"No, the character's name?" Smitty was lining up another target.

"Peter Quill?"

"Yea! That guy! I'm him right now!" Smitty laughed and engaged the laser again. "Pew! Pew!"

On the Serbian communications network, a senior sergeant noncommissioned officer jumped on the radio. "They're shooting out the tires! Turn off the fucking lights!"

Major General Dučić ordered the lights out and authorized return fire on any perceived enemy activity. Small arms fire erupted as the lights went dark. It wasn't clear what anyone was shooting at.

A loud bell blared from the command post. It could be heard for well over a mile. Curt and Smitty assumed it must have been the signal to turn out lights, as that action happened immediately after. "Oh, you wanna play in the dark?" Smitty said rhetorically. He dropped his night vision device over his eyes and quoted a famous line from "It's a Wonderful Life." "Look, mommy! Every time a bell rings, an angel gets its wings!"

Smitty locked up another vehicle tire and fired. "Atta boy, Clarence!" Smitty continued the movie quote. Curt sat in his over-watch position growing concerned Smitty may be having a bit too much fun. Smitty would keep shooting out tires until twenty vehicles had flats randomly scattered throughout the formation. At the end of shooting vehicles, he said, "Curt, Buddy! I gotta get me one of these! Han Solo, eat your fucking heart out!"

At 2130Hrs the Commando Solo transmitted, "WE WON'T LET YOU GO FIGHT. WE BEG YOU, GO HOME TO YOUR MOTHERS, FATHERS, SISTERS, BROTHERS, WIVES AND CHILDREN. IT WILL ONLY GET WORSE THE LONGER YOU STAY."

Major General Dučić screamed at his forces and pleaded with Belgrade to act. There'd be no response. The EC-130H Compass Call was flying south from Papa Air Base. The wireless communication networks were again inoperable, being heavily jammed from the EC 130s massive power. The Major General was alone. This time, however, the Compass Call would not make it to Skopje. Over Bulgaria, the aircraft made a call to airspace control and requested a return to Papa Air base through Romanian airspace. The reason used was 'mission needs,' with an intent of keeping the flight plan open and depart again later. After about a half a minute, Bulgarian air traffic cleared the aircraft as requested. Near the North Macedonian border, the Compass Call slowly turned north, continuing its mission, heading now to Papa Air Base.

Smitty looked at his watch. It was time to change targets. Using a small joystick, Smitty moved the laser and locked it on a large tree next to the vehicles. The laser would center around fifteen feet in the air. He fired the laser, and within seconds, the tree started to smolder. After another twenty seconds, it erupted into flames.

Serbian soldiers rapidly moved to put out the flames, while others tried to figure out where the incoming rounds were originating from. There was no explosion, no indications of rockets or mortar rounds. The tree just spontaneously combusted. They'd seen nothing like it before. When the Serbian army's small arms fire ceased, it was eerily quiet, until another tree erupted into fire.

Smitty would shoot the laser at ten trees, then power down the HEL. He called Curt, "Dude. I don't know how much this thing costs, but we need about a dozen! I'm complete, let's go." Curt pulled back from his over-watch position and stowed his weapon.

The two raced back to the Land Rover and sped down the hill. Their return to the hotel was unnoticed in the midst of all the commotion.

As they walked into the hotel, the air defense officer stopped them. "Hey. What the fuck! The radar still doesn't see anything! Where were you guys? What are you doing?!" He yelled in Serbian, a language neither understood.

"Nick!?" Curt said as he pointed up the stairs. "Get Nick?" Neither understood Serbian and needed a translator.

The air defense officer obliged, and they all walked up to Nick's hotel room. The air defense officer pounded on the door.

"Nick! Nick! Open the fucking door!"

Nick opened the door, staring at a screaming Serbian officer with Smitty and Curt standing behind him. There was only one thing to do. Smitty looked down the hotel hallway. They were alone. He smashed his previously concealed sidearm on the officer's head. He collapsed immediately as Curt and Nick caught him. They dragged him into the hotel room and tied him up.

Downstairs, Major General Dučić ordered his lower commanders to control the fires. Company, battalion, and brigade commanders were reporting fleeing soldiers.

Dučić grated his teeth. He was less than 24 hours away from becoming Serbia's newest hero, who returned Kosovo to its rightful owner. He would not stand for desertion.

"Wolf Commanders. This is Wolf Six. You are ordered to 'Shoot to wound' any soldier who appears to be deserting."

Seconds later, scattered small arms fire erupted. Screams from fleeing soldiers could be heard across the valley. That lasted for roughly fifteen minutes. Eventually, the desertions ceased. Other soldiers who witnessed the mayhem looked on in utter fear.

The tree fires were contained and there were no further communication intrusions. Magically, Major General Dučić could again communicate with Belgrade. He reported in detail what happened, and again, Belgrade confirmed there were no aircraft overhead. Belgrade could hear the frustration in the Major General's voice, continually asking him to calm down. That message was not well received by the Major General and he decided, perhaps, it was not wise to share his last order. Belgrade would not know Major General Dučić ordered his military to fire on their own soldiers. He would tell them later once he was a hero.

At Papa Air Base, two C-130s were on the ramp with their engines running. One was the EC-130H Compass Call. The other C-130 had departed Aviano to deliver some goods, and then would return to Aviano. It was a basic 'slick' C-130 flying one of the many mundane missions C-130s around the globe perform.

It, however, would serve a valuable purpose for the night's mission. The two C-130s sat next to each other on the ramp. At the prescribed time, both pilots in their cockpits looked at each other and nodded. As they did, their callsigns and transponder IFF (Identification Friend of Foe) squawk changed. The basic C-130, which arrived from Aviano, would continue onto Skopje and the EC-130 would go take the other mission back to Aviano Air Base. To air traffic control up in the tower hundreds of meters away, the swap was unnoticeable.

*************************************

As social media lit up with posts about the ongoings in Serbia, the U.S. Ambassador to Skopje could take no more. He demanded to go meet the C-130 on the ramp and question the aircraft commander. Eventually, the Ambassador and defense attaché were notified the aircraft was approximately an hour away. They departed the embassy and parked on the ramp. The two stood there awaiting the aircraft, both remaining silent. Off in the distance, on the approach profile, the lights of the aircraft became visible, and it landed uneventfully. The distinct sound of a C-130 reversing its props and revving the engines could be heard across the airfield, decelerating the aircraft to a crawl.

An airport ramp handler taxied the aircraft back into the parking spot. The defense attaché was amazed. It was a basic cargo C-130, not the airplane that departed. All the antennas, wires, blister pods were gone. He didn't say a word. This fight was gonna be between the Ambassador and the pilot. Not him.

The engine shut down, and the Ambassador walked up as the crew door opened. "Hi. I'm the U.S. Ambassador. Who's in charge?"

A young captain looked down from the flight deck, "Hey, Mr. Ambassador! It's an honor! I'm the aircraft commander, Captain Cundiff. They call me 'Chewy!'"

"Fine, captain, can you tell me what you're doing?"

"Yes, sir." With that, Chewy got up out of his seat and walked down off the flight deck. "Come with me, Ambassador." Chewy led the Ambassador to the cargo area, where three pallets stood neatly in a row, tied down, all marked with USAID. "Sir, we are flying back and forth in the region with food and other necessities. Our mission is classified, but some leadership well above me believes there will be an imminent humanitarian crisis and they want this stuff pre-positioned in Eastern Europe when needed. As you can imagine, asking nations to preposition humanitarian aid could alarm our allies, which would be undesired. Hence, we keep flying it. Frankly, it doesn't make sense to me to keep flying it around, but I don't make the orders, and I get to log flight time. I guess they wanted to keep it moving for some reason."

The Ambassador looked at Chewy. Then at his defense attaché. None of it made sense, and he was right. "I want to talk to a flag officer at U.S. EUCOM Headquarters tomorrow first thing!" He barked at his attaché.

"Yes, Mr. Ambassador," he responded. The attaché understood the Ambassador's frustration, and honestly, he too did not truly understand what was going on, but sometimes, that was the way of the special operations world.

At Aviano Air Base, the EC-130H would be landing and parking next to the Commando Solo, her sister aircraft. The two would be tucked to sleep that night and immediately start their flights back to the U.S. in the morning. Their part of the overall mission was complete. Admiral Hershey and General Etcher would pray few would ever realize their presence in Europe.

*****************************************

In Kosovo, the reports of exploding tires, trees igniting, and fratricide quickly circulated. Kosovar Albanians may speak primarily Albanian, but most understood Serbian and had enough folks with 'ears' to the ground to know what was happening. They would rejoice in the streets, crediting the fallen Kosovo Liberation Army soldiers with the nefarious actions, not the fallen Serbian soldiers. Such was the way of the Balkans. In Kosovo, however, the narrative didn't matter.

Intel assets from Montenegro, Croatia, Romania and Bulgaria were also reporting the oddities of the evening. Baffling their leadership, all who privately harbored their belief it could be the ghosts of fallen soldiers, but would not publicly acknowledge it.

\*\*\*\*\*\*\*\*\*\*\*\*\*\*\*\*\*\*\*\*\*\*\*\*\*\*\*\*\*\*\*\*\*\*\*\*\*\*\*\*

This night's social media and news reporting surpassed the previous one. Allison and her group of friends did all they could to keep generating buzz. At this point, however, mainstream media was reporting near constant breaking news on the Serbian forces, far outpacing social media.

## *Chapter Fifty-Three*
# The Aftermath

Major General Dučić was up all night, talking to his staff and Belgrade. He could not find his air defense officer, another likely deserter who'd get punished later. He had little time to try and solve that mystery now. Morning rose over the encampment and resolute soldiers were trying to change out flat tires and quell the remaining brush fires.

Back at the command post, the battalion commanders slowly walked into the briefing room and stood behind their chairs. Minutes later, Major General Dučić would enter. The room would be called to attention, he would sit, then the others would follow. The morning brief was a disaster. Desertion rates were over 50%, and there were over 300 injured for trying to flee. After the meeting, Dučić contacted Serbian Defense Chief General Bojović and relayed the unfortunate news, but desperately argued the case he could continue with the mission. The defense chief did not provide an answer, but rather said he needed to speak to his superiors. The two hung up, and the general asked his staff to connect him to President Sokol.

"Mr. President. I regret to inform you we've had another incident last night at our staging area."

"General, I am aware, as is the media. The rampant speculation of superstitions and ghosts is flooding the papers and the people are drinking it down like water. How bad is it?"

"Sir, over 50% desertion; however, Major General Dučić believes he can continue."

"With less than half the force? Most of which are only there out of fear from the far greater consequences of desertion. I don't believe that's possible. General, tell me, did you authorize Major General Dučić to fire on our own soldiers?"

The general was stunned. "Sir?"

"There are reports he ordered the officers and noncommissioned officers to 'shoot to wound' those that were fleeing."

"Sir, I know nothing of this."

"If it is true, he cannot lead our force. Do you understand?"

"Yes, sir."

The phone line cut off. The Chief of Defense was furious.

\* \* \* \* \* \* \* \* \* \* \* \* \* \* \* \* \* \* \* \* \* \* \* \* \* \* \* \* \* \* \* \* \* \* \* \* \* \* \*

A hotel cleaning lady in Kopaonik entered a dirty hotel room in the late morning. Inside, bound and gagged, was the air defense officer. She screamed and ran out of the room, trying to find another soldier. Soon, he would be untied and share his horrible experience. Major General Dučić could not see straight. His security officers discovered CCTV video of all four men, and he ordered them to be stopped at all costs.

As that order began circulating, the Raytheon HEL, driven by Nick and Jerry, was already in North Macedonia, on its way to Pristina airport where a waiting C-17 would fly it back. Jerry, who hadn't said or done much the entire trip, was elated. As the lead engineer, HEL was his baby. While he had dreams of it shooting down planes and drones as well as engaging in many other aspects of conventional warfare, his 'baby' proved worthy in irregular warfare. If he had a cigar, he'd have lit it. Much further north, outside of Belgrade, Curt and Smitty were in the Land Rover. All four had departed Kopaonik at 0500Hrs, well before light. It would take hours, but photos of the four would be plastered on every Serbian police station wall with 'Be on the lookout' reports flooding Serbian police channels.

Serbian authorities were too slow to stop Nick and Jerry. They'd fled the country already based on recent CCTV video analysis., But it was clear that two of the four remained in the country. Quickly, Nick and Jerry's images were removed from the BOLO, but Curt and Smitty remained. An all-points bulletin circulated from the highest levels, to every ministry, department, and agency from the office of President Sokol. Officers walked the streets of major cities with photos in hand, asking citizens if they'd seen these two men. The hunt was on.

At Aviano Air Base, the two EC-130s took off five minutes

apart. They would share an airborne tanker somewhere near Shannon, Ireland. Then the Commando Solo would speed up home back to Harrisburg, while the Compass Call would require one more airborne refueling to make it to Tucson. The crews would not speak of their missions to anyone. From that perspective, Admiral Hershey and General Etcher's secret remained safe.

******************************************

The late morning breeze through Belgrade was pleasant, as Nikola and Katarina sat drinking coffee, reading the paper, and scrolling through the craziness of social media. While Katarina was concerned, Nikola dismissed the stories as overblown hype and soldiers' jitters before the big fight. There was little to worry about.

A buzz from his phone vibrated the table, and he picked it up. "Hello?"

"Nikola, this is Aleksandar." It was President Sokol. "I am sure you've seen the reports. Things are not going well, and we will have to postpone the attack."

The news struck Nikola in the heart. "No! You can't! We had a deal!" He was furious. Katarina watched. She knew exactly what was happening. A tear trickled down her cheek. In her mind, this story ended just like every other Balkan story. They were all tragedies.

"I'm sorry Nikola, but it will not happen today. I did not say never. Just not today. We cannot risk it."

Nikola hung up the phone. He was enraged. Katarina slowly got up from the table and walked back to her apartment. She'd lay down and cry. Nikola dialed Steve's number back in D.C. Clearly the U.S. had interfered, and he wanted answers. Steve never heard the call. It was 0430Hrs local time. The phone sat on his nightstand, set to silent.

Arriving in Belgrade, Smitty and Curt drove the streets, talking to each other about the lay of the land, noting one-way streets, and choke points, checking stop light timing and other things. There was only one piece of the mission left unaccomplished. Every time they passed a police car, they'd look down. At one point, they pulled up to a four-lane stop light. In the lane next to them was a police car. Smitty tried to avoid eye contact, but it was clear the police officer was looking at him. Eventually, the light changed. Smitty would never know, but that officer was not aware of the manhunt yet.

The two had seen enough. There was little reward for taking more risk. They checked into a low-end hotel and prepared for their evening expedition.

*****************************************

As D.C. awoke, so did New York City. The Ambassador of the Russian Federation called an emergency meeting of the U.N. Security Council for 0800Hrs. Someone or something had attacked Serbia, and they wanted answers. Because of this emergency meeting, Admiral Hershey was summoned to the White House along with the Secretary of Defense. In Tampa, at SOCOM Headquarters, General Etcher canceled his morning staff meeting to dial into the White House Video Tele Conference. His morning staff meeting would have to wait, as would the pending intelligence assessment regarding the previous night's events.

Standing outside the Pentagon at the helipad, Admiral Hershey and Secretary Gerzema stood as they could hear their helicopter approaching. "Strange happenings in Serbia," the Secretary said.

"I agree, sir. Strange indeed."

Secretary Gerzema stared at the Chairman. Trying to assess if he knew anything. Admiral Hershey's face was as solid as a stone. There would be no tell shared.

The helicopter flew to the White House, and the two entered the National Security Council meeting. Soon after, the President walked in. Along with the normal characters, the EUCOM and SOCOM Commanders were on a Secure Video Conference Screen, hanging on the wall. Sitting next to General Etcher at his table was Moose, who was far less composed than his boss.

"OK, what do we know?" The President wasted no time.

"Mr. President, Good Morning," Director of National Intelligence Greg Cromwell started. "Sir, there are confirmed reports that Serbian military vehicles had their tires explode and trees surrounding the staging area ignited. Numerous Serbian soldiers deserted, and intelligence assets were able to intercept a transmission of one commander authorizing soldiers to actually fire on fleeing deserters."

The table was quiet. Most already had heard this news and wanted to know the 'how' not so much the 'what.' DNI continued, "Sir, yesterday we assessed the erroneous transmissions to be from Montenegro and Romania. On further examination, we now believe that is incorrect." Admiral Hershey's and General Etcher's stomachs churned.

"The theory we are now tracking down is a possible saboteur within the Serbian military. While we assess that radio transmissions could theoretically come from anywhere with line of sight, exploding tires and tree fires had to originate much closer to the Serbian forces staging area. We have no indications that Kosovo sent any special units into Serbia, nor any indications from other neighboring countries."

The President looked at the director of the CIA, "You agree?"

"Mr. President, I don't agree or disagree at this point. Our folks are still running the traps, but I believe that DNI's assessment is about the only logical conclusion."

"Good." The President turned to the Secretary and Chairman, who both oversaw the Defense Intelligence Agency. "John, Admiral, what do your guys got? Anything different?"

Secretary Gerzema spoke up. "No, sir. Nothing different."

White House Chief of Staff Steve Lewis stood against the wall and could not believe his ears. It was as if God had given the President a golden lottery ticket. Steve had yet to return the call from Nikola, for good reason. He needed some excuse, and he now had it.

Also, on a VTC screen, the U.S. Ambassador to the U.N. was tuned in. "Mr. President, Russia will seek to blame the U.S. for all of this. How would you like me to respond?"

"Yes, Ambassador, I am sure they will. We will draft you a statement quickly. In essence, the statement will demand Russia present facts of such activities or stop their constant rhetoric of blaming the U.S. Got it?"

The Ambassador nodded.

"Anyone else in the room have anything?" The President asked. Everyone remained silent. No one knew exactly what to say about the previous night's events. "Good. Let's go listen to the Russians complain." With that, the President rose and soon after, so did the rest of the table.

\* \* \* \* \* \* \* \* \* \* \* \* \* \* \* \* \* \* \* \* \* \* \* \* \* \* \* \* \* \* \* \* \* \* \* \* \* \*

At Fort Bragg, a gorgeous Harley Davidson Ultra Glide Classic sat outside the 4th Psychological Operations Group. Lieutenant Colonel Monk Baylis walked up to it, wearing his leather vest and chaps. Slowly, he would strap on his helmet and then put on his gloves. He straddled the beast of a bike and checked his left rear-view mirror. For a brief moment, he caught a glimpse of himself, and he just smiled. Monk had crafted a mission that pitted two C-130s and four individuals against an army of 10,000, and it worked. The grin lasted for a few seconds. He started the bike, and it chugged beautifully with the distinctive Harley sound. Monk kicked the shifter into gear and rode off the base. Neither National Defense University, nor his family, nor anyone would know of his efforts. Had the University learned of his accomplishments, he would have graduated with honors. To Monk, it didn't matter. Because that's just the kind of guy he was.

\* \* \* \* \* \* \* \* \* \* \* \* \* \* \* \* \* \* \* \* \* \* \* \* \* \* \* \* \* \* \* \* \* \* \* \* \* \*

A shiny Gulfstream G650 flew through the night from Dulles International to the airfield in Tivat, Montenegro. It parked in the line with all the other private jets, as Tivat was the airport for the rich and famous oligarchs who harbored their ridiculously large yachts just a few miles away in the Bay of Kotor. Andrew Denney was the only passenger aboard the private jet. His funding the plane was part of the deal he struck with Smitty in private days before the activities began. Upon landing, Andrew would depart the plane and catch a cab to the Port of Montenegro. A hotel reservation awaited him where he'd be able to grab some rest. He'd be expecting a call, eventually, if everything went as planned.

## Chapter Fifty-Four
# The Ugly American

After the U.N. Security Council video cast ended, Steve stepped away and finally returned Nikola's call. He didn't want to, but he also didn't want to ignore the man extorting the President.

"Nikola, it is Steve. Can you talk?"

"Steve, what the fuck did the U.S. do? We had a deal?"

"Nikola, calm down. We didn't do anything. Our Ambassador even challenged the Russians at the U.N. to provide proof. No one knows what happened, but to blame the U.S. is rich. Let's be clear, Serbia hasn't been the best neighbor in the neighborhood. The coup attempt in Montenegro, a war with Croatia. If you have any evidence to prove this was the U.S., let's hear it. Can you?"

Nikola could not, but the entire saga of the last 48 hours could not be placed at the feet of dead soldiers and superstitions. "Fine. But this isn't over. Once we find out what happened, Serbia will again mass forces and we will execute our deal then! Do you understand?"

Steve was just happy to fight off the alligator in the boat. The invasion planned for today was aborted. Alligators on the shoreline were menacing but far less dangerous. "Yes, Nikola. I understand." Steve hung up and breathed a sigh of relief.

"Who was that?" The President asked as he stood behind Steve.

"Sorry, Mr. President. I didn't see you there. Well, it was our challenge in Serbia. He's quite angry."

"I can see why. I'd be angry if I were him, too. Did he say anything about his blackmail information?"

"No, sir. He said that Serbia will, at some point in the future, refit their forces and commence the attack."

"Of course they will, Steve. Yes. Of course." Steve could not tell if the President was being honest or sarcastic. It was 50/50.

\*\*\*\*\*\*\*\*\*\*\*\*\*\*\*\*\*\*\*\*\*\*\*\*\*\*\*\*\*\*\*\*\*\*\*\*\*\*\*\*\*\*

Evening fell upon Belgrade. Serbians followed their normal routine of socializing in cafes and restaurants. The Russian Tsar Restaurant was packed and full of life. Standing at the door, attempting to get a seat, was a tall man, shoulder length hair, with an obnoxiously loud American flag T-shirt, Bermuda shorts, and flip-flops. The hostess and the other guests scowled at him. In Belgrade, it was OK to be American. It was not OK to be an ugly American.

The man sat down at a table and immediately ordered two beers, both for himself. He then began talking on his phone loudly. He mentioned NATO, U.S. military, a new weapon system, and much more. Eventually, one waiter overheard the conversation. He exited the restaurant, standing just out front, then placed a call on his cell phone. "Hey. We got one here if you're interested. Looks like a clean kill."

On the other end of the line, Katarina said, "OK. I'll be there soon." She knew the place. It was where she and Nikola always had their late morning coffee. Katarina considered not going. She was still destroyed from the earlier news, but she also knew her winning lottery ticket didn't deliver, and she needed to make a living.

As the obnoxious American ate, Katarina walked into the Russian Tsar. She looked stunning. She sat at a table next to the American, specifically reserved by the waiter whom she'd pay handsomely later.

After a few bats of her eyes and a few flirtatious smiles, she struck up a conversation. "So, what brings you to Belgrade?"

"Uh, wow! Are you talking to me?" The man replied.

"Of course, handsome. Who else would I be talking to?"

"Uh... well. I'm here on a bit of vacation from my company. We are a defense contractor for the U.S. military. We've been assessing a new weapon system for NATO in Croatia, and I always wanted to come to Belgrade, so I'm here just for the night."

It was everything Katarina needed to hear. "Mind if I join you, then? I know the best tour guide of Belgrade."

"I'd love that! Who is it? Are they working this late?" The man was clueless.

Katarina smiled. "It's me." She slid sideways to sit across from him at his table. "And I can promise you a night you will never forget." Her foot slid under the table, up along the leg of the American, and she buried it gently in his groin; the entire time staring him in the eyes. It was intoxicating. They drank more alcohol and spoke. He was an idiot and could have left an hour ago, but still was trying to seduce her. Finally, she'd had enough. "What do you say we get out of here and go back to your hotel room?"

The man's eyes bulged. "Check please!" he loudly proclaimed. The two walked arm in arm back to his hotel that was just around the corner. On the elevator up, Katarina kissed the man passionately. He dropped his room key out of nervousness. As they stood in front of the hotel room door, he said, "Man, stuff like this NEVER happens to me!"

As he put the key in and opened the door, Katarina said, "It must be your lucky day."

He gently led her into the room and closed the door, where she was greeted by Curt and a syringe. "No, Natalie, it must be your lucky day."

Curt quickly injected her in the neck, and she fell to the ground. Smitty ripped off his disguise, pulled out the photo that Buck said was Natalie. It was definitely her.

Curt departed the room and walked down the hall, looking for CCTV cameras. He found two and from behind smudged Vaseline onto the lens, blurring the image. He then opened the service elevator, doing the same. Holding the door, he softly called for Smitty, who ran from the room with Katarina over his shoulder. Within seconds, he was on the elevator and going down to the service entrance, which was empty at this late hour. Quickly they sprang from the elevator and into the waiting Land

Rover, pre-positioned behind the hotel. Katarina was loaded into the back seat and the two men jumped up front.

The drive to Tivat would take nearly nine hours. They started out cautiously as they transitioned away from downtown Belgrade, not to bring undo attention. Once outside Belgrade, the route would be through back country, small villages and up over the Montenegrin or 'Black Mountains' range.

After four hours, they approached the border checkpoint between Serbia and Montenegro. It was the only place they'd have to talk to someone. The border patrol officers at the Jabuka crossing were nice young men. Both lived in a nearby village and were happy to have work. Few people crossed during the night shift, so it was a simple job with plenty of time to watch Serbian national television, mainly soccer games. As the lone vehicle approached, one man got up out of his seat, frustrated to have to work. He waved his hand for the car to stop. Curt did as instructed.

"Passports." The border officer said in Serbian.

"I'm sorry. We don't speak Serbian," Curt said softly. He also raised his finger to his lips, making the international sign for 'Shhhh,' pointing at Katarina in the back seat, who appeared to be sleeping.

"Passports," the officer said, this time in English.

Curt and Smitty passed over their British Passports, the officer waited for the third. "Hey, buddy look. She had a bunch to drink, and we don't know where her passport is. Can you just let it go?"

The officer looked at her. "I'm sorry. I need to see her passport."

Curt kept his cool. "I understand. Hey, can you just quickly look at our passports and see if they are good?"

The guard opened Curt's passport and two hundred euros fell out.

"Sir, what is this? Are you trying to bribe me?"

Of all the border guards in Serbia, Curt and Smitty had found one that was ethical, a rarity in the Balkans. The guard told the two to wait in the car as he went into the border patrol building.

On the bulletin board, the guard saw images of Curt and Smitty. He nudged his buddy, pointed at the photos, and then out to the car.

After a minute, the two border officers approached. As they did, Curt began to make a commotion. "Aw! Come on, guys!" He shouted. "Look! We just want to get outta here! You don't understand!"

The two raised their hands as if to calm him and the situation. Then one said, "Sir, please get out of the car."

Curt, still being loud, put the car in park and turned off the engine, all the while talking, continuing his fuss and drawing their attention. The guards had not noticed Smitty was no longer in the vehicle. As Curt opened the driver's side door, Smitty emerged like a flash from behind the car, pointing his Glock 19 at the high ready and aimed directly at the two border guards with the laser clearly painting the chest of the nearest guard. They turned to look at him and tried to draw, unfortunately turning their attention away from their closest threat, Curt.

Curt forcefully bent the arm of one guard backwards. Hearing the 'pop' of it dislocating from the shoulder joint, he quickly felt the sound resonate through his entire skeletal structure. The wracking pain caused the guard to drop his sidearm. As that happened, Smitty closed quickly on the second, pointing his gun at the man's head. If he drew his gun, the guard knew he would be dead. There was no chance. Curt and Smitty were in control.

It took an additional thirty minutes to tie up the two men, destroy their radios, and cut their phone lines. After that, Curt gave Katarina another injection, and they continued to Tivat. At roughly 0600Hrs, Smitty called Mr. Denney. "Andrew, we are 30 minutes away. Please have everything ready."

"I am already here. The jet is fueled and ready to go."

Like clockwork, the Land Rover pulled up next to the Gulfstream. The private guards at the Tivat Airport sat idle as the large luxury SUV drove in, blaring house music as if it was returning from one of the nightclubs in Budva, the local beach town. The guards watched uninterestedly as Smitty and Curt danced getting out of the car, acting as if they were quite inebriated. For them, such activities were common occurrences. Curt and Smitty threw their gear into the plane's cargo hold, then shook Katarina. "Hey, Natalie! Come on!! We're here! Natalie!"

She would not wake up. On board the aircraft, the two private pilots had seen far worse. Flying the rich and famous could have been a great opportunity to write a novel, if it weren't for all the non-disclosure agreements.

Eventually, Smitty and Curt lifted Natalie into the aircraft, handing over their passports as well as a poorly made fake one for Natalie that Andrew had crafted. Within 20 minutes, they were airborne on their way to Dulles International Airport.

Andrew Denney stared at Katarina, who was still asleep. He turned to Curt. "She's the one. Thanks."

"We did this for Buck as well." Curt paused, then continued. "Mr. Denney, can I ask what you're thanking us for?"

"For avenging my son's death. I owe you a debt. Please. Call me Andrew."

"Andrew, you're welcome." Curt wasn't fond of receiving appreciation from someone he saw as part of the D.C. swamp he despised.

"Son, you don't have much of a poker face. I can see from your reaction that you aren't very fond of my kind."

"You're correct, let me ask you. Were you proud of Don when he graduated from West Point?"

"Yes, of cou..."

"Why?" Curt cut him off.

"Excuse me?" Andrew was taken aback.

"Why? It's a simple question. Why were you proud? Was it simply a father's pride in a child's success? Or was it deeper? Were you proud he'd become part of an entity revered by the American public?"

Andrew thought about it for a minute. "I guess both, but I don't get why you ask."

"Well, it's not rocket surgery." The phrase was one Curt had grown fond. It combines 'rocket science' and 'brain surgery,' two phrases often used to reference intellect. "You, your company, and your kind are the antithesis of the military. The Army's 'Duty, Honor, Country.' The Air Force's 'Integrity, Service, Excellence.' The Navy's 'Honor, Courage, Commitment,' and the Marines 'Semper Fi.' He'd become something better than you, and I mean no disrespect by that, sir. Yet, after his education and service, those morals, those benchmarks for life. Why would he abandon them? Do you have any idea what might have caused him to stray?"

Andrew knew exactly what Curt was getting at. While the question was blunt, there was merit to it. It left a very unpleasant taste in Andrew's mouth. "I see your point." It was as much as Andrew would give Curt.

"Sir, you owe me nothing. I appreciate your thanks, but if you truly want to avenge your son's death, work to clean up D.C. Our Capital is a global embarrassment, and I'd argue the trend line is going in the wrong direction."

"Son, I don't disagree with you. But there is little one person can do to remedy the problem."

"Yup. That's the common answer. 'It's too hard.' Sir, I'm a former SEAL. I live by the motto 'The only easy day was yesterday.' I don't know the word 'hard,' and I'd suggest Don didn't either."

As difficult as it was to hear, everything Curt said was true. "Yes, Don didn't know the word 'hard.' I'm proud of him, and I am very proud to have been his father."

"I'm sure you are, sir. You should be. Do you think Don is proud of you?"

Andrew wouldn't respond. He just stared out the jet's window, looking out over the clouds. The discussion was over.

\*\*\*\*\*\*\*\*\*\*\*\*\*\*\*\*\*\*\*\*\*\*\*\*\*\*\*\*\*\*\*\*\*\*\*\*\*\*\*\*

In Chicago, Allison's phone rang. She was worried about Curt, and she'd answer numbers she didn't recognize, hoping it was him. The number had a 312 area code, likely Chicago.

"Hello, Allison Donley."

"Ms. Allison. Hey. It's Wanda from the hospital."

"Wanda. Is everything OK? Are you alright?"

"Yes ma'am. I'm good. I'm sorry to bother you, but the hospital administration is being a pain in my ass."

"Wanda, it's no bother at all. What's wrong?"

"Well, the hospital cleaned out Curt's office. Everything is in boxes and at my nursing station. I've tried to call him dozens of times, but he doesn't answer."

"Yes, Curt's out of the country right now."

"Well, these boxes is in the way. I'd really like to get rid of 'em."

Wanda didn't need to talk anymore. Allison would go get the boxes immediately. There was no need for Curt to go back to the hospital and carry out his belongings in front of his former colleagues. Allison jumped in the car, drove to the hospital and parked at the E.R..

"Ms. Wanda, good to see ya." Finding Wanda was easy. She was a big black woman who exuded attitude in spades. She was also one of the most loving individuals Curt knew.

"Hey, Ms. Allison. That was fast. Let me help you carry out da boxes."

"Thanks, Wanda. I appreciate that." The two each carried one box, then Allison walked back in with Wanda to retrieve the third. Before she could grab it, Wanda picked it up and the two would walk back out to the car. Wanda's shift was over, and she enjoyed Allison's company. The two chatted for a while as Wanda stood at Allison's car with the third box in her hand. It was only half full and partially open.

Wanda said, "Ms. Allison. That's all of it. I really appreciate you coming. I packed that box myself. It's just the last few files from his desk as well as his recently received mail. Please tell Dr. Nover I miss him, and I wish he could come back. But I guess since the hospital packed up his stuff in boxes, I don't think dat's gonna happen."

"I will do that, Wanda. And just so you know. You were always his favorite at the hospital. He'd want you to know."

The two hugged, and Allison drove away. Once back at the condo parking, Allison grabbed the last box Wanda brought and took it upstairs. She was concerned some of Curt's credit card bills delivered to his work address were likely going to be overdue. As she got to the condo, she sifted through the mail. As she suspected, one credit card was three days past due. Also in the mail was a manilla envelope, with handwritten to and from post markings. It was addressed to Curt, but the return address name was only D.D. with a Washington D.C. address.

## Chapter Fifty-Five
# An Unraveling Lie

Through the night, the intelligence community gathered, trying to recreate the events in Serbia. No one was left out of the meeting. Personnel who worked with space-based assets, the National Reconnaissance Office, DIA, CIA, the meeting was near unruly with sixteen different intelligence agencies trying to work together. If it was a saboteur, there had to be clues left behind. As they continued to work, the notion of the saboteur was collapsing.

Plots of the radio intrusion transmissions were confusing, as they originated from multiple locations along the Croatian and Montenegrin coast. Analysts assessed the transmitter must have been moving. Additionally, the jamming signal blocking communications from Kopaonik to Belgrade was also coming from multiple places in Bulgaria and Romania. That, too, was assessed to be moving. None of it made sense. As the analysts continued to plot the transmission locations, it was clear these transmitters were not only moving, but moving far faster than ground assets were capable of. Well into the day, intel analysis would continue to try and figure out what happened.

\*\*\*\*\*\*\*\*\*\*\*\*\*\*\*\*\*\*\*\*\*\*\*\*\*\*\*\*\*\*\*\*\*\*\*\*\*\*\*\*

As Mr. Denney's private jet crossed into U.S. airspace, Curt placed his call to Allison. He missed her dearly.

"Hey baby. I missed you. Before you ask, I'm fine."

"CURT! Thank God! Oh, sweetheart! I missed you, too! It's so awesome to hear your voice. Crazy shit was going on in this world. I don't know if it was you, but someday if it was, I wanna know what happened!"

Curt laughed. "Yeah. Frankly, I wanna know what happened too!"

The two chatted for about fifteen minutes. Allison eventually brought up that the hospital had cleared out Curt's desk and that Wanda helped Allison retrieve the boxes. She then brought up the envelope. "It's from whom?" Curt said.

"A person with the initials D.D.," she responded. The only 'D. D.' Curt knew of was the man who'd recently tried to kill him.

"Can you open it, please?"

Allison did as Curt requested. The first document she pulled out was a two-page typed letter. She began scanning through it. "Curt. Holy mother of God."

"What is it?"

"It's from Don Denney. It appears he wrote you this right before he killed himself. The letter is an apology as well as a detailed explanation of how Don and the White House were extorted. The blackmail plot is laid out." She paused, then continued. "And all the supporting evidence is in the envelope!" It was partially true. Don only shared what he knew, which was the same extortion information that Steve Lewis did. It was a great deal, but it did not include information about the video of the Ambassador's granddaughter. That information resided with the Russians, and Don was never exposed to it.

Curt took a deep breath. "OK, Baby. I'm gonna need you to scan that for me and send it out. I'll pass you the email address." Curt hung up and looked at Andrew. They hadn't spoken more than 10 words since their last exchange. "So, Mr. Denney. Interesting news..." Curt shared what he'd learned from Allison. Andrew shared what he knew, as did Smitty. Between the three, the full picture became clear during the last two hours of that plane ride. The unknown pieces to them were conveniently filled in by Katarina, who feared for her life and sung like a bird.

\* \* \* \* \* \* \* \* \* \* \* \* \* \* \* \* \* \* \* \* \* \* \* \* \* \* \* \* \* \* \* \* \* \* \* \* \* \* \*

The work in the Pentagon was exhausting. One of the intel analysts, Lieutenant Colonel Brian Austerman, needed a break. He stepped outside into the building's inner courtyard and pulled out his iPhone. He checked his personal email and scrolled through his social media account, something he hadn't done in about five days. As he did, a post from an old colleague caught his eye. Posted two days ago, was a selfie photo from Aviano Air Base that said, "Check it out! My old girl, the EC-130H, right here in Italy!" In the background, clear as day, was Compass Call aircraft. Brian knew the airplane well. He was the lead intelligence officer for three years at Davis Monthan Air Force Base. *'Son of a bitch!'* he thought. Lieutenant Colonel Austerman ran back into the intel analysis room, pulling flight data. Within an hour, he'd know the truth. In true intel analysis fashion, he'd push it up to his leadership, who would also push it quickly up to their leadership. It would eventually be on the President's and Secretary of Defense's desks, along with all the other National Security Council members. Admiral Hershey was a dead man walking.

Admiral Hershey returned from a lunch workout down at the Pentagon athletic center. It was a good workout and while the insubordination upset him, the averted crisis in Kosovo made up for most of it. Walking into his office, both of his executive officers stood. "Hey, team!" The Admiral belted out. The lead exec tried to speak before the Admiral walked from the waiting area into his private office, but it was too late.

As the Admiral turned to enter his office, he saw Secretary Gerzema sitting in his chair.

"Good morning, Squirts."

"Good morning, Mr. Secretary."

"I presume you know why I am here."

There could be only one reason. "Yes, sir."

"Admiral Hershey, you may wish to put on your best service dress. We will depart for the White House in a half hour to meet the President. He will expect your resignation." With that, Secretary Gerzema got up out of the Admiral's chair and walked past him, providing a glance of disdain as he walked by.

The Admiral closed his office door and began changing clothes. He'd draft the letter of resignation later.

A soft knock emanated from his office door.

"Not now, please."

Thirty seconds later, the knock grew louder.

"God damn it, not now!"

The door opened, and it was the junior executive officer, a bright young female Air Force lieutenant colonel. "Admiral, I am very sorry to bother you, but the man on the phone says it's urgent."

"For Christ's sake. OK, put him through."

The phone buzzed in, and the Admiral put the call on speaker as his executive officer exited and closed the door.

"Yeah. Hershey here."

"Admiral! It's Curt! I'm really sorry to bother you, but I have some critical information."

"Curt. It's over, son. But I want you to know what you, Smitty, and Monk pulled off. I couldn't be prouder."

"Sir, what do you mean, it's over?"

"The intel analysts appear to be too good at their jobs. They identified the EC-130s. I'm going to resign in 30 minutes to the President."

Curt was pissed... "No freaking way. The hell you are. Admiral, can you access your private email in your office?"

"Yeah, I can get to it here. Why?"

"Tell me the address. Don't go to the President until you get an email with an attachment from Allison Donley. Print off the attachment and take it. Do you understand?"

"Yes, but..."

"Admiral. Trust me." Admiral Hershey gave Curt the email address, and he passed it onto Allison, who was already prepared to push the scanned PDF.

The Admiral sat down in his chair, printing off the file.

"Hot fucking damn!" He screamed as he read through the letter. The Admiral continued to put on his service dress as if he was preparing for a wedding or graduation, far from a resignation.

No words were spoken as Secretary Gerzema and Chairman Hershey flew from the Pentagon to the White House, both expecting drastically different outcomes. As they walked into the Oval Office, the President stood looking out the window.

"Mr. President," they both said.

"Yes, please. Sit down." The President did not look at them. Secretary Gerzema and Admiral Hershey took seats on the sofa as Steve stood in the back of the room, silent.

The President was conflicted. His senior most military officer clearly disobeyed a direct order, but by doing so, thwarted an imminent invasion; something the President clearly would have done had it not been for Nikola. It would be painful, but the President had to force the Admiral's resignation.

"Squirts. Ya fucked up."

"Yes, Mr. President."

"I presume the Secretary of Defense shared you need to tender your resignation."

"Yes, Mr. President."

"Do you have your resignation letter?" The President inquired.

"No, Mr. President."

The President's head turned somewhat rapidly from the window and looked at the two of them. The Secretary of Defense was also surprised but not shocked, given Chairman Hershey's recent insubordination.

"Excuse me?" The President said.

"Mr. President, I don't intend to tender my resignation," Admiral Hershey said with growing confidence.

"Admiral Hershey. Please do not make me fire you."

"Mr. President, I don't believe that will be necessary either. If you do not mind, sir, I'd like a moment to speak with you and your Chief of Staff alone."

The Admiral's request was unusual, but the President saw no harm in it. The request was likely a desperate plea. Secretary Gerzema left the room.

"Well, Admiral, the floor is yours."

"Yes, sir. Well. I think you both would like to read this letter I received and also look at its supporting documentation." Admiral Hershey handed duplicate copies to both.

Steve finished first. "Where did you get this?"

"Aw, come on, Steve. It's not that hard. The letter is

addressed to Dr. Curt Nover. What's your next question?"

Both Steve and the President had no more questions.

The Admiral continued. "The way I see it, if I make that letter and associated documents public, it would be a terrible day for you two."

Steve responded. "Whether you or Nikola that release it, you mean. You're not the only one holding these documents."

"True, but I also know someone who is currently holding Nikola's sister, a known secret espionage agent for both Serbia and Russia on U.S. soil, ready to turn her over to someone. If we can come to an agreement, perhaps we can make that entity be the FBI, and a big win for the President."

"You're bullshitting," Steve responded.

Chairman Hershey pulled out his cell phone, opened it and showed Steve a photo of Curt, Smitty and a gagged Katarina clearly in a private jet. Two individuals in the photo were smiling happily. One was not.

It was either an elaborate hoax or true. The President was leaning towards the latter. He thought for a minute. "Steve, call Nikola. Put him on speakerphone." The call rang through.

"Nikola here."

"Nikola, it's the President. How are you doing?"

"You know the answer to that. And I absolutely made clear to Steve, this is not over."

"Yes, yes. He told me. Hey, how is your sister?"

"She's fine, why?"

"Hmm. I'm not so sure. You see, I believe she's on U.S. soil right now, and the FBI is on its way to arrest her for espionage and also charge her with the deaths of two NATO officials."

"Bullshit."

"OK. Call her. I'll again call you in five minutes." Steve disconnected the line.

Thirty seconds later, Katarina's phone rang. Curt answered it. "Dr. Curt Nover, can I help you?" The other party remained silent. "Curt Nover here. Who is this? The caller ID says 'Nikola. Is this... is this Nikola? Hey! Do you want to say hi to your sister? Oh, wait. She's got a gag in her mouth, and don't go thinking anything kinky. This isn't one of the fun ones." The line went dead.

Nikola hung up and desperately waited for the President to call back. Eventually, the phone rang. "If you hurt one hair on her head, I'll…"

"You will what? Nikola? Look. This is over. Do you understand? Your sister, in exchange for a confession from you that you falsified numerous documents in an attempt to extort the President and were caught. That you have absolutely no proof of wrongdoing and that any and all pieces of evidence were forgeries."

"And in return?"

"Your sister walks free. But I need an answer now. I can't hold off the FBI. Forever."

"It's a deal." Nikola was done. Checkmate.

"Good. Please go to the U.S. Embassy in Belgrade. Someone there will take your confession and notarize it. Thanks, Nikola." And with that, the President hung up.

"OK, Admiral. It seems you still have a job. Now where's Katarina?"

"Not so fast. I do have some requests. First, you're going to give a press conference. You'll say you ordered the operation and that because of the sensitivities, many in the military were left out of the loop. Details can remain classified. Do you understand?"

"Admiral, there is no need…"

Admiral Hershey cut him off. "Mr. President, with all due respect, bullshit. The reason you forced Nikola to make a statement is the same reason I need a press conference. Forgive me, sir, but it appears your word is not what it once was, if ever."

Steve ground his teeth. *'How insolent of that little prick,'* he thought.

The Admiral continued. "You'll replace the Secretary of Defense within six months. He's become untenable to work with and this is the straw that broke the camel's back."

"You want Gerzema fired? Ha. That's easy. I only gave him

the job because I felt bad about how his Presidential campaign exploded when news of his affair decades ago surfaced. Tell ya what." It was clear the President had no firm feelings towards Secretary Gerzema and even Steve sat idle as the simple discussion to fire him progressed.

"Steve, can you get the Secretary of Defense?" Steve got up, fetched Secretary Gerzema, and brought him back into the Oval Office.

"John," the President said. "I want you to know I truly appreciate all you've done for me and, more importantly, our country." The Secretary of Defense was confused and growing irritated. He could sense where this speech was going.

The President continued. "I think at this point, especially considering all the things that happened in the Balkans, we need some fresh ideas in the Defense Department. Because of that, I'm asking for your resignation."

John Gerzema was dumbfounded. "Mr. President?"

"John. This isn't the end of the world. Look, we both knew you weren't going to be Secretary of Defense forever. I plan to announce your resignation in an hour when I address the press. Do I have your word you'll resign?"

It was D.C. politics at its finest. John Gerzema had no cards to play. Stuttering and internally furious, he said, "Yes, Mr. President."

Within an hour, the President held a press conference. "Fellow Americans, over the past 72 hours, I directed a surgical and precise special forces mission in the Balkans. To be clear, no U.S. forces EVER entered sovereign Serbian territory. The mission was so classified that I couldn't even share it with the full National Security Committee or the ambassadors in the countries we operated in. Only a select few leaders were aware of the mission in order to maintain secrecy."

He continued. "As you see from the outcome, the mission was a huge success, the crisis in Kosovo has deescalated and I've now ordered our military to do everything they can to bolster U.S. Forces in and around the Balkans as well as deploy five thousand U.S. Forces to the NATO KFOR until our other allies can reconsider their commitment to this vital mission. I'm proud of Secretary Gerzema, Admiral Hershey and General Etcher for a job well done."

During a brief pause, the President looked at John Gerzema with a smile, then started speaking again. "I must also share that it is with great regret I am accepting Secretary of Defense Gerzema's resignation letter. John has been an exceptional servant of this magnificent land and he will be sorely missed. But John said he wants more time with the grandkids, and I can't blame him! Right, John?" The President turned his attention to Secretary Gerzema standing off camera in the back of the room. The press instinctively turned around to see his reaction. John was a seasoned politician. He smiled, waved his hand and nodded as if he was flattered to be called out by the President during a live press conference. Inside, he wanted to knife the President at least 50 times in the heart.

The President was not done with the speech and the press turned back around. "Next week, I will hold a special ceremony awarding the Presidential Medal of Freedom to Secretary Gerzema, Admiral Hershey, and General Etcher. May God bless you and may God bless the United States of America." The President would take no questions.

After the press conference was complete, Admiral Hershey shared Katarina's location. Soon, the Gulfstream would be refueled, and once Nikola signed the confession, Katarina would be flying again on her way back to Belgrade. This time, however, she'd not be jumping out of the plane.

Secretary Gerzema stood in the White House hallways for a while. He'd watched the press conference as if it was spoken in a foreign language. 'What just happened,' he thought. He was the Secretary of Defense and somehow, the President and chairman had crafted a Special Forces mission he was not privy to? How could this be? And now, he was fired for doing nothing but backing the President's position? That's what loyalty in D.C. gets you? John knew he'd recover, though. He just needed some new cards in his political hand.

## Chapter Fifty-Six
# For Whom the Bell Tolls

Memorial Day weekend weather was beautiful in Virginia. Allison and Curt were packing their last items in the hotel before they set out to the Annapolis Yacht Club. They had an invitation from Admiral Hershey and his wife for a day of sailing on the Chesapeake. Downtown in Annapolis, Smitty and Buck were drinking Bloody Marys at Middleton Tavern, eating Chesapeake Bay crab dip, working off their hangovers from the night prior.

A cab would bring Allison and Curt to the tavern, and the four would grab one last drink before the Admiral's yacht pulled into 'Ego Alley,' a narrow strip of water only forty feet wide that boaters could bring their boats in to 'see and be seen' in the heart of Annapolis.

At 1100Hrs, a 60ft monohull traditional sailboat slowly made its way into Ego Alley. Docking perfectly, the Chairman of the Joint Chiefs, wearing Bermuda shorts, playing Jimmy Buffett tunes, emerged from the boat. "Welcome, shipmates!" he bellowed to the four.

As the sailboat sat idle next to the dock, the Admiral would give all who gawked at Ego Alley the show they deserved. He emerged from the aft section and grabbed hold of the H.G.A.U.'s bell pull. The bell was gorgeous, freshly polished brass with a spotless white hand braided bell pull. For each guest, it would ring twice, as the Admiral, in true Navy fashion, 'officially' rang his guests aboard.

Ding.

"Allison Donley, arriving."

Ding, Ding.

"Curt Nover, arriving."

Ding, Ding.

"Mark 'Smitty' Smith, arriving."

Ding, Ding.

"Mark 'Pooh Bear' Thiessen, arriving."

Buck shot a puzzled look at Curt, Smitty, and Allison, all who shrugged, wondering why the Admiral misidentified Buck's actual nickname as 'Pooh Bear.' No matter, it was perhaps just a mistake. After all, one doesn't just go correcting four-star admirals willy-nilly.

After a few greetings and settling in, the Admiral exited Ego Alley just as smoothly as he entered and his ship, 'H.G.A.U.,' sailed out of Ego Alley and set out into the Chesapeake Bay.

Back at the helm, the Admiral addressed the three who were standing there with him. "Curt, Allison and Smitty, I am grateful you took me up on the invite for a sail today," Admiral Hershey said. Buck was wandering around the ship.

"Sir, how could we say no?" Curt responded.

"True, the weather is spectacular, isn't it?"

"Weather? Who said anything about the weather? You're in charge of the most lethal fighting force in the world. Our life expectancy would drop to near zero if we refused."

The entire group laughed at Curt's joke except Buck, who'd wondered off to another part of the sailboat. After approximately 30 seconds, Buck began yelling from the midship in front of them. "Curt! Smitty! Allison!" They, along with the Admiral jumped up from the helm and looked towards where the screams emanated. There was Buck, standing with his back to the mainmast and hands locked around it, as if he were tied to the pole. Once he saw everyone looking at him, he proclaimed, "Look at me! I'm sailing…. I'M SAILING." It was his horrible attempt at a Bill Murray impression from the classic film "What About Bob." It didn't matter. Buck was Buck. Besides the Admiral, everyone laughed.

Admiral Hershey turned to Curt and said, "Is he really your friend?" This was actually the first time the Admiral had met Buck.

Curt smiled. "He may be a knucklehead, Admiral. But he's our knucklehead. There's just something about him. It's infectious."

"OK," Admiral Hershey responded, "But I think that guy is nuts."

After an hour or so and making their way across the bay, the

Admiral along with help from his new crew, hoisted the mainsail and threw out the jib. The beautiful sailboat gently settled to one side and was now at the mercy of the wind and the hand that sailed her.

Mrs. Hershey served a few more drinks, along with some appetizers. The Admiral looked at her and said, "Sweetie, Pooh Bear's beer is empty. Can you get him another?"

Buck believed this was just a continued error, but decided to nip it in the bud. "Excuse me Admiral, perhaps you didn't know, but my nickname is Buck."

"I'm aware on land you're known as Buck, but on my ship, you are Pooh Bear." The Admiral looked out in front of the ship, hand on the wheel, not phased at either Buck's or his comments.

Buck looked at his three friends, who again shrugged.

"OK, sir. Your ship, your rules, but can I ask why?"

"Sure, Pooh Bear." The Admiral licked his lips and took just a small pause. He'd waited quite a while to deliver this joke. "You and Winnie the Pooh are the only two I know who can't resist a sweet honey pot."

Curt, Allison, and Smitty's jaws fell in unison and their eyes bulged. They howled in laughter. The joke was perfect. The timing, the presentation, the punch line.

Buck, not amused, realized he'd been had.

"Buck," the Admiral continued. "That's how you deliver a punchline, my friend. Now, can my lovely wife get you another beer?" The Admiral reached out his hand to Buck. They shook. It would be the best joke told all day.

The group continued chatting and laughing. The men hinting at what had transpired, edging around the classified constraints, and the women trying desperately to put the puzzle pieces together.

Just then, a small twin turboprop aircraft, low on the water, started heading towards the yacht. Admiral Hershey pointed it out. "Will you look at that idiot. He's way too low!" The entire group watched as the aircraft closed on the sailboat. Buck yelled, "Hell! That's a Twin Otter, my old aircraft!" At the last minute, it changed heading and flew down the starboard rail of the H.G.A.U. As it did, the paint scheme and tail flash were easily distinguishable. There was a dark blue strip down the fuselage and on the tail was the very recognizable NATO star.

Buck was confused. "What the... that plane has a NATO paint scheme."

"Yes, it does Buck," Chairman Hershey said.

"Like my old aircraft," Buck said sadly, recalling the aircraft he lost.

"I think you mean, just like your new aircraft," Chairman Hershey responded.

Curt, Smitty, and Allison couldn't take it anymore. Buck was not one to catch onto things quickly, case in point was his honey trap. "CONGRATS, YOU IDIOT!" They all yelled.

"What!? That's... That's MY plane?"

Curt jumped in. "Yes. And it will meet you back in Europe in a week or so. After helping with the little Kosovo issue, it appears someone was gracious enough to give you a new airplane."

"To be clear, it was NOT the Defense Department!" Admiral Hershey quickly jumped in, ensuring there was no hint of impropriety.

They all raised their glasses and toasted him.

"Smitty," the Admiral said, "I hear you lost your job at the Steel Mill."

"Yes, sir. That's true. But it really wasn't for me, anyway. I'll find something. I need something more exciting than just watching TV monitors in a guard shack."

"I see," Admiral Hershey said. He continued, "You wouldn't be interested in joining my private security detail, would you?"

Smitty's eyes lit up. "You gotta be shitting me?" He said. "I'd fucking love it!"

"Good, it's settled. You'll start training in two weeks. My staff is briefed. Just do me a favor. Try not to kill anyone."

Smitty grinned, "You mean, 'that doesn't deserve it.'" Everyone joined in the laughter.

"And Curt. I owe you a great deal and I hear you lost your

job as well at Cook County Hospital."

"I did. But sir, you really don't have to do anything. Allison and I are fine. Really. The medical board ruled that the heroin introduced into my body was not of my own will, so they are allowing me to keep my medical license."

"Well, that's good. Because you'll need it."

"Excuse me, sir? I don't understand."

"Congressman Donegan, Smitty, and Allison gave me all the details of your challenges this past spring. I want you to know I'm not only proud of you for your efforts in the Balkans, but also your fight in the daily struggle against PTSD."

"Thanks, sir, but I don't reall...."

The Admiral continued his sentence, "Really like to talk about it. Well, I hope that changes. I've asked Congressman Donegan to work with the Department of Veterans Affairs. Within a week, you will be offered the lead position helping our homeless veterans deal with their demons. He and I can think of no one better qualified. I mean that."

Allison began to tear up. She knew it was exactly the job Curt needed. He'd make a world of difference. She grabbed him and hugged him.

"Baby! Easy. I haven't even said yes, yet," Curt quipped.

"If you don't say yes, I'll throw you off this freaking boat!"

The Admiral looked at Allison, "Uh... It's a ship."

"Whatever. Not the point right now. Curt, please take the job."

"Allison. I don't know. It would mean I'd have to move to D.C., and we'd have to talk about whether you'd come with me. There are tons of issues. Plus, I'm somewhat disappointed in the Admiral."

Allison looked at him like he was an asshole. "Why on EARTH would you say that?" she questioned him.

"Well, for one, the Admiral has offered something to every one of us, but you. And to me, you're the most important thing in the world. Frankly, I find that offensive."

"Curt, I don't care about the Admiral's dumb gifts. I care about us."

Admiral Hershey had heard enough. "OK, wait. First, you insult my ship by calling it a boat. Now you're alluding to a new aircraft and two new jobs as dumb gifts. I guess you don't want this then." With that, the Admiral reached in his pocket and pulled out a beautiful diamond studded wedding band that matched her engagement ring.

Buck dropped his beer can on the deck in shock. Allison's eyes lit up. She was speechless. Mrs. Hershey began sobbing in happiness.

"According to maritime law, we are far enough away from shore now that I, as the captain, can legally conduct a marriage. So, is it a ship or a boat?"

One of the things Allison wanted most in the world ever since she met Curt was to be Mrs. Curt Nover. She threw her arms around Admiral Hershey and cried, "It's a ship! It's a ship!"

Mrs. Hershey tried her best to prep the aft end of the ship for a wedding. Curt looked over at Buck, who oddly seemed disappointed. "Buck," he asked. "What's wrong?"

"Dude... When you asked me to be your best man, I kept thinking I was going to give the most excellent best man speech in the world, because frankly, you deserve it. Now, I haven't prepared, and it's gonna suck."

Curt just smiled. "Buddy, I kinda think you're missing the point of being a best man. It's not about a speech on one given day, no matter how good it is. It's about being in Allison's and my life forever."

"Alright. If you say so, but I'm serious. This speech is gonna be worse than Sally Field at the Oscars." Curt laughed and hugged his big ol' friend.

The Admiral conducted the ceremony. Curt was with the folks that mattered most to him, and Allison was with Curt. They'd have another wedding later with family and friends, but this would be their day. It was magical. "I now pronounce you husband and wife. You may kiss the bride." Curt and Allison kissed for many seconds. It wasn't awkward at all. Smitty popped the champagne. It was a perfect day to be on the H.G.A.U.

Buck was right. His speech was far from exceptional, but it didn't matter. The day was perfect. As he ended his speech and proposed a toast, Smitty manned the H.G.A.U.'s bell, and he rang it for what seemed like minutes. The clang of the bell echoed across the Chesapeake, clearly signaling this was the boat to be on that day.

\* \* \* \* \* \* \* \* \* \* \* \* \* \* \* \* \* \* \* \* \* \* \* \* \* \* \* \* \* \* \* \* \* \* \* \* \* \*

Months later, back in Arizona, former Secretary of Defense John Gerzema bounced his smallest granddaughter, Georgia Lynn, on his knee. She was a beautiful little child, dressed in a wonderful Christmas dress which blended nicely with all the house decorations. He'd been out of the Pentagon for over a half a year and enjoying time at home, plenty of time for him to have calmed from the forced resignation.

"Here, dad, let me take Georgia. It's time for her feeding," his daughter said. Georgia raised her arms as momma came to take her away.

"Sure, just when I'm really starting to have fun," John said. He reached over to the coffee table next to his chair and grabbed his phone. An email came in from what appeared to be a mid-level diplomat at the Russian Embassy in D.C.

> 'Secretary Gerzema,
>> On behalf of the Russian government and our Ambassador, I wanted to thank you for your service to your nation as well as the global community. May you truly enjoy your time in retirement.'
>> Anton Mazur

The email was signed, and there was a video clip attached at the bottom of the email. The title of the clip was 'Ambassador's Granddaughter Skating.'

John opened the video file only to learn it had nothing to do with a skating granddaughter.  He smiled.  His political hand was just loaded with four aces.

                                        The End.

# Glossary of Acronyms

| | |
|---|---|
| AB | Air Base |
| ABL | Administrative Boundary Line |
| AFSOC | Air Force Special Operations Command |
| AG | Attorney General |
| AMCIT | American Citizen |
| AWOL | Absent Without Leave |
| CAG | Commander's Action Group |
| CCTV | Close Circuit Television |
| CIA | Central Intelligence Agency |
| COMKFOR | Commander, NATO FORCES Kosovo |
| DIA | Defense Intelligence Agency |
| DNI | Director of National Intelligence |
| DoD | Department of Defense |
| EMS | Electromagnetic Spectrum |
| EUCOM | European Command |
| FAA | Federal Aviation Administration |
| FBI | Federal Bureau of Investigation |
| FBO | Fixed Base Operations |
| FS | Flight Station |
| HE | High Explosive |
| ICAO | International Civil Aviation Organization |
| ID | Infantry Division |
| JWICS | Joint Worldwide Intel Comm. System |
| KFOR | (NATO) Kosovo Forces |
| KSF | Kosovo Security Force |
| LCDR | Lieutenant Commander |
| LTC | Lieutenant Colonel |
| LtCol | Lieutenant Colonel |
| LTG | Lieutenant General |
| LtGen | Lieutenant General |
| MajGen | Major General |
| MFP-11 | Major Force Program - 11 |

| | |
|---|---|
| MG | Major General |
| NATO | North American Treaty Organization |
| NDA | Non-Disclosure Agreement |
| NSC | National Security Council |
| NWC | National War College |
| OSCE | Organization for Security and Cooperation in Europe |
| PAX | Passengers (on Aircraft) |
| POTUS | President of the United States |
| PTSD | Post-Traumatic Stress Disorder |
| RSO | Regional Security Officer |
| SACUER | Supreme Allied Commander, European Forces |
| SATCOM | Satellite Communications |
| SOCOM | Special Operations Command |
| SOF | Special Operations Forces |
| TACC | Tanker Airlift Control Center |
| UN | United Nations |
| UNSCR | United Nations Security Council Resolution |
| USAID | United States Agency for International Development |
| VADM | Vice Admiral |
| VTC | Video Tele-Conference |

To all who struggle with PTSD, please remember, help is never further than a phone call away.

The National Suicide Prevention Lifeline: 988, then press 1.

The Veteran's Crisis Help Line: 1-800-273-8255, press 1.

### *You are not alone*

\*\*\*\*\*\*\*\*\*\*\*\*\*\*\*\*\*\*\*\*\*\*\*\*\*\*\*\*\*\*\*\*\*\*\*\*\*

Thanks for reading.  Please consider leaving a review on Amazon.  Just scan the QR Code for a direct link to the book.

# THE AUTHOR:

Colonel (Retired) Jeffrey H. Fischer is a 30-year aviator with seven combat tours in Iraq, Afghanistan, and the Balkans. Additionally, he served at the U.S. Air Force Headquarters, the Pentagon, as well as a senior defense official in U.S. Embassies Vienna and Pristina. Jeff ended his extensive military career at NATO Special Operations Headquarters, Mons, Belgium. He currently resides in Austria with his wife Barbara and son Tobias.

Made in United States
Orlando, FL
11 August 2023